SEASON ONE

SEASON ONE

AN ALL ABOUT THE DIAMOND ROMANCE

NAOMI SPRINGTHORP

Season One goes back to the beginning of my baseball series. The story of catcher extraordinaire Rick Seno and loyal baseball fan Sherry collected into one book.

This collection is dedicated to my original supporters, readers, and baseball ladies everywhere.

Season One
An All About the Diamond Romance
Including: The Sweet Spot (Book 1), King of Diamonds (Book 2),
Diamonds in Paradise (Book 3)
Copyright © 2022 Naomi Springthorp
Published by Naomi Springthorp
Print Edition ISBN 978-1-949243-64-2
Cover Photographer: Randy Sewell of RLS Model Images Photography
Cover Model: Chris Mayo
Graphic Designer: Irene Johnson johnsoni@mac.com
Editor: Katrina Fair

THE SWEET SPOT

AN ALL ABOUT THE DIAMOND ROMANCE BOOK 1

CHAPTER ONE

"Sir, will you please sign my ball?" The sweet, innocent voice I project frustrates me. I've been here before and I recognize the symptoms. My brain automatically switched to autopilot. He's got me tied in knots. I've got it bad for this ball player and I've never even spoken to him! Last time this happened was when I met my teenage heartthrob. I'm in trouble, but it's too late now—no turning back.

"Hi, I'm Rick. Put the ball away and have a seat. I don't want to be a baseball player tonight." He reaches his hand out to shake mine and directs me to sit across from him in the booth.

"Joni." I reply as I shake his large masculine hand. "I'll do my best not to talk about baseball."

"I hope the part about not talking about baseball is true," he doesn't release my hand. "Start over. That's not your real name. I already checked to see if you're one of *those* women," he says with an irritated look of disdain.

"Sorry, I don't give my real name to men in bars. It's not my scene. I'm Sherry," warmth gathers on my cheeks.

"What else do you know about me?" I ask curiously. He has a dark beer in his hand and the bottle has a yeti on it. I laugh to myself because bearded guys remind me of yetis and I'm never attracted to them. Except Rick Seno, who has the best beard in the league.

"You've been a Seals Ticket Member for years and have never chased a player or dated a player or fucked a player. By all counts, you're a loyal fan and not a stalker. You understand the game better than most and you're older than me," he states true facts, unless you count my dreams and even then it's only him.

"Do you have an instant background check service or what?"

"The front office and the membership team take care of us. We're all in the public eye and can be targeted for all kinds of things, especially by women. It's why I never accept invitations."

A moment later he loosens his grip on my hand and slowly pulls his hand away. He stands up abruptly and excuses himself to the men's room.

That's it. He's not coming back. He already has me pinned as a crazy fan and who could blame him after that opening line. *Sir, will you sign my ball?* Where was my brain?

A few minutes pass and he returns to the booth. He slides in next to me on my side of the booth and pushes me into the corner with his kiss. Immediate heat runs through my body like bursts of fireworks lighting up the night sky. This man. Oh, this man! His rough hands in my hair, holding me where he wants me. I reach out to his muscled upper

4

arms and find myself stroking them. His lips are greedy with want and his tongue dances against mine with needy desire. I'm in heaven. Who am I to disagree with what he wants?

We break for air, both completely out of breath and he looks into my eyes with a heat I've never seen before. His fiery gaze makes me nervous and I search for an escape. "Want to shoot some pool?" Almost unable to get the words out between my ragged breaths.

He nods silently, offers his hand to help me out of the booth and leads me to the back room with the pool tables. I can't help but sway my hips to the music playing when we enter the room. Anything with a groove has always driven me to dance and the bass line from "All Right Now" by Free has me moving. His hands are suddenly on my hips and his warm body behind me, directing me out the back door of the Locale.

It's dark, with only a dim light in the far corner of the parking lot and most of the other patrons have left for the night. Rick leans against the exterior wall of the bar and pulls me back against him. His breath warm on my neck sends tingles down my spine.

He whispers in my ear, "Are you teasing me with your hips?" He kisses my neck from the back to below my ear, and gives my earlobe a gentle nibble. The whole time holding my back to his body snugly, with his interest pressed against me.

The heat of my body overwhelms me and I respond with a shaky voice I can't believe is my own, "Not a tease, just love music."

"You're giving me mixed signals. You obviously wanted me to stop kissing you in the booth. I doubt you're a pool shark with a master plan to swindle me." He turns me around to face him, and searches my eyes. "So, what's the deal?"

Okay. So, I'm having a moment. Quite possibly, a fanatic moment I may never recover from. Rick Seno is gazing into my eyes, his thick arms wrapped around my shoulders and he has no plan of releasing me. I've got goose bumps and it's not the weather. He has the most gorgeous bright blue eyes, I could get lost in them like the unending sky on a sunny day. He smells fresh and clean with a hint of something woodsy. Like heaven.

His solid muscles are all around me and I want to explore him. He screams man without opening his mouth. My brain and heart are arguing with each other, while my body wants them both to shut up and enjoy themselves. Run away or...

"Well? I'm waiting for a response." He shifts his eyes and focuses on me, "Are you okay in there?"

"My brain wanted to stop kissing you, it doesn't think I should move too fast," I state matter-of-factly. "My heart is afraid of getting hurt, but knows you have to take risks," my heart swells in my throat. "My body has wanted you from a distance for years and doesn't want to wait any longer," I gaze up into his eyes. "I don't know how to play pool, but I've always wanted to learn... I want to want you for you, not because you're a baseball player. Because you're Rick Seno."

A devilish grin takes over his lips, "Then we're both in luck because I'm not a baseball player tonight and I've always wanted a woman who wanted me for who I am." He kisses me and I'm his.

My heart and body beat my brain into submission. Two out of three isn't bad. Hopefully, my brain won't come back with "I told you so."

He laces his fingers with mine, "This isn't my style either, but something about you seems to change the rules for me."

"Want to go to my place?" I ask and his eyes light up. "I live a couple blocks away and it's a nice night for a walk."

"I'm not interested in walking anywhere at two in the morning, seems like asking for trouble."

"Funny, I thought that's what I just did," I retort with a smile and gaze up into his eyes.

"I'll show you trouble!" He scoops me up over his shoulder and carries me to his car, while I laugh uncontrollably.

Normally I'd complain about the manhandling, but the view of his strong tight ass is worth the price of admission. I grab it and hold on as if for dear life for the walk across the parking lot. I wonder if his guttural groan is a sign of appreciation, or possibly his realization of what he's gotten himself into.

He drives us the two blocks to my place, and through the parking maze at my complex. He parks his car and walks around quickly to open my door. He offers me a hand out of his car and doesn't let go. We take the elevator up to my one bedroom penthouse and I unlock the door. Urgency kicks in out of nowhere. I push him against the door, run my fingers through his hair and he eagerly meets my lips halfway to find his. He lifts me up to his height and holds me there, taking control of the kiss. I wrap my arms around him and kick the door open. He carries me in and closes the door behind us without breaking our kiss.

His lips on mine are soft, tender, and needy. His tongue lightly strokes my lower lip and moves into my mouth a little at a time. He puts me down and runs his hands slowly over my body. His hands caress down my arms as he moves his kiss to my jawline. Slowly, taking his kisses down my collarbone as he palms my breasts. I feel his smile on me and grab his head, redirecting his kisses to my mouth while encouraging his caressing of my breasts with my body.

I've wanted him for years and this will be a one time thing, so I do what I can to keep a steady pace and make the experience last as long as possible. I want the night I have with Seno to be a memorable one. Tomorrow morning he'll be gone.

I slide out of his embrace and lock the door. I open the window to let the cool breeze blow through and turn on an oldies station as I excuse myself to the bathroom. I change into my only oversized San Diego Seals jersey with Seno and a big 6 on the back, and comb through my hair with my fingers as I walk back to Rick.

He turns to watch me walking toward him in his jersey and gets the dirtiest expression on his face, "You're so mine tonight."

I reach out to him and start to pull his shirt off. Impatiently, he takes over, throws his shirt across the room and toes off his shoes.

His eyes are intense and the bulge in his pants is trying to break free. I grasp his belt, intending to remove it, and he quickly grabs my wrist.

Doing his best to maintain control, "Are you sure about this? I don't want to go any further if you're going to change your mind."

I rub his rock hard cock with my free hand and he releases my other hand to continue removing his belt. I unbutton his jeans, and reach into his pants as I unzip them and free his obvious desire. I drop to my knees for a better view, wrapping my hand around him at the base of his cock and licking his shaft from end to end while he trembles and becomes harder. He's silky in my hand as I take his head in my mouth and swirl my tongue around him. As I begin to suck and stroke him, he grabs my head and makes me stop. I stare up into his eyes, holding his gaze and suck him into my mouth as far as I can. I moan with my lips firmly around him. He watches me for a few moments and gives in, letting his head fall back. I stroke his thighs and continue my tongue game until his breathing goes ragged. Slowly, I stand, wrap my arms around his neck and begin to kiss his lips gently. I hold his need between my thighs. As I squeeze it, his tongue takes over and deepens our connection. I pull him toward me as I walk backward towards my bed. He lifts me and I wrap my legs around his waist. He takes control. Rick pins me against the wall with his bare chest and continues to kiss me as he drops his pants to the floor and steps out of them. Suddenly his hands grasp my bare ass and lift me. He rubs his tip against my wetness and slides his shaft across my clit, setting my body on high alert.

His lips move to my neck and I breathe into his ear, "Let's take this to the bed. I want your hands on me."

He tosses me to my bed, while I giggle like a nervous schoolgirl. I creep up to my pillow and lay on my side watching him, waiting for his next move. The moonlight is shining in from the open window behind him. He's an absolutely phenomenal sight, built all over of solid muscle and his cock standing at attention for me.

I should've expected no less because he's a professional athlete, except he's not a baseball player tonight. He climbs into my bed and lies on his side facing me. He unbuttons my jersey as I lean in and kiss him roughly. I want to encourage him and feel his sexy grin on my lips. This night has been perfect, I'm in a happy haze waiting for whatever will come next.

He squeezes my breasts and my nipples harden. He unhooks my bra and suddenly I'm naked, my jersey sent flying across the room. His touch sets my skin on fire as his tongue lightly caresses my left nipple, and he gently begins to suck. He runs his hands down my body and lightly strokes my inner thighs, moving toward my promised land. He rolls me onto my back while his motions continue. Closer and closer, he teases me until he touches my wet folds.

"May I?" he asks in a low out of breath tone.

"I thought we already determined I'm *so yours tonight*," I purr.

He presses his lips to mine and delves his tongue into my mouth engaging in a delicate tango with mine. His passion grows, his cock at my wanting sex and I push towards him needing to have him hard inside me. He refuses to let me take control and pulls back, insistently taking me for his own and burying himself deep in my heat.

My every nerve endings are active live wires as he drives into me slowly, repeatedly and deliberately. I appreciate his gaze on me in combination with the weight of his delicious body and allow myself to selfishly indulge. I memorize everything about the experience, so I'll remember it as clearly as basking in the sun near the ocean shore. His strokes begin to quicken and I arch into him. He drags his tongue across my collarbone and up to my ear, gently tugging and nibbling on my earlobe. He moves his hand between my thighs and fists his cock tightly while he continues to fuck me. I'm lost in sensation until he releases his hand and allows his dick to slam all the way into me while he circles my clit with his finger. I explode like a cannon, shouting his name.

Rick follows me over the edge as he watches me come. He makes a few low groans and whispers, "Fuck."

We stay connected as he rests on top of me. Both of us are breathing heavily and trying to regain control. He strokes my hair and kisses me softly. He stirs inside me as he begins round two. I'm a ball of overactive nerves on high awareness when he starts slowly stroking into me and putting pressure on my clit. He carefully rolls us over so I'm straddling him, riding him, bouncing on his hard cock like it's my own personal joystick. His rough hands guide my hips in a way that's more him touching me and enjoying me moving on him. The whole time he's watching me, taking in the vision of me riding him to ecstasy. I squeeze him with each stroke, almost as if I'm milking him with my body. His body tenses, his heartbeat grows faster and his cock hardens, growing hotter inside me. I close my eyes and let my head hang back as I luxuriate in the moment. He increases his pace, pounding into me wildly. Orgasmic screams repeat over and over, interspersed with calling out his name for what seems like hours. I uncontrollably tumble over the edge and he holds me tight in his arms as he continues to stroke into me with wild abandon. My orgasm keeps going as he fucks me. I bite into his shoulder, sucking his skin into my mouth and send him into wild detonation.

It's early Sunday morning and I'm in bed, sleeping all snuggled with my favorite soft blanket. I've been dreaming about my favorite professional baseball player and I'm in a wonderful mood. Love, love, love those dreams about my favorite guys—musicians, actors and especially ball players.

The combination of the squawking seabirds, the breeze rustling the trees and the white noise from the freeway is relaxing. I don't want to open my eyes. I'm relaxed and slept better than I can ever remember. Yet, something is different. I'm on sensory overload. It's almost as if...

"Are you going to wake up?" I hear this deep familiar voice whisper in my ear. "I've been rubbing my cock against you for the last hour. I have to be at the stadium in less than three hours and I want to visit your warm happy place again, now." His rough hand skims down my side and over my hip.

Now, could it be possible I wasn't dreaming? Is my current baseball playing heartthrob right here in my bed and... I was wondering what was poking me, trying to slip between my legs? Did I mention it was a great dream?

Must investigate.

I'm experiencing Phil Connor's Groundhog Day euphoria, the day isn't repeating itself again. It's not a dream. His facial scruff on the back of my neck and his lips kissing below my ear bring memories of last night to mind. His hot breath on my neck intensifies my early morning, dream preheated mood. I rub my face on my pillow trying to get a glimpse of the man wrapping his arms around me from behind without being obvious, and discover I have some serious whisker burn, but that's not important. My favorite catcher has his hands on me with the same intensity he plays baseball and a dirty glint in his eyes that says he wants more.

"I'm not a morning girl, but I guess I'll let you have your way with me," I say glibly into my pillow.

"After the way I had you screaming a few hours ago, I expected you to be more willing," he says questioning.

"I told you I'm not a morning..." The sensation of his

tongue on my clit is all it takes, I no longer have the ability to speak and the orgasmic screaming is back. This man! Is the screaming me? He has control over me.

Licking and sucking on my nub, he runs his finger over my folds and presses into me, stroking me and adding a second finger.

Breathing heavy, I reach for him as I start to yell, "Oh, home run, Home Run, Home Run! Oh, Rick!" And buck wildly.

He immediately stops, climbs up to kiss me and pushes his hard length into me. Pounding hard and causing me to orgasm again almost immediately. I wrap my arms and legs around him, meeting his every thrust. Kissing him is amazing, unthinking entanglement I wish would never end. His intensity pushes me forward and drives us to passionate hours of explosive sex I've never even imagined.

My body is jello as he spoons me closely and nuzzles into my hair. Our legs are entwined. We're naked. This is how it's supposed to be, not like this was... I don't know what this was. A date? Booty call? Whatever it is, it's right.

I must've fallen asleep, I'm suddenly startled by an alarm. A strong warm arm pulls away from me, a tender kiss is planted on my cheek and the bed moves as Rick gets up. I'm torn at the idea of a one-night stand being over and waiting for my brain to claim victory over my heart and body. I can't decide if I should play ostrich, bury myself in blankets and hide under my pillow or get moving for the day.

Since I've never been a passive person, I get up and make sure he remembers who I am. I find my jersey in a wrinkled heap on the floor and put it on anyway, leaving the top buttons undone. I go to brush my teeth and find him already dressed and hot as sin on a stick. How did he do that so fast? His clothes had been strewn across my apartment.

"Good morning," I say with a yawn, "How about some breakfast or coffee or me?"

"Yes, I would like all three. But..." he starts and I cut him off.

"...you need to get out of here as quick as possible, so you aren't stuck in a weird moment with a one-night stand?" I finish for him.

"I was going to say, I only have 45 minutes to get to the stadium. The game starts in less than three hours. Sorry I woke you."

"So, you're a baseball player today and that makes me a crazy fan?" I ask only halfway joking.

"You are wearing my jersey." He states with a smile and adds, "I had no idea my jersey could look as good as it does on you." He checks the time, "I need to go, as it is I'm walking into the clubhouse in the same clothes I left in."

"Walk of shame?" I ask with a laughing smile.

"No shame here, but the rookie might get a kick out of it," he plants a wanting, passionate kiss on my lips with no warning.

He turns and walks out the door, leaving me in a lust-induced coma of wonder.

CHAPTER TWO

I'm 35 and single for a reason. I'm independent. I take care of myself and don't need or want someone to support me financially. I've always scared men off, for some reason they're intimidated by me. I've got my friends, my support system. But, I appreciate having time to myself to do what I want to do and not having to change plans to suit somebody else. I guess I'm selfish that way. Guys always want to tell you what to do and take control of your life, it doesn't fly with me. My way or the highway. If you want me, you want me the way I am. The problem is sometimes I want a man to take care of me—naked. Sometimes I want to be spoiled. Sometimes I want to be loved, not used.

What was I doing getting involved with a ball player? Okay, admittedly my brain allowed my lust to take over like those things that make smart girls stupid. You know, the V shape at their hips? But I digress... Actually, I guess that's what it's all about. It's not like I love him or anything. It was one night. It was sex. Above average sex. Amazing sex. Okay, fine. It was mind blowing and his hands, lips, tongue lit me up like lava flowing down a volcano. It was one night. It's probably over now. I want him again.

He's not just any ball player, he's Rick Seno. The man I've been crushing on hard in my private world for over five years. In my world, nobody compares to him. In my world, he's perfect. In real life, he blows every previous conception of him I had to smithereens. In real life, he's better than anything I've ever imagined.

Damn it! I'm not going to be a needy girl! I'm not going to be one of those women that chase baseball players! Not even one ball player. Not even Rick Seno. Maybe. What am I thinking? This all depends on his next move. Crap! He doesn't have my phone number. He'll find me if he wants me and he can probably have the Seals Investigator Team get him whatever information about me he wants. I bet my seat number would be a no brainer.

I'm going to the game today, so it's all fine. I can sit in my normal seat and drool over my guy behind the plate while replaying the last 18 hours in my mind in great detail. (Note to self: Set replay to start at about midnight last night.)

The lineup for today's game pops up on my social media and he isn't on it. Fuck! He's going to be pissed. He can't stand sitting out and rarely misses a game. Worse yet, I can't watch him from my comfortable distance.

LAST NIGHT at the game I wandered down to the dugout in an attempt to get an autograph. The game was just finished and we won in walk-off style with a three run homer. The team was hyped up and Gatorade was flying everywhere. The current cute interview girl, Hannah, was on the field trying to get the attention of a few guys to do her post game field interviews, but the team was busy chasing each other around on the field. A win is always better than a loss. For an autograph collector like me, this big win gives me an opportunity to add to my collection because the players are happy, they were a success today and they are on the field longer which makes them more accessible. There were other fans around me calling out to different players, trying to get their attention. Some after the attention of whoever happens to be easiest and others, like myself, are on a specific mission.

My collection is missing autographs from four of our current players. Mark Rock is one of my all time favorite outfielders, but he's out injured and not even in the building. Chase Cross, a rookie that gets played wherever they need him and is happy to get any playing time that he can. Joe "Bubbles" Bravo, a veteran outfielder that spends more time thinking about blowing bubbles with his bubblegum than actually paying attention to the game and therefore I don't give a shit about him. And of course, Rick Seno— catcher extraordinaire, Renaissance man, star in most of my dreams, and my baseball boyfriend, well, at least in my mind. That is until last night. My focus was on Rick Seno and Chase Cross, and I had two clean baseballs just waiting to be signed in the sweet spot.

Seno is a hard autograph to get, this is the sixth season I've been attempting it and that's a problem because the longer it takes, the less likely I get it before he gets traded. He's all business and impossible to get an autograph from pregame because he's always warming up the pitcher.

I've heard Chase is a sweetie, but he doesn't usually get to start the game and he's rarely available at the autograph wall—which means he gets mobbed by the young gold diggers that want to be a baseball wife. The young gold diggers are at the stadium exits by now waiting for players to come out or already went home bored, this should be my opportunity.

Hannah grabbed a couple guys for her interviews, first my Rick and then our first baseman, the hunky, lanky with legs that never stop and look good in those pants—Kris Martin, who provided the game winning hit. While I was gawking at my catcher as he talked with Hannah, I was able to get the attention of Chase Cross before he snuck off into the clubhouse and got one of the autographs I was after. Chase looked at me funny, I must have had starry eyes focused on Rick because he followed my sight line and smiled.

"Thanks for the autograph! You're looking good out there and I hope you get more starts." I said to the rookie.

With a goofy look on his face, Chase asked, "Are you okay, ma'am? I'm afraid you're going to fall the way you're leaning over the rail." I realized my drool was showing and tried to recover quickly.

"Oh, yes... Seno is the only autograph I'm missing from the current team and I've been trying to get it for years."

The antics had moved to the dugout and Kris got doused with blue and red Gatorade. Now starting to look like the Grape Ape, he took off to the clubhouse skipping his interview. Luckily, this saved me because she pulled in the rookie to cover her interview spot. I stood and watched the rest of the interviews. There was a quick exchange of words between Rick and Chase between their discussions with Hannah, and they glanced my direction. I thought this could be good! Maybe the rookie put in a good word for me and I would finally get the elusive Rick Seno autograph! Or, maybe he warned him about the crazy look in my eyes and the drool running down my chin.

Rick smiled at me when he walked right by me and didn't give me his autograph. A batboy hands Chase a note while he's being interviewed and continues on with his duties.

The interviews were over and I turned to check out the remaining crowd before I started my journey home from the game. I hate being in the middle of the rush of people. When I hear someone yell out "Hey blonde in the Seno jersey!"

Chase was calling me and had something to hand to me. I met his reach and before I even had the chance to recognize what I had in my hand, he was gone. Chase had handed me a folded piece of San Diego Seals Stationary that had "only for the blonde" scribbled on the outside and immediately disappeared.

I am blonde. He did smile at me. Me? I unfolded the note quickly and read:

> *I'm not interested in meeting crazy fans. It always turns out bad. Rook thinks I need to get away from the team this evening and vouched for you. Meet me at the Locale on Midway at midnight.*

> *Rick*

Does he really think I will just jump at his command and meet him? At midnight, no less? I'm not into booty calls, but this is Rick Seno. Will I regret not going and not knowing? What if he's a jerk and ruins my completely made up view of him? What will he think of me if I do go? I wonder what he wants? Crap! I have less than two hours to get home, get the public trolley system smell off of me and get to the Locale. If nothing else, I'm going to get his autograph!

I got home as quick as I could and scouted the Locale on my way, luckily it's only a couple blocks from my place. I've heard of the place before, but never visited the establishment. I know it's a local hangout that has a bar and upscale bar food.

So, do you wear your Rick Seno jersey to meet Rick Seno? Is that overkill? Is that expected? Does that make me a crazy fan? Does it draw more attention to him than is necessary? I'm so excited and nervous that I'm thinking at over a hundred miles per hour, can't even keep up with myself! Too many questions, no jersey. I'm going with my basic night out ensemble: tight dark wash jeans, black fringed boots and a low cut black V-neck that fits perfectly snug around my chest. I toss a baseball and pen in my purse, and do what I can to eliminate the hat head I'm sporting from the game. I notice I'm going to be late and head out the door.

I pull into the parking lot at the Locale and easily find a spot. It doesn't appear to be a very busy place tonight. Makes sense, everyone would stay downtown after the game, except Rick who wants out of the limelight. I step through the front door and take a look around the dimly lit room. I make my way to the back booths and find Rick sitting alone with a dark beer. It was the beginning of an unexpected and memorable night.

––––––––

THERE'S NO BETTER place to be than at the game, but this one has been tame and I'm preoccupied. It's the top of the

4th and we've been tied at 3 since the hour long 1st inning. Certain *scenes* from the replay reel in my head seem to be stuck on repeat. Not the best combination on a warm Sunday afternoon when I'm sitting in the sun. The game is going slow. I'm antsy and hot. I wander up to the concourse to hang out in the shade, but go for a walk to find the gelato vendor instead. Not because the gelato guy is on the other side of the stadium which would provide a great view of the dugout and possibly a glimpse of Seno. Fine. Maybe so, but they do have yummy milk chocolate and peanut butter swirl gelato, and on a hot day a girl deserves a splurge.

I get my gelato in the miniature plastic baseball helmet and happily walk over to get a peek at what's happening in the dugout. Rick is sitting there with his cap pulled down over his eyes and his legs stretched out, he's damn sexy in his Sunday uniform. The team gets the third out and heads to the dugout. Rookie Chase Cross beelines for Rick and razzes him about something, grabbing the cap off his head and flipping the collar of his jersey back revealing a huge hickey on his collarbone. I did that! Hickey plus trying to nap in the dugout plus same clothes as when he left the clubhouse last night equals Seno got lucky. The grin on his face in response to his teammates ribbing makes me smile. I did that. I make my way back to my seat because I'm satisfied with myself for now.

Top of the 7th inning, 1 out, runners at 1st and 3rd, 2-1 count and the score is tied at 3. Our number two catcher has been calling a good game and keeping the visiting team off the base paths. The fourth pitch of the at bat is a 94 mile per hour fast ball, the hitter goes for it full on ready to take it out of the park and smacks our catcher with his bat. There's an audible gasp throughout the stadium. Catchers are tough guys. He stands up out of his crouch to walk it off, but it isn't going to happen. I'm suddenly warm all over because Seno will be out in all of his gear at any second.

"Now replacing the injured Antonio Saben, Catcher Rick Seno!" The public address announcer blares through the stadium speaker system.

And there he is, a warrior walking out to the plate in his full armor with that intense expression I assumed was only for baseball until hours ago. He gets to his position and warms up with a few tosses to the pitcher followed by throws to each of the bases. I swear he glances toward my section and Kris Martin must have caught him, too. Instead of throwing the ball back to the plate, he walks it back to Rick and has a quick chat. There's no way it's about me—it must be my imagination. Time runs out on the injured player replacement warm up and the game gets going. With Seno behind the plate, the pace picks up. Rick throws the runner out trying to steal 2nd, we strike out the hitter and it's time for the Seals to bat. Three up and three down, no hits and we're back on the field for the top of the 8th inning.

"Miss," an usher is trying to get my attention. "What's your name?"

I gawk at the young usher and give him my name.

"I wanted to make sure because I have something for you." He hands me a bag and walks away.

I find this odd, but the more I examine it I get excited and anxious like a child on Christmas morning. It's a small duffle bag, big enough for a trip to the gym and it's used, a bit worn round the edges. I unzip the bag to find a warm baseball glove embroidered with Seno holding a baseball that's autographed by every player on the team, featuring Rick's autograph in the sweet spot followed by a heart. My heart beats in my chest like it's trying to escape. After closer inspection of the bag, it's embroidered with a big rounded RS monogram on the end. I hear cheers and find they're showing me all giddy up on the big screen. I focus on the field and see Rick lift his catcher's mask. He smiles at the sight of me on the big screen and gets right back to business.

My seat section buddies swarm me to find out details, not the guys, the girls and mostly Dina, Samantha and Meli. I had greeted them when I got to the game, but kept to myself today, other than my incessant yelling and jumping out of my seat like a jack in the box. The looks I get are priceless. What is the girl who goes to the games by herself up to? What is a stadium employee, not a ticket representative, bringing to her? The eyes were on me. My eyes were on the game and trying to ignore them. To be clear, I'm ready to spill my guts like a teenage snitch. I'm not sure what to make of the gesture. Is he trying to make up for the fact he wouldn't sign a ball for me last night? Is this his "Take this, go away, and leave me alone because we both got what we wanted?" Something to remember me by and peace out. I want to retreat into the game and forget about all of it, but I can't because it's all right there in front of me. After all, he's catching the game and everything hinges on him. I focus on the heart he drew on the ball after his name and it gives me hope.

After all this commotion, the Seals are coming up to bat in the 8th. No score change. We need to hold the other team and we need to score. The rookie, Chase Cross, is stepping up to the plate and Seno is scheduled to bat second.

Cross takes the first pitch outside, ball one. Shows bunt on the second pitch and smacks the ball foul, one and one. He gets the bunt down toward the third baseline on the third pitch and legs out the throw from the third baseman. Chase is safe at first.

Rick walks to the plate with so much intensity it should be illegal. He nods at his teammate on first. He takes the first pitch up and inside, a little close to his handsome face for my liking. He continues to crowd the plate. The next pitch is a low passed ball and Cross advances to second. It's a 2-0 count. The third pitch is a fastball on the inner half of the plate, Seno swings and connects. It's a beautiful sound off the bat, fresh and sharp. The horn sounds and the fireworks fly, 2 run homer! Seals are ahead 5-3. The next three hitters were struck out at the plate and we held the other team to 3 in the top of the 9th. Seals win 5-3.

Seno and our veteran closer Doug Houck are the heroes. I watch the on field interview girl, Hannah, trying to get their attention for interviews. She has Houck, but Seno is nowhere to be found. I sit in my seat watching the interview, I catch the rookie's eye and he waves at me. No need to go down by the dugout when I have every autograph. I wait for the crowd to thin out and walk back to the trolley for the ride home.

CHAPTER THREE

I usually go home and relax on Sunday after the game. Maybe read or go hang out at the beach. Today I'm stuck in baseball mode. I turn on the TV and load up one of my favorite past games. Seno's major league debut.

The team is away for the next three days playing the Arizona Assmunches. No, that's not their real name, I'm a huge fan and the other teams suck no matter what! Thursday is an off day. Friday they'll be back at home playing the Denver Douchebags for another three game series. Today is a get-away day, the team has probably already had their post-game briefing and they're packing up for their trip to Phoenix.

I'm wishing I would've at least thanked Rick for the duffle bag, glove, and autographed ball. I can't do it now because I don't have his phone number or email address. I jump on the internet to see if his email address is public on his social media, but it's a futile attempt. He's not a social media guy, but the rookie is! Cross is on Twitter right now giving his run down of the plays he made today. I message him:

> Sherry: Hey Chase! This is the blonde from Saturday night who needed Rick Seno's autograph. Will you please thank Rick for sending me that awesome gift at the game today? I didn't want to be in the way after the game, since I obviously don't need any autographs. Hope you don't mind me messaging you, Seno doesn't have any social media. My thanks to you and the rest of the team.

Better. I want to show him my appreciation, but still leave the next move for him to take or not.

I turn some music on and review my work schedule listening to my favorite 80's station. Might as well get a jump on this week and get caught up on what came in while I was enjoying my weekend. Nothing better than belting out "Voices Carry" by 'Til Tuesday to help clear your mind and set you to concentrate on work. Luckily, I don't have to worry about work clothes or a boss or anything. I run my own travel service from home and most of it's done by email, so I'm in control of my schedule and my dress code. I've gotten a few emails from customers since I signed off late Friday afternoon, two thanking me for planning them such fabulous trips, and another asking me to plan a trip for their group. I specialize in beach locations, but I can arrange itineraries for anywhere. I reply to the emails, asking for pictures from the fabulous trips and request additional details for the group trip. My calendar has a few follow up items that will need to get taken care of on Monday and I need to do my social media updates. I'll be ahead for the week and have time to work on my fantasy baseball stadium tour vacation.

I start some laundry, because it's a vicious cycle and consider dinner. The 80's station continues with the Pseudoecho version of "FunkyTown" and it has me dancing around my kitchen. I check the refrigerator, but there's nothing I want and a girl cannot live on Dr. Pepper alone— I've tried. I settle on the half pint of Chocolate Chip Cookie Dough Ice Cream I have left in the freezer and a trip to the grocery store sometime in the near future.

I get a social media ping from someone who's not on my list and shows as a brand new account:

Notabaseballplayer: I've got this song stuck in my head and I don't know what it is, but it made this girl's hips swing and it's driving me crazy.

Sherry: Girl's hips swing when there's good music. You might need to contact a doctor.

Notabaseballplayer: My doctor can't cure this problem... he doesn't have the right equipment.

Sherry: The song is "All Right Now", it has a great swinging groove to it's bass line. Does that help?

Notabaseballplayer: I just checked with my doctor and he prescribed time with hips.

Sherry: What doctor is available on Sunday night? Quite an odd prescription.

Notabaseballplayer: Dr. Cross

Sherry: Is that Dr. Chase Cross?

Notabaseballplayer: Yes.

Sherry: He's a baseball player, not a doctor. He's cute though and does make a mean diving catch.

Notabaseballplayer: You think he's cute?

Sherry: Every female in the Northern Hemisphere thinks he's cute and some of the men do, too.

Notabaseballplayer: Do you think he's cute?

Sherry: Absolutely. He's one of my favorite players and a real cute kid.

Notabaseballplayer: Who's your favorite player?

Sherry: This catcher guy. He's a total hunk and a real man. Calls a great game and holds the record for throwing out the most runners from behind the plate.

Notabaseballplayer: Tell me more about this guy. He sounds interesting.

Sherry: He's 28 and single. Stands about 6'1". Has blue eyes and looks sexy in his catcher's gear.

Notabaseballplayer: Do you have a thing for baseball players?

Sherry: There's one baseball player I've got a thing for. The rest of them I cheer for because they're on my team.

Notabaseballplayer: On my team, huh? Are you part owner or something?

Notabaseballplayer: You mean you only have a thing for one player now, right?

Sherry: I've had a thing for the same player and only that player since his major league debut. I never had a thing for any player before him.

Sherry: Don't be a smart ass! I just claim the team as my own! Go Seals!

Then the messages stopped. I determine then and there I should prepare for next weekend. Positive attitude to get positive results. Manicure, pedicure, facial, waxing—all on the agenda this week. I need a new dress for Wednesday night karaoke, too. This girl deserves some pampering.

I add the games for the week to my calendar and block out the time so I won't be disturbed. I get ready for bed and find myself putting on my Seno jersey. My bed smells like him. (Note to self: Don't wash the sheets.) I strip naked, wrapping myself in his scent and memories of the last 24 hours.

CHAPTER FOUR

M onday morning came quickly and I hit the snooze a few times before I force myself to open my eyes. Not tired or lazy, simply upset the alarm went off while I was dreaming. Wait. I drag my hand across the bed checking for someone there with me and roll over to get a visual on the situation. This time it's a dream, though it sure seemed real. A video of scenes from our night together, set to music and on a continuous loop. I smell my coffee is ready and roll out of bed, pulling on some denim shorts and a purple tank top. I visit my coffee maker and thank it for preparing my morning caffeine.

Coffee in hand, I head to my desk to check my schedule, email, and social media. The game starts at 6:10 today. I have confirmation calls to make this morning and I need to review itineraries for anything last minute a couple of my regular customers may need. I need to call and check in on three clients who are currently on trips, make sure they're enjoying themselves and there are no hiccups. Only one new email this morning, photos from a trip to Oahu one of my repeat customers recently returned from, they'll be perfect for updating the website this week and sharing on social media. Nothing new on social media this morning, not surprising—it's Monday.

I call the salon and schedule their Pamper Me Package for Wednesday. I spend the rest of the morning and early afternoon handling business. I'm not a Monday person, but then again who is? I hit the mall in the afternoon to shop for a dress, but nothing jumps out at me and says "buy me!" I stop off at the thrift store and there's a vintage dark purple suede mini dress circa 1980's on the mannequin in the window. It's absolutely perfect for the songs I've chosen, it screams 80's Rock Ladies. I go inside and immediately climb into the window display to investigate. It's the right size and only $15! Having it! I drop off my new-to-me dress at the dry cleaner, stop to pick up dinner, and hurry home to watch the game.

I check my messages while the announcers do the pregame show and sit down to eat while I watch my team prepare to take on Arizona. The lineup is about normal. Cross is leading off, followed by Martin. Seno is hitting sixth. Arizona has their ace pitcher on the mound tonight and they're on a five game winning streak.

The game starts off good with Cross getting a base hit, but it gets erased when Martin hits into a double play. Repeat that a few times and it sums up the game. We lost 4-0. It was painful to watch. They're my team and I stand behind them either way. There are 162 games in a season and you just don't win them all. Seno did his job behind the plate and got on base twice, but nobody brought him in to score.

I grab a book to read and relax for a bit. I've had my favorite author's new book waiting for me about a week now and that's unacceptable. About 50 pages in I hear my social media ping.

Notabaseballplayer: Did you watch the game?

Sherry: I never miss the game.

Notabaseballplayer: You could've missed tonight's game.

Sherry: Any day with baseball is better than a day without it.

Sherry: Noticed you have a nasty bruise on your collarbone. Did you get hit?

Notabaseballplayer: Like a truck. Don't you remember how that hickey got there? I've been the target of all clubhouse fun since I walked into the stadium Sunday morning wearing the same clothes that I left in Saturday night.

Sherry: I did that?

Notabaseballplayer: You have no idea what you've done.

Sherry: Thank you for the autograph. I especially like the heart after your name.

Notabaseballplayer: I'm glad. Now, no more baseball. Okay?

Sherry: Scouts honor. Would you like to buy some cookies?

Notabaseballplayer: I want your cookies. That's for sure.

I didn't respond for a few minutes. Not sure what to say. I don't want to be a booty call. Then again...

Sherry: Chocolate chip or peanut butter?

But, he was already gone.

TUESDAY MORNING IS a happy busy blur, four new trips to plan and the details for the group trip came in. I work my ass off to get it all done, because I'm basically planning to ditch on Wednesday between my appointment to get pampered, the early baseball game, and karaoke night. I pick up my suede dress from the cleaners and make a stop at the grocery store. I toss all the usual suspects in my cart plus a few sandwich fixings, pick up a pizza, and go home to watch the game.

Tuesday's game went much better. Same lineup again, but the Assmunches couldn't do anything right—they had two errors in the first inning and we were capitalizing on them. Cross finished the game with a single, a triple, and a home run—only a double shy of a cycle. Martin had two doubles. Seno hit a homer and everybody else was on the hit list at least once. We won 7 – 0 and used up their bullpen. It was fantastic!

After the game, I spend time in my closet putting

together my karaoke outfit. The purple suede mini dress is very 80's, it needs appropriate shoes and accessories to make the statement I'm striving for. It's a cool dark purple, so I choose silver accessories: a shiny metal belt made entirely of misshapen links that will leave links dangling once it's around my hips, a few bangle bracelets and a two inch wide faux chainmail choker with a teardrop amethyst charm hanging from it. The dress itself is short, but not so short it will reveal too much when I'm on stage. It's fitted and feels like it was custom made for me. The top is low cut in a sweetheart neckline and snug like a bustier with two thin straps of ribbon over each shoulder. My black leather thigh high boots will be perfect.

I hear my social media pinging.

Notabaseballplayer: Can I take you out Thursday?

Sherry: What do you have in mind?

Notabaseballplayer: Dinner. I feel like I owe you.

Sherry: You don't owe me anything. Thanks.

I log out. I don't want to see anything else he has to say. How does he make me such an irrational girl? He's going to buy me a meal after we already fucked because he didn't do it beforehand? Not on my time. His loss.

Five minutes later my phone starts to ring. The caller ID says Phoenix, AZ.

I answer the phone nonchalantly, "Hello?"

"Hey! This is Chase. Seno is being a stupid ass, so I looked your number up on the internet and I'm calling you so I can hand him the phone."

"Hi, I don't want to talk to him right now..." and I get cut off.

"Sherry?" comes over the phone in the voice I've been dreaming about.

"Yes," I reply curtly.

"Please listen to me. I'm sorry my message didn't come out right. I feel like I owe you because I invited you out and didn't even buy you a drink," Rick's sincere tone attempts to melt me. "Will you go out with me Thursday? I want to spend some time with you and get to know you."

"Look, I don't know what you think. I'm not a booty call. I'm not a player chaser. I'm not your San Diego sex. I have more respect for myself than that," I spout off irritably.

"Just stop," he says with a sigh. "I can't stop thinking about you. Yes, I want to see and feel your hips, but its more than that."

"I need to sleep on it. I'm not sure about going out with a baseball player."

"Remember, I'm not a baseball player with you and I don't want to be." He hangs up.

I immediately log on to my social media and message him...

Sherry: What time are you picking me up on Thursday?

Notabaseballplayer: I'll be at your place about 6:30.

Sherry: See you then.

Notabaseballplayer: Can I have your phone number?
Cross won't give it to me.

Sherry: 619-555-1269 Tell Cross he can call me anytime, and you can too.

Notabaseballplayer: You don't need to talk to Cross.

Sherry: Yes, I do. You wouldn't be messaging me right now if he didn't call me.

Notabaseballplayer: See you Thursday.

Late to bed and I need to get up early for my pampering. Not the best combo. I'm going to need an afternoon nap to make it through karaoke.

CHAPTER FIVE

I wake up Wednesday morning before my alarm goes off and jump out of bed. I've been waiting for karaoke night because it's not just any karaoke night —tonight will decide who moves forward to the final five. I'm excited about the 80's Rock Ladies theme, totally my genre. I've been competing every other Wednesday for three months, with a different theme every round. It's down to ten of us performing tonight, when we started there were thirty of us. I'm going to dress the part and I'm going to rock it! Rules for tonight say I'll be singing three songs and to have a fourth song ready in case there needs to be a tie-breaker. Here's my set list for tonight, but I haven't decided which one to save for the tie-breaker:

"Shadows of the Night" by Pat Benatar

"Alone" by Heart

"The Warrior" by Scandal

"Kiss Me Deadly" by Lita Ford

I've had fun singing karaoke with friends over the years, but it's always been fun and good times. I'd never signed up for a competition and I'd avoid the bar on competition night. My karaoke buddies all decided we should sign up for the competition and I fought it, but in the end I went along with them. If we're all going what could it hurt? Well, believe it or not it can hurt. I'm competitive by nature and let's just say challenge accepted. Five of my buddies and I signed up to try out. Three didn't make it passed the try out round. My remaining two friends got dropped in week 1 and week 2. Here I am, its week 6 and I've been accused of taking it too serious. I've made it this far and I'm going for it. My friends still love me and will be there tonight, even though they've all made excuses and told me they won't.

I get to the salon ten minutes early and check in for my Pamper Me Package. First, I'm getting a Brazilian wax, then a full-body massage, and I'll be left wrapped in tropical leaves with essential oils while I get a facial. Next, an all over sea salt scrub. Then I relax in the most luxurious spa robe ever while I'm served tea, water with fruit essence and fancy sandwiches in a private room with relaxing music and a fountain. Thirty minutes later I'm joined by two women, one does my manicure and the other does my pedicure. It's wonderful and I've been pampered until I'm glowing, but I'm running late for the game.

When I turn the game on there are already two outs in the top of the first inning. I check the lineup and wonder why our back-up catcher, Saben, is playing first base and Kris Martin is playing right field. Our utility guy, Lucky Lucine is playing shortstop and the order is all mixed up. I'm not sure if I'll ever understand it. Right now, Seno and Saben are both on base—second and third respectively. First base is open and it seems the rookie pitcher for Arizona has been challenged by runners on base. They're running a replay of Saben and Seno both stealing at the same time. I love my guys tearing up the base paths! Martin is at bat and draws a walk. Cross comes up to bat, lays a bunt down toward first base and legs it out. Saben scores and Seno moves to third. Martin safe at second, watching and waiting for his opportunity to cause trouble makes eye contact with the third base coach and Seno. He starts for third and gets caught in a pickle, runs back toward second, then toward third, back toward second. Seno runs for home, shortstop throws for home not in time, Seno scores. Martin is safe on third and Cross moves up to second. 2-0 Seals. Lucky is at bat next and grounds out. Seno caught an awesome game assisting our pitcher, John Birmingham, to his first shut out. Quick game at only two hours and thirty-eight minutes, with a final score of 3-0 Seals thanks to Lucky's home run in the 7th inning.

I turn on some music and decide to sing through my set a couple times before I relax and take a nap. I'm relaxed after my morning and want to be fresh tonight. I set my alarm for 5:30, close all the blinds, and sack out.

I wake up in time to hear my alarm go off and notice my social media has been pinging.

Notabaseballplayer: Did you watch the game?

Notabaseballplayer: It was a quick one and done.

Notabaseballplayer: Hello?

Sherry: Hi!

But it's too late. He's gone. He keeps saying he doesn't want to be a baseball player with me, but he always asks if I watched the game. I must be missing something.

Time to get ready. I get my set music playing to get me in the mood. I strip naked and start with black satin bikinis and a strapless black satin push-up bra. I brush out my long blonde hair, wipe some metallic eye shadow across my lids, put on some black eyeliner, apply a couple extra coats of black mascara, and dab some of the same dark red lipstick I use on my lips on my cheeks. I slide on my black thigh high stockings and attach the garters as I get my black lace garter belt situated on my hips. One of the things I love about the structure of lined suede is it doesn't show panty lines and such, a perfect opportunity to go for the garter belt and thigh highs. I pull on my black leather thigh high boots and they come up about seven inches short of the stockings. The three-inch heels on the boots elongate my body and add an arch to my posture. I pull on my dress and I'm transformed into a sexy rocker. I arrange the silver belt at my hips, slide the bangles over my hand and fasten the choker around my neck. I check my outfit in the mirror and I love it from the large teardrop amethyst to the thigh highs, but I'm missing earrings. I find my two inch misshapen silver hoops, they're exactly what I need and match the belt perfectly. My hair needs to stay simple, so I can shake it out when it gets crazy on stage tonight. I toss my lipstick, brush, and mints into my small black purse and take off for the bar.

CHAPTER SIX

I arrive at the Batter Up Sports Bar and walk to the back bar near the stage to check-in. Now, I use the term "stage" loosely. It looks good to the audience, but they put up a curtain to divide the backstage off from the rest of the bar, built a plywood cover over some pallets and painted it black. There's a milk crate performers use as a stair step. On competition night, all contestants are required to stay backstage (which includes the alley for air and smoking) until everyone has finished singing. They do provide a continuous flow of appetizers, water, and tea for us. If you want anything else you have to pay and the server only checks on us every thirty minutes. At 8pm sharp the karaoke competition host will step up on stage to start the night off by belting out "Living on a Prayer" by Bon Jovi, he does the same thing every time. Then he'll welcome all the Batter Up patrons and give them the low down on the competition tonight and what they can do if they want to sing karaoke later this evening. Our host and karaoke DJ for tonight, Mike with the Mic, announces all of our names and explains we will each be invited to the stage in random order based on names pulled from a hat. I'm not sure about the random name drawing, but it does keep you from getting too nervous because you don't have any warning. They call your name and you get on stage. Three songs each breaks down to 10 to 12 minutes per contestant, so it will take a couple hours to get through all of us. I don't talk to my competition backstage, other than "Nice boots" and "Did you change your hair?" Mostly, I review my lyrics, take advantage of the free meal, and listen to the other vocalists.

It's Wednesday night and the Batter Up is all regulars. No crowds from the game or weekend partiers. During the fourth singer I notice the crowd gets a bit louder. It's about 8:45 and I'm waiting for my name to be drawn. So far, I'm not impressed with my competitors. It's 9:30 and there are only two of us left to sing. The host draws the name and I'll be singing last. I take advantage of the ten-minute warning to use the ladies room and touch up my lipstick. I make sure Mike has my songs in the correct order:

"Shadows of the Night" by Pat Benatar

"The Warrior" by Scandal

"Alone" by Heart

"Please welcome our last singer for the night, Sherry!" announces Mike.

I make my way up the milk crate. I scan the room, there's a crowd way on the other side of the bar by the TVs, and mostly past competitors and friends around the karaoke area. I smile and wait for "Shadows of the Night" to load up on the karaoke machine. It starts dramatically with vocals only, the karaoke machine begins with a metronome to give me the beat, the lyrics come up, and I sing. Back up vocals join after a few lines and the music kicks in at the end of the first stanza. It's all me for the first fifteen seconds. I love the lyrics and show their intensity in my voice from the promise they'll make it through together, through the getting to know you phase, to the begging for acceptance. I've listened to "Shadows of the Night" countless times and every time I enjoy the freedom rushing through me with no regard for the unknown. I chose my set list before Rick, yet tonight as I'm singing I find I'm somehow listening to the meaning of the lyrics for the first time and applying them to my life. While I'm singing, the hope that we're real runs through me. I want to know everything about him, I want to know his dreams. It's moving way too fast, and yet it's my dream coming true. I try to keep my emotions in check, and use my voice to make the song dramatic.

I hear the applause and notice some of the crowd has moved into the back of the room, but don't pay much attention to it since I have two more songs to sing. I wait for "The Warrior" to load up on the karaoke machine and start with power. I realize I'm singing to myself, I can be strong and I can do this. I'm a warrior. I need to put my heart out there and not be afraid. I'm the stereo jungle child, but I don't know if I'm the hunter or the game. I love that in the end two hearts will win. I let loose in the second verse and the emotion hits me. I wail for the reprise of the last six lines and it's freeing.

I have the most exhilarating feeling as the crowd moves toward the stage, more men have entered the Batter Up and there's an electricity in the air.

"Please give Sherry a big round of applause, she's closing out the competition tonight with Heart..." Mike rambles in DJ style as "Alone" loads on the karaoke machine.

The rhythmic opening piano makes me smile inside. My mom had this Heart cassette when it came out in the late 80s and I remember her having to replace it when the tape broke because she was constantly rewinding to play this song. I take a deep breath, the plan is to start with a tender tone and then let it rip. Reading the lyrics as they print across the screen is like reading my life, my internal infatuation trying to be real and yet still a secret. I build volume at the first chorus, but bring it back down for the second verse. The words come out with my heart and plant themselves on my sleeve for everyone to see my naked emotions during the last chorus, loud and forceful, yet questioning. I feel raw as I step back from the mic and turn my focus down to my feet, hiding my eyes and letting the piano solo gently end the song.

As I finish my set, the crowd has a deep roar. It's encouraging and I'm pleased with my performance. None of my competitors got a response like I did. I don't think I missed any notes and I stayed in key. A different type of cheer fills the bar with more manly sounds. I start to check myself and make sure my boobs aren't hanging out or something, when I look up and instantly know where the electricity is coming from—Rick Seno is in the room with most of the team. He's staring straight at me with fire in his eyes, his heat drawing me in. Chase is waving at me with a big grin on his face and calling me over.

"Thanks, Sherry. All of our singers did a great job tonight. They will be joining the bar in about 15 minutes, after we handle some business," Mike with the Mic closes out the contest for the evening.

I go backstage and hang out for a few minutes, waiting for the results. Only half of us will continue to the finals. There's a three-way tie for the number six spot tonight, but no sing off because number six doesn't move on. I made the top five! Now I wait for them to contact me about the finals.

I step out from behind the curtain and Seno is waiting for me, "You surprise me. You were extraordinary and look fucking hot."

Within a millisecond his lips are on mine. Lightning shoots through me. His hands appreciating the suede that's perfectly fitted to my ass, roaming up and down my back, and pulling me against him. His heartbeat is strong and his eyes are hooded. When did he get here? Did he hear my whole set? I'm thirsty after my performance and need to break away to get some water. I put my hands on his shoulders and step back.

I smile uncontrollably while I gaze into his eyes, "I'm surprised you're here. Can you give me a minute to get a drink and I'll meet you at your table?" I need to transition out of performance mode and unexpectedly having him right in front of me is a shock. I love his positive reaction to me, but it's still a switch flip in emotions.

"I'm not leaving you alone while you're dressed like this," he says firmly. He takes me in from head to toe, setting me on fire with his gaze.

"It's fine. I can handle myself," I retort.

"You're beautiful. You make me want to mark my territory and hide you from every other man here. Don't bother arguing with me, I'm not leaving your side. Or, maybe your rear since it's so fine. What's with going to the bar dressed like this anyway?"

"I wanted to dress the 80's Rock Ladies part to go with the competition."

"You're driving me crazy," he whispers in my ear and his hot breath sends tingles through my body. "You're a great singer. I love your voice."

I grab his hand, walk to the bar for some water and over to Chase. He tries to stop me before I get to Chase, but I'm not having it.

Chase winks at me as I walk up and asks jokingly, "Why are you hanging on to this loser? I'm more fun."

I laugh. He grabs me away from Seno to give me a hug and a kiss on the cheek. He whispers in my ear, "Happy to meet you outside the ball park. Seno has it bad for you and the longer I hold you close, the more furious he's getting. You're all I heard about on the Arizona trip."

I give him a wink and mouth thank you to him, while Rick pulls me into his gravitational field—claiming me as his and sending Cross a look that could kill.

It's 10:30 and I'm in no mood to go home. I want to dance and stay out late. I don't know what Rick is planning, but he's glued to me and I think he'd like to leave. The Batter Up opens up karaoke to everybody until midnight and patrons dance to the karaoke music.

With my body against his, I reach up and put my arms around his neck, stroking his hair. "I can't stop thinking about you. Will you dance with me? Then go back to my place and I'll make you breakfast," I gaze into his eyes coyly and fully aware of what I've asked for.

His smile widens and twists, "I don't dance, but the rest is exactly what I was hoping for."

I pull him to the dance floor anyway as "Thinking Out Loud" by Ed Sheeran starts to play. Perfect, a slow song. He doesn't fight it. He reaches around me and holds me tight while we sway together to the beat of the music. Gazing into each other's eyes. Gently kissing. Each of us caressing the other's back. I relax into his body and rest my head against his chest, feeling his heartbeat and mine. It doesn't matter if the guys are here or anybody else for that matter, we're in our own world and the rest has faded away. I lose track of how many slow songs play in a row, but when a fast beat hits he laces his fingers with mine and leads me out the door.

We walk hand in hand around the restaurant and club scene of the Gaslamp Quarter in silence. He leads and I follow to see where we're going, in more ways than one. We walk under the Gaslamp sign on Fifth and cross Harbor toward the convention center. He puts his arm around me as we walk along the marina toward Embarcadero Park South where the concert venue is set up. He leads me through the chained off entrance to the closed venue and up into the grandstand seating. The moonlight over the bay is bright, glowing and romantic as it reflects off the water's surface. My face in his hands, he kisses me tenderly and attentively. His lips soft and full of desire as they move over mine. His hands possessive as he holds me near. The heat is overpowering. He stops kissing me. His breathing is ragged. His face is red and he searches my eyes as he leans his forehead to mine. We sit together, silently in the moonlight and just be.

Eventually he speaks, "We should go to your place now," Rick offers his hand and leads me back to the Gaslamp Quarter.

CHAPTER SEVEN

We get to my place and the mood is calm, but full of intent. Cross' words give me confidence and alleviate my insecurities.

"Want to play a game?" I ask.

"What do you have in mind?" he inquires with a dirty glimmer in his eyes. "Strip Poker? Naked Twister?" he offers and wiggles his eyebrows.

"Sherry Says. It's like Simon Says, but better and I promise you'll love it."

"I'm in," he answers.

"You're not in yet, but you will be. I can promise that," the naughty girl inside me taking over.

"Sherry Says: Run your hands through the length of my hair." His fingers in my hair are light, sexy and somehow cooling.

I turn on my music with a groove playlist knowing I won't be able to help myself, my body will want to dance.

"Sherry Says: Unhook my belt and let it fall to the

floor." Rick finds the latch and lets the belt fall, skimming his hands over my swaying hips while he does it.

"Sherry Says: Unzip my dress." He finds the zipper at my back and unzips it slowly down to where it ends, right at the curve of my ass.

"Sherry Says: Kiss my cleavage." Seno's eyes glitter and he settles in at the rise of my breasts, kissing, licking, and fondling them appreciatively.

"Sherry Says: Push the dress straps off my shoulders." One shoulder at a time he picks the straps up off my shoulder and pulls them down to hang over my arm.

"Sherry Says: Give the bottom of my dress a quick tug." My suede dress puddles around my feet leaving me to stand there in front of him in my thigh high boots, stockings, garters and black satin under garments. I watch his face and body heat as he admires my body. The power and sexual need running through me is unbelievable.

"Sherry Says: Take off my panties." This might not be the easiest thing to do since I'm still wearing my boots, but it will give the best results. He gets down on his knees and starts to pull down my panties... The next thing I know his mouth is on my bare, sensitive, just-got-the-Brazilian-treatment-this-morning pussy and *Sherry* can't say anything. I simply whimper and give myself to this hot, sexy man's desires. His hot wet mouth sucking at my clit and his beard rubbing against my delicate folds are so much all at once, but he continues by sliding two fingers into me deep and separating me so he can dive his tongue in straight to my core. My body tingles almost immediately. Everything becomes more sensitive and starts to tighten, and he continues— knowing exactly how to play my body, as if he had a map and detailed instructions on how to bring me to ecstasy.

As he strokes me deliciously with his fingers, he glances up at me, "Is this bare pussy for me?" He smacks my sex.

I can't put any words together.

"Answer me." He says and smacks my sex again, "Or I'll stop fingering you."

"No. No! Don't stop! Yes, it's for you. Only for you," I say emphatically. I'm so far gone, I can barely keep my eyes open. I can't focus. All I can do is exist, living by the contact and warmth of his body with mine. The next thing I know I'm bent over with my feet spread apart in my thigh high boots and garters, holding my ankles as he plows into me hard from behind. I pant and scream out his name over and over and over. He reaches between my legs and strokes my clit while he slams his hard cock into me.

"I'm so close, baby. I need you to come for me. I need you to come for me now." He puts more pressure on my clit and I fall over the edge uncontrollably, tightening on his cock as he fucks me and pulling him over the edge with me. His deep release echoes through me. He's holding me up to keep me from falling. He carries me to the bed still mounted on his cock and holds me. Both of us staying connected as one, he kisses my hair and wraps his arms tightly around me.

"I'm staying here with you all night and I'm not leaving tomorrow," he whispers as we fall asleep.

I WAKE up at about 4am Thursday morning. Rick has released his arms from around me, but his body is still up against mine. I carefully get up to use the bathroom and get a drink of water. I'd managed to sleep with my boots on, so

I finally take them off and strip down to skin. I climb back into bed to find Rick asleep on his back and still buck naked from last night. Memories from the evening and our personal after party roll over me.

Did he say he's staying and not leaving? Snap out of it. Don't go all mushy now and start reading too much into it. It's simply his off day.

I move toward him and take his cock in my mouth. He hardens almost immediately as I stroke his shaft with my tongue and vibrate him with my moans. He groans appreciatively, but doesn't open his eyes—Could he still be sleeping? Dreamland? I suck lightly and tenderly love on him for quite some time, when he finally opens his eyes and focuses on me. I climb up him and kiss him like I've never had the pleasure of kissing him before and may never get to kiss him again. He wraps his arms around me and holds me while we kiss. My naked body on his, as if it's how it's meant to be. I rub my bare sex against him and his cock is ready for me. I lean back and take him in. His cock completely buried in my wet heat.

Something new and different shines in his eyes, "I love the way this feels. I love the way you feel."

It makes my heart kick and I'm not ready to hear any more, so I squeeze him inside of me and begin to bounce up and down on his hard cock.

He sits up and embraces me while I ride him, stopping my motions. He makes eye contact, "Something just changed, what happened? I want to be in the same place together, not different worlds."

I bite my lip nervously and try to ignore his question, but he turns my face to him and forces me to look directly into his eyes while he's searching for an answer, "Sherry?

You fell asleep in my arms last night. You were mumbling in your sleep. You said the sweetest things and made me believe I'm special to you. You make me happy, but now you're running from me."

"You make me happy, too. It's just all so fast and it's been only me for so long. What did I say?" I ask, though I'm not sure I want him to tell me.

"You told me you've been waiting for me and you told me not to leave. The rest of your sleepy words aren't important right now," he says, but his expression says something different and he isn't sharing.

"I talk in my sleep? Apparently, I'm honest because that's what I feel in my heart," I reply as I gaze up into his eyes.

I sigh and put it out there, "Your words caught me off guard. We haven't spent much time together, and the time we have been together has had a lot of naked. Yet, my heart has a long history with you."

"Sherry, you drive me to say things I've never said before. Things I can't imagine ever saying. Your honesty, tenderness and playfulness—there's nobody else, only you."

"How can you say that when all we do is kiss and have sex?" I throw at him rather thoughtlessly. What woman doesn't want to hear these things from her imaginary boyfriend? And there it is. Reality. My baseball boyfriend in my mind for the last few years is actually here. Breathing. Live and in person. In my bed. Saying sweet things. Naked. Inside me. Better in every way than I thought possible. I immediately wish the words didn't come out of my mouth, at least not with the accompanying accusing tone.

"I'm sorry. I..." and I'm cut off again.

Holding me tightly with one hand on each of my upper arms, he's almost shaking. "I could get mad and leave right now, but I'm not going to let the one person who makes me happy be the one who ruins my day. Look, I understand what you're saying, but I also feel you and your heart. This, right now—it's not just sex. What are you scared of?" he says with a strange, almost angry tone.

"I am scared. My fantasy world became real. You don't want to hear it, but you've been my baseball boyfriend for years. You were a fantasy who didn't have real life implications or any of the real issues around having a relationship with a baseball player. I'm scared you'll leave, then I lose both you and my fantasy." I stop and take a deep breath. He's still hard inside me and I want to move on him, grind against him. "I get it. You're not a baseball player with me, but you do play professional baseball for a living."

He puts his hands on my hips and holds me still, "I'm not leaving." He kisses me senseless and encourages me to continue my movements, grinding together where we're joined.

We kiss and grasp at each other for purchase, full of genuine need while we make love. He's right, it is different. We come together with no effort at all. No words directing one another, it's how it's meant to be. The ultimate climax, both of us going off like slow burning gun powder with unending orgasms. Simply mind blowing.

We held each other and he fell back to sleep while I recapped in my head. He isn't leaving because I'm the one person who makes him happy. His words sink in and my heart is full. Tears roll down my face and I sniffle, waking him from his almost sleep.

"What's wrong?" he asks.

"Nothing. Nothing is wrong. Happy girl tears," I say with a crooked smile and relax into his arms.

WHEN I WAS FINALLY ready to get up, Rick was already awake and having a quiet conversation with himself.

"Good morning. Hungry? Coffee? How long do you have this morning before you need to leave?"

"I told you, I'm not leaving today and I meant it. I need to be at the stadium tomorrow by 2pm and I'll be back after the game tomorrow night. Very hungry, and coffee sounds good."

"Let me whip up an omelet for you. Coffee is brewing."

"Are you going to cook breakfast for me naked?"

"Yes. Cooking naked. Is that a problem?"

"Not at all, as long as we have some time to shower together after breakfast."

"Is your plan to be naked all day today? I was asked out on a date for tonight at 6:30."

Our conversation continues as I go to the refrigerator to gather what I need for the omelet. I beat a half-dozen eggs with milk, a shake of salt and a pinch pepper. I let the eggs rest while I chop up part of a ham steak and half a basket of cremini mushrooms. I break down half of a red bell pepper, ending up with pretty strips of red. I roll up a few basil leaves tightly and give them a thin chiffonade. I cut the green ends down about four inches off three stalks of my scallions that are growing in my kitchen and chop them into little rounds. I put my skillet on to warm, rub it down with a tiny bit of butter and add my ham and mushrooms. I give the pan a toss, flipping everything around and add my bell peppers. I give my egg mixture a quick beat and dump it all into the pan. I give the pan a swirl to make sure everything is coated quickly. After a few minutes I flip it over and add some Colby Jack cheese as well as the scallions and basil. I turn off the burner and let the remaining heat cook it gently for a few minutes. I fold the omelet in half as I slide it out of the pan. It looks about perfect.

Rick had already helped himself to coffee and poured some for me. I hand him the plate with a napkin and fork.

"This is my take on an omelet, enjoy."

He sits down to eat. "So, you cook, you sing, you know baseball, you're beautiful naked, and you aren't shy. What don't you know how to do?"

"Play pool, hit a baseball and I'm not very good at catching either," I reply bluntly. "How's your breakfast?"

"It's delicious. Thank you."

I wasn't questioned on my baseball skills, so I'm calling it a win.

"How about I stay here with you while the team is home this home stand? Since I'm special and you don't want me to leave," he states more than asks.

"I do have to work, but I guess you do, too," I reply with an accepting smile.

"I'm still taking you out on a date tonight, so how about a ride to the stadium? I need to get my car and pick up a few things. I'm not leaving you."

"Don't we need to shower first?" I ask with a wink and a dirty smile.

Rick wraps his arm around my waist, picks me up and carries me to the shower. We're both already naked. He turns on the hot water, I dash out of the shower to turn on my steamy music playlist (you would guess its dirty, sexy, and maybe even kinky by the name, but it's my shower mix) and avoid the cold water that's going to come spraying out. He finds out the hard way it takes a minute for my water to heat up and I laugh as he jumps and curses at the cold water hitting his bare ass. With an ass as hot and hard as his, the water must have been almost instantly hot. It doesn't take long for the shower to get steamy. We're both wet all over. Droplets of water beading on his eyelashes. All I can do is admire how sexy he is, so damn sexy.

This hard everywhere, solid man with muscles on his muscles and he only wants me. I must be crazy if I believe I'm the only one he wants. I would buy that I'm the only one he wants right now, maybe even this week. Or, maybe he's crazy for being a professional baseball player who can have almost any woman he wants and choosing me. I think pretty highly of myself, but I understand reality and I've met it face to face on more than one occasion. Let's face it, I'm seven years older than him and in my mid-thirties. Nothing is sagging yet or anything and I've got some great curves, but I'm not one of those perfect twenty somethings. Then again, they'd be lucky to have an ass as nice as mine. I'm not blind and I'm not stupid, so I must be crazy to keep walking forward into whatever this is. Maybe I'm thinking about this the wrong way. Maybe I need to consider this an opportunity or a once in a lifetime experience. But, if I consider him my hot baseball boyfriend and truly the fantasy—that makes him a baseball player—which is definitely not allowed according to Mr. Seno's rules for this... this thing. All I know is I'm taking this ride until I'm road rashed, black, blue and bloody, because I will regret it if I don't.

I reach for my shampoo and Rick gives me a funny look, until I start washing his hair. Massaging his head, neck and scalp with my fingertips, causing him to close his eyes and sigh with relief. I rinse his hair out and repeat the process, making sure to thoroughly massage his head and rub my naked body against his front in the process. I soap up his muscled torso, shoulder to ass, front and back. Its like taking a trek through a forbidden place, touching everything that has a "Do Not Touch" sign on it and pressing every red button that says "Emergency use only". Bathing him, my hands on him, is turning us both on. Both of us hot and slippery soapy. The exotic tropical coconut and warm vanilla scent from my shower gel engulfs us as "Never Tear Us Apart" by INXS starts playing on my steamy playlist (who knew? I actually had something somewhat steamy on there). He pulls me close and kisses me with intent I feel all the way to my toes. This is a new kiss. Lingering, promising, claiming. His hands skimming over my wet nakedness. Holding me with his strength, yet as if I were breakable. Making me feel cared for, loved. I reach my arms around his neck and he lifts me up, so I wrap my legs around him. He backs me to the shower wall, the water spraying down over us as he kisses me deeply. Sucking on my tongue and stroking it, then darting in and out of my mouth—showing me what he wants to do next. I deepen the kiss and push myself up higher on him, allowing him access to my opening that's already spread and waiting for him with my legs wrapped around him. His erection in the perfect place, we work our bodies back to one slowly, tenderly, until he's completely seated inside me. Slowly, he moves in and out, sensuously stroking himself with me. It builds inside me with each thrust, over and over. His kiss alternating between sucking and stoking my tongue. His hands grasping my breasts while he continues to thrust into me, pinned to the shower wall. His pace begins to quicken, he moves his kiss to my neck and bites down hard, sucking on my neck, sending me into an immediate spiral as he comes so hard inside me I can feel his cock pounding and his fluids fill me. He pulls out quickly and sets me down before we both fall over. He leans against the wall and slides down to sit on the floor. He gazes at me across the shower, both of us completely sated and in uncharted territory. At least I'm not alone, unable to stand, heart beating out of my chest, with no words.

CHAPTER EIGHT

I drive up to the stadium to drop him off and he directs me to the employee entrance. He waves to the gate guard and I find myself driving into the player's garage. I've never been here before, so I need to take a moment and note the details. There are only about a dozen vehicles parked here right now, but it's an off day. I wonder how many of the guys are here and how many are doing exactly what Seno is doing, left their car here for safe keeping. Are the coaches here or are some of the players here to get a work out in on an off day? Maybe some front office people are taking advantage of the parking? I stop in the middle of the garage with my car still running to let him out.

"What are you doing? Park," he says gesturing with his head to the right.

I pull into a parking space on the right and turn off the engine. Not sure why he wants me to park. He's not taking me into the clubhouse with him or anything.

He turns to me, "I'll be back at your place in a couple hours."

"Okay," I say with a sweet girly smile. What the heck has gotten into me? Sweet girly smiles make me want to yack! I must be losing it.

He gets out of my car and starts to walk into the stadium, then turns around all of a sudden. "I forgot something."

I roll down my window to ask what he forgot, but he's kissing me before I can speak. He's kissing me hard and long, with serious sexual intensity. He breaks away, "I don't want you to forget about me." He disappears into the building, leaving me wondering if being punch drunk could cause me to get pulled over for drunk driving. I gather my senses and decide to use part of that couple hours for some shopping. I can still be back and working by the time he gets to my place. But, his kiss inspired me to go panty shopping.

I check out the main stream fancy underwear stores and find a short red satin robe with a matching lace up corset and string bikini set. I stop in the department store and hit the jackpot with fun panties. One pair is black with lips like the Rolling Stones logo and says "Bite Me" in big letters across the butt. Another pair is pale pink and printed with lollipops, candies, and the words "Lick" "Suck" "Sweet" all over them. But, my favorite pair is bright blue with the Cookie Monster on the front eating a cookie and "Eat Me" in bold print across the butt.

I hurry home to get going on my work before he gets there.

I walk into my small penthouse and it smells like him. I take a deep breath and enjoy the scent. I put away my new purchases, open the window, start up my work playlist, and do my best to focus on business as Rick Springfield's Beach Reggae Mix version of "Jessie's Girl" floats around me. What can I say? Beachy, reggae style gets me in the beach vacation-planning mood.

I update my website with the vacation photos I received earlier this week and share them on my social media. I make a few calls to check in with my customers who are currently vacationing and everybody is happy. In fact, the Crane Family is having such a good time Mr. Crane wants me to see if I can extend their vacation home rental on the beach of Oahu another week. I'm good, but I'm not a magician. Beachfront rental homes get booked up early and rarely have any openings for something as spontaneous as extending a stay after you are already there. It's not a hotel, there are no extra rooms. I check with the property owner and they can extend, but only one additional night. I check the last minute travel specials for hotels and discover the Sweetheart Rock Resort on the Island of Lanai is offering free airfare round trip from Oahu and Kona with a minimum 5 night stay and price it out. I call Mr. Crane and let him know we can only extend the house one night, but we can fly his whole family to Lanai where they can stay at the Sweetheart Rock Resort for a week for only $2,800. It's a steal and he can't pass it up. I love those last minute things. Hotels have too many empty rooms and come up with some great offers.

There's a knock on my door, I look up and realize how quickly the time has flown by. I check the peephole to see Rick waiting at my door. I play with him. "Who is it?" I call through the door.

"You know who it is. I saw you look through the peephole."

"No, I don't recognize you," I say jokingly.

"Maybe if I pulled out my huge cock that would jog your memory," he says loudly so all the neighbors can hear.

I quickly open the door and glare at him.

"You started it." He laughs and comes in, greeting me with the same kiss he left me with. I could get used to that.

He brings a duffle bag and garment bag in with him. "Go ahead and hang your clothes up in my closet, there's some room on the close end," I tell him and immediately wish I'd think before I open my mouth. Too late. I hung my new red satin purchase there, next to my jerseys and base-ball shirts.

A comment comes from the closet, "That's hot." I grin to myself, I knew he'd like it. A few minutes later he returns in a T-shirt, shorts, and running shoes, with a black iPod shuffle and ear buds clipped to his shirt.

"I'm going for a run, while you finish working. Be back in a bit." Followed by another one of those don't-forget-me kisses and he's out the door.

I still have some work to do, but now I'm distracted and want cake. I tell myself no cake, you have a date tonight and work to do. Okay, no cake until you get your work done.

I get back to work, checking my email, making sure I haven't missed any phone messages and of course I must see what's new on my social media. I send out an email with options and prices for my group trip request and finish booking a honeymoon I've been corresponding with the bride-to-be on for about a month. Lastly, I check social media and everything work related is current.

I go to my pantry to see if I have ingredients for cake, and I have a box mix that'll work if I doctor it up. Setting the oven to preheat, I empty the chocolate cake mix into my mixing bowl and add a small box of instant cheesecake pudding mix, give it a quick whisk and add the eggs and oil as directed on the package, replace the water with milk and stir to see if I have the correct consistency. I add a bit more milk and stir again, much better. I drop in some semi-sweet chocolate bits and look around the kitchen. I check the refrigerator and the freezer. I don't know what I'm searching for. I find some leftover cream cheese, put it in a separate mixing bowl and toss it in the microwave for a few seconds to soften it up. I add some powdered sugar to the cream cheese and stir until it's smooth. I pour my chocolate cake mix into a nine by thirteen baking dish and add spoonfuls of my cream cheese mixture evenly throughout the cake, making pools of deliciousness. I get a butter knife and drag it, zigzagging across the cake causing a swirl affect. I stick it in the oven and set the timer for thirty minutes. Waiting for cake to bake is the worst, it's a big tease! You know it's there and you want it, it makes you wait. It teases you with its delicious smell while it's baking.

I wander out to my balcony and see Rick running along the river path. I clean up my kitchen mess and wash up a bit, so it's not obvious I licked the bowl the raw cake batter was in... and the bowl the cream cheese mix was in. Well, I couldn't waste it. There's still a few minutes left on the cake when he comes back in from his run.

"Cake? I thought you were working," he says.

"I finished up for the day and wanted cake," I say, used to doing whatever I want.

I'd been dreaming about our date and wondering where he's taking me or what I should wear, "What's the appropriate attire for our date tonight?"

"You wear whatever you want. You're beautiful no matter what," he says. "I'm going to take a shower and clean up from my run. But, I want to talk to you and now would be best," he continues. "I will not be having sex with you tonight. I want you to know now, so you don't read anything into it. I want you to know it's more than sex," he sounds like there's more.

"I don't know why you're punishing me by withholding sex, but whatever," I say laughingly, waiting for him to say more. He simply turns and walks away, releasing an exasperated sigh.

Rick gets cleaned up, while I take the cake out of the oven and sample it—Yum!

When he emerges from the shower he's dressed in extra dark jeans and a navy blue long sleeve dress shirt with turquoise pinstripes that set off his eyes—and smells ah-mazing.

"I'll be back in an hour to pick you up." He gives me a sweet kiss on the cheek and he's out the door.

I check my closet and decide to go with my new Cookie Monster panties, tight black jeans and a tie dye printed flouncy deep V-neck tank that just meets the top of my jeans, with my black gladiator sandals. I apply a light amount of make-up and curl my hair. Checking my accessories, I choose a simple leather wristband, gold diamond stud earrings for some bling, and leave my neck and chest bare, accentuating the deep V-neck. It's exactly 6:30. I walk through a spray of my favorite perfume as the doorbell rings.

I open the door to find a gorgeous man with a fragrant bouquet of mixed tropical flowers in a beautiful vase that reminds me of beach glass.

"Hi, come on in," I play along with the date as if we haven't spent most of the last eighteen hours naked. "The flowers are lovely."

"I noticed you like tropical," he gestures around the room.

"I love anything on the beach, near the beach, smells like the beach, or simply reminds me of the beach. That's why I'm a travel agent specializing in beach vacations. Someone once told me I should do what makes me happy. The beach makes me happy," Providing more information than necessary. I swear, diarrhea of the mouth sometimes. "I like to make others happy by helping them with beach trips."

"That's a smart person who told you to do what makes you happy," he replies.

"It was a woman I met on Oahu who was running a small souvenir shop. She said she had worked in corporate America, but she was only happy in her town by the beach," I sigh remembering my friend, Malia, and wanting to go visit her.

Rick reaches for my hand, "We need to get moving or we'll be late for our 7pm reservation."

I follow his lead to his car and he opens the door for me. "You look beautiful." He kisses me on the cheek.

He gets in the car and we take off toward the freeway. I don't know where we're going, other than out to dinner. I can't remember when I've been on a date before when everything was already planned and I was simply along for the ride. I could get used to this. We get off the freeway in Del Mar and head toward the beach.

We park along the side of the road and walk up to a restaurant on the beach. He reserved us an ocean side table with a view of the sunset. And, we're here at the right time to witness it. He sits next to me on the same side of the table and holds my hand, lacing his fingers with mine. He orders a Mai Tai, a Ginger Lime Fizz and Parmesan Truffle Potato Chips.

I focus on him, "What do you do?" Pretending I don't

know and going along with him not being a baseball player.

"I have a non-profit organization that provides money to send teenagers from financially challenged families to camps for sports and arts. I volunteer at the sports camps, providing special baseball skills training to the campers. But, the art campers are already ahead of any artistic skill I have, so I speak at the art camps about following your dreams," he states proudly.

I see him with a different perspective, "That's a great thing."

"I'm also a professional baseball player. I'm thankful for everyday I get to play. Baseball has provided me the ability to fund my organization, get additional donations from my contacts and charity events. My name helps with the publicity and so do my teammates," he says, going along with the date and admitting he's a baseball player to me for the first time. Interesting that being a baseball player is secondary in importance, but the means to his non-profit.

"You're a baseball player? I had no idea!" I say feigning shock.

Rick looks at me and smiles sincerely. Appreciating that I've been going along with him not being a baseball player with me.

Our drinks and appetizer arrive. I take a drink of the Mai Tai and ask him, "Are you trying to get me drunk?" laughing as I ask.

"No, I just want to get to know you. I meant it when I said no sex tonight. I have to tell you, it's not because I don't want you." He leans in and whispers in my ear, "I want to take you right here on the table, then again down on the sand with the waves at our feet. I need your tight wet body around my cock. I need to taste you. I need to hear you calling out my name. I need to feel your heart beating against mine. I need to kiss your perfect lips." Turning my face to his, he puts his lips to mine softly and sits quietly with his arm around me while we watch the sun paint the sky with shades of pink and orange as it sets into the ocean.

We order dinner and our conversation flows. The food is well plated with tropical flowers as accents on the plates and delicious. His steak looks mouthwatering and my heirloom tomato bisque with ricotta grilled cheese is over the top luxurious. We talk about our families, where we're from and where we consider to be home. His parents still live in the small Colorado town where he grew up, his sister is happily married with two children, and in his heart San Diego is home.

"My dad disappeared when I was young, it's been me and my mom since I was ten. I can't imagine it being any different. I grew up in Orange County and moved to San Diego because I've always been drawn here. Mom brought me here for vacations every summer. She lives about sixty miles North right at the edge of the Orange County line," I tell him.

After dinner we walk down to the beach and go for a barefoot stroll in the sand. He laughs at me when I can't stay out of the water and end up wet to my knees. The clear night is brightly lit by the stars and moon, multiplied by the light bouncing back off the ocean. The beach is empty except for a couple of groups with bonfires burning. In our own world, he stands at my back and wraps his arms around me while we absorb our surroundings.

His warm breath at my ear is killing me, but I try to stick to his no sex rule. I'm not sure about all of his rules.

He speaks calmly in my ear, "I wish you were always in my arms. Nobody has ever made me want to just hold them. I just want to be with you. We don't need to do anything, but simply be together. You make everything right in the world." His words melt straight into my heart.

He holds me tightly, wrapping his body around me to keep the chill of the ocean breeze from my arms. Light kisses go down my neck as he holds my hands in his. It's perfect. I don't need to speak.

"I know how you feel about me and I know you're scared. I want you to know that I'm scared, too. I don't want to ever leave you. The kiss I give you when I leave is selfish and all for me, so I can have your taste on my lips when we're apart. The next road trip is ten days long and I don't want to be away from you." He makes my heart beat faster with his words. I had already checked the schedule and I'm dreading Sunday—Get-away day.

We walk back to the car and Rick asks if I want to go to a movie or dancing.

"Actually, I'm starting to get cold. Can we go back to my place? I'll share my cake with you and we can play a game or something with clothes on," I suggest.

"Your wish is my command. Leaves us more options for our next date." He drives to my complex. "Are you available Saturday night after the game?"

"I'm available all day Saturday, that's my laundry day and I'm happy to put it off."

"Can you meet me at the dugout after all the kids run the bases post game Saturday?"

"No. I don't usually go to Saturday games and I don't have a ticket."

"Okay, I'll have a ticket added to your account for Saturday's game. Will that work?"

"Sure. Any special instructions?"

"Wear your tennis shoes."

We get home and it's going to be a challenge to keep my

hands off him. I wanted to unbutton his jeans and give him a hand job or suck him off the whole ride home. Something about him keeps me turned on and wanting more. Maybe it's the time I've spent drooling over him as my fantasy or maybe it's his special brand of pheromones or maybe it's simply the presence of a cock in the same room with me. Maybe I'm horny and easy. Maybe I'm one of those baseball skanks. That's it. I've got to get control. If it's important to him, then it needs to be important to me if I'm interested in making this real. Or maybe, in reality, I know this won't last and I want all of his time that I can have and as many memories as possible.

I get the cake, a fork, and a can of whipped cream, and we sit next to each other on my love seat.

"So what exactly do you see happening here?"

"Just watch and see. Don't worry, no sex." I unbutton his shirt, because I want to. Then I take a small bite of cake in my mouth and it makes my eyes roll back in my head, it's so good. Next I get a bite of cake and feed it to Rick, then I spray some whipped cream into his mouth... and by some I mean as much as will fit. I repeat this a few times until he takes the whipped cream away and starts squirting it into my mouth. It's getting warm in here, whipped cream and licking and... I put the whipped cream and cake away. Trying my best to be a good girl, because I don't think I can lick whipped cream off anything else and not have it turn into sex.

"How about we play a game?" I ask.

"No, last time I agreed to a game—well, I still haven't gone home," he says with a dirty glint in eyes.

"I promise. Nothing dirty. No sex. No Sherry Says," I say solemnly. "No fun."

"What's left?" Rick looks at me questioning.

"Board games? Cards? Music trivia? Video games?" I offer options.

"Tell me more about Music Trivia."

"Really? Nobody will ever play any kind of music trivia with me. We have a couple of options. We can turn on the radio and see who knows the artist and title of the song first, or I can get out the music trivia cards." I say with a grin.

"How about you pick between board games and video games? I don't feel like getting my ass handed to me on a night I'm not getting laid and I'm pretty sure that would happen with music trivia."

"Not to be smug, but you would be correct on that assumption. Though you're the only thing keeping you from getting laid tonight. I choose board games," I say as I get out Sorry, Clue and Trouble. Okay, maybe this will be fun.

"We're in for the night. Would you like to have a drink with our board games?" I ask. "I promise not to have sex with you."

He smiles, "Yes. Which game are we playing?"

"All of them," I reply as I pour some Screwdrivers. "When does the ban on sex expire? And, does it include everything or only the actual deed?"

"All of them?" he questions.

"Yea, they don't usually take very long to play. Don't ignore the other questions," I prod.

"If we do anything it will turn into everything, because I can't help myself."

"Okay. So, it turns into a pumpkin at midnight like Cinderella or?" I want an answer. "You're kind of punishing me here. Staying here with me and being near me and having a hard-on like that. Like having a toy and not being able to play with it."

"Should I leave?" he asks quietly.

Surprised, "No, it's not like that. I want you here with me. I want your arms around me. I want you to sleep with me in my bed. I don't want you to leave. I'm trying to understand what you want and help you make it happen."

He straight out says, "We need to be able to spend time together without getting it on."

"So, getting naked would be okay, but it's not okay to have sex?" I couldn't help myself. "You sit on your side of the board and I'll stay on my side of the board."

He sighs, almost a grumble. "You know what I mean."

And I did. I shouldn't be adding to his frustration.

We start with two Screwdrivers each and Clue. I'm always Miss Scarlett and apparently I did it with the candlestick in the library. By the time we find out I'm the murderer, I need to make more Screwdrivers and Rick sets up Sorry. Sorry takes forever and I can't stop laughing. Buzzed much? I do whatever I can to send his little marker dudes back to home base and start over instead of trying to get my marker dudes home. It's more fun that way. I've been accused of cheating at board games. However, I don't use any of those skills tonight because of the sex ban. Rick is irritated with the game, but laughing and needs another Screwdriver.

Its Screwdriver number six that pushes me over the edge and makes me go back to the cake. Rick turns red with laughter at me as I sit Indian Style with the whole cake pan in my lap, fork in one hand and whipped cream can in the other. Fork of cake in right hand, slide cake off into mouth, left hand comes in with whipped cream, squirt onto cake in mouth and yum. Suddenly he's on my side of the game board and takes everything away from me. He keeps the whipped cream and takes over with his own process. He fills my mouth with whipped cream and eats the whipped cream out of my mouth, licking with his tongue deep inside and sealing my mouth with his lips while he sucks the whipped cream from me. It's amazing. (Note to self: Always keep a can or two of whipped cream in the refrigerator.)

The next thing I know, he says, "It's after midnight, it would probably be okay for us to have sex now."

"No. Not until tomorrow after the game. But everything else is fair game. It's important for you not to give in. I get it. But, if you want to strip me naked and cover me in whip to your heart's content, I'm up for that and even have some chocolate sauce," I say, catching him off guard.

He looks at me and his mouth drops. That's when I remember I'm wearing the Cookie Monster panties that say Eat Me across the butt. I strip down to my panties and stand in front of him giving him my rear view as I bend over, pointing my ass at him. Basically commanding him to eat me. He turns me around and covers my nipples in whipped cream, one at a time. Taking his time to lick and suck every trace of whipped cream off of my breasts, then going back and doing it again... and again... and again. He draws a line with the whipped cream from my breasts to my navel, then to my sex, covering my sensitive nub and folds in whipped cream. He licks the cream from my belly and navel, heading directly to my sex.

"No sex," I remind him. "But, I'd be happy to lick whipped cream off your dick." His eyes hooded, I know I'm in dangerous waters if I'm going to hold him to his no sex request. Besides, I really want it and I'm drunk. Not the smartest thing I've ever done. He licks the whipped cream from my sex and I take control. I undress him slowly, starting with his shirt and then his pants to find he's going commando. His cock comes jutting out to meet me and I immediately greet it with my tongue, giving him a suck. I cover him in whipped cream and go to work licking and sucking him all over the hard length of his shaft. I take the can of whip with me to my bedroom and he follows me without request. Lying together on my bed we kiss, facing each other on our sides. I change position and squirt whipped cream on my sex and his cock, putting us both in the perfect position to clean up together. His tongue on my clit drives me to suck him harder and faster, taking his cock completely into my mouth. Groaning and moaning with pleasure. Adding to his pleasure, I start to feel his shock waves and know he's close. I'm on the edge, but my focus is on making this man come uncontrollably in my mouth. I pull my sex away from him, so he doesn't have the distraction and can't help but concentrate on the pleasure I'm giving him with my hot wet mouth and tongue stroking every inch of his cock. I suck on him harder and move on him faster and faster until he goes off like a fire hose in my mouth. I swallow and swallow again without stopping. He reaches for me to make me stop, but I refuse and go back to licking him clean. Rick takes control of me by tonguing my sex and licking my clit, pulling away his cock.

"Did you make me cum in your mouth and swallow?" he asks.

"Twice." I answer. "Am I a bad girl?"

"Fuck, more like amazing," he says in a guttural tone. "Now what should I do to you?" and his grin turns dirty. He slowly sucks and licks my clit over and over repeatedly. It goes on forever and feels spectacular. We fall asleep naked in each others arms and somehow manage to not actually have sex.

CHAPTER NINE

Waking up with Rick Seno wrapped around me buck-naked has got to be one of the best things on earth. Scratch that—it's the best thing in the universe. He has his arm around me, holding me close to him, legs entwined with mine. Somehow during the night he pulls me in so close, all I can hear is his heartbeat, he's better than white noise and the sound of the ocean put together. He becomes my blanket and my pillow. Then it hits me. He's still here. He's not leaving. Two nights in a row. We didn't have sex last night, at least we didn't do the deed. I have a date with him on Saturday after the game and of course, Sunday is a get-away day. Reality can be a confusing bitch, happy, shocked, and sad—all at the same time. For now, he's not awake yet and I'm going to soak in as much of him as I can. I'm going to commit this to memory, so I can have him in my dreams. I'm also going to change his pillow case when he leaves, so I can have two with his scent to get me through the ten day road trip.

Somebody should market pillow cases scented as your

favorite professional athlete, actor, musician. Fantasy Pillow Cases. They could have the athlete's picture printed on them. Maybe even matching sheets with full body photos and body pillow cases, too. Then buyers would have to order scent replacement for when they washed the sheets. This is the crazy that runs through my head when I'm in bed with my athlete. I want to share the euphoria, but not the man.

Bitter, chocolaty notes of my coffee brewing reach my nose and it means I should get up. But, it's a game day and I don't want to disturb whatever mojo he has going on. My team needs to win and maybe I don't want to leave his arms. He's awake because his morning wood is after my ass. He squeezes me tight and holds me.

"I know you're not a baseball player with me, but I'd like to know what your pre-work ritual is on game days. Coffee or no coffee? Do you always eat the same thing on game days? Are there any rules? Is sex banned on certain game days? Stuff like that." I ask because I want to make sure I have the right supplies available and don't plan a meal he can't eat or something.

"I'm not as superstitious as many of the guys I've played with. I wear clean socks every day and don't recycle the same dirty ones until I strike out or anything. I don't drink more than one cup of coffee per day unless I'm recovering from too much alcohol. Coach doesn't like it when we have sex on game days, but he knows most of us do it anyway. I try to only have sex after the game. I need a lot of protein and calories just to be me, but especially on game days. I try to stay away from too much fat and sugar. Sugar is a big one today, because I ate a lot of sugar last night with the cake and whipped cream." He stops and gazes into my eyes. "Do you remember the whipped cream?" He gets a happy, sexy expression on his face and I feel his cock get harder against me.

"Of course," I smile uncontrollably. "We ran out of whipped cream and I've already mentally added it to my shopping list. I'm going to buy two cans," I reply happily. "What can I do for you this morning?" I ask.

"I'd like to stay in bed until I have to get up and go to the park. Can we do that? Will you stay in bed with me?" he requests.

I snuggle back into him and do as he asks. There's nothing that can't wait a couple hours.

WHEN RICK finally climbs out of bed, he's in a hurry to get ready and go to work. I stay in bed and out of his way. I watch and listen as he gets ready to leave. He'll be back. He's only going to work, but the mere loss of his body near mine hurts. I don't understand what he's done to me. I'm not a wussy girl. I'm typically relieved when a guy leaves. Okay, so I haven't had a guy over in months. Fine, years. That doesn't change anything. I enjoy the warmth of my bed and hold the pillow he was using, taking in his scent.

Rick sits on the bed next to me to put his shoes on, "Are you going to the game tonight?"

"Yes," I reply, "I'm going to the next three games. The whole Colorado series."

"Do you have any plans for later, after the game?"

"Actually, I do. I'm dating this great guy who said he's spending the weekend with me and I'm hoping he'll be back when he gets done with work tonight."

"Do you want him to come back tonight?" Rick asks.

"Yea, I can hardly wait," I reply anxiously with a smile.

"What are you going to do if he comes back tonight?"

"I'm going to make him a sandwich in case he's hungry after work. Then we're going to lie in bed together, holding each other and watch a movie. We'll probably make out and strip each other naked. Honestly, as long as he's here with me I'll be happy. It doesn't matter what we do. He does give sex that's off the charts explosive, best I've ever had."

Rick leans over and gives me one of his amazing kisses. He lingers with his lips to mine and runs his hands along my outline under the blankets, remembering I'm still naked. He makes a low groan, "If I had the option of calling in sick, I'd do it today. I could stay here with you naked and we could just be us with no world out there."

I have no words. He makes me believe I'm important to him, and not just another girl.

"I'll see you later, babe." He says with a smile as he leaves for work.

Now, I could stay in bed and hide under the covers. Eventually, he'll come back and find me here waiting for him. Or, I'll die of starvation. The smell of coffee wins, even though it's gotten bitterer, and I roll out of bed. If only I could stay in my Rick Seno haze all day, every day. The world would definitely be a better place.

I turn the shower on and let it heat up while I get my coffee. I'm a bit sticky all over and I need to get on with my day. I shower and talk to myself... Okay, I know last night was real and I know the night before was real and I know he's real and I know I need a reality check. First, this has gotten deep faster than I thought possible. Second, I haven't made a pros and cons comparison for or against dating him. Third, I stayed in bed instead of getting up to work and that doesn't keep me in business, pay my bills, support my base-ball habit or keep me in cake. I need to settle this here and now. I get out of the shower and with a towel wrapped around me sit down to make a list. I write "Pros" draw a line down the middle of the paper, then I write "Cons". It goes like this:

Pros
He's a baseball player
He doesn't want me to think of him as a baseball player
Best sex ever
He isn't leaving
He can't keep his hands off me
He's still here in the morning
I like him
I want to keep him

Cons
He's a baseball player
He doesn't want me to think of him as a baseball player
He travels for work
Trade deadline
His rules
His presence causes me to go brain dead
He makes me think silly girl things
Boys are stupid

My coffee is gone and I start another list. A list I never considered before...

Reasons Not to Date a Baseball Player

Travels for work
They get traded
Other women are after them
They get traded
Gone half the time
They get traded
They get hurt
They get traded

The facts are a slap in the face. He could get traded and the trade deadline is coming. Fantasy baseball boyfriends can get traded, which is a huge downer. But, having my own baseball player boyfriend, live and in person—well, add a few complications and multiply by infinity. Technically, he's not my boyfriend, that's just another girly fabrication in my head. Maybe that's why he doesn't want to be a baseball player to me. He wants a woman to want him for him and not his money, notoriety, status. Baseball player reality.

I look at the clock and it's almost 3pm! I haven't gotten any work done, and I'm not even dressed! Add he's a distraction to the cons list. I'm meeting my section peeps for our pre-game pow-wow at 6:30 and I still need to replenish the whipped cream supply. I have to be waiting at the trolley stop no later than 5:30.

I manage to get everything done, and to book another vacation client. I grab my Seno jersey and put it on over a strappy tank with my blue jeans. I drive to the trolley station, and get to the platform in time to watch my trolley roll away. I'm stuck waiting fifteen minutes for the next one. The trolley is crowded with commuters, standing room only and the funky smells are in full force. The combination of body odor and skunk weed is nauseating. I wander through the sea of people to get away from the stench. I end up standing near an older woman wearing dark glasses and a wide brimmed floppy hat, she appears to be talking to herself. I eavesdrop on her conversation...

"In your heart you love him. He's a good man. Don't let your brain ruin it. Trust your heart over your eyes. You will want him in the end." She turns to me, "Good luck with your man," as she gets off the trolley at the next stop.

What the hell? Public transportation can be an adventure.

I get off the trolley and get a text message from my section peeps, meeting at the lounge pre-game. That's code for $5 beer and free popcorn, which is fine with me because I'm not going to have time to get food and meet them in time. Beer and popcorn wins.

It's Friday night and that makes the stadium full of energy. "My Songs Know What You Did in the Dark" by Fall Out Boy is blaring throughout the park and it's a party atmosphere. I get to the lounge right on time and find my peeps with beers in hands. Yes, they're two fisting. Tonight is obviously about the beer and not the pre-game conversation. That's probably good, I'm not ready to be questioned about Seno yet. We each get round two and walk to our section in time to watch the players stretch and warm up for the game. Ed the usher, waves as we go to our seats. I can't remember the last time he checked our tickets. Sandy and his wife are already in their seats waiting for the game, as always. We all comment and share our opinions on the recent trades, review the players on the disabled list and recap any shifting between the Seals and their farm teams. Nothing too crazy going on right now, feels like the calm before the storm—the trade deadline.

Seno is already out in the bullpen helping the starting pitcher, Corey Grace, warm up. Grace the Ace starting tonight should lead to a victory. I always enjoy the process of a game. Everything from the pre-game with friends and the National Anthem to the fireworks when we get a home run and the post-game interviews—even the occasional Gatorade baths. Tonight it all seems to hang out in the background because I'm focused on Rick Seno. His deliberate, catlike moves behind the plate. The control he has over the whole event, calling the pitches and leading his team. The crouched position he spends most of the night in while balanced on the balls of his feet and ready to throw anybody out that tries to steal second. His sheer overall strength and ability. He was my fantasy, but now he's real and he makes me proud of him. My desire to be with him is greater now than it's ever been.

The game was going well. We had a couple of home runs and had taken control of the bases early, Cross and Martin had been stealing bases all night. The opposing team scored three in the top of the ninth inning and tied the game. Bottom of the ninth inning with one out and nobody on, Seno steps up to the plate. First pitch: Ball. Second pitch: Ball. Third pitch: Grounded foul down the right field line. Fourth pitch: Strike. Fifth pitch: Smack! Straight out to Center Field, home run. Walk-off! Seals win! Rick doesn't dally, he rounds the bases at a good trot and meets his teammates at home plate for their winning celebration scrum. I'm standing and cheering and yelling and clapping. My peeps stare at me like I'm crazy. I don't get it, we always cheer our team on. When Sandy turns to me, "Did you just say *That's my man?*"

I can't contain my happiness as I see Seno searching the stands and finally pointing at me. I make my way down to the autograph wall to watch Hannah interview him, all the while he's focused on me. He finishes the quick interview, walks over to me, grabs my hands and leans in to whisper in my ear, "I heard you yelling for me through the whole game and I love it, my own cheering section." He kisses me at my ear. "The guys want to go drink, but I like your plan better. I'll be at your place in less than an hour to celebrate the win with you."

"It takes me longer to get home after the game. I wait for the third trolley, so it's not packed and standing room only."

"I'll be ready in less than thirty minutes. Hang out and go to the team store or something. Meet me at the employee garage entrance and you can ride with me. I don't want you on the trolley," it was more a command than anything else. He planted one of those crazy don't-forget-me kisses on me and took off into the dugout.

My peeps are usually gone by now, but apparently decided to stay for the show tonight. I walk up the stairs to my section and let the questioning begin. They all want to know what's going on with me and Seno. Who could blame them? I'd like to know, too!

"He's a great kisser and we're kind of dating," Giving them somewhere to start.

Sandy starts in, "You're dating a baseball player? You should know better than that."

"I'm dating Rick Seno, not a baseball player," I reply. "I've got to get moving, he's giving me a ride home." I excuse myself from the questioning with looks of awe following after me.

CHAPTER TEN

I walk up to the employee garage entrance and some of the players are wandering out into the garage to find their rides. Taking in my surroundings, there are quite a few people hanging around, mostly women. Baseball skanks. This is uncomfortable.

Text to Rick - Not comfortable out here with all the baseball skanks. Taking the trolley.

I wait for a reply and as I start to walk off I get a text:

Text from Rick - Chill thirty seconds

Cross comes out to get me, puts his arm around me and says, "How are you doing, baby?" loud enough for everyone around us to hear. Nasty remarks and pure jealousy from the skanks ensue as Cross leads me into the stadium. He has a way of making a scene and making me smile while he's at it. Such a good kid.

"Seno was in the showers and I saw your text, so I went for the assist."

"It seems to be your calling." We stand and talk for a few minutes inside the stadium, until Seno walks out of the clubhouse.

"Hands off my woman. I've got it from here. Thank you." He says, not really joking. He picks me up, and kisses me stupid.

"Dude, you've got it bad..." I hear trailing down the hallway as Cross makes his way back to the clubhouse.

"Let's get out of here," he says and basically drags me to his car. I didn't notice the limo tint on his windows before. Nobody can see in, complete privacy, and I decide to take advantage. I love how his car has a bench seat. I scoot over next to him, and run my hand up and down his thigh. I move up his leg and find he's very happy to see me. I unbutton and unzip his pants, safely releasing his cock to come out and play.

"What are you doing?"

"I must be doing it wrong, if you have to ask," I reply as I grasp his hard length in my hand and begin to stroke him. I lean over between him and the steering wheel to kiss his tip and lick the bit of moisture off. I drag my tongue around his tip and shaft as I go down on him, taking him completely in my mouth.

"I'm trying to drive here," he says and hesitates. "But, it's a short drive. You keep doing what you want with me."

I hum, intensifying the affect of my lips and tongue on him. I feel the reaction in his body, his heart beating fast and hard. He pulls over to the side of the freeway and slides over to the passenger side, where I quickly mount him to take a ride. He's so hard he fills me completely and I have to work my way down on him the last couple of inches. Stretching me to make room for all of him. Not much time when it comes to freeway quickies, the police could stop to check the car at any time. Rick smells yummy and I want to eat him up. I ride him hard like the rocket he is, ready to shoot me off into space. Grinding against him and getting off on the whole situation. He thrusts up meeting me in time. The windows fog. Harder and faster we pound together. He kisses me deep and pinches my nipples. He gets harder inside me, and we both explode carelessly. His name on my lips and mine on his. He quickly gets back to the driver side and drives off toward my place.

The last few miles of the nine-mile drive from the stadium, "I'm going to make you a sandwich and I bought more whipped cream, just in case." I ask him to pick a movie to watch when we get back to my place, while I make us some sandwiches. French rolls layered with ham, prosciutto, hot capicola, pepperoni, provolone, Italian herbs, black pepper and a drizzle of olive oil, then placed in the oven for a few minutes to toast up. I sliced the two sandwiches into thirds and arranged the pieces on a plate with some pickles and raw baby carrots.

I find Rick asleep on my couch when I walk in with the snacks. Now what? I was only gone a few minutes. (Note to self: Postgame snacks need to be pre-made.) He's obviously tired. He did work all day. I wrap up the snacks and snuggle up against him on my couch. It's late and I fall asleep next to him.

I wake up being carried to bed. Rick sweetly puts me in bed and climbs in bed next to me. I open my eyes to find him gazing at me contently, and it makes me smile.

"We fell asleep on the couch," he says softly.

"You were sleeping on the couch after I made you

snacks," I corrected. "I figured you were tired and sat with you."

He pulls me close and squeezes me tight. Uncomfortable still wearing my jeans, I work my way out of them and slip off my bra. Rick starts to play with my string bikinis and I discover he lost his pants at some point. I help him lose his shirt.

"I was planning on some long drawn out, teasing, sexual activity tonight. Your quickie move in the car threw me off, but I'm not complaining." He runs his finger along the edge of my panties. "No car fun tomorrow. Tomorrow you're mine to play with."

"Yes, sir," I reply. "But, what about now?"

The heat in his eyes ignite, he received the invitation he was waiting for. He moves toward me slowly while searching my eyes and touches his nose to mine before he kisses me sweetly. He kisses my eyelids. He kisses his way across my forehead and down my cheek to my ear and neck, leaving a trail that gives me chills when he blows on it. He meets my lips with his tenderly, just feeling and hardly moving. He sucks lightly on my lower lip as he moves his hands to my breasts. My breasts are a bit more than a handful for him and I can tell he appreciates the creamy softness. Massaging them thoroughly while he continues to kiss me. He's so freaking sexy, I can hardly stand it. I want to jump him. I do my best to maintain control. What is it about this guy that makes me always want him inside me? I'm like a cat in heat. He separates my lips with his tongue and keeps his slow pace with his tongue against mine. Squeezing my breasts and playing with my nipples. It's all so exquisite, and all I can focus on is how much I want him right now.

"Not yet," he says.

I must have been talking out loud again. Not sure what I said.

"Please, I want you inside me now. I need you," I plead needfully. Did that come from me? I swear something takes power over me. He deepens his kiss and my plea is getting to him. He slides a finger under the hem of my panties to explore me. A groan rumbles through him and he speaks against my mouth, "You're so wet, is that for me?"

Unable to speak, I manage, "Uh-huh... Rick please."

He slides his finger inside me while his other hand continues to fondle my breast and he moves his mouth to suck on my nipple. He sucks my nipple into his mouth hard, nibbling on my breast and occasionally biting my nipple. I'm hot and overcome with sensations. I can't control myself and without warning I come hard. Rick immediately plunges his cock into me, sending me into a further spiraling orgasm. I scream out over and over, calling out his name as he continues to stroke his hard length into me, hitting all the right spots. It's as if he'd been holding back and is finally giving me all of him. His pace grows quicker and he flips me over for an angle with deeper access.

I scream out, "Oh, oh, Rick!" panting heavily as he reaches down to touch our connection. He reaches around me, pulls my back to him, squats back into that catcher's position and holds me on him. Moving me up and down on his long thick cock, almost bouncing me in the best position ever. His powerful legs allowing him the ability to drive me out of my ever-loving mind. It went on and on, with sounds of his pleasure being ripped from his mouth. I'd become a rag doll for his pleasure, completely sated and unable to even count how many times he brought me to orgasm. I was still experiencing aftershocks when he bent us over and continued to take me from behind, pounding with wild abandon. Instantly tightening up, his release taking over and out of his control. The bed slamming against the wall with his final thrusts. Unable to hold himself up, he falls on top of me. His heart racing and breathing heavy as he tries to regain control. The feel of his body and weight on me is delectable. A few minutes pass and he rolls to his side pulling me with him. I fall asleep with him spooning me tightly.

CHAPTER ELEVEN

"Baby, are you awake?" Rick whispers. "You're so beautiful and peaceful when you sleep. I love the way you give yourself to me. I want you all the time. I want your heart and your body." Always easier to talk to someone who isn't listening. Rick wakes me with a squeeze and says, "What are we doing this morning?"

I rub my ass against his cock.

"No more sex until after the game tonight."

I make fake pouty noises at him and pretend to go back to sleep.

He smacks me with the pillow. I'm up and at him in full on pillow fight war in a split second. There's something inherently wrong with a naked pillow fight war when you've been told you can't have sex. Especially when your opponent has an appendage standing at attention.

"Hasn't he been told he doesn't get any?" I ask.

"He hopes he gets control instead of my brain," Rick says.

"I'm on his side," I tease.

"You're killing me." He pulls me to him and kisses me senseless. I take advantage of the closeness, maneuvering his willingness and embracing him with my thighs.

"Fuck," he says. "You know I want you. I'm not supposed to have sex pre-game and over exert myself."

"Come with me and let me do the work," I suggest.

"You know I don't work that way," he says. "I'm an active participant. I promise I won't fall asleep tonight."

He starts to get dressed. I wonder if he wants to leave or simply have a layer of protection from sex.

"Would you like to walk over to the Yolk for breakfast before I have to go to the stadium?"

"Sure, I'm starving. Can you drop me off at my car before you go to work?" I ask. "It's still in the transit parking lot from last night and I'm not walking or taking the bus to get there this afternoon."

"No, you're not. I'm getting you a parking pass."

When I get to the game on Saturday and scan my membership card, the ticket that prints out is row 1 seat 6 in Field VIP Section 103—right behind home plate. First thought in my mind is I'm going to have the best view of his ass for 9 innings. I should've brought my camera. It's nice to watch the game from a different vantage point, but it's not my normal seat that I've spent many games in over the years—I'm not complaining about being closer to my man. Where did that come from? My man? I'm losing it.

I've been a baseball fan since I was a kid and I've had my favorite players over the years. You might see a guy walking down the street and think, "oh baby, he's hot!" Granted there are some super hot baseball players. But with me, it's always the music. Admittedly, I have musician issues, but the baseball players on my team have held my heart. The walk up music is the first attraction that grabs me. My favorites have walked up to the plate accompanied by Motely Crue's "Kick Start My Heart", Quiet Riot's "Cum on Feel the Noise", Metallica's "Seek and Destroy", Black Sabbath's "Iron Man" and good hard rocking power. On the other hand, there have been a few players I would never even notice if they had legs all the way up to their neck because they walk up to a whiny, mushy, emotional song. I will never get what they're thinking with that, there's no way a song like that's at all threatening to the opposing team—unless they're afraid he might need a hug rounding first. Seno fits into the hard rock walk up music category. Funny thing, hard rock is not the music I find myself listening to when I think of him, in fact I can't get "Thinking Out Loud" by Ed Sheeran out of my head since we danced to it at the Batter Up.

A few times he turns around and smiles at me when he's adjusting his mask and leg guards. I never knew leg guards were sexy, but they most definitely are.

In the middle of the first inning a server comes to me and says she would be happy to get me anything to eat or drink that I want from anywhere in the stadium and hands me a note on Seals stationary:

Sherry,

Sorry we won't be able to go out to dinner on our date tonight because of timing issues. Please order whatever you want and it will be charged to my account. Consider it part of our date. I'm sure this makes it hard to not think of me as a baseball player. You do like baseball, so maybe this is in my favor.

Rick

I decide not to fight it. I order a chocolate vanilla swirl ice cream in a mini helmet, a bottle of water and a bag of peanuts—dinner of champions. Usually I throw peanut shells at fans of the opposing team, but not today since there are no rows of people in front of me.

The game is going well. The best catcher ever calling the game. The pitcher, Tommy Knight, on point and hitting his spots. Not shaking off Seno's calls. Cross is a catching machine in centerfield, seems he has a magnet connecting the ball to his glove. Everybody on the Seals lineup has scored at least once this game. During the seventh inning stretch, my ticket representative comes by to visit and gives me a bag from the team store.

"I'm helping a friend. He would like you to change into these before you meet him after the game," she smiles and leaves before I can say anything.

I consider objecting and meeting him without changing, but I do have ice cream all over my shirt.

The Seals win 12-5, and the fans are ecstatic. The kids are lining up to run the bases and the rest of the fans are slowly making their way out of the stadium. As soon as there is room to move, I go to the ladies room to check out the contents of the bag and change.

Okay, I admit opening the bag is better than getting a

surprise box from Amazon filled with everything in your saved for later cart. Leggings that say Seals down the left leg, a V-neck T-shirt that says Seals across the chest and Seno across the back with his big six, a Seals zip up hoodie customized like a jersey with Seno and his number on the back and the front, and a Seals baseball cap with the number six embroidered on the back. Everything fits properly, but the T-shirt is the best—the way it stretches across my breasts, yet isn't too tight around my middle, is perfection. I make sure all the tags are removed and put my original clothes for the evening in the bag. I stop to use the mirror and make sure my cap is on without my hair sticking out everywhere and head toward the dugout.

When I get to the dugout, there are about two-dozen kids still waiting to run the bases. I hangout leaning on the dugout until one of the ushers comes to ask me to leave because the game is over. Right at that moment, Rick pops out of the dugout and says, "It's okay, she's with me," and opens the gate onto the field for me. Smiling as he takes me in from head to toe, "You look good in my number."

"I feel like you've marked your territory with your name and number on me," I say giggling.

"Well, if I'm going to have you on the field then you need to represent and I don't want any of the guys getting any ideas about you. In a way, I guess I am marking my territory," he says as he pulls me into the dugout and kisses me silly. In no time our hands are all over each other and the heat level is stupid. Sucking on his tongue and his hard length pressed against me, trying to break free. He pulls away, "We have to stop this or we won't get to what I have planned."

"I'm happy with this, maybe the plan doesn't matter," I say red-faced through ragged breaths.

"We have limited time and can pick up this part after we're done," he says and leads me out of the dugout to the bullpen.

"Are you sure? We could handle the getting done part now," I suggest.

He laughs as we walk to the bullpen. The stadium is empty and there's nobody left out at the bullpen. The grounds crew is working on the field, otherwise we're alone. As we walk into the bullpen, one of the grounds men calls out to Rick "about 40 minutes."

"You told me you aren't very good at catching and can't hit. Since I'm a catcher, I thought we could play some catch and I can help you learn how to catch and throw better. Maybe hitting another time. What do you say baseball fan? Do you want private lessons from your major leaguer?" he plays.

"I definitely want private lessons, not sure catching and throwing is what I want the lessons in right now," I reply jokingly.

He smiles, tosses me a glove and hands me the ball. "Now, throw the ball to me."

I throw the ball overhand toward him, but it bounces about five feet short and a bit to the right. We continue to play catch until the grounds men kick us out, I was getting better with each toss. I'm not sure what I appreciated more, getting to observe his happiness playing ball firsthand, playing with him or the thought behind the date plans. I love how he thoughtfully plans dates and takes me along for the ride. By the end, I was throwing the ball far enough and within his reach. Progress.

At this point, the stadium is pretty much a ghost town. A few maintenance people roaming about and maybe a couple of players in the video room watching footage of the game. The music has become silent and most of the lights are off. Rick intertwines his fingers with mine and we walk to the dugout the long way, on the warning track. He pulls me with him into the dugout and down the stairs into the locker room. There's nobody in the locker room but us. He walks to his locker to drop off his gear and leads me through the work out room to the players parking. He drops me off at my car in the parking lot across the street from the stadium and says, "Separate cars tonight, so you can't take advantage of me. That's good because I have plans for when we get back to your place." The fire in his gaze and intentions in his tone are undeniable and make my body yell yippee internally. He leans into my window and plants one of his don't-forget-me kisses on me.

We meet up in the parking lot at my complex and take the elevator up to the top floor. He has his hands on me before the elevator doors close and backs me up to the wall, lifting me to raise my neck to the same level as his mouth. Holding me there and sending me into a state of heated bliss with his kisses. The way he's taking control. Something tells me the catcher will be calling the game tonight.

As the elevator door opens, he takes my keys from my hand and lets us in. Probably the only way we'd get in since I'm in La La Land. He leads me to the bedroom, puts his arms around me and holds me close to him for a long time. Eventually he turns to tend to my neck, nuzzling tenderly, licking and nibbling until it makes me shiver. We make out in each other's arms for hours. The heat is palpable. His tongue controlling me as I do everything I can to encourage him. The softness of his lips on mine almost hypnotizing. His hands on me like they belong there and I belong to him. I want him to be in control. I want to give up control. I want to lose control with him. My head is racing in circles distracted by the facts: Tomorrow is Sunday, Sunday is a get-away day, Sunday games are early. Which means I will be alone tomorrow night—No Seno. I'm already dreading it. Is it possible to miss someone before they leave? If it is or not, doesn't matter—I'm missing the man who has his arms around me and is kissing me right now. This is all pure insanity! I can't miss him if he's here! I don't let any man have control of me! I don't need a man! Or, maybe I do. How did this happen? It's got to be because he's a baseball player. And, now I'm back to he's not a baseball player with me. Except he was a baseball player with me tonight. Private lessons from my own major leaguer and all. Damn! I start to freak out as my emotions take over and I'm in deeper than I thought. I escape with a fake "need to use the bathroom" and lock the door behind me. A total girl move.

A few minutes go by and Rick is at the door. "Are you okay?"

"No. Yes. I mean, I will be," I reply through the door.

"What's the problem? Do you want me to leave?" he asks.

May I claim the girl card now and not answer? "I don't want you to leave and that's the problem. Tomorrow is get-away day, then this will probably all be over. I can't believe how much of a big freaking girl I'm being right now. I blame you! It's all your fault!" I say pouting.

"Sherry, come out here please," he says in an authoritative voice.

I think about it, but make no action.

"Sherry. You know I leave tomorrow. You just said so. Let's not waste the time we have tonight."

I don't like the way that sounds. Tonight is our last night. "I'll stay in here, so I don't get hurt more than I already will be."

"I'm leaving for work. I'm not leaving to be away from you. I'll be back to you," he says.

"Say more things like that last part," I say through the door.

"Not until you unlock the door and come out of there, like an adult," he says.

I open the door and gaze up at him doe eyed.

"There's nobody else. Only you, Sherry. I only want you. I want to spend more time with you. You're the only one who makes me lose control. You're the only one I can't keep my hands off of. There's never been another woman who drives my desire to be with them, protect them, take care of them and, yes, sex them the way you do." He stares at me waiting for a response.

"You mean tonight or this weekend or this week, right?" I try to confirm.

"I don't know how long. More than tonight or this weekend. More than this week. More than this season. Sherry, there's nobody else while I'm with you and I hope there's nobody else while you're with me. I can't tell you how long. All I can tell you is I can't see an end right now," he spews irritably.

"Are you saying you want us to be exclusive? Like you're my boyfriend?" I question, looking like a teenager.

"Yes, I guess I am," he confirms.

"That might be okay," I say with a huge grin. I need to break up with my baseball fantasy boyfriend. It seems he's become real.

"Don't you get it? I love having you in the stadium during games. I love hearing you yelling and cheering for me. I love that I'm not going home to my empty apartment, I'm going home with you. You won't be on the road trip with me. You won't be in the stadium. I won't be able to hear you cheering for me. I'll be alone in a hotel room. I won't wake up to find you next to me, saying sweet things in your sleep. I won't start my day with the taste of you on my lips or the feel of your silky skin under my hands. Damn it! You're not the only one in this!"

"You're the only woman I can be a baseball player with and you want to be with me for me. I want to be a baseball player when I'm with you and nothing else. You're making me fucking crazy!"

"I need to go for a run," he says and goes to change.

"You just said we shouldn't waste the time we have tonight. Use me to release the frustration," I say demanding.

He walks back to me, burning with flames in his eyes and heat radiating off his body. He takes complete control immediately. His strong hands gripping me tightly, his mouth claiming me like never before. I tingle down to my toes and the heat builds in my happy places. He stops and searches my eyes, unsure. As if, his plan changed and he has no ability to keep his original course or even chart a new one. Some other force is influencing him and he can't deny it's powerful requests. He wants me and he wants me now, but it's different. He needs me. He says more with his hands on my body than any words could convey. Claiming me with his lips, his hands move on me, undressing me with a light touch. He guides me mindlessly to the bed and there are no words for his body on top of my nakedness. He removes his pants as his kiss grows more demanding. His tongue dives deeper into my mouth. His passionate caresses. His body a pure ball of fire. I want him so bad it's unbelievable. He drags his rock solid cock across my opening, and he releases some type of caveman response to my wet heat against my lips. He very slowly slides in until he's buried all the way inside me. I shudder, whimper, not of my own doing and he stops to enjoy the moment. Continuing to claim me with his mouth while we're one, he starts to move slowly on top of me. His eyes closed, fully invested in our connection, our smooth skin moving against each other, the heat between us that neither of us seem to be in control of. He pulls his lips away from mine and watches me with the happiest face I've ever seen, as he strokes slowly, deeply, deliberately, without growing intensity. His forehead leans against mine, his breath is uneven and sends tingles down my neck as each breath reaches my skin. The slow sensual connection has taken over. Each stroke pulling us closer. My hands on his back, tracing the definition of his muscles up to his shoulders. He puts his arms around my shoulders and holds me tight to his chest. His heart beats strong and steady. He sits back on his feet, pulling me with him and continuing the pace, guiding my hips with his hands. My mouth is at his neck and I can't help myself, I lick him across his collarbone, nibbling along the way. My hands on his head playing with his short hair and rubbing his head. The fire between us is an inferno waiting for the house to collapse.

"Sherry, tell me there's only me," he says softly.

"It's only you, Rick," I reply trying to find my voice.

"More, tell me more," he requests out of breath.

"You're the only man that's ever been in my bed. I've never brought anyone else home with me." I admit without thinking. "No one has been inside me for years except you —even in my dreams," man I need to shut up. I start to wonder what I say when I'm asleep if I say this when I'm awake. But forget it and blame it on the man currently making love to me for making me brainless. Stop and listen to your thoughts, Sherry! My brain tries to get my attention. Deeper than you thought? Duh, you're in love with this guy and he's going to leave! Your dream man may be real, but real life comes with it and he'll leave taking your heart with him. I ignore my brain because I don't want to give him up. I want this. I want this moment. He's only going to leave for work. He said he's not leaving me.

"Oh, Sherry. I love the way you feel on me. Your every shudder and shake is driving me crazy. I'm losing myself." He says low and raspy. "I love your hands on me."

I search for his eyes and reach up to kiss his lips. We close our eyes as our lips meet and I see stars. Stars shining everywhere against a dark night, shooting stars flying through the background. Our kiss breaks. We both cry out as we lean on each other and whisper to each other.

"Never think I don't need you," he rasps sincerely.

"I'll always be here for you. Only you," I promise.

"Only you," he repeats to me as he lays me down. He bends over me, continuing to slide in and out of me, and absorbing every orgasmic pulse as we ride it out together until we are no longer able.

This was different. We went to bed and he held me close like he has the other nights. There were no words, but the noise from all the thinking was deafening.

CHAPTER TWELVE

Rick wakes me by kissing my neck and running his hands over my naked body. I open my eyes to see the daylight of early morning clouded by marine layer out my window. He rolls me to my back and disappears under the blanket to play with my body. He starts at my breasts, squeezing, licking and sucking them into his mouth.

"You said no sex on a game day," I remind him.

"I'm a rule breaker when it comes to being away from you for the next ten days," I hear mumbled under the blanket.

Rules are made to be broken, so who am I to argue? I enjoy the attention he's giving me. Loving his hands and tongue on me, in me, everywhere. He kisses me from my breasts down my side, all the way down the outside of my thigh and leg to my toes. Repeats the process on my other side, then starts alternating from right leg to left leg kissing his way up the inside of my legs. He gets to my knees and stops to lick and suck. Continuing he drags his tongue up the inside of my thigh, stopping to kiss me there just before he reaches my promised land. Licking and sucking on the uppermost part of my inner thigh. Driving me up the freaking wall with sensation. He cradles my ass in his hands, lifting me for his mouth to pleasure. His mouth on me is exquisite, kissing, licking, sucking my clit. His tongue delving inside me, tasting my wetness. He slides a finger inside me, and bends it at the knuckle to reach the perfect counter point to his tongue on my clit and I combust hard without warning, screaming out his name. He peeks out from under the blanket and puts his lips on my neck, sucking lightly as he enters me, filling me immediately. I'm already on the edge of a second explosion when he starts to move, dragging his cock across my clit with each stroke in and out. Harder and faster with each pass, I come over and over. No longer in control and his to play with, he tosses the blanket to the side and lifts my legs up, then pushes them back so my feet are at my ears. Allowing him to push in deeper than ever before. Once he's there he pounds into me hard, separating my legs for as much access as possible. His balls start to smack against me and he bends me even further. He's so deep with each stroke, I'm uncontrollably releasing cries of pleasure every time he pounds into me. I'm grasping at the bed with my fingers wrapped in the sheet, wanting to reach for him and unable to move. He circles my sensitive nub and sends me skittering into darkness. He falls over the edge, my body pulling him with me. I hear him call out my name and there's only darkness.

The alarm goes off a couple hours later and I never open my eyes.

"Babe, I need to get to the stadium early. I'll miss you while I'm gone and I'll be listening for you to cheer for me today. Don't get up. Thank you for the best sex ever. I'll call you tonight," he whispers. I smile and he kisses my cheek. Then he was gone.

I don't want to face it, so I stay in bed and sleep until I smell coffee.

WHEN I finally get up Sunday morning, Rick had already left for the stadium. I find an envelope with my name on it and a box left next to my "Everything is better at the beach" coffee mug. I open the envelope to find a card with a modern art style palm tree and a hula girl on the front. Inside the card was preprinted simply "Aloha" and he had written:

Sherry,

Aloha means hello, goodbye and love. I hope you know which definition I have in mind. It's get-away day and I'm not wanting to leave, but it's my job. I want to take a trip with my woman in the off season, something for us to look forward to being just us. I'm thinking somewhere with a beach for maybe two weeks. I think you know a travel agent that can take care of this for me? I will do anything to make my girl happy, so whatever she wants goes. I prefer a resort with room service and a gym. I hope you like this small gift and don't forget me while I'm on the road.

Love,
Rick

The small square box was simply a white cardboard gift box with a bow stuck to the top. I open the box to find a baseball bracelet made with baseball stitching on baseball leather. I've always loved those when I see them at the stadium. As I take it out of the box, I notice he has hand-written on the inside of the bracelet, a hand personalized inscription. It's the two lines from "Thinking Out Loud" that confess his love. I scream out in joy and tears instantly run down my face. I love that he quoted Ed Sheeran—it must be our song.

I reread the note and he's planning on spending time during the off season with me, he's not leaving. And, I'm going to Hawaii for two weeks with my Seno. I can't wait to plan the trip! He's going to love it as much as I love him! Stop! Hold the phone! Back that up! I love him?

I jump in the shower, get ready as quick as I can, throw on my Seno jersey, fasten my new bracelet around my wrist and head to the stadium. The trolley is pretty empty because I'm going earlier than most of the crowd, but that doesn't keep it from feeling like it's taking forever to get there. I'm at the gate waiting to get in when it opens. I check the field and the bullpen to see if Rick is out, but it's Sunday and there's no batting practice on the field. I make my way to the first base wall where the players sign auto-graphs, hoping he'll notice me there when he comes out to warm up the pitcher. He never signs autographs at the wall. He's all business before the game. But, it's the autograph wall or waiting in the stands next to the bullpen and I can't put my hands on him through the chain link fence of the bullpen.

A few minutes go by and the players start coming out to stretch. Saben walks up to the wall to sign autographs. I check to make sure Rick is in the lineup today, and he is.

Saben gawks at me oddly when I don't want his autograph. The starting pitcher, Josh Kranston, walks out of the dugout and straight toward the bullpen. A couple more of the players not in the starting lineup today come over to the wall to sign autographs. Finally, Rick comes out of the dugout focused on his pitcher who's stretching outside the bullpen. He didn't turn and notice me there, so I yell his name—but he doesn't turn around and why would he? Fans do this every game.

"Rick! I love you!" I yell at the field. He keeps walking toward the bullpen, but the rookie is there for the assist yet again. Cross runs to catch up with Seno as he approaches second base, they exchange words and he points at me standing at the wall. Rick turns and runs toward me.

He reaches for me at the wall and says, "Rook says you were yelling "I love you" to me. Is that true?" His face is twisted up.

"Yes. I love you."

"I love you, too..." I cut him off and see his smile climb into his eyes.

"Now, go get to work," Before he runs to the bullpen, he grabs my face with both hands and plants a kiss on me like no other. At least three times more potent than his don't-forget-me kiss. There's hooting and hollering around me, from the players stretching on the field and from my peeps in my seating section. Apparently, the stadium had started to fill up while I was on my mission.

CHAPTER THIRTEEN

The game was great! Nothing better than a sweep! Though, I must admit the details are fuzzy. My brain may be sex-fried or is there such thing as a sex hangover? Anyway, Seno went after one of the opposing players who was trying to steal home, doing his best imitation of dodge ball on the base path and tagged him out. A fantastic play, they replayed it on the big screen three times. Rick also hit a double, getting two RBIs, walked and grounded out to short. Martin was a triple short of a cycle and the rook, Cross, hit a 2 run homer as well as stealing second base and then third base when the catcher tried to throw him out and ended up airmailing the ball to center field. The final score was 7-2 Seals.

The cleaning crew at the stadium gets into it and supports the team when they get a sweep. Awesome to see them wandering through the crowds of people as they leave the stadium with brooms, sweeping up in front of all the fans for the visiting and losing team.

I walk down by the dugout to watch Hannah do her on

field interviews. She's got Cross and Martin to interview today. Seno sees me and waves me closer to the dugout surrounded by a sea of people trying to get autographs. He tosses me a ball and gets this dirty grin on his face. The ball has a message scribbled on it:

Meet me at 317 in twenty minutes. Love—R

I give him the okay sign and he disappears into the locker room.

I watch the interviews, and hoot and holler for them both, especially the rookie. Cross waves and walks over to me when he's done with his interview. He reaches up to the stands and gives me a big hug. "Great work today, kid!" I say to him encouragingly. "Soon all the other teams will be scared to have you on the bases."

"Thanks, I appreciate the support." He looks around and continues, "Is what's going on with you and Seno real? It's so quick."

"Yes, it's real. It's scary because it is so quick. I guess when it's right, it's right. Thank you for getting him to go out last weekend. It seems like so much longer than a week." There I go rattling on again. "If you need anything, just let me know."

"He looked at me like I was crazy when I told him you were yelling at him pregame. Like you'd never say those words to him and then after he basically attacked you at the wall, he was walking around like the king of the field," he laughs.

We parted ways and I went to the elevator, trying to make my way to the top deck and section 317. I press the call button and the elevator is already going up. The door opens and looking back at me is Rick. I step into the elevator and it continues to go up. Rick pulls the stop button and the elevator stops between floors, only us in the elevator.

"I want to talk to you before I leave for the road trip, but I have a thing about elevators..." his words drift off as he grabs me and holds me against the wall of the elevator with his body, kissing me hard and full of desire. He stops kissing me and holds me close, whispering in my ear, "I love you, Sherry. I've never said that to another woman. I don't want to be with any other women, only you."

"You make me crazy happy and I'm scared of how much I need you. I only want to be with you. I love you, Rick," I listen to the words come out of my mouth and can't believe they're mine. I never thought I'd be in this place. In love. Let alone needing a man or experiencing my fantasy in real life. Right there in the elevator I start to sing to him. The lines from "Thinking Out Loud" that resonate with me because love is mysterious and I'll never forget the first touch of his hand or kissing under the stars on the bleachers at the Embarcadero.

He cuts me off with his hands and lips on me, dancing in the elevator to the song running through my head. Our song. "I don't have much time and I don't want your last memory of me to be sex. Please know we're more than that, you're special to me and I never want to hurt you." He releases the elevator and walks me out of the stadium.

Tears roll down my face because I'm such a fucking girl and I can't help it. I don't want him to leave and he has to for work, so my team can keep winning. I don't want to be upset. I don't want to be a whiny girl and I definitely don't want him to see me like this, but it's too late. His face twists at the sight of my tears streaming down my face. It's not what I want him to remember. I'm independent and don't need anyone, or maybe didn't need anyone until him. He puts his arms around me one last time and squeezes me tight.

He whispers in my ear, "It'll be okay. I promise. I'll be back. I'll call you when I get to the hotel tonight. I love you, baby." He gives me a quick kiss on the forehead and turns to run back to the clubhouse before they send the hounds out to hunt for him.

The trolley is pretty much empty on my way home. At least that's in my favor, less people to witness me blubbering like an idiot.

CHAPTER FOURTEEN

I get home and throw myself into my work. It's Sunday, but I'm behind due to being distracted by a certain baseball player. I check my emails, my social media and phone messages. Everything is going smooth. I do have a few clients to plan vacation options for, including my new client the professional baseball player who wants to take his woman on a trip for a couple weeks during the off season. Whatever his woman wants she gets, he said. I'll start with trip options for that vacation. I research the locations I want to go to and ultimately end up with a couple different options, both Hawaii. I type up an email and send it out to him:

Mr. Seno,

I'm sure your woman will love either of these options, without any of the upgrades. I'm sure she'd be happy just to be with you.

Option 1 $6,457

2 Weeks in North Shore Resort Cottages on the beach
(with full resort amenities including a gym, room
service and a spa/salon)
Roundtrip airfare for 2
2 weeks of Rental Car – Jeep Wrangler
Lei Greeting for 2 at the airport
Add upgrade to First Class Airfare +$780
Add Oceanside couples massage +$240
Add Surfing Lessons $200/person
Add Hawaiian Welcome Basket Small $60
Add Hawaiian Welcome Basket Large $100

Option 2 $7,340

10 Nights in North Shore Resort Cottages on the
beach
4 Nights Lanai Sweetheart Rock Beach Spa Resort
Roundtrip airfare for 2
Roundtrip airfare hop to Lanai for 2
10 days of Rental Car – Jeep Wrangler
Lei Greeting for 2 at Honolulu Airport
Lei Greeting for 2 at Lanai Airport
Lanai Transportation Fee for 2
Add Lanai excursion package +$200-$500

Additional options available including Maui, Waikiki,
and other locations. However, I've found going to more
than two islands becomes too much travel and not
enough vacation. Cost may vary based on exact travel
dates. These rates are based on travel departing after
October 31 and returning before Thanksgiving week,
avoiding holiday crowds.

If you have anything else in mind, I'm happy to
research it for you.

Please let me now if you have specific dates in mind,
so I can provide exact costs and get you booked.

Thank you for the opportunity to help you with your
travel plans.

Aloha,
Sherry
Beach Vacations

I finish up my other work and immediately have tears
rolling down my face. I need a distraction, I guess I should
clean and do laundry. I wonder who does Rick's laundry
and cleaning? He probably has a maid service. I don't even
know where he lives. There are so many things we haven't
talked about. I hate cleaning. I'll cook dinner instead, or
maybe I should bake.

My social media pings at me...

Notabaseballplayer: Messaging from the airplane

This is the opposite of a distraction. This is right smack
dab in the middle of it.

Notabaseballplayer: Are you okay? I don't want you to
be upset.

Sherry: I'm fine. Sorry, I didn't want you to see me like
that. Don't worry. It's not your fault.

Sherry: Okay, well it's kind of your fault.

Notabaseballplayer: I didn't want to leave you. I wish I was on my way to you right now.

Sherry: Say more things like that.

Notabaseballplayer: I want to wrap my arms around you and hold you against me while I kiss you for hours.

Notabaseballplayer: I want to taste you on my lips.

Notabaseballplayer: I want to smell your hair while I hold you in bed and nuzzle my nose into the silky strands.

Notabaseballplayer: I want to bury myself deep inside you until I lose myself in you.

Now this, this counts as a distraction.

Sherry: You're good. I feel better already.

Notabaseballplayer: It's easy when it's the truth. I don't have to be creative. It's just what I want.

Sherry: Have you noticed we don't do very good at talking when we're together?

Notabaseballplayer: You make me lose track of my thoughts. When we're in the same room, I can't concentrate.

Sherry: Can we talk now?

Notabaseballplayer: Sure. What do we need to talk about?

Sherry: I don't know where you live, where you like to vacation, what your favorite food is, and we've never said the words birth control—I want to be with you. I love you. I guess that's enough.

Notabaseballplayer: I'll take you to my place when I get back from the road trip, you should know where I live. I like your place better, it feels like home. I prefer steak. I like Italian food and Mexican food, and you can never go wrong with pizza. Cake with whipped cream recently became a favorite. I haven't traveled anywhere other than with the team, so I don't really know where I like to vacation. I just want to be with you. Anywhere with you will be perfect.

Notabaseballplayer: I know I missed part, but I'm not sure what to say.

Is Seno seriously one of those guys who doesn't worry about birth control? Is it my problem? Or, is he trying to knock me up?

Sherry: Okay. I'm glad you like my place.

Notabaseballplayer: I've broken many of my rules with you and I don't know why or how. I just seem to get caught up in it and I'm not able to stop. It feels right. You feel right. I don't even consider stopping because I want you so bad and my dick takes over my brain.

Sherry: Of course it does! You're male!

Notabaseballplayer: It's not like that. I've never gone bare with anyone else. I know better. It's you. I should be protecting you. You do something to me.

Sherry: Lucky for you, I'm on the pill.

Notabaseballplayer: I'm lucky because I met you.

Damn it! How does he always know the right thing to say!

Sherry: Would you like to come over when you get back in town? I want to cook dinner for you.

(Note to self: Find the perfect side dish to go with steak.)

Notabaseballplayer: I was already planning on it.

Sherry: What do you think of the vacation options?

Notabaseballplayer: They're both great. Whatever my woman wants, she gets. Upgrade to first class. Add the Oceanside couples massage and anything else you want. I'm happy to stay at the one place, gives us more time to be alone.

Sherry: When you say alone, do you mean naked?

Notabaseballplayer: Yes

Notabaseballplayer: Landing. Gotta go. I love you.

And he's gone. My tears are under control. I don't understand how I miss him so terribly, when he's new in my life. Maybe it's because he's not new. I've had him in my world for years, I just wasn't in his world.

Where was I? Needing a distraction. Really don't want to clean. Oh yea, dinner or baking? Maybe both, I've got the whole evening. Either that or I should go to bed now. I make a sandwich and while it's toasting in the oven I start my dough. I'm craving chocolate chip cookies. I get the dough brought together and wrap it up, putting it in the freezer to chill. I turn the oven up to get it preheated for the cookies and sit down to eat my sandwich. My sandwich is the same as the sandwiches I made the other night for Rick. I inhale some potato chips on that thought and retrieve my dough from the freezer. I line my sheet pans with parchment paper and proceed to dollop out three-dozen equal sized mounds of cookie dough. I put them in the oven to bake and set the timer for ten minutes. I scrape the bowl with my finger, I don't want to waste any dough. The timer goes off and it smells yum. I check the cookies and they need a couple more minutes in the oven to be perfectly gooey. The longest two minutes ever. It's like watching a pot and waiting for it to boil. I set my cooling rack out on the counter and take my cookies out of the oven. I give the cookies a few minutes to solidify and move them to the cooling rack, so they don't continue cooking.

I grab a few cookies and a mug of milk for dunking them. I settle in on my loveseat with a blanket to watch a movie. Of course, I get sucked into a sappy love story and I'm full on bawling when the phone rings. Crap!

"Hello," I answer trying to hide the tears.

"Hi, baby," that deep voice that drives me crazy comes through the phone.

"Hey! Did you get checked in and everything already?" I ask without knowing why.

"Yea, just another hotel. I wish you were here or even better, I was there."

"Me, too. What are you wearing?" I decide to have some fun.

"Actually, we have travel attire guidelines and I'm still wearing my travel clothes," he says matter-of-factly.

"You know that's not what I meant," I scold him.

"Well, what are you wearing?" he asks.

"Oh, nothing special. I'm lounging around in my black lace string bikini panties, a snug fitting low cut black strappy tank and my Seno baseball cap." A low groan comes through from the other end of the phone. "So, do travel attire guidelines allow you to go commando?"

"You're a bad girl."

"Me? I'm a sweet girl."

"A sweet girl that's killing me right now. I take it back. You're my girl and I love you the way you are," his tone changes from playful to sincere. I imagine the claiming look he has in his eyes though I can't see them and it's making me hot.

"I miss you and I'm here when you need me."

"The guys are dragging me to the bar before we call it a night. Know I'm thinking about you." He says and the rook is in the background rushing him.

"Goodnight," I make a kiss noise into the phone and hang up.

I wrap up my cookies, a dozen in the freezer for Rick and go to bed on a high note. My bed smells like he's here, like us together, like sex—it's wonderful. I'm going to use his pillow and wrap myself in the blankets, like he's here holding me.

My alarm goes off, telling me to get my ass out of bed and I slam the snooze button. I'm not ready to face today yet. Monday, the worst of all the days. I hide under the blanket and hope it goes away and forgets about me. Unfortunately, the problem with the snooze button is in its name—it's a "snooze" button, not a "forget about me" button. The smell of the coffee brewing is sour today or maybe that's just my mood. Time to be a big girl and start my day.

I check my calendar for today's schedule. It's the normal Monday business routine, and the game is at 6:10 since the team is away in Colorado. I pour my coffee and sit down to get working. Starting with my email, I have a couple of interesting items and two new requests for beach vacations. I send my reply email with questionnaire to the vacation requests and move on to the others.

From: RS6

We have early practice this morning, so I didn't call and wake you. Waking up in a hotel room alone is depressing compared to waking up listening to your sweet voice, saying sweet things to me in your sleep. You build my confidence and my ego. When I'm with you I feel like a king.

6:10 game today, but I'm sure you already know that and I know you'll be watching.

I miss you, babe.

Love,
Rick

From: MikeMic

Here are your details for the karaoke finals at Batter Up! Same reporting time and day as all the other Wednesdays, sticking with the every other Wednesday schedule. There will be multiple rounds, as follows:

Round 1: Each of the five finalists will sing two songs that were released in the last five years. One originally recorded as a male vocal and one originally recorded as a female vocal. Both songs should be upbeat. Top three will advance.

Round 2: Contestants choice. Your chance to bring down the house! Top two will advance.

Round 3: Wild card round. You will not know what song you're singing until you get to the stage. You will be provided a choice of three songs to choose from. Time to show your true karaoke skills without time to prepare and memorize the song.

Remember, no songs you have already done for the competition.

Good luck singers!
Mike with the Mic

So, do I reply to Rick or wait until I talk with him later? I'll wait until after the game, he's busy with practice.

I'm not sure about the rules for the karaoke finals. I've never done multiple rounds in one night before. I know immediately I want to do "Love Runs Out" by OneRepublic and "Ex's & Oh's" by Elle King for round one. I can't worry about the round three wild card, nothing I can do about that. Contestants choice, unlimited options, no category to stick to—this is going to take some time.

I choose a random playlist and start on my weekly business updates, photo changes on my website and social media, tweets and Facebook posts scheduled for the week. I try to talk myself into signing up for Instagram and promise I'll do it later, just like I've done for the last two months and I still haven't created an account. I check in on current travelers and everybody is enjoying their vacation. I review the new price drops for the week and add an extra blurb about the great deals available on theme park packages and Hawaiian Cruises to my social media.

Satisfied with my updates, I head out to the grocery store to get food for the next few days and restock some basics. I need to replenish my baking supplies, or I may not make it through the week. I pick up some Mexican take-out on my way home, it's almost time for the pregame show to start. I get everything up to my place and put away. Someone bangs on my door, scaring the crap out of me. I look through the peephole and there's a guy with flowers. I open the door.

"I have a delivery for Sherry."

"That's me," I say not able to hold back my giddiness.

"These are for you, ma'am. Have a great day!" He hands me the arrangement and moves on to his next delivery. The flowers are beautiful and perfect. One dozen roses —half red and half baseball leather with stitching, all in a ceramic vase that's shaped like a baseball bat. I find the card and read it:

Sherry,

I can't be away from you for ten days. Will you spend this weekend with me in LA?

Love,
Rick

Squeeeeeeeeeeeeeee! I text Rick a picture of the delivery and a quick message:

Text to Rick - The flowers are beautiful. I love the baseball roses. I can't wait to spend the weekend in LA with you!

I sit down with my take-out and settle in to watch the game. Right now, that means watch my man play baseball and drool over him in his uniform. The way his blue eyes pierce the metal grate of his catcher's mask. The way he holds himself on the field. I double-check the lineup to make sure he's playing and everything is as expected. The first inning went well, but no score for either team. The second inning, Seno got beaned with a bat on the helmet and hit in the instep with a ball. Still no score. The third inning, our pitcher is shaking Seno off—never a good thing when the pitcher doesn't go along with the catcher's calls. It's a sign of pending disaster. Seno misses a pitch completely, it bounces off the backstop and he gets it off the carom, but not before the runner on third comes in to score. He's pissed! The silent communication on field says the pitch wasn't what was called. The catcher is still supposed to catch it. The rook and Kris run in to home plate to have a quick pow wow and try to calm Seno down. But, it's all downhill from there. Cross stole bases and got to third base twice, but never scored. Seno got picked off at first and tagged out at home. The team couldn't pull it together for anything and it all fell on Seno for starting the bad streak with the passed ball. Final score 3-0 Colorado.

After that game, I wasn't sure Rick would call tonight. I had already resigned myself to the fact that he wouldn't, it's okay, and not my fault. Don't mess with baseball stuff, OCD, superstitions, streaks, whatever—stay out of the way. A couple hours after the game, I'm climbing into bed when my phone rings.

"Hello," I answer quietly.

"Hi, did I wake you up?" he asks.

"No, just climbed into bed. I have some reading to do. Thank you for the flowers. Sorry the game sucked," I say not judging.

"The game was bad and I don't want to talk about it.

I'm glad you like the flowers, but I'm even happier you'll be spending the weekend with me. I miss being near you. I like that I can talk to you and not get distracted by sex, but I miss holding you, kissing you, waking up with you," a soliloquy from his lips.

"I miss you, too. I tried not to bug you today, I don't want to be a distraction while you're on the road."

"Babe, you can call me, text me, whatever you want whenever you want. You make me happy. Anything new today?"

"Actually, yes! I got the details for the karaoke finals this morning and it's going to be three rounds of elimination in one night. I've never done more than one round in a night. I need to have two songs for the first round and I know what those will be. The second round is contestant's choice, so I'm working on that and have too many to choose from. The third round will only be the top two finalists and it's going to be wild card, which means they'll give the finalists a choice of three random songs after they're on stage and they'll have to show karaoke skills with no song practice. I'm open to suggestions for the contestant's choice," I say happily.

"When are the finals?"

"It's the Wednesday you're in Pittsburgh. I don't expect you to be there or anything," I say nonchalantly.

"I might be late, but I'll be there. Are you wearing the purple dress again?"

"No, I haven't put together my outfit yet. The first two songs are both current, so nothing retro. I'm thinking all black with bling, but that'll probably change."

"It wouldn't hurt my feelings if you didn't wear something so revealing. I don't like to share," he says selfishly.

"Is that so, King Seno?" I say jokingly.

"Yes, my queen. I'm the only man who'll be worshiping you," absolute truth from his soul. His tone rips right through me. He isn't joking at all. He means it with all his heart and soul. I'm the queen to his king.

"And in case you're wondering, I plan to worship you like the royalty you are this weekend. Our room will be at the Universal City Hilltop and it'll be reserved under King and Queen. Do you mind sitting in the friends and family box with the player's wives and girlfriends? I don't want you to be by yourself, it's not your hometown stadium," he elaborates.

"I can't wait! I trust your judgment, but I'd rather be behind home plate so I can look at your ass!"

"I can hear you better from there, too. All the wives will already know who you are, it's a rumor mill and somebody got a video of me kissing you Sunday at the first base wall."

"Can I get a copy of the video?"

"Seriously?"

"Yes! I want to see what it looks like when I get one of those mind-blowing kisses from Rick Seno."

"I'll check with the rook, I think he has it."

"Cool! I'll be dreaming about you tonight, my king."

"I love you, my queen. I miss you, babe." He hangs up.

CHAPTER SIXTEEN

I 'm beginning to hate my alarm. Every morning it taunts me. "Get up, you're in bed alone." It's just rude. I snooze three times and try to get the alarm to go away. But as always, eventually the aroma of the coffee brewing wins. I wake up needing baseball and decide to watch the recap from last night, only to find out the skipper blamed Seno for the team's horrible performance. I hate to see that. It can't all be his fault, it's a team effort after all. Rick takes those things to heart and he's harder on himself than most players. No wonder he didn't want to talk about the game last night. I run through my morning routine and make sure business is caught up. Mid afternoon I hear my social media ping...

RookCross: Sherry?

This is not what I expected when my social media pinged.

Sherry: Cross?

RookCross: I'm not sure I should be doing this, but the skipper said he's going to bench Seno if he doesn't get his head straight and I'm pretty sure you're the only one who can make that happen. Skip went off on the whole team about last night's game, but focused the problem as starting with Seno.

Sherry: I've been talking to him every night. Are you saying I should avoid him or ignore him or what? I'm a huge fan and a team player, but I don't think I can do that.

RookCross: I think the opposite. You need to come to Colorado. How soon can you get here?

Sherry: Really? Isn't that overstepping my boundaries?

RookCross: Yes. Really. The team needs you, more importantly Rick needs you. That's still weird to me, he never needed anybody.

Sherry: Where is he staying? Let me check for flights. Don't say anything to him. I'll message you my arrival time, so you'll know when I'm getting there. There's no way I can get there before the game today.

RookCross: We're all at The Downtown in Denver. I'll get you his room number. Thank you.

I check flights to Denver and the next flight is leaving San Diego in thirty minutes, that won't work since I won't make it through security before the plane takes off. There's a 4:45 with a layover. Bingo! 5:30 departure nonstop to Denver arriving about 8:50 with the time difference. I should get to the hotel about the same time as the players after the game. I book the flight, get dressed and primped so I'm ready to see my Rick, pack up quick and get the complex maintenance man to give me a quick ride to the airport (he'll do about anything for a twelve pack without judging, so I keep a couple on hand just in case). When I get to the airport, I send the rook a quick message...

Sherry: Landing in Denver at 8:50 Denver time. Best I can do. At the airport now.

RookCross: Got it. Thank you. He's in room 823.

I get through security without any trouble, I used the tip sheet I provide to my clients and it was perfect. I find my gate and have a few minutes to browse the newsstand before boarding. I purchase the new issues of Cosmopolitan and Hawaii magazines for my in-flight entertainment, as my flight starts boarding. I lift my carry-on into the overhead and keep my huge purse with my electronics, snacks and magazines with me in my seat. I try to get comfortable, but no matter how many times I fly I'm nervous at take off. I go for my iPod, ear buds in my ears, and start listening to music on shuffle—I've got to figure out what my round two song is going to be. It's an easy take off, I'm in the air and on the way to Denver. I flip through the Cosmo looking at the current fashions, perusing some interesting "How to please your man" and "Is he a keeper?" type articles I may go back to at some point. The flight attendant comes around offering drinks and pretzels, which I accept willingly. I try to relax, but I'm going to see Seno and he doesn't know I'm on my way. So exciting and spontaneous. I take the Denver Magazine from the plane for future reference, I doubt I'll have time for it while I'm here. The plane has started its descent and I'm starting to get anxious. What if he doesn't want me here? What if he's irritated because I didn't tell him I was coming? What if he wants to kill Cross for contacting me? What if I'm in the way? What if I make the problem worse? What if he decides I'm too clingy? Probably all things I should've considered before I got on a plane. But, I didn't. Cross said Rick and the team need me. That's all it took.

What the fuck am I doing? How could I be such an irrational and impulsive girl to just go jet set off to see her big league baseball boyfriend because his teammate called her and told her she should? For the team? For a win? For the emotional girl he's caused me to become, that's apparently unable to conduct herself like a rational human being? For the sex? You don't know what you'll find when you get there. You don't know what he's really doing on the road. You don't know if he's secretly married. You don't know if he has a girlfriend in every town. My insecurities have taken over my inner voice, but my heart insists on taking the risk. I need to be here.

The landing is smooth, which is not what I usually hear about Denver. I quickly get my things together and get off the plane. I send a quick text to the car service I requested and stop off in the ladies room to freshen up. I get a message from the car service and have ten minutes before they'll pick me up, so I walk to the pick-up area and get there right on time. I give the driver the hotel name and we're on our way. I check on the game and it's not good. Top of the ninth inning 7-2 Colorado, bases loaded with

Seals, two outs, 3-2 count and Martin strikes out ending the game.

In no time at all, I'm in front of The Downtown in Denver. The hotel is a beautiful building, modern and easily twenty stories. I walk into the lobby at straight up 9pm and get my bearings, bar, coffee shop, elevator. I beat the team to the hotel, and go on up to his room to be there waiting when he gets there. Avoid the whole team seeing me. I take the elevator to the eighth floor and I'm flooded with visions of being pressed up against the elevator wall by Rick's hard body and held there while being kissed sense-less with his hands on me. My cheeks get warm at the imagery in my head and I'm thankful there's no one in the elevator to witness my blush. I reach the eighth floor and step out of the elevator to a huge mirror. I check myself out and I know Rick will love me in my short denim skirt, low cut black strappy tank, black sandals and my Seno baseball cap (yes, the black lace bikini panties with matching bra, too!). Then again, he loves me regardless of what I'm wear-ing. I walk toward his room and there's a voluptuous, fake-boobed, red head, wearing a skintight black mini dress with cut-outs in the hallway. She's attempting to use a key card to go into one of the rooms and not having an easy time with the technology. I judge her choices internally and keep walking toward Seno's room. As I'm passing her, "Can I help you with the door?"

"No, these cards are temperamental. Thanks though," she says dismissing me.

I look at the door and she's trying to unlock room 823, Rick's room. "The problem is you have the wrong room," I suggest.

"No, this is the right room. I'm sure of it," she says, doing her best to ignore my existence.

"I'm sure it's not. I'm meeting someone here," I say as I swing my hair around like a schoolgirl.

Fake boobs stops and turns to me, "Honey, he's out of your league. He's not interested in anyone like you. You need to get out of here before you embarrass yourself and let the women handle this." Her key card finally works and she slides into his room. I look at the door as it slams in my face and the number on it is 823.

Now what? This can't be right. This can't be happening! There's no way my Rick is interested in that baseball skank! Am I going to put him in the position to have to explain why she's in his room? Do I want to stay here and watch him go in his room to find her and have his way with her? Do I want to have a scene in the hall? This isn't helping. This is just going to make it worse for the team. Or not, maybe this is how he gets his head straight. I can't pretend this isn't happening. My tears stain my cheeks. I can't be here. No matter what, he doesn't deserve to see me cry over him.

I run for the elevator to get out of here before the team shows up and ride down to the lobby. I beeline for the ladies room and plant myself in the ladies lounge room where none of the guys will run into me. I gather my senses and search for a flight home before it gets too late. Nothing. I use my travel agent secrets and still nothing. I call in a favor and the best I can do is get on a waiting list. I'm starving, but don't want to go into the lobby until I know I won't be spotted. I check the time and I've been hiding in the bathroom lounge for almost two hours. I can't believe I'm so stupid! He's a professional baseball player! He's probably in his room banging her right now! She had his room key! My anger takes over, I shove my Seno cap in my bag and wash my face.

I walk out to the lobby and head toward the coffee shop to find food, but it's closed. The only other option is the bar. It can't hurt and they probably have a bar menu. Sure enough. I sit in the corner of the bar and check out the limited menu. I order cheese fries and a shot of Jack with a Coke back. I can't believe I'm here. The server delivers my drink order and I know better than to do any shots when I haven't eaten, but it doesn't stop me. I use logic, food will be here soon. My server checks on me and brings me a second shot before my food order is ready. I'm warm all over and not caring so much about that red headed bitch. The server stops to chat with me when she brings out my cheese fries and actually has me laughing. I look up to see Cross standing over me.

"What are you doing here?" he asks.

"You told me to come to Colorado, remember?" I say.

"Why aren't you with Seno?" he specifies.

The fun server drops off a third shot for me with a wink and asks if Cross would like anything. I tell her to bring him some shots, too. Just laughing.

"Have a seat," I offer to Cross and he sits across from me.

"Are you drunk?" he asks.

"I'm getting there. I can't believe I hopped on a plane to Denver because you told me Seno needs me! No matter what, you guys will always be my team, but you sucked tonight!" I toss back my third shot and eat a few fries.

"Okay, obviously I'm missing something here," Cross looks at me bewildered.

"Yes, you need a shot to catch up with me, so I'm not drinking alone," I suggest.

"Are you kidding? I don't want Seno to beat my ass for getting drunk with his woman. I'll be on the DL for the rest of the season," as he tries to reach Seno by text. "Does Seno know you're here?"

"I have no idea. He probably can't remember me with his dick buried in that fake-boobed red head!" comes out louder than planned.

"Sherry, that doesn't sound like Seno," defending his teammate.

"She had his room key and I watched her use it," I glare at him deadpan.

"There's got to be a logical explanation, this doesn't make sense," Cross says refusing to believe it.

"There is. I should've known better than to get involved with a baseball player. I should never have flown to Denver. What did I think happens when you guys are on the road? I'm an idiot. A broken-hearted idiot," and the tears stream.

"I preferred you mad," wondering why Seno hasn't responded to him. "I'll be right back." He goes to the bar for a drink and he's trying to use his phone, possibly leaving a message. I work on my cheese fries until the rook returns.

"So, what's your plan?" he asks.

"I'm going to toss back another shot, finish these fries, and go sit at the airport until there's a seat available on a flight home. I'm on a waiting list for a flight departing at about noon," set on my decision.

"That's not going to work. I'll get beat that way, too. I can't allow you to spend the night in the airport. You can stay in my room with me," he suggests.

"Excuse me? Did you just invite me back to your room? You're a baby!" alcohol talking instead of my brain.

"I'll sleep on the couch and you can have the bed," he made his intentions clear. Fingers working his phone. "I'm not giving you a choice."

"Fine. But, you can't make me talk to Rick," I put my

foot down as I walk toward the elevator with him. Of course, we get off the elevator on the eighth floor. What the hell? Is the whole team on the same floor? I can't help it, I glance toward Seno's room. There's nothing to see, but a closed door. Luckily, Cross leads me the opposite direction to his room.

"Okay, you make yourself comfortable and use the bed. I'm going to shower and change in the bathroom, so you have plenty of time to change or whatever you want. I'll knock before I come out. Does that work for you?" the rook was trying to control the situation.

"None of this works for me!" I spin around angrily with my hands in the air like the wicked witch.

"Okay, I'm glad we have an understanding." He went into the bathroom, shaking his head and talking to himself as he closed the door behind him.

I consider changing, but decide it'll be easier to simply leave my clothes on. I check out the rook's room and discover the minibar. He said to make myself comfortable. I'd be more comfortable if I had a couple more shots. Looky there, two mini bottles of Jack sitting there waiting for me. I shoot one of the bottles and take the second with me just in case. I climb in bed and try to relax. Big, comfortable, white, fluffy bed. I sink underneath the sheets and appreciate the silkiness on my legs, as I consider how great it would be to have sex in this bed.

"Chase! Chase!" I yell.

Cross comes running out of the bathroom with a towel wrapped around his waist, "Sherry! Sherry!" He examines my squeamish expression. "What's wrong?"

"Spider."

There's a knock on the door and Cross goes to look out

the peephole. He opens the door immediately and says, "Where have you been..." and gets cut off.

"Where is she and why are you calling out her name?" Seno storms in as Cross directs him to me laying in his bed. "What the fuck is going on here?"

"Whatever I want! Cross said so!" I volunteer.

"Dude, she's drunk," Cross offers.

"Why is my woman drunk and in your bed, while you're in a towel? And it better be good, or I'll put you on the DL for a year," Seno had turned red and was making tight fists, ready to give the beat down.

"Because that's what I want!" I shout. Entertained that Cross was going to be on the DL longer than he expected.

"Sherry, you aren't helping. Cool it a second." Cross gestures for her to calm down and turns back to Seno. "I found her in the bar. I messaged her earlier today and told her she should come see you. When she got to your room there was a woman with your room key going into your room. Not sure how many shots she's had, but I can tell you she likes Jack and Cheese Fries, and she gets louder and bolder as she takes shots. She's a handful, dude." Cross says shaking his head.

"Why is she in your bed and in your room, while you're wearing only a towel? I'm still waiting for the explanation," Seno ready to blow.

"Oh, yeah. She was going to go sit in the airport all night until she could get a flight home and I knew you wouldn't want that. I brought her to my room and told her she could have the bed. She yelled and I came running out of the shower to see what was wrong and that's when you knocked. Swear dude, I'd never touch your woman. Honest, I don't think I could handle her. She's hot and spunky though. I totally see the attraction." Cross should have stopped while he was ahead. "And, she got into my minibar while I was in the shower." He sighs.

Cross looks at Sherry, "Why did you yell?"

"I told you! Spider!" I point to the eight-legged creeper on the wall.

Cross turns to Seno, "Where have you been? I've been trying to reach you since I found her in the bar."

"Yeah! And how was the fake-boobed, red headed, baseball skank?" I yell at him in pain.

"Thank you, Cross. I'll take care of this," Seno says as he stalks toward the bed.

I hold the sheets tight around me because he's coming for me and I don't want to go with him. The sheets are suddenly ripped away from me and I'm over his shoulder being carried out of Cross' room.

"Traitor!" I yell at Cross. Seno slaps me on the ass and I squeal. "I don't want to go anywhere with you! Where are you taking me?"

"Stop being difficult. No more Jack for you. I'm taking you to my room and I don't care if you want to go with me or not!" Rick kind of turns me on with his power trip.

"I don't want to go to your room. I'm not going to be your sloppy seconds. I'm the only one or I'm no one. I don't need to see that skank or your messed up sheets!" I went off, kicking my feet.

Seno persists, unlocking his room and taking me in to his clean room, with the bed still made and nobody else in the room. "Now, you can see the bed is obviously not messed up and there's nobody else here."

"It doesn't mean anything. You could've had shower sex or did it on the floor or on the bathroom sink. Damn it! Why did she have a key to your room?" I cry out. I don't want to care. It needs to be over.

"Do you trust me?" He asks.

"Yes, but..." and he cut me off.

"Then, that's all that matters. Yes, there was a woman in my room when I got here after the game tonight. It appears someone who works at the hotel gave her my room key. I already filed a complaint with the hotel and they're taking care of the problem," he explains.

"More importantly, I've been trying to reach you for hours and getting nothing. It's been killing me. I want to know when you're traveling. If you're getting on a plane or going for a long drive or not going to be accessible for more than an hour, please let me know. I'm not worrying about you like that again. Where's your phone?" Seno lectures. There's a knock at the door and Seno goes to investigate. He opens the door to Cross.

"Here are her things, have a good night." Cross was out of there quick.

Seno brought in my big purse, my sandals and my carry-on. He looks at me, "What were you planning?"

"I brought everything I need to work from the road and stay with you for the rest of the Colorado series and maybe not go home before our weekend in LA," I reply soberly.

"You took a plane from San Diego to Denver dressed like that for me?"

"Not exactly." I took my bag from him and put on my Seno baseball cap. "More like this, except I had my sandals on and my hair looked nicer and I had my make-up on."

"The only part that matters to me, is you came for me," he says with a new heat in his eyes.

"I beg to differ." I say as I drop my skirt to reveal my black lace string bikini panties. "It seemed you appreciated this ensemble when I described it to you last night." I know it's asking for trouble. This was only the first of many challenges in loving a major leaguer. But, he's right—I trust him. More than that, I love him.

Rick comes at me and claims my mouth with his, running his hands up and down my sides. He puts one of his hands in my hair and holds me where he wants me while he kisses me passionately. This. This makes it all worth it. His pants drop to the floor and his fingers push my panties to the side, feeling my wetness and dragging a low guttural sound from him. He rubs his head in my wetness gently and suddenly plunges in with need, drawing a scream from my mouth. Needing me wrapped around him. He lifts me up and I wrap my legs around him wantonly, my hands in his hair as I break the kiss and whisper with my ragged breath in his ear, "I trust you completely. I know you only want me. I know you love me. I'd do anything for you. I don't want any other man to ever touch me again, I'm only for you to worship, my king. I love you, Rick." My breathing gets harder and I've lost control, I call out, "Oh, my king! Rick! Rick!" and scream out over and over.

Someone in a neighboring room beats on the wall and says, "Turn down the porn."

Rick immediately takes us to the bed and slams into me over and over causing me to keep screaming and making the bed slam the wall, "Say my name, baby, say my name and say it loud, tell me how you want it."

"Rick, Rick! Rick! Oh, baby, Fuck me hard! Yes! Yes!" If he wants to put on a show for the neighbor, I'm in! Seno's got the biggest grin and went off like a bottle rocket yelling at the top of his lungs. I'm surprised the windows didn't shake. He doesn't stop, he changes his pace and leans over me to kiss me. His intensity with different meaning. Slowly and deliberately pushing in and pulling out, pushing in and pulling out, absorbing everything, memorizing every stroke, appreciating me tight around him, pushing how deep he can bury himself inside me, using our connection, drawing his orgasm out longer while pulling mine from me.

His mouth at my ear, he whispers, "I love you, my queen. Tell me what I can do for you."

"You've already given me everything I wanted. I only wanted you and you're better than I dreamed you could be," I need to work on keeping my tongue in check. I blame him, when he's buried this deep inside me and driving me crazy touching that spot he can only reach with his cock over and over, how is a girl supposed to think straight?

"I'm going to come again and this time you're coming with me," he says. He reaches between our legs and strokes himself a few times, then rubs my clit as he pounds into me hard. "Come for me loud, baby. Come for me now!" And I go off on command with no control, screaming out repeatedly at the same time as he calls out my name and pulls me tight against him. He whispers in my ear, "Thank you for coming to me. I need you with me. I love you."

"Can I stay with you for the rest of the Colorado series?" I ask.

"I'll get you a room key and a ticket to each of the games, please stay with me." He smiles and relaxes on the bed with me.

"I forgot, I brought you something," I open my carry-on and unpack quickly, grabbing what I was digging for.

"I like your stuff unpacked and mingled with mine," he comments on the mess I made in his room.

"Here, I made these for you," I hand him a dozen of my chocolate chip cookies, tied with a ribbon and a copy of my house keys.

"You didn't need to make cookies for me, but I'm glad

you did," he says as he opens the cookies. He notices the keys and turns to me with big eyes.

"They're your housewarming gift to go with the keys to my place. I want my place to be like home for you."

He looks me in the eyes, "You're my home. There's no one like you, my queen."

I fall asleep in my favorite place, his arms.

CHAPTER SEVENTEEN

I wake up with my man's arms wrapped around me from behind, both he and his cock wanting some good morning love. He enters me slowly and starts whispering the sweetest things in my ear as he strokes in and out, "I feel like you were made for me and I want to be with you always. Whatever you want, I want to give it to you."

It reminds me of "The Flame" by Cheap Trick. It's my contestant's choice song! I sing the next lines of the song and the rest of the chorus in a soft, sweet voice. I move my ass against him while he's in me and reach down between my legs to find our connection. He cusses and reaches around to rub my clit, but I smack his hand away. My left hand on his shaft where he enters me and my right hand on my sensitive nub.

"Do you like to feel me entering you?" breathing hard.

"Yes."

"Are you touching yourself?"

"Yes, is that okay?" I ask for permission.

"Oh yea." He's limited.

I move with him, my body lighting up and ready to go off like a roman candle. "I want you to come hard, I want you to come with me," I command him and squeeze him as I go off at the same time. His whole body shakes and I feel his orgasm roll through him. He bites down hard on my shoulder through his release.

About 45 minutes later Rick jumps out of the bed cursing. He only has thirty minutes to get to the stadium. "Babe! Game is at 1:05 today, different time zone. I gotta run. Order some room service or whatever you want. Stop at the front desk and they'll have a room key waiting for you, tell them your name is Sherry Seno. I don't want to leave you."

"Don't worry. I'll be at the game and I'll be here after the game. I'm not leaving you. Play hard, babe! Make it a win!" I encourage him.

"Um, Rick... Sherry Seno?" I question cautiously.

"The hotel will treat you better if you're my wife and not a groupie," he replies quickly on his way out the door and I let it go. I lie in his bed, in his hotel room, and review all the things I need to do, but can only focus on him. How he breaks rules for me. How I'm his home. Can I travel with him on road trips?

The problem with the hotel room is the coffee doesn't make itself. You have to get up and make it yourself or order it. I get up and get ready for the game. I take advantage of the time I have to explore the area for my baseball stadium vacation tour. I'm sure I'll find some coffee somewhere.

The stadium isn't far from the hotel, so I walk and take in the scenery. The streets are busy and the closer I get to the field, the busier they get. The fans are all gathered in the restaurants enjoying pregame libations. I consider myself lucky I'm not hung over. I enjoy window-shopping the kitschy gift shops. I step into a typically touristy shop, everything says Colorado on it. I browse around and find the cutest picture frame with a crown and rhinestone tiara on the top, and it says Colorado across the bottom. I gotta have it! I leave the store with my purchase and continue my stroll toward the stadium. I find a baseball shop with all kinds of cute tops, and nothing team specific. I'm concerned I might max my credit card, but I go in anyway. So many things I simply adore! A deep V-neck T-shirt in black with the words "This girl loves diamonds" outlined with a baseball diamond on it in shiny crystals. A pullover hoody that says "Keep swinging MY catcher likes the cool breeze" and they customize the back with a name and number. Shit! It's almost game time. I get it in gear and somehow manage to get to the stadium as I hear the National Anthem. I check my phone and I'd missed a call from Rick, but he texted me:

Text from Rick - Your ticket is at will call. I was late. Skip scratched me from the lineup. I'm working him because I'm going to make it a win for you. Wish you would answer your phone. You make me worry.

I don't know if he'll get my response if I text him back now. I don't think they can have their phones in the dugout, but I text him anyway:

Text to Rick - Sorry, I didn't hear it ring. I'm setting my phone to ring and vibrate when you call. Walking up to will call now. I'll be watching for you. I didn't mean to get you in trouble. Go Seals!

I get an immediate response from Rick:

Text from Rick - It's not your fault. It was worth it.
You're worth it. You should set it to just vibrate for me.
Skip had already heard about the "porn" in my room
when I got to the clubhouse, so that didn't help and
that was all me. The team is all over it.

He's killing me! Just vibrate! I should expect no less. I should be embarrassed by the porn stunt getting around, but I'm not. Proud to have him as my man and they can all know it. I walk up to the will call window and give the girl my name.

"Miss, are you sure there's a ticket waiting for you? I don't have a ticket for that name. Who left the ticket for you?" trying to be helpful.

"Rick Seno left the ticket for me. He just did it today," I offer hopefully.

"I do see he left a ticket here. Ummm... Does he maybe call you something else? Possibly a title?" she suggests trying to give me a clue.

"Queen Sherry," I say with a blank look.

"Better, and ah, what is Queen Sherry's last name?" she asks with big eyes.

"Queen Sherry Seno," I say and bang my head on the counter repeatedly.

She passes the ticket envelope to me, "Don't worry, these guys are always up to something. Enjoy the game."

I walk away from the window with my ticket, wondering what just happened. I get through the metal detector, pull my ticket out of the envelope to pass through the turnstiles and find a note in the ticket envelope. It's crowded and there's nowhere to stop, so I hold the note until I get to my seat. When I get to my seat, the rook is leading off and has walked up to the plate, waiting on the pitcher to get the game started. My seat is field level, the first row right behind the visitor's dugout. I get settled and finally read the note:

The player's family and friends have a suite, but I didn't get you a ticket there because my family is there. I want to be there when you meet them, and we're going out to dinner with them tonight. It's the closest stadium to my hometown. Don't freak out. It'll be fine.

Freak out? Who's he kidding? I'm not ready to meet his family! I can't even handle how he puts things under Sherry Seno. That's it. This is how my life ends. Heart attack while I sit in a baseball stadium, comatose at the mere thought of meeting my fantasy's parents. Imagine my nervous tongue showing itself when I'm meeting the parents... "So, Mr. Seno did you teach your son that great move he has when he pounds his cock into me?", "Yes, ma'am. He's very polite and courteous. He's made sure I get my orgasm before he gets his, every time except for once and sometimes you can't help it. A real gentleman." Or worse, what if one of the players comes by the table at dinner and says "Hey porn star!" I wonder what he's up to with the Sherry Seno thing. I know what he said and I understand the logic behind it, but why doesn't he use a cartoon character name or something as an alias? Then again, Sherry Seno does sound good. Crap! That's what he wants! He wants me to want to be Sherry Seno, a not so subliminal message. Damn it! I kind of do! This is absolutely insane. What is he doing to me? I'm acting like a dumb girl!

I check the scoreboard and it's already the bottom of the third inning. No score. I lost three innings! Where the hell was my brain? Maybe I was unconscious. Makes sense, right? Being told about a horrifying event you're going to screw up and you can't avoid that could potentially affect you for the rest of your life, could definitely cause a brain melt down. I'm sure there's a technical term for it. Mental Paralysis, maybe? Neurocircuitstoppus? I scan my surroundings mid-meltdown to see if my mental state is obvious to anyone around me. Perfect timing, the red head bitch from last night is in the stands. Obviously, the logical thing to do is to ignore her right now, considering the current stability level I'm exhibiting. She's walking up the stairs toward the bathroom. I want to go after her and tell her to stay away from my man. I know better. I simply hope she gets run over by a truck and throw myself into the game. The game will rescue me.

Today's lineup is the norm, other than Seno being a late scratch. Funny, since he was scratched for being late because he fell asleep after scratching an itch. The team is doing well, but Saben's skill doesn't compare to Seno behind the plate. He's missed a couple of pitches, he threw the ball into the outfield when he was trying to get a guy out at second base and he couldn't catch the ball to get a guy out at home. The team has displayed exceptional defense, keeping his errors from allowing the other team to score. End of the sixth inning and we're tied at 4. The rook sees me when he's running to the dugout, waves, and tosses me the ball. A few seconds later, Rick steps out of the dugout and waves at me with a huge smile. It makes it all worth it. I can do this. I start cheering on my team, "Go Seals!"

Bottom of the eighth inning and Seno comes out replacing Saben as catcher. "Wooooooooooo! Go Seno! Let's Go Seals!" I stand up and scream at the top of my lungs. He looks at me. His expression tells me he can hear me and he loves it. Colorado scored twice in the seventh, so we're down by two. We need to hold them there and come up in the ninth ready to do some damage. Skip did a double switch when he put in Seno, so he's fourth to bat in the ninth inning. I hope we get a fourth hitter in the ninth. Seno is focused, I'd say he's got his head on straight—nothing is getting by him, he's the backstop of all backstops. His calls are on point and he's set up perfectly for every pitch. It's a 1-2-3 inning, including two strike outs and a pop fly out. Seno comes out of his crouch position and walks toward the dugout like a man on a mission, the warrior is in and it turns me on.

Top of the ninth inning and we need to make some action to win this game. The pitcher's spot is up at bat first and Skip debuts a rookie who was brought up today from the farm team. Jones Mason is a 23 year-old center infielder that's been knocking balls out of the park all over the Mid-West. He's comfortable in the batter's box and he doesn't give a crap about Colorado's closer. First pitch he's caught looking, strike one. Second pitch he fouls it off into the stands down the right field line. Third pitch—Smack! I watch anxiously to see if it has enough on it to get out of the park, but it bounces and goes over the wall. That's a double! Every Seals fan in the place yells! Top of the lineup brings Cross, Martin and Seno. Cross digs in and butcher boys the first pitch down the third baseline perfectly, legging out the ball and safe on first. Mason still on second. Martin turns to hit from the left side for the first time today, you have to appreciate the value of a switch hitter. First pitch is a ball on the inside low. Second pitch is a ball in the same place. Third pitch, strike right down the middle of the plate. Fourth pitch is a ball outside. Count is 3-1 when the fifth pitch of the at bat goes out of control and hits Martin in the leg. Kris walks it off and takes his base, pushing Mason and Cross around to fill the bases with no outs. Seno walks up to the plate and before he chokes up on the bat, he points at me and smiles. There's a play on, I see the signs getting thrown around the field. My experience tells me they want Seno to put on a hit and run, so they can steal home and move up a base—but he's shaking them off. Not the best idea when you've already been scratched and brought in late. He points at me again. The first pitch is a fastball down the middle and Seno is ready for it. The sound of his bat connecting with the ball tells me it's out of the park. It's a beautiful sound, sharp, crisp. A no doubter. A grand slam! Mason scores, followed by Cross and Martin. They wait at home plate for Seno to get there and all four of them high five before they head into the dugout. Seno steps out of the dugout, points at me and winks— reminding me he said he would get the win for me. It makes me giddy. 8-6 Seals, still no outs. The next three hitters strike out. Bottom of the ninth inning, Seno marches back out to his position behind the plate and pulls his mask down, he means business. He makes eye contact with our closer, Houck, and it's on. First batter watches three fast-balls fly by him and never even swings. Out! Second batter smacks the first ball and pops it up to our second baseman. Out! Third batter works it to a full count 3-2 and fouls off a few more pitches protecting the plate. He hits a ground ball and gets thrown out at first base. Seals win! I yell "Wooooooooo!" so loud the people around me turn and give me a dirty look. I don't care!

The team celebrates on the field and Rick calls me down to the end of the dugout. I make my way there and he reaches out, puts his arms around me, and lifts me into the dugout with him. As if nobody else is there, he sets me down on the bench and claims my mouth, all hot sweaty man. He takes me to another world and everybody around us doesn't matter.

I break the kiss and gaze into his clear eyes, "Meet me in our room, so we can celebrate."

"We only have time for a short celebration before we meet my family for dinner, but we will have all night after. Skip said I'm allowed to have sex before any game I want to," he smiles deviously.

"You deserve special permission. Are you sure you want me to meet your family?" I query.

"No doubt in my mind. They're going to be asking me about the woman I pulled into the dugout. They'll love you," so confident.

"Okay. I'm going to make a quick stop on my way back to the hotel and I'll meet you there. You rocked it today," I smile proudly.

He smacks my ass as I head up into the stands. I should be offended, but it shows me he loves me and wants me.

CHAPTER EIGHTEEN

It takes me longer than I want to get to the baseball shop, mostly due to the crowds from the game. I grab one of the *This girl loves diamonds* shirts and a *Keep swinging* hoodie. Then I find the cutest shirt with gathered material and ties at the bottom on the sides and no sleeves, printed in foil lettering with "I just want to hold hands and watch baseball"—it's a must have! I take my items to the register and they add the big number 6 to the back of the hoody along with Seno. It's ready and I'm out of there, walking quickly towards the hotel in less than ten minutes. Before long I'm in the hotel lobby, needing to stop and get my key. I walk up to the front desk.

The front desk clerk looks at me, "How can I help you?"

"Mr. Seno had a key left for me, Sherry Seno," I say to her and the name rolls so naturally off my tongue.

"Yes, Mrs. Seno. I have the key waiting for you right here," she says as she hands me the key card.

I take the key and thank her as I walk to the elevator

with "Mrs. Seno" echoing in my ears. I wonder if he knew what was going to happen, if this was his intentional plan. I'm standing in the elevator contemplating when the door opens and Rick is standing there. He steps into the elevator with me and looks at me funny.

"Why are you standing in the elevator?"

I never pressed the button to go up to the eighth floor, stuck imagining what it would be like to be Mrs. Seno. But, I can't tell him that, can I? "I must've gotten lost in deep thought."

"Why don't you tell me about it?" he says as the elevator takes us to the eighth floor and he moves toward me unable to keep his hands off me.

"Umm, I don't think I should," as I encourage his hands and hope he forgets about it.

"How about you tell me while I kiss your neck right here, then I won't be looking at you when you tell me?" he says.

Sounds logical. Well, it sounds logical when he's kissing my neck. I would do anything he asks when he's kissing my neck. "The desk clerk called me Mrs. Seno when I picked up my key. I was Queen Sherry Seno when I picked up my ticket at will call. The name I gave the clerk to get my key was Sherry Seno. The baseball cap I'm wearing says Seno on it. I get it, it's to make people treat me better than a baseball groupie." I take a breath, "I'm just such a fuckin' girl. You make me act like, feel like such a girl."

He whispers at my ear, "I like that you're a girl. Does my name bother you?"

"No. That's the problem." Crap! Here I go with the diarrhea of the mouth again, "I love it! Listen to it—Sherry Seno—Queen Sherry Seno—Mrs. Seno—Mrs. Sherry Seno

—Mrs. Rick Seno—Rick and Sherry Seno—It's perfect! It's you!"

He pulls the button to stop the elevator between the floors and doesn't say a word. He really does have a thing about elevators. He claims my mouth with new intentions and pushes his body against mine. His hard length proving how much he wants me. He spreads my legs with his feet and I drop my bag. I hike up my skirt, so he gets a view of the Cookie Monster on my panties peeking out at him and put his hand there so he knows I'm wet for him—My panties are soaked. He stops what he's doing and steps back with a lustful caveman stare, like he's waiting for permission. "Rick, will you please fuck me in the elevator?" I ask sweetly and his face changes. He does nothing. I step away from him, pull my panties off, unbutton his pants, turn away from him, and bend over in front of him, holding my own ankles for balance.

He steps toward me, puts his hands at my waist, and pulls me to his hard waiting cock—sliding his length into me slowly, "How are you so perfect? Fuck." As he pulls out and slides in again. He pushes in harder and I brace myself against the elevator wall. He stops.

"Come on baby. Do what you want to do. Take me hard and fast and dirty, or however you think it should be on an elevator. I want it the way you want it," as I push back against him.

I hear a low groan as he slides in deeper then pulls out all the way, before he pulls me back against him, plunging in hard and fast. Keeping it fast and hard, over and over, pounding into me, controlling everything with his hands on my waist. It's amazing and I don't want him to stop. He's so big inside me, larger than before. I cry out and he smacks my ass, setting me off instantaneously. I yell out his name over and over with every stroke in, as I tighten around him, grabbing at his hard thick cock trying to bring him over the edge with me. He tenses up, then lets go, holding me on his cock. He's seated deep inside me and his hot fluids fill me as his tip finds that deep spot while he comes. Fucking amazing. He leans back against the wall to recover, and the glazed look on his face tells me he isn't with me. I quickly grab my panties from the floor, button his pants and get the elevator going to the eighth floor. After all, we are still in the elevator. I take his hand and the elevator stops. I lead him to our room and lock the door behind us.

He hasn't said anything and simply follows my lead back to our room. "Are you okay?" I ask him and kiss his cheek. He puts his arms around me and holds me, not talking.

"I love you. You do crazy things. You make me think crazy things. We should talk about what we want from this," he says softly and kisses me tenderly on the lips.

I stiffen, afraid of what he's going to say. "It's okay," he says. "I think I'm the one that's out there on this. I need to say things to you before I can't go back. Shit, I'm already too far gone."

He's nervous and I don't want him to be, so I interrupt. "Babe, I love you. I'm in this for as long as you'll have me and for whatever you'll have me for. One more night or years. I'll do anything I can to make you happy. I don't need your name. I don't need your sperm. I just need you."

"What if I want more?" he says gazing into my eyes.

"As long as it's not illegal and there are no other women in your bed, I'm probably okay with it."

"I can't believe you did that in the elevator. I've wanted that for years," he says remembering.

"I knew you wanted it and I want to make you happy. No brainer."

"So, if I asked you to marry me you'd say?"

"Yes."

"And, if I asked you to move in with me?"

"I already gave you my keys and you said my place feels more like home, so I'd suggest you move to my place."

"I just want to know you're with me and we want the same things. I want to get married someday. I want a family someday. I only want to be with you. I want a partner. I want to move in with you. I want to take care of you. I want you with me on road trips. I might want elevator sex again sometime. I don't mean now, I want to be on the same path," he leans his forehead against mine, heart bare.

"The fact that I love you means I want you to have those things with me. Some of it we have now and some of it we'll grow into." I change my tone and question, "Why do I feel like I'm missing something?"

"I was engaged and she dumped me for a guy who makes more money. Since I've been with you, I know that wasn't love—it didn't feel like this," he kisses me and I tingle down to my toes. "I know this all sounds stupid, we've known each other less than two weeks."

"We can be stupid together because I want to be with you, too. Do you want to start moving in with me when you get back from your road trip?" I wait for his response.

"Yes, Mrs. Seno, I'd love to," his smile shining into his eyes.

"I'm going to stay home while you're in Pittsburgh, to prepare for you to move in," I give him a heads up. "You need to stop with the Mrs. Seno stuff."

"And you need to prep for karaoke, right?"

"Yes, but it's the last time. Finals."

"Why do you want me to stop the Mrs. Seno stuff?" he asks.

"It makes me want to be Mrs. Seno and makes me do dumb girl things," I explain. "Like tears for no reason."

"What if I want to pretend you're Mrs. Seno?" he says quietly.

I take a deep breath and respond quietly, "I can't pre —," and I'm cut off by his phone ringing.

Rick walks into the bathroom to talk on the phone for a few minutes. He returns and says, "My sister got out of the house without her kids and wants to start in the bar tonight before my parents get here. I told her about you and she wants to meet you. I need to get cleaned up from the elevator. Can you go meet her? I'm sure she'll love to tell you stories about me," he entices me.

"Am I allowed to ask questions about you?"

"Yes," with a deep sigh. "But no shots of Jack, you're meeting my parents tonight."

"I won't forget I'm meeting your parents. What if your sister wants to do shots of Jack?" I say joking. "I need to get cleaned up, too... I don't even have any panties on!"

His eyes heat at the thought, "I think you should go commando tonight. I like the idea of knowing you don't have any panties on."

I give him the evil eye and change into my skinny jeans with my new *I just want to hold hands and watch baseball* shirt, "Not when I'm meeting your parents. I'm already worried I'll say the wrong thing."

"Don't worry. Go find my sister. Her name is Sam and you'll know her when you see her. I'll be down as soon as I shower," he disappears into the bathroom.

CHAPTER NINETEEN

I make sure I actually press the button for the lobby and make my way to the bar. His sister shouldn't be hard to find, she's female and alone in the bar. Then I see the bright blue eyes like the eyes I've been gazing into, but with long brown hair and make-up. It must be her. I walk up to her and ask, "Sam?"

"Yes. Short for Samantha. You must be Sherry! I'm so happy to meet you! I knew something was up when my brother didn't call me for a few days, then he was playing like shit!" directing me to sit on the bar stool next to hers.

"He's showering and will be down soon."

"Oh, then we need to make the most of the time we have before he gets here. He won't let us girl talk," she says.

"Then, we should talk about him and get to know each other after he's here," I say laughing.

"Exactly! There are a few things you should know. I'm his older sister and always looking out for him. He isn't the typical baseball player, he doesn't live that player life off the field. He did for a bit at first, but he got engaged because his longtime girlfriend told him she was pregnant with his baby. He thought he loved her and knew it was the right thing to do, he figured he'd marry her at some point anyway. He was really happy for a couple of months and accepted the path he chose. He was looking forward to being a father and doing everything for her. But, then he caught her with a player from another team who was in a higher income bracket and found out she was chasing players on the visiting teams when they came to Colorado. He doesn't come home as often any more. Now it's only when he's playing Colorado or it's a holiday. You're the first woman he's mentioned to me since they broke up and it's been almost two years. It means a lot to him that you came here to be with him on the road trip. He still thinks about what could've been and the whole experience made him want those things more than most men, I think." She takes a breath, "I probably shouldn't have unloaded all that. I suffer from DOTM."

I laugh, "I have the same problem and at the strangest times. I hope you have my back when I meet your parents!"

We laugh and order a drink.

"I know he's not a player. I still have moments of shock that we actually ever went on a date. He told me today he'd been engaged and got dumped for a guy who made more money, but he left out the rest. I suspected there was more. It makes more sense, I couldn't under-stand how income was a factor when you're a professional baseball player and it didn't seem like I should be prying. He has asked questions men don't usually ask when you've been together less than a month. I don't mind. I love him and I want to make him happy." I look at her sincerely, "Honestly, I'm not looking for a man to take care of me. I had satisfied myself with a fantasy baseball boyfriend and that was good enough. Until my fantasy man entered my real world and reality blew the fantasy away."

"Stop! I don't want to hear about my brother," she says laughing. "I know what its like to accidentally find someone you never want to leave and the connection you have. It's scary and wonderful at the same time."

Rick walks into the bar and gives Sam a hug. He puts his arms around me from behind and holds me, joining our conversation. "Two of my favorite women laughing together and getting quiet when I walk up is kind of disturbing." Leaning over he kisses my cheek.

"Your sister is great," I say as I try to turn back to him.

"I knew you two would hit it off," he stops. "Not sure I should've given you time alone."

"Don't worry, no embarrassing stories were shared," Sam says and glances at me knowingly.

Rick cringes, "Did you tell Mom about Sherry?" he asks Sam.

"No, but you should've before you grabbed her like a wild man and dragged her into the dug out this afternoon after the game. I got questioned like I'm your keeper, baby brother. Mom was shocked to see you do that and started rambling something about as long as you're happy, she guesses you're an adult and can be a player if you want. I reminded her you aren't a player and she mumbled something about more grandchildren."

Rick tightens his arms around me, letting me know he likes the thought and whispers in my ear, "I love having you as part of my someday." He softly kisses me below my ear and orders shots of Jack for the three of us.

Sam glares at us shaking her head, "You need to get a room! I guess you two will be ditching me and the parents right after dinner. No way to get you to hang out for karaoke in the bar? I never get out of the house."

I look at Rick with big eyes and he sighs, "Karaoke will be fun, but we might not stay all night."

I smile and clap like a fool. Yay! Karaoke!

The three of us shoot the Jack and continue with easy conversation until their parents show up. His father is a handsome older man who still has a full head of hair, dressed in a Seals polo shirt, and jeans. His mother is blonde with the same bright blue eyes he shares with his sister, she's showing her age, and thicker than she should be. She's dressed in capri length gauchos and a peasant style top, well put together except for the look of worry on her face.

His mother walks in and goes directly to him, pulling him from around me to hug him. "When did you start dragging random women into the dugout after the game?"

"It's nice to see you, too. Mom, this is Sherry and she's the only woman I've ever pulled into a dugout—not a random woman," making a direct point.

His Dad shook his hand, "Good game today. You were on point when you finally came in to play. Weren't you on the original lineup?"

"Yeah, Skip scratched me as a punishment for being a few minutes late getting to the stadium this morning. I worked him until he put me in. I told Sherry I'd make it a win today, so I had to make it happen."

"I approve of any girl that has a positive impact on the game, and being a beautiful blonde doesn't hurt. It's nice to meet you, Sherry," Mr. Seno says politely.

"It's nice to meet you, too, sir," I reach to shake his hand, but he pulls me in for a hug. His Mom is not so easy. Apparently, he's still her baby at age 28.

We eat in the bar since Sam wants to do karaoke. We sit down at the table and Mrs. Seno starts with the questions.

"So, Sherry, what do you do for a living?"

Does she think I'm a gold digger trying to take advantage of her son? "I'm a travel agent. I run my own online travel business, specializing in beach destinations."

"At your age, you must be new in business. I bet it's a challenge to cover expenses," she says digging.

"Actually, I've been in business for about ten years and consistently generate enough income to cover my expenses, as well as go on a trip or two each year and have my season ticket to the Seals in the lower field section," I don't know why I had to prove myself to her. It was all I could do not to tell her flat out "Look lady, I love your son and I don't care if he's a baseball player or if he even has a job or any money." I should've stuck to the no Jack idea. Rick slides his arm around me and I know everything will be fine.

"My dear, you don't look old enough to have a business for ten years. Did you take it over from a parent or something?" she says trying to demean me or get something out of me, and she does.

"I started my business when I was 25 and turned 35 earlier this year. I do better in business online because I don't look my age. In person, clients don't take me seriously." As it came out of my mouth I could see Sam mouthing DOTM at me and realized I gave their Mom something to harp on. I'm seven years older than her baby. That probably makes me a cougar in her eyes.

Rick rescues me, "I love that Sherry is a woman and not one of the whiny girls who have always hung around trying to get my attention. She's even more beautiful than any of them, inside and out." He pulls me closer to him and gives me a sweet peck on the lips, but doesn't pull away. He holds his lips on mine, worshiping my lips softly for a few seconds. My body turns to jelly.

Rick whispers in my ear, "I love you, my queen." I know my face lights up and I can't help it. I lean my head toward him and give him a hug.

"Sam, what do you know about the karaoke they have here?" I ask anxiously needing something I can rule.

"The KJ just started setting up. He has books with the songs he has available tonight and a sign-up sheet," Sam says as she scopes out the guy setting up behind me. Sam grabs one of the books and brings it back to the table.

We start flipping through the pages and Rick interrupts, "You should let me and Sam pick the songs for you, so you can get practice with songs you didn't pick." I see the questioning look from Sam and Rick continues, "My Sherry is in the final round of a karaoke competition. They've always chosen their own songs and have time to practice beforehand, but for the finals they'll be given a song when they're already on stage. No time to practice and she may not even know the song."

"I will know the song, as long as it's not country," I say. "Challenge accepted. Do your worst." I push the book away and leave it to them. Hopefully, Rick will pick something in my wheelhouse—I'd like to blow out my nerves and impress his family, even though I know it doesn't matter. It matters to me.

Rick and Sam discuss the torture they'll be putting me through amongst themselves and sign me up to sing. Sam signs up to sing and Mrs. Seno (whoa, weird) takes the book to find a song to sing as well.

We order all the appetizers on the menu and snack on them throughout the evening. I've been hitting the songs out of the park and my confidence is up. My last song of the night and the intro to Ed Sheeran's "Thinking Out Loud" starts playing. Rick did this on purpose, he smiles at me and my insides turn to goo. I decide to show what I've got and feel it all the way through. Let his Mom and everybody else witness how I feel about him. I look to him with questioning eyes and he nods at me in approval. It's an amazing release to put it all out there. To lay my heart out there bare for everyone to see it beat raw with my love. The words are so simple, tender and meaningful. I think about how he didn't let go of my hand when I met him that first night at the Locale. I think about that first unexpected kiss in the corner of the booth. I think about kissing under the stars on the bleachers at the Embarcadero. I think about the way he hasn't been able to keep his hands off of me since, and how I came here because he needed me. I think about how we found love and I look at my bracelet. At the end of the song, Rick is standing in front of me. He picks me up off the stage and holds me up over him, looking up at me and kissing me like he needs my lips on his to survive, not caring who is around us.

He carries me back to the table and holds me on his lap with my arms around his neck. Focused on each other in our haze. "You're amazing and I'm not just talking about your singing. That was probably the best I've heard you." The emotion made a difference in the performance, in me.

His parents sit there silently, in shock at our connection. Sam chimes in, "I'm staying in town tonight, so get my number from Rick and we can meet for coffee in the morning," she says to me.

"Bro, get a room before you combust. The heat off you two is insane. I'll take care of the parental units." She watches him and he makes no action. "Go. Now."

He picks me up over his shoulder and says goodnight,

then turns around. "Nice meeting you all," I say as he carries me away.

He carries me into the elevator and pushes the button to take us to the eighth floor. "I know what you're thinking. I'm trying not to stop the elevator," he says as he distracts himself by smacking my ass. All of the sudden his phone lights up with texts and I read them over his shoulder:

Text from Cross – Saw you in the lobby. Looks like you've got your hands full again. Let me know if you need help with that. She's hot and spunky.

Text from Skip – Good work getting your head on straight. Make sure you bring that girl to the game with you tomorrow and do whatever you did last night again. You'll be in the lineup tomorrow. Don't want to see that shit again in LA.

Text from Houck – You let me know if you need help closing that deal. That's a nice ass!

Text from Martin – Fuck, dude! You've got it bad. Hey, is your sister here? I'd like to tap that.

Text from Kranston – As a thank you for your help behind the plate, I'd like to offer my services in teaching you how to handle that woman. I know you're still a virgin. Don't worry, I won't tell.

Text from Rock – That's a description of my dick, not just my name. You know where to find me if you can't get it up.

Text from Mason – I know I'm new, but is that the way we treat women on this team? I gotta get me one of those. Know any you can suggest?

Text from Bravo – Bravo, baby, Bravo... way to make a scene in the lobby... caveman style. That's going to be all over the internet.

Text from Sam – Dad is handling Mom. He really enjoyed the evening. He's relieved and happy you have someone. I am, too. I like her. This hot player Kris Martin just gave me his number. I think I might call and have some fun.

Text from Dad – Was afraid I wouldn't see you happy again, son. Do whatever you can to keep her. It doesn't matter if it's only been a week. When it's right, it's right. From what I saw, it looks right. She loves you. Do what's right for you.

"Nobody ever texts me. I don't even remember giving the new guy my number. Now they decide to play with me and Sam is in on it," he says as he walks from the elevator to our room.

"Well, you managed to get to the room without stopping on the elevator. I'd say that's a step in the right direction, but I kinda like the elevator stuff," I mutter.

"Fuck me. You like the elevator make out sessions?" he asks surprised.

"Oh yeah, but not as much as the elevator sex. Best quick fuck ever," tormenting him on purpose. He puts me down, standing facing him.

"That stuff does it for me, but tonight can it just be you

and me, let me love you..." He kisses my neck, sending tingles down my spine. I know better and can't help myself, "One more thing, then I'll stop... So, our first daughter should be named Elle because she was conceived in an elevator?"

"I know you're being funny, but that works for me. Also, Elle can never know why that's her name. Kids don't need to know their parents are elevator freaks," he replies seriously. He picks me up and kisses me passionately, carrying me to the bed. He sets me down and lies down next me, pushing my hair out of my face, "I really do love you, I didn't think I'd ever feel like this. I've been alone for so long. I didn't think I'd trust anyone again. Now I know I didn't love anyone until you." He gazes into my eyes and kisses me softly, tenderly brushing his lips against mine, lightly sucking, and claiming me all the way to the depths of my soul. Running his fingers through my hair, wrapping his strong arms around me, and all I can focus on is having him inside me. I want him closer. I squirm out of my jeans while he's kissing me and start to unbutton his, but he stops me and stops kissing me. He searches my eyes, finding my need and desire. He pushes his pants off and pulls his shirt off over his head. He wants me. He leans over me and kisses me, until I reach to stroke his hard length.

"Please," I say against his lips. "I need to have you and love you. Make love to me." I must have said the right thing. He got harder. Kissing me more deeply. He slowly slides inside me until he can go no farther. My every nerve ending a frayed electrical wire. But he doesn't move. He keeps kissing me and exploring me, while he's buried inside me. I push the kiss further, forcing my tongue into his mouth and drive him to move inside me slowly as he moves his tongue deeper into my mouth. The kiss becomes uncontrolled and heavy, hard to breathe, our hearts beating hard against each other, I move to meet his slow strokes. He pulls away from my kiss, licking my lips, kissing my eyelids and moves to kiss by my ear.

He whispers in my ear, "Baby, feel how deep inside you I am. That's my love for you. Feel my heart beating hard against yours. That's my heart trying to reach yours, so it can finally be whole. Feel my breath on your skin. That's the heat you make inside me. Taste my lips. That's your sweetness rubbing off on me. Feel how hard I am inside you. That's the strength you give me. Listen to my voice, my words are only for you. I want to be closer to you, but I don't know how to get any closer."

I reach for his hands and lace his fingers with mine, pulling his lips back to mine, rubbing my hips against his, driving him to need more, our hands together above my head, neither of us wanting to let go. The friction between our bodies growing slowly. The heat intensifying into hot sweaty bodies against each other.

"I can't help myself," he says as he moves faster inside me. Pushing harder, pounding his love into me.

"It's okay, baby, it's the intensity of our love," I tell him on ragged breaths. He pulls me up with him, kissing me, sliding my naked body against his. Taking my words as permission to show me what he wants. "Whatever you want is right. Feel me wrapped around your love, my hands exploring you and holding on. My ragged breath telling you I've lost control. My trust allowing you to be in control of my body. It's only us, baby. Nothing for anybody else. No judgment. No lies. Only Love. Only us together." I push him back, so I'm on top of him. Riding him. He reaches up to squeeze my breasts and doesn't object to the change. He's pushing up into me while I come down on him, meeting each other at the best point. Working together to reach our climax and making noises I've never heard. The intensity grows as both of us get close. I can't stop. I can't help but move faster, plunging myself down on him. I need him. I need all of him. He cries out his release. I can't stop my actions, I want more, I need more. He reaches for me and takes control, slamming into me until I explode with his name from my lips. He slows down, but keeps going until I've come down from my high. He pulls me down to him, laying me on his chest, and caressing my back while he holds me.

"I love you, Sherry. I will love you as long as you will let me. I will take care of you as much as you will let me. I will love you more than any other man is capable. I promise. I'm the only one for you. I'll even be a baseball player, but only for you—you make it okay."

I lie there silently on his chest, listening to his heartbeat for what seems like hours before I speak, "That sounds a lot like a proposal."

"It's the promise before the proposal. If I had a ring, I'd probably propose to you right now. I don't want to take any chances on losing you. Whatever I need to do to keep you, I'll do it. You make me happy and I'm not losing my happiness."

"You don't have to do anything, but be with me. I'm not rushing you or pushing you, and I'm not leaving you. I'm happy with you the way it is right this moment and I can't wait to take the ride with you, travel to our destination together. I'm on the trip at your pace, when you're ready. I do want two things."

"Anything for you, my queen."

"I want you to keep calling me Sherry Seno, I've thought about it and I like the way it sounds. And, I really do want you to move in with me, you should be where your home is and I'm your home, right?"

"Absolutely, Mrs. Seno. When do you want me to move in?"

"Mrs. Seno reminds me of your mother."

"No problem, my queen, Sherry Seno. You'll be Mrs. Rick Seno."

"We can work on that when you're moving in."

CHAPTER TWENTY

Thursday morning comes early. Mostly because I don't want to be the reason Rick is late to the stadium today. I didn't tie him up and lock the door to keep him from going yesterday, but I did let him break his rules about pregame sex. I definitely wasn't complaining or stopping him. Honestly, I don't think I ever will. The game is at 11:15 today and I had planned on going home when he left for the stadium, but that's no longer an option. Skip told him to make sure I was at the game and that he did the same thing he did the day before. Plus, he got me a ticket for the game. So, maybe I can be a rule follower today, they sound like my kind of rules and I'm not one to turn down a baseball game. I'll have to change my travel plans, but there's time for that after he leaves for work.

I roll toward my man, to snuggle into his neck and I'm greeted by his sweet kiss on my forehead. He rolls to his back and holds me near, with my head on his chest. May be my favorite place, solid just like the beat of his heart I feel when I lie on it. I run my fingers over his abs, tracing the outline of each of them, working my way down until he bumps my hand with his cock. Before I can touch him or make another move...

"Come here, baby. I've got something for you." He says as he pulls me over on top of him. His expression changes as he changes his plan. He props himself up against his pillow and pulls me close until he can suck at my breast, and he goes for it. Licking my nipple and sucking my breast into his mouth, while squeezing the other. Then switching just to drive me crazy. Somehow he manages to get a hand on my sensitive nub while he's driving me insane and I'm a bundle of raw nerves, more sensitive to his touch than I've ever been. I feel his tip at my entrance and he makes a low groan when he finds my wet heat. He pushes in and his obvious pleasure is my undoing. The sexy expression on his face, eyes closing and automatically sucking harder—I'm done like never before.

"Oh, Rick. Oh, baby. Oh my god! Rick!" I whimper uncontrollably.

He flips us over, pushes in deep and hard. He bends down to go back for my breasts. I'm on sensory overload and he keeps going. I cry out again, louder than I intended. He releases my breast and asks, "Who am I? Tell me who I am, my queen." Slamming into me and slamming the bed into the wall.

"The king," I say breathlessly.

"I can't hear you."

"The king! Oh! Rick!" I yell out uncontrollably.

"Who's king am I?" he demands roughly squeezing my breasts as he pushes into me deep.

My incoherent brain finally understands where he's

going. "Oh, my king! You're my king! I love you, my king!" as stars burst before my eyes in the darkness.

"That's right, baby. Only your king. Grrrrrrr..." he growls as he follows me over the edge. Leaning down he searches my eyes and says, "I love you, baby. Always you. Only you, my queen." He kisses me softly, worshiping my lips.

We hear applause from the room next door, "Alright already. You're in the lineup today Porn King!"

We laugh out loud together and he gives me a quick kiss, as he gets up and hits the shower. "I need to be early today to secure my spot. Your ticket for today's game is on the nightstand. Also, what are your travel plans?"

I walk into the bathroom to continue the conversation and enjoy the view of my super hot baseball player boyfriend naked in the shower. "I may need to leave the game early to catch my flight back to San Diego," knowing he's not going to like it and I don't either.

"How about you change your flight and go directly to LA?" he suggests.

"My plan is to fly home to San Diego and drive to LA. I want to stop and visit my Mom."

"Fly to LA and I'll rent you a car to drive home, so you can visit your Mom on Sunday after the game. Then you can stay the night with your Mom, or whatever you want. I know you can't go to Pittsburgh with me. I don't like it, but I know it. It will give us more time together in LA. I'll even take you shopping. I know you want a new outfit for karaoke finals."

"Bribery!"

"I'm not beyond bribery. It's in my arsenal. I'll do what-ever it takes to get what I want." He says being demanding on purpose. "And, what I want is you with me."

"All you had to do was ask. You don't need to bribe me. You're all the bribery I need. I don't even need you to rent me a car, I'll take the rail."

"Is your Mom a baseball fan?" he asks.

"Yea, but... she's an LA fan," I say in shame.

"Well, then its time to change that. I'll get you two tickets to the Sunday game, so you can bring Mom. I'll even send a car to pick her up for the game."

"No."

"No?" He turns to me questioning selfishly, "Why not?"

"I haven't had time to talk to her about you yet. That's something we would do in person and I was going to do it on my way to LA." My cell phone rings and it's my Mom... say the name three times and they show up or call, never fails. I walk out of the bathroom to take the call.

"Hi, Mom. How are you today?" I ask cheerily.

"I was fine until my neighbor showed me a picture on the internet of my daughter being carried over some guy's shoulder through a hotel lobby in Colorado," she says in shock.

Fuck! "It's no big deal, Mom. That guy is my boyfriend. I want to introduce you to him, but his schedule is a bit crazy right now. I was planning to visit you this weekend and tell you all about him." I cover the phone and stick my head into the bathroom, "There's a photo of you carrying me through the lobby on the internet, according to my mom."

"Sorry, not a good start with the mom."

"Sherry, are you listening to me? What kind of man doesn't have time to meet your mother?" using all her mom powers.

"A professional baseball player who's on a ten day road

trip. I happen to be visiting him in Colorado right now," trying to show my inner adult.

"What are you thinking? A ball player! You know better," upset with my choices.

"Stop! I know. It's not like that. He's not like that. You need to meet him. I promise, you will love him as much as I do, Mom." Shooting myself in the foot with my DOTM.

"You love him? Crazy girl."

"Yes, I do and I'm keeping him! Believe it or not, Mom, I'm 35 years old and an adult in control of my own life. At least he plays for my team and isn't an LA fan! I'll call you later," I hang up.

"Rick, now your phone is ringing and saying, 'answer the phone damn it!'"

"Answer it, that's Sam," giving me permission.

"Hello, this is Rick's answering service and he can't come to the phone right now," I say laughing and Rick rolls his eyes at me.

"Hey, I'm hungry. Meet me at the hotel coffee shop in about twenty minutes? That give you long enough to get off my brother?" she says giggling deviously.

"For the record, I'm not on your brother. He's already in the shower. I'll be there in twenty," I hang up.

"I never should've introduced you two," shaking his head.

"She wants to talk about the hot ball player she was with last night," I say getting his goat.

"What? She's married with chil...," I cut him off.

"Kidding! She didn't say anything about him. But, you can bet I'm going to ask!" as I quickly get ready for my breakfast date.

The shower shuts off right when I'm ready to leave our room. I peek into the bathroom to find my man with a towel wrapped around his waist and quickly snap a photo with my phone.

He turns to me, "What are you doing?"

"I don't have any pictures of you or us for that matter, unless you count whatever is on the internet," I say thinking of the cute frame I picked up yesterday. "This is personal, only for me."

He shakes his head at me and takes my phone away, holding it up out of my reach. I fight him to get it back, I don't want him to delete the picture I took. He grabs me around the waist with one arm and pulls me against his more than half naked, muscled, wet body. He leans his head against mine and kisses my cheek—taking the most perfect selfies the whole time. He even manages to get a picture of him claiming my mouth with his before he set the phone down, needing to have both of his hands on me.

Fine. It took me thirty minutes to get to Sam, but I had a huge smile on my face and I was able to get my flight changed as I walked through the lobby.

"Good morning and it's about time," she glances down at her wrist as if there was a watch there.

"Sorry, I had a, uh, delay. Blame your brother," I say laughing as we sit down to eat in the coffee shop. It's nice to have some girl talk and know she's there to back us up.

"Thanks for running block last night with your parents."

"You make my bro happy. Last night, you were singing that last song to him and there was some type of gravitational pull drawing you together. Nobody else mattered. I swear he floated to the front of the stage to be with you. I've never seen him like that. I'd been worried he'd never be happy again, he's been so guarded. Take care of him. It's obvious you love him and care about him. So, you won't hurt him and I won't have to make your life miserable. I am the protective older sister," Sam says with a smile. "Though, you may need my help at some point and you know where to find me."

My phone vibrates. Text from Rick:

Text from Rick - I won't be back at the hotel, flying out right after the game today. I put your name on the room and got a late check out, so you can check out whenever you want. Hope you got your flight changed. I want you with me.

I message him right back:

Text to Rick - Flying direct to LA. Won't miss any of the game unless it goes to extra innings. 6pm flight, landing at 7:35pm LA time. I'll get checked out before I leave for the game and leave my bags with the bell-man. See you at the stadium! Make it a win, babe!

Rick replies quickly:

Text from Rick - Perfect. Just like you.

I smile and Sam starts in, "Seriously? All he did was text you and you're all googly eyed! You two are in trouble!"

"It's not trouble if it's right," I reply. "I need to get packed and take care of an errand before I go to the game. I'm flying to LA after the game to spend the weekend with Rick."

"Kris was right, you've got it bad," she said reminding me about the Martin text last night.

"About Kris, what's up with you two? You're married right?" rhetorical and questioning.

"Have you seen him? He's hot! A girl can dream you know," Sam says playing all dreamy.

"Be careful with that dream, sometimes fantasies come true. Rick is my proof," I say as I walk away.

I get back to our room to pack and head toward the stadium. I stop at the corner drug store to use their photo printer and print out copies of the photos from earlier this morning. I look for a greeting card, but nothing is right. I write notes on the photos and grab an extra photo envelope as I leave the store.

I get to the game in time and my seat is behind home plate today. That's where he wants me to be. He sees me as soon as I get there and he's ready for battle. Happy to be in the lineup and gear on, ready to go. It's going to be a great game. Rick is warming up the pitcher pregame and Chase comes over to talk to me through the netting.

"Hey beautiful! Nice seat you've got there. Will you cheer for me, too? I need as much help as I can get."

"I always cheer for you, just not as loud as I cheer for my Rick. I'll make an extra effort for you today. Can you do me a favor and give Rick an envelope for me when you guys are on the plane to LA? Without opening to look at what's inside and without the whole team knowing. Please." I slide the envelope to him through the netting.

"No problem. I'll go stash it in my carry-on right now. What is it? Dirty pictures?" he says wiggling his eyebrows like a creep. A cute baby-faced creep, but a creep nonetheless.

"No. Not dirty pictures," I blink my eyes at him and sigh. Cross gives me a wink and runs off to stash the envelope before the game starts and hopefully without Seno noticing. I stand for the National Anthem and it's game time! Seals are up at bat first, with Cross leading off followed by Mason and Martin. I make sure to cheer extra loud for Cross, "Let's Go Cross! Wooo!" and he connects with the first pitch sending it straight up the middle, base hit! I continue to cheer when Mason walks to the plate, "Wooo! Go Mason!" and he had a good eye on the ball taking a four pitch walk to first and pushing Cross to second base. Martin steps into the batters box, "Knock it out, Kris! Wooooo!" First pitch: ball low. Second pitch: strike straight down the middle. Third pitch: ball high and inside. Fourth pitch: hit foul into the Colorado dugout. Fifth pitch: ball high and inside. Full Count. "Let's Go Kris!" Sixth pitch: he connects, breaks his bat and it goes sailing through the air like a javelin toward shortstop. Grounder right between the legs of the shortstop and Martin legs out the throw, safe on first and bases are loaded with Seals, no outs. My Rick steps out of the on deck circle, swinging his bat like he means business as he steps up to the plate. "Let's do this, baby! Slam it! Wooooooooooo, Rick!" Cheering even louder than I was before. The people around me are staring at me funny, like I should be quiet or something. Not happening. First pitch: way inside. Second pitch: way inside and high. This pitcher is pissing me off, trying to throw at my man! "Get some control meat!" Third pitch: called strike, but it was a bad call. I could see it was inside. That's the call the pitcher is hoping for. "Slam it, Rick!" Fourth pitch: Smack! It's that sound I love and I'm up out of my seat waiting for the ball to come down from the heavens and be the grand slam it sounds like. Rick takes off around the bases and the ball lands in the upper deck right field about the same time he touches first. Cross scores. Mason scores. Martin scores. The three of them wait at home plate for Seno to catch up, they all high five and belly slap when he gets there. He turns to me and points. I scream out, "Go Seno! Wooooo!" 4-0 Seals. The Seals scored two more times, both at Rick's bat. Rick hits a double, batting in Mason and Martin. Then in the ninth inning, he hits a line drive solo home run to the third row in right field. Colorado got on base a couple of times, but the only time they got a player to third he was tagged out at the plate. The batter struck out and the ball had gotten away, Rick snatched the ball up and dove in front of the plate tagging out the runner trying to steal from third. Amazing play! Final score: 7-0 Seals, Seno 3 hits, 2 home runs, 7 RBIs. I could not possibly be prouder. I make my way to the dugout to congratulate him, but Cross and Mason are each dumping Gatorade on him. He's a nice shade of pink and getting pulled onto the field by Hannah for the postgame interview.

"Rick, you played a great game today both offense and defense. This game was all you!" Hannah starts her interview.

"This game took the whole team. We all need to get on base, so our teammates can bring us home. This is a team sport and without the lead-off hitters doing their job and getting on base, this would've been a very different game," Rick never takes all the credit—it's the team.

"What do you attribute the sudden turn around in your game to? You've been playing well all season, but had a few down days earlier this week. You seem like a new man coming into the game late yesterday and for the start today," Hannah continues.

"I always do my best to play at the top of my game, but my love for the game has been reignited," he says as he looks over at me.

Hannah follows his gaze, "Are you sure that's love for the game and not a new someone special in your life?" she asks Rick.

Rick smiles and walks straight for me, grabbing my face

with both hands and planting one of those you-are-so-mine-and-don't-you-forget-it kisses on me that goes on forever—I love it, even when they put us on the big screen. He breaks the kiss and whispers in my ear, "I love you, baby. You really do make a difference."

I can do nothing, except smile like a fool. What this man does to me, it must be pheromones or something. I'm not complaining because he's magnificent, but seriously where does my brain go when his lips are on mine and when he's whispering with his sexy deep voice in my ear?

He takes off into the locker room and I start my way back to the hotel with a little bit of extra time before I need to be at the airport. I take advantage and utilize the hotel business center to get some work done and call the car service to pick me up. The ride to the airport is a quick one and I get through security with no hang-ups. My phone vibrates with a text from Rick as I'm walking to my gate:

Text from Rick - Charter bus is taking us to the airport now and we should be landing about the same time you are. See your beautiful face in a couple of hours, baby.

I message him back:

Text to Rick - Is it stupid that I miss you already? See you in LA. Love you.

CHAPTER TWENTY-TWO

I need to call my Mom. I know she won't understand until she meets Rick. When I look at the situation from the outside, I think it's crazy. The schedule this weekend doesn't have enough time in it to get Rick to my Mom's to meet her. I don't want to make the phone call that will get me nowhere and leave me upset on the plane. There's got to be a better way.

I board the plane and nobody sits next to me. I take advantage of the two and half hour flight, set my iPod to my nap playlist and recharge.

Two hours later the flight attendant wakes me to prepare for landing. "We'll be landing in a few minutes, do you need anything?" he asks, looking at me funny.

"No. Actually, where's the new hot place to eat in LA? And, why are you looking at me like that? Do I have dumb ass written on my forehead in permanent marker or something?" I ask after determining he seems like an LA guy in the know.

"You look familiar. Let me get the plane ready for

landing and I'll sit next to you for the landing," and he was gone.

What did I start? Who is this guy? I don't need a flight attendant hitting on me. A few minutes later, he returns and it's extremely obvious he wasn't hitting on me. He sits down, buckles himself in, crosses his legs, "I'm happy to provide my LA knowledge, but first you'll need to tell me how you landed the baseball beefcake. That was you getting carried through a hotel lobby over hottie Rick Seno's shoulder, right?" He hands me a plastic cup half full of wine and is sipping on the same.

"I'm Joey, by the way," shaking my hand.

"First, that story requires Jack," I say laughing.

He pulls a mini bottle out of his pocket, "It's always good to be prepared," pouring my wine into his cup.

I give Joey the Reader's Digest version of how Rick and I got together, and confirm Seno looks as good out of his uniform as he does in it.

"Sweetie, you can't lay all that on me without a warning! I've been single for too long!" he says fanning himself.

We exchange numbers as the plane is landing and Joey is going to text me some great places in LA.

I turn off airplane mode and send Rick a quick text:

Text to Rick - Just landed. Calling the car service and I'll see you when you get to the hotel.

Almost instantly I get a reply from Rick:

Text from Rick - I have a better idea. It's date night. Picking you up outside the terminal in fifteen minutes.

Date night? I could get use to this hunk of man making

unsolicited plans for me. I stop at the ladies room to freshen up and make sure I'm presentable for whatever it is he has in mind. I walk through the airport and step out of the terminal to find Rick leaning on a convertible Porsche 911 with the top down.

I walk up to him and give him a quick kiss, "You're much better than a car service."

Rick grabs me around the waist and pulls me close, "That's not acceptable..." and plants his lips on mine as if he needs me to survive and hasn't had me in days. I hop in the car, tie my hair back and put on his baseball cap, ready for the next step in the adventure. Rick takes off with a destination in mind and his hand on my knee. "How about a drive and dinner at the beach before we go to the hotel?"

"I'm up for whatever you want," I give him my sexy eyes.

"Don't make me go straight to the hotel. It's date night," he says and takes off northbound on Route 1.

We cruise through Marina Del Rey, Venice, Santa Monica, and Pacific Palisades, staying on Pacific Coast Highway until we get to Malibu. The cool ocean breeze against my skin and the majestic ocean feet away with it's rolling thunderous sounds. The fathomless clear night sky glittered with stars and the moon reflecting off the water. It couldn't be more perfect. I lean my head on Rick's shoulder and place my left hand on his upper thigh. He pulls into a parking lot on the edge of the water and parks, putting the top up on the Porsche. He comes around to my door, offers me a hand out of the car and takes the baseball cap off my head, tossing it back into the car. I take my hair down and shake it out as we walk up to the restaurant. It's a Hawaiian themed place called TuTu's and Rick leads me to the patio bar in the back. It's a lanai built over the water with mostly bar food and shoes are optional. The palm trees, palapa umbrellas and ukulele music send the atmosphere over the top. He picked another beachy thing for me and even went Hawaiian now that he knows that's my favorite destination. This man never ceases to amaze me. He chooses a table on the edge, with a great view. We sit down on the same side of the table and he puts his arm around me, as the song changes to Iz's version of "Somewhere Over the Rainbow". The waitress walks up and he orders the Kalua Pork Nachos, a Lava Flow, and a Ginger Beer.

"That sounds delicious," I look at him hungrily.

"I hoped you'd approve and I thought you might want to share dessert. One of the guys said they make an amazing coffee and macadamia nut pie, and I know you have a sweet tooth," he smiles and pulls me close.

I will never get tired of this. I had no idea men like him existed. I'd resigned myself to think they were all fictional tales. Caring, thoughtful, masculine, handsome, and, well, just plain hot? Lethal.

Rick takes an envelope out of his pocket, "So, do you happen to know anything about this envelope the rook passed to me on the airplane?"

I grin at him, "You're a great photographer, or maybe a selfie master? I wanted pictures for me, but I thought you might want a few pictures to take with you on the road. If nothing else, I wanted something I could look at to prove this is real and I'm not dreaming."

"You're not dreaming, baby. This is real. We're real," he gazes into my eyes and kisses me softly, lightly sucking on my lip.

The shock he sends through my body at his contact is something I've never experienced before. "It must be a dream, you're my fantasy." I reach for him, running my

184

hands through his hair and claiming his mouth passionately. Something about him and the beach extends my personal boundaries. He turns his chair toward the water and pulls me into his lap. We sit together admiring the ocean, appreciating each other's heartbeat and heat.

The waitress drops off our order and stays away, leaving us to our own world. The Lava Flow adds to my mood. There's something sensual about sharing the nachos, we feed each other different bites and I help him by licking sauce from his lip. All I want to do is get out of here, so we can be alone together.

"Do you think we could order dessert to go?" I study him with heated eyes and see the flames reflected back at me.

Rick leaves cash on the table, leads me out of the restaurant, and down a path to the beach. A soft white sand beach, hidden from the highway by custom homes, secluded, empty, and lit only by the moon at this time of night. He holds my hand, intertwining our fingers as we walk down the beach. I turn to him and go up on my tip toes to kiss his lips. The need between us is burning as I kiss him deeper and bring him down to me. All the way to the sand. Rolling in the sand, kissing, exploring each other, with the waves lapping at our feet. We're on a public beach, but we're alone in our private haze. I take my shirt off, kick off my shoes and slide out of my pants, leaving me in my matching bra and panties with little pink bows all over them.

"Swim?" I offer, wanting to dive into the ocean.

"No," he says with glazed eyes as he slides his finger along the edge of my bra, releasing my nipple and sucking me into his mouth. He rolls me underneath him and rubs his hard cock against my almost naked body. I don't care where I am, I want him. I reach into his pants and he works with me to get his length accessible. Spreading my legs with his, he drives his hard love into me slowly. Pushing and pulling, sliding in and out, with a painful passion I've never witnessed. His body shaking with each breath he takes and trembling with need. His desire taking over. I draw his mouth to mine, trying to soothe his need and tell him I'm right here with him. Our heat burning hotter than ever before. He runs his hands along my body and I quiver at his touch. Matching his desire. With both hands he holds my lips to his, kissing me erotically, imitating his pelvic actions with his tongue, claiming me in every way he can. Both of us out of control and on the edge. He muffles my screams with his mouth. Kissing me as he moves faster and harder, needing to come. He pushes me over the edge and my orgasm is earth shattering. Suddenly I'm squeezing him and his size almost hurts. I encourage him to push in farther, but can't control myself and end up on top of him riding him, screaming out in need. He looks up at me in the moonlight and comes so hard I feel it leaking out of me. He reaches for me and pulls me down to him, rolling me back under him. Soothing me with his lips and getting us both through.

"Babe, you need to put your clothes on now and we need to get out of here." I put my shirt on and grab my pants, but he scoops me up and carries me down the beach quickly, back up the path and to the car. We were turning out of the parking lot when I saw the police vehicles shining lights down on the beach. I pull my pants on in the car, grab my hoodie from my bag and snuggle up against Rick for the ride to the hotel.

Rick is back in control. He calls ahead to the hotel to check in and make sure his luggage got delivered to our room. He asks to have two keys ready for him to pick up at the front desk and tells them he'll be valet parking.

When we pull up to the hotel, we're greeted by the valet, "Welcome, Mr. Seno, here are your room keys. Please let us know if we can be of service."

"Thank you," he says as he tips him and grabs my carry-on out of the back seat. Rick reaches out for my hand and laces his fingers with mine as we walk into the hotel and through the lobby.

"I'm trying not to make any more bonehead caveman moves tonight." He brings my hand to his lips and kisses my fingers. "Something about you, or me and you together, just... I can't think, I don't know what it is that takes over my brain."

"The same thing happens to me." I find myself anticipating the elevator, distracted and wondering. "For the record, I don't think you've made any bonehead moves today and I like your caveman moves."

"You could've at least waited until we got off the elevator to tell me that," he mumbles and he's hard again. We step into the elevator and he hits the button for the fifteenth floor. The door closes. He stops and focuses on me in torment.

"Fuck it!" and he's all over me. He pushes me to the corner of the elevator and stretches my hands up above my head while he kisses and nibbles at my neck, pressing his hard cock against me. "I want you. I just had you naked on the beach screaming my name and I need more of you." He claims my mouth with his, kissing me hard. The elevator dings and we're at the fifteenth floor. He pulls me with him urgently to our room and unlocks the door.

We walk in our room and it's well appointed with dark wood and a huge bed. With hooded eyes he says, "Let's clean up," as he walks into the bathroom and turns on the shower. Not a bad idea since I've got sand in interesting places. I stand there and watch him undress. His muscular legs and arms, with those abs and tight round ass only catchers have. He walks over to me, "Don't you want to shower with me?" He kisses me softly. "I want to show you how much I love you. That was my intention tonight."

"You did."

He glares at me strangely, "Are you kidding? I couldn't even wait to have dessert and bring you to our room. I had to fuck you right on the beach. I can't control myself around you in an elevator to save my life!"

"I loved every second of it because I was with you. I love how you pick restaurants for me. I love the extra passion you get in elevators as odd as it is. And, I have never felt closer to you or as raw with you as I did on the beach tonight. The way your body trembled for me said it all."

"If anyone else treated you disrespectfully, I'd beat the crap out of them because you deserve better."

"The fact is, there's only you in my world. Your passion for me makes me feel loved." He steps toward me and I undress quickly, moving for the shower.

Rick joins me under the hot shower and holds my wet naked body against his while he puts his lips on mine. "I love you, baby. You make it okay to be me." He slides down my body to his knees and puts his mouth on my sensitive nub. Sucking and licking me insane. I'm backed to the wall, leaning to stay upright and he slides a finger inside me sending me over the edge. He's the only thing that keeps me from hitting the ground. He wraps his arm around my waist, "I've got you, babe," and holds me to him standing under the shower, letting the water fall over us.

CHAPTER TWENTY-THREE

I wake up early and I'm alone in bed. "Rick," I call out and don't get a response. I find my phone to see texts from Joey and Rick previewed on the screen.

Text from Joey – Hey sweetie! I'm off Friday and Saturday, let's get together.

Text from Joey – I'm staying in LA. Let me know what works.

Text from Rick – Why are you getting texts from some guy named Joey?

Text from Rick – Went for a run

I check the time. It's 6:11am and I hear the door open. "Rick?"

Rick walks over and stares at me. Hurt written all over his face.

"I've been through this before, but I never really loved her. Tell me you're fake. Tell me you're what I think you are. Tell me who Joey is."

Fuck, the last thing I ever wanted to do and I did it unintentionally. Everything was perfect and I broke it, well Joey broke it but I enabled it to happen. "Rick, I'm exactly who you think I am and I only love you. There's only you. Come sit here with me and let me make it better," I say patting the bed next to me.

Rick paces the room.

"Fine, then listen to me. You have to trust me and not go crazy off the deep end. I do have male customers that contact me. Joey was the flight attendant on my flight to LA yesterday, and we hit it off so we exchanged numbers. He said he knows some great places in LA and he loves baseball."

"Damn it! He was hitting on you!"

"Stop! In fact, he was jealous of my beefcake baseball boyfriend because he recognized me from the picture on the internet with you carrying me over your shoulder through the lobby in Colorado. He asked how I caught you, because he wants to get him one of those beefcakes."

Silence.

"Did you hear me? Rick?" I pick up my phone and dial Joey on speaker.

"Hello? Who the hell is this? It's too early. I need my beauty sleep," Joey says sounding like his eyes are still closed.

"Hey Joey, sorry to wake you. I have you on speaker phone. Will you please explain to my bonehead boyfriend that you're not interested in me for anything other than shopping and maybe lunch?"

"Oh, hi sweetie! I'm actually interested in more... what

do I need to do to borrow that beefcake of yours? Just kidding! But, I would love to find one of my own! Any of the guys on the team swing my way?"

"Joey, you're not helping here."

"Oh, sorry. I thought you might have some free hours while your man is working and I know some great second hand shops," Joey says.

"Joey, you want to go to the game with my woman tonight," Rick asks.

"Yes, please. Can we have seats behind home plate? There's a great view there," Joey says laughing.

I take Joey off speaker, "I'll give you a call back when it's a decent hour, so we can make plans. Bye."

"Now, I'm going back to bed and I'm going to try my hardest to forget this happened. I never want to wake up in an empty bed again." It was either be mad and lay it out there or cry. I'll be damned if I'm going to cry. I hide under the blanket and pretend I didn't blow up my life. I hear the shower in the bathroom and a few minutes later, my naked man crawls in bed with me and digs in the blankets to find me. He uncovers me to find me naked from last night and tear stained from the disaster today has already been. He doesn't say a word, he simply runs his thumbs over my cheeks like he's wiping away the tears and holds me.

A couple hours later when I wake up for the day, it's all right there in front of me and I can't forget it. Fresh tears run down my face. I escape his arms for the bathroom and turn on the shower, hoping the water falling over me will hide my emotions and no one will ever know they have the power to make me cry. That's it. It's over. Once you break it, you can't go back. Damn it! I don't want to regret this. I don't want to make the wrong choice. It hurts just thinking about being away from him, let alone never being near him again. Never kissing him again. Never feeling his lips on me. Never tasting him again. I refuse to be one of those women who cries all the time. Suck it up and get over it. Shit happens. If you love him, isn't that what matters? All over a text message. I even appreciate his jealousy, in a way it shows how much he cares. But, not if he doesn't ask about it like a human being. Not if he runs and gets mad. Not if he doesn't trust me.

I don't know how long Rick was standing there watching me in the shower when he finally spoke, "How can I fix it? How can I fix us? Please."

"I don't know. You don't trust me. I don't know how to fix that. I don't think I can," I say into the shower as the tears flow. "I know she hurt you. I know she lied to you in the worst way. I know you only ever did the right thing by her. You never deserved to be treated that way. You deserve a woman that cherishes you. You deserve the family you thought you had. You deserve everything you want. I'm sorry for what she did. I'm not her!"

He walks closer to the shower, "I know who you are. You're perfect. I'm a bonehead that can see the future with you in his life, but doesn't know how to keep you in it and doesn't have a future without you. I know you're not her. You would never do the things she did. What do I need to do to keep you? What do I need to do to keep us? I want the rest of my life with you." His tone sad and quiet.

"That's what I wanted, too."

He steps into the shower with me and puts his arms around me.

"No. Not now. I need to clear my head," I say and he backs off. "I need you to trust me. The other night in Colorado, the only thing you did was ask if I trusted you and it was all that mattered. I got over the woman I watched use a key to go into your hotel room. I trusted you and believed you were only for me. This morning you don't trust me because I got a text. You have to trust me."

"I trust you."

"You don't act like it."

"Will you be at the game later?" he asks.

"Yes, if you want me to be there."

"Please come to the game. Nothing is the same without you. I know we belong together and we will be fine."

I want to ask who he's trying to convince, but it's not the time. I don't know if I want him to go or stay with me until he needs to leave for the stadium. He's been the only man I wanted since I first saw him set foot on the baseball field. It's the first time I've thought I might rather spend time somewhere other than with Rick in years. He's gone on the road trip on Monday and I'm wasting time I should be with him. Unless, I'm done being with him.

"Sherry, I love you and you're the only one I've ever loved. I don't want this to be over. You're my life." He leaves and I hear the hotel room door close.

I bawl my eyes out in the shower and get myself together. I'm strong and I don't need a man. Shopping therapy may be what the doctor ordered. I text Joey and make plans for lunch, shopping, and the game, trying my best to understand where Rick is coming from. Joey picks me up from the hotel and is a wonderful host around LA. He's entertaining, upbeat, and we like the same styles. We hash out my anger, sadness, general pissed off state over lunch because He says you should never shop angry. He tells me I have every right to be upset and reminds me Rick is male. It was the oddest conversation, Joey telling me how stupid men are and how they have a much harder learning curve than women do for almost everything. He sums up with the fact my man is a hot piece of beefcake and he deserves a pass for that alone. I'm not so sure, but he made my afternoon fun and reinforced he was on Rick's side at every opportunity. I'm still tender on the subject, but I want to keep my catcher and I go with Joey's reasoning.

> Text from Sam - I'm getting a bad feeling about a call I got from my brother. I'm here if you need to talk. I promise not to beat you up. Boys can be stupid and they usually are.

> Text to Sam - I was pissed and still am. Trying to get over it. I think it will be okay.

> Text from Rick - Your tickets are at will call. BP was early, I'd love to pick you up and give you a ride to the stadium. I would be picking you up about 4:30.

> Text to Rick - Don't pick me up. I'll get there on my own. I'll be at the game. I'm out shopping with Joey. Doing my best to get over it. I love you, my king.

> Text from Rick - I'm sorry. I trust you. I love you, my queen.

Joey and I get to the stadium early to pick up our tickets from will call, get beer, and find our seats. We're behind home plate and about ten rows back. I'm surprised he managed these seats in LA. He sees me as soon as I get to my seat and waves. Joey waves back energetically and Rick's expression changes, he realizes how stupid he was and finally relaxes, sure that Joey isn't a threat. I yell out,

"Make it win!" and I'm happy to feel a real smile creep across my lips for the first time today.

"Have you tried bouncing a quarter off his ass yet? My god he's so hot. He's so much better in person, the internet doesn't do him justice. They never show enough ass." Joey comments on our view behind home plate. "How do you get anything done? I'd spend all my time trying to get him to strip."

I laugh and it feels good, "We tend to discuss things when we're apart because we get distracted when we're together in the same room. That's not a complaint. He's simply magnificent."

"He scores pretty high."

"He puts his all into the game. His bat is above average for sure."

"I didn't ask you about his peen, but if you want to talk about it I'll listen. I'm talking about my scoring system. He gets points for his tight round catcher's ass, his sexy beard and the way he holds himself—always in control and ready to fight. Were you really talking about his hitting?" He goes on talking about my man.

"I was talking about his bat. I'm not telling you anything about my man's peen, but it is above average and he knows how to use it—just like his bat."

Bottom of the 2nd inning, Joey starts in on the players, "This guy leading off for LA, such a baby. He needs to work on his arms and some squats wouldn't hurt. Do they require their players to have boney asses? It's disturbing."

I listen as he goes on describing each player, one by one. Finding something wrong with most of the LA players. The Seals are up at bat and he continues with his scoring. "Is this guy new? Jones Mason? I don't know him."

"Yea, he just got brought up this week."

"He's a cutie, kind of a Mid-West babyface thing going on. Not that it matters when you get to his thighs. What does he do in his free time to get those thick muscular thighs? I wonder what he presses. I'd let him press me. His pants are perfect, snug and showing off his lower half assets. OMG! Did you catch the side view. He's packing! He's so young. Maybe it's time for me to try a younger man, a couple years is really nothing." He glares at me waiting for me to call him out on his age, but I don't. Joey must be a decade older than Mason. "Younger is easier to train." Mason ducks to keep from getting hit by the first pitch. Joey stands and has a fit, "Don't throw at my cutie pie! He needs to keep his brains to balance out his little head!" He sits back down, fanning himself. Mason gets a base hit and Joey jumps up out of his seat clapping. "This is too much for me, I'm going for more beer."

Joey continues to dis on the other team, and comments on the Seals though he's obviously focused on Mason. "Cross is fast in the outfield, but I'm not a fan of skinny butts. He does have nice shoulders. He could use a haircut. Their shortstop looks familiar, I think I've seen him at the bar. What's with your guy Martin? Does he play for my team?"

"I don't think he plays for your team."

"How do you know?"

"He's a flirt and acts like he wants Rick's sister."

"It could be a cover."

"I suppose. She's married, so it is safe flirting. At least, I think it's just flirting."

"Get me his number. She's his beard. Actually, get me Mason's number. I like him better." Mason stretches and bends backwards while he's playing out behind second base. "Those pants. He wears the hell out of those pants. I bet he has to have a tailor let out the thighs in his jeans." Joey starts to turn red and I give him my water.

Joey knows baseball and baseball players. It's an enjoyable experience to watch the game with him and have an intelligent baseball conversation, granted it did include a lot about individual players and their asses. Most importantly, I have fun and it allows me to block out the horrible morning. I'm looking forward to spending the night in bed with my man and this morning I would've bet good money against it.

As far as the game itself, we lost 4-3. Joey's scoring system is better, based on player hotness we win by a landslide.

Joey takes me back to the hotel via surface streets through Hollywood, trying to talk me into going out and enjoying the Hollywood scene since it's Friday night. It's a sight to see with all the crazies wandering the streets and people lined up to get into clubs. People dressed up as superheroes and princesses, but my favorite was the guy with the hat, antenna, and cloak—all made from aluminum foil. I explain I want to beat Rick back from the game and he couldn't argue with wanting to be ready for my beefcake. He drops me off at my hotel and says he'll be calling. Felt like a date when you know the guy isn't ever going to call you, but Joey will.

I go up to our room to take a quick shower and be ready for Rick when he gets back. We need each other and after today, we'll need to be close to let each other know we're still us. I don't think it's quite the same as make-up sex, but then again maybe we can do that, too.

I walk into the room to find that skanky fucking fake-boobed, red head—naked in our bed. Are you fucking kidding me with this? How does she get room keys? How does she find out the room number she's looking for? My common sense left and I'm at a loss. I love Rick. I want to trust him, but the same skank only a few days apart waiting in his room for him? Questions fly through my head and I can't make them stop.

I straight up yell at her, "Get the fuck out!"

"Oh, hi sweetie. I didn't expect to see..." I interrupt her.

"Shut up and get out, now!"

"It would be better to let him pick who he wants. The hotel clerk gave you the key, too? I told you he isn't interested in you. This is going to be embarrassing for you. You should go before he gets here. Unless you want to have a threesome. Rick can handle it. He's good. Very good. It's those catcher's legs and what he can do while he's in that crouch position."

"Rick gave me the key. I'm his girlfriend. Get the fuck out!"

"He didn't say anything about a girlfriend when I talked to him on Tuesday. Remember I was in his room then, too."

The door opens and Rick walks in taking in the scene.

"I said, get out!" I yell at her again, more agitated than when I found her.

Rick gazes at me and smiles, concern in his eyes. He turns to the red head, "Ava, what are you doing here?"

What the fuck? He knows her name? This is the same skank from Colorado. He obviously knows more than her name. I can't believe I trusted him. I need to get out of here. I pack at a frantic pace. This can't be happening. I should've left in Colorado. Fuck, and he doesn't trust me getting texts from a guy? I don't need to know anything else. I'm out of here.

Rick grabs my arm, "Stop. You don't need to pack. You're not going anywhere."

I try to pull away from his strong grasp, yelling at him, "I'm not staying here with her. Get your hands off me!" I turn to her and scream, "Why are you still here? Get the fuck out!"

Rick pulls me to him with both hands, holding me tight against him. "She's a friend. She visits me sometimes on road trips when she's lonely. Sherry, she's only a friend. She's not you. I love you, my queen. It's okay."

"Fuck you. That bitch told me to leave so I wouldn't embarrass myself, then suggested we have a threesome because apparently you're 'very good' and can handle it. I bet she visits you a lot during baseball season and I bet you fuck her brains out." My anger takes over, but my heart hurts and tears are going to fall at any second. "I bet you touch her like you touch me. I bet you don't use condoms with her either. Fuck, now I have to get tested, who knows where that skank's been!"

"Sherry. Stop!" Pain and anger in his eyes as he tries to get through to me.

"Get out, Ava. Sherry is my everything and I love her. Quit being stupid and causing trouble. Get out."

"You don't love her!" Ava continues to be trouble.

"She's right. You don't love me. You don't trust me." I pull myself from Rick's grip, grab my bags and make a dash for the door.

"Sherry, please!" Rick blocks the door, trying to keep me from leaving.

I stare into his eyes, "I loved you with all my heart. I only wanted to be with you. I would've given you anything." I look at the floor, needing to gather strength and not giving either of them the privilege of my tears.

"Please, my queen. I love you."

I push past him, leaving quickly. I yell back at him when I walk out the door. "Enjoy your evening with the skank." I run for the elevator, needing to get out of the hotel as fast as possible. I hop in a waiting taxi and see Rick running across the lobby as I pull away.

I don't know where I'm going. Usually, I would say home. I'm not in the mood to go home. I text Joey and get dropped off at the bar he's at, luggage and all. Joey scans me head to toe as I walk toward him in the bar.

"Sweetie, you look wrecked!" He knocks on the bar top to get the bartenders attention. "Jack shots and line them up."

I tell Joey what happened and he offers to let me stay at his place in LA. He's gone most of the time anyway, flying somewhere. He puts my luggage in his car and takes my phone from me. "We should turn this off for now." He's right. I don't want to talk to anyone. Honestly, I don't want to be at a bar. I want to hide in a corner, somewhere nobody who knows Rick can find me. My head is filled with images of him fucking her and how they're probably doing it right now. Joey puts his arms around me, "Sweetie, don't think about those things. You'll get through this. You don't need him. There's always another man. Trust me, I know."

"It was only me before. I don't need a man. I wanted him. I'll be fine and back to my old life soon." I listen to my voice and it doesn't sound confident and independent. I don't understand how I got here. He was a fantasy. I was satisfied with the fantasy. My life was perfect. I had everything I wanted. Now, I don't know if I can go back to that.

"Sweetie, you need to hide at my place for a week or so. You need to be away from the memories and somewhere he can't find you. Joey will take care of you. I know what its like."

I have everything I need with me for work and I need to be home for the karaoke finals on Wednesday. Hiding for a few days might be a good idea and I want someone to take care of me. I shoot the three shots of Jack lined up for me, then I do two more. Jack and Joey get me through the night without crying and make sure I'm safe.

I wake up about noon on Saturday in an unfamiliar bed and remember I'm at Joey's. I don't get out of bed until I have to or I'm going to wet the bed. Yes, I'm being a self-indulgent, pouty baby. You would, too. Joey hears me rustling around and walks in with a cup of hot coffee and a full container of chocolate chip cookie dough ice cream. This is definitely an eat-a-whole-quart-of-ice-cream kind of day. I settle on cheesy old romance movies and spend the day being a girl. Joey indulges me, even sitting with me and crying at the movies. We don't turn on the game.

I spend the next few days at Joey's, concentrating on work and coming up with ideas to increase business. I'm also researching trips, specifically cheap vacations, local getaways, and staycations. I need a get-away. I need alone time. I need the beach.

We go out to the bar every night, getting wasted so I can make it through the night without crying. I refuse to allow a man control over me. It's never happening again.

I call my season ticket representative and turn in the rest of my tickets for the season for a refund. It's not their normal process, but she made an exception for me because she understands and it's not a typical scenario.

Monday night, a hot guy with toned arms, sits next to me at the bar. He's clean cut and smooth shaven with dark almost black hair and light grey-blue eyes. He smells good, woodsy with a hint of citrus, and I ignore him. I order another shot. A few minutes later, the bartender brings hot guy two shots and he slides one over to me, "Hi, I'm Adam."

I don't want to talk to him. I'm not interested in men. I'm done with them. But, I'll take the drink. "Thank you. I'm not interested." I toss back the shot.

"So, I'm-not-interested, do you have a nickname that's shorter?"

I can't help it and I smile, "No."

Joey, paying close attention, kicks me and whispers in my ear, "He's hot! Have some fun, you deserve it."

He examines me for a few minutes, taking in every detail. "I'm going to call you Angel. You might be able to save me tonight."

"Call me what you want. I probably won't answer."

"Give me your number and I'll call to ask you out."

"No, thanks."

A slow acoustic song starts playing on the juke box and he reaches for my hand, "How about a dance?"

Joey kicks me, almost knocking me off the barstool. "Fine." Adam's hand is warm and callused, strong holding mine as he pulls me over to the juke box where a few couples are dancing. He puts his warm hand on my back and doesn't release my other hand, watching me and not pulling me close.

A couple minutes into the song, he leans into my ear and I tense up at the thought of another man's lips on me. He whispers, "You're so beautiful. I don't know why you're sad. Let me help you bring the shine back to your halo, Angel."

I go back to my barstool immediately when the song is over, but not before I reach up and kiss his cheek. I don't know why I did it. Joey pats my leg when I sit back down and orders us another shot.

Adam puts his hand on my shoulder, turning me toward him. "I'm only in town for a few days. Can I take you out to dinner?"

"I don't live here. I'm visiting."

"Why do I think it's more than that? What are you hiding from?"

"Who, not what." Joey kicks me again and I'm starting to worry about bruises on my leg.

"It's only dinner."

Joey butts in, "She'd love to."

"Joey!"

"What? You need to get out. Let the man buy you dinner." Joey looks at Adam, "You, keep it just dinner. She's already heartbroken."

Adam smiles at Joey, "Let's go, Angel."

"Now?"

"Like I said, I'm only in town a few days. I'm hungry. What do you say?"

I consider the jeans and old T-shirt I'm wearing. "I guess."

"Good girl. Have fun, sweetie."

Adam covers my tab, takes my hand and leads me out of the bar. We walk down the street, finding an all night cafe a few blocks down. "I'm guessing it's a guy who has you sad?"

"I don't want to talk about it. Why are you picking up a woman in a bar when you're away from home and it's just dinner?"

"I travel a lot. I don't have a home unless you count my parent's place and I rarely go there. Nothing wrong with having another friend."

His words trigger something in me and I burst out,

"What kind of friend? I'm not the kind of friend who shows up at your place waiting for you naked."

He holds his hands up, "Only dinner, Angel. I might want to touch you and kiss your lips, but I don't jump. It takes time to get there. I don't share much of me often."

I admit it was nice to sit and have dinner with him. We talked about places we like to go. I told him I love the beach and I'm planning on a trip somewhere along the coast soon. I've been planning a slow road trip along the West Coast, stopping somewhere different every night.

"I'm traveling to San Francisco in about a week, maybe we can cross paths again. I'm busy with work tomorrow, but how about a late night dinner or maybe breakfast? I'd like to see you again."

"I'm going home tomorrow morning. I have to be home on Wednesday."

"Where's home?"

"San Diego."

"I go there for work sometimes, too. I'm in LA until Thursday, then I've got a couple stops across the mid-west before I go to San Francisco. Can I have your number?"

I don't respond. We get up and leave the cafe, walking back toward the bar we started at. Joey is still there when we walk back in, he gives me a nod. I start toward my barstool, but Adam has my hand and doesn't let go. He pulls me to the juke box and plays the same song from earlier, "Can I Be Him" by James Arthur. He places his hand on my back like before and we dance slightly closer. He pulls me closer and closer as we dance, and the song repeats on the juke box. Guilt consumes me because another man has his hands on me, it's not Rick. I remind myself it's over. Why should I feel guilty? I reach my hands around his neck and run my fingers through his hair. His smile brightens and he pulls me against him. He's solid muscle and it feels good to have a man against me. My body is needy and I'm not going there. It might make me a tease. It doesn't matter. I gaze into his eyes and he leans in, kissing me softly and chaste on the lips. It's not Rick. It's not electric. But, it's nice and I want to kiss him again. I stretch up to him, me in my jeans, T-shirt, and flip flops, to him in his long sleeved dress shirt with his loosened tie and turned up sleeves. His lips meet mine, we're both needy. His lips are soft. His kiss is open-mouthed without tongue and I want more. I wonder if it can be electric. I want to know there can be somebody else. I need to have options other than going back to my old life alone. I push it though I shouldn't, I lick his bottom lip and suck on it lightly driving him to deepen the kiss and he moves his hand to the back of my head, holding me where he wants me and playfully kissing me.

The music stops and I'm suddenly brought back to reality. I break away and run out of the bar quickly. I lean against Joey's car and hope he follows me out. I need away. I can't do this.

"What the hell?" Joey yells across the parking lot while he walks toward his car. "Why are you running away from the hottie?"

"I'm not ready. Can we go home?"

"Yea, but we're walking." I'm good with that, it's not far back to his place.

CHAPTER TWENTY-FOUR

Tuesday morning, I need to be an adult. No more hiding at Joey's and letting him take care of me. No more letting Joey handle my phone, edit my email and texts, sheltering me from the problem. I'd still be a blubbering idiot, sitting on his couch wrapped in a blanket and eating junk food, without him and his help. If nothing else, I've established a plan and I'm sticking to it. I'm taking the rail home today. I have to do laundry. Tomorrow is karaoke finals.

The Seals are home on Thursday and I want to be away. I've already mapped out my road trip and I'm leaving Thursday morning. I'm packing enough clothes for two weeks and I'm breaking out my unused back up credit card to cover rooms and gas. I'm making it all a business expense, trying different hotels, checking out different beaches and taking photos along the way. Hopefully, I'll make friends at the hotels I stop at. It'll be great to link them to my website and social media.

I start Tuesday walking with Joey to get his car and

taking him to breakfast, a thank you for taking care of me and letting me stay with him. He drops me off at the rail and I'm on my way home. I plug into my iPod and hit shuffle. For the first time in four days I look at my phone, social media, and email. A text pops up at me:

Text from Joey - You can do this, sweetie. I'm here if you need me. I didn't delete the messages and emails you don't want to see, I hid them for you until you're ready or you can leave them hidden forever.

I smile, knowing I've got this and get some work done on the rail. I start with email and choose which messages I want to read. I've been keeping up on daily work email, but not others and thankfully I can pick up with today's and not have to see anything about Rick. I have a couple new emails from customers and a message from Mike with the Mic.

From: MikeMic

Sherry,

Finals are postponed. Batter Up was rented out for a party and they used the stage as a dance floor. It wasn't made for that and collapsed. It'll be a few weeks. I'll update you when I have the new date for finals. Hoping they upgrade the stage and maybe the backstage area in the process. Thank you for your patience.

Mike with the Mic

Wow! Well, that makes my life easier and gives me more time to get ready for my trip. When it's time for the karaoke finals, hopefully I'll be more emotionally prepared.

Text from Rick - It's been four days and you haven't responded to anything from anybody. I know you don't believe me. I know you turned in your Seals tickets for the rest of the season. You will have a seat to every home game waiting for you behind home plate for as long as I'm a Seal. This is killing me. I know you're hurting. We don't need to be hurting. We could be together. I love you.

I feel it in my chest and in my eyes. He still has control of my emotions. I've made it this far and I'm not giving up. I can be me and I don't need him. I don't respond. I set an alarm and set my iPod to my nap playlist. I can sleep the rest of the way home and ignore my life.

I get home to find delivery notices stuck to my door. Two from florists dated Saturday and Sunday, and one from the Seals on Monday. I ignore them all and unpack, immediately doing laundry and getting ready for my trip. I get my camera equipment together and update the music on my iPod. I pack multiple bags of clothes, so I have what I need no matter what the weather—nothing baseball other than my old Seals cap.

I spend Wednesday getting errands done, baking, and preparing snacks for my trip. I get a text from an unknown number.

Text from Unknown - This is Adam. I hope you don't mind me texting you. I ran into your friend at the bar and he gave me your number. May I call you sometime?

Text from Adam - I don't have much time right now. If you're still going on your trip, I'll be in San Francisco next week. We could meet.

Text to Joey - Joey! What did you do? You gave Adam my number! Why?

Text from Adam - Is this Angel?

Text from Joey - He's hot

Text from Joey - You need the distraction

Text from Joey - He paid my tab LOL

Text from Joey - Nothing wrong with having another friend

Text to Adam - Yes, it's me. I guess you can call me.

Text from Adam - Will you go out with me Monday night in San Francisco?

Text to Adam - I'm not dating right now

Text from Adam - Plan on seeing me Monday. It's not a date.

Shit!

Text from Rick - Plane just landed in San Diego and I would love to see you

I continue to ignore Rick and hope he'll go away. It's strange to think that. He's been my only for so long, even my fantasy. I never thought I'd want him to leave me alone.

CHAPTER TWENTY-FIVE

I spend the next few weeks driving the California coast in search of beautiful beaches, relaxing motels and unique resorts. I stop at all the scenic view points. I get my feet wet at every beach. I explore every kitschy town and outlet mall. I make notes and take photos along my way, documenting everything and scheduling social media posts for a week later.

Texts continue to come in from Rick daily, and occasionally I get one from Sam saying something about how he bribed her to text me hoping I'd respond to her, but I won't. I ignore them all.

Adam has been tracking my location, which is thoughtful and creepy at the same time. He calls me and talks to me while I'm driving. On my first weekend, he made sure I was going to meet him on the Monday. I did. He lied. It was a date. After talking to him on the phone for a few days, I didn't mind. He's a nice guy. He held my hand while we walked along the wharf and we went to dinner at a restaurant with a view of the bay. At the end of the night, he gave me a chaste kiss and waited to see if I'd take it further like I did at the bar. I didn't. He told me he had the whole day off in San Francisco on Thursday and asked if I'd spend it with him. When I told him I'd be in Northern California on Thursday, he said he'd meet me there. Wednesday night he called and asked where I was staying. Thursday morning he calls at 8am.

"Good morning," my eyes are closed.

"Good morning. Did I wake you?"

"Yea."

"Are you hungry? Can I take you out to breakfast?"

"I want coffee. I just woke up. I'm not ready." My eyes still closed.

"Breakfast comes with coffee."

"What time?"

"Now, I'm sitting in my car in the hotel parking lot."

"It's too early. What?"

"Should I sit in my car and wait until you want to get up? I thought you'd be up and wanting to go explore early. I'm here to go exploring with you today."

What the hell? I'm not ready for this. "Why did you drive here?"

"Isn't it obvious? I came to spend time with you."

"You don't even know my name."

"Get ready and we can talk about it over breakfast."

I'm hungry now. "Fine, but I'm getting ready quick and I'm not primping for a date or anything."

"You're naturally beautiful. You'd look amazing in a bag or nothing. I'm sitting in the black convertible with the top down and a baseball cap on."

Did he just hit on me? "I'll be a few minutes. Find a place for breakfast and make sure they have acceptable coffee." I hang up, pull on my denim shorts, and a black tank top. I brush out my hair quickly and tie it up in a knot, putting my Seals cap on with the knot sticking out the back. I grab my bag with my hoodie, sneakers, and necessities, and walk out to find Adam in the parking lot sitting in a shiny black Jaguar F-Type Convertible—a hot and sporty two-seater. I walk up to the car and lean on his door looking down on him and judging him for wearing a San Francisco Sissy's cap. "Nice car. Did you rent it for the drive?"

"No, it's mine. I don't drive it often, but San Francisco is my working home base right now. I thought it'd be nice to take it for a drive, maybe have a hot blonde with me and take her to breakfast."

"Should be easy for you to find a hot blonde. This is California."

"I meant you, beautiful. Get in and let's go to breakfast."

My hunger and desire for coffee wins over my want to be difficult and make him go away. It doesn't make any sense. Adam is a nice guy and hasn't done anything to make me dislike him. He hasn't pushed me. He's been polite and went out of his way to pay attention to me and talk to me everyday. I'm not comfortable with it. I'm sure it's because he's not Rick. How can a mere mortal compare to a man I fantasized about for years? I don't want a rebound guy. I don't want a guy at all. Joey's not wrong, he's hot.

We pull into a coffee shop a few blocks away and have a leisurely breakfast, starting with coffee. We talk about my trip and my plan for the day. He drives me to today's destination and wanders through a forested area to find the beach with me. I take photos along the walk, as well as up and down the beach before I play at the edge of the water and relax in the sun.

"Is this what you've been doing all week?"

"Pretty much. Exploring beaches and towns. Sometimes I need to sit down and simply absorb what's around me to get the whole atmosphere of a place. When I stop for a few minutes, everything comes into clear view and makes sense."

"How often do you go exploring?"

"This is the first time I've done it on the mainland. I've explored on most of the Hawaiian Islands and I've done many day trips around San Diego."

"Why are you exploring California now?"

Without thinking, "The beach keeps me focused and I can work from about anywhere. It's an opportunity to get better at what I do and forget my life."

"Seems like a good life to me. Why do you want to forget it?"

"I guess I want to forget my life the way it was with someone. I don't want to talk about it." I strip down to my bikini. "Want to go swimming?"

Adam takes in the view of me in my bikini, head to toe and back.

"Your loss. Just going for a quick dip." I yell as I wade into the ocean and swim out to bodysurf. He's watching me every step of the way. He wants more, but he hasn't tried to get it. Maybe he knows I'd turn him down.

I walk out of the water, spread out my beach towel and lie on the warm sand to dry off. Adam takes his shirt off and uses it as a pillow, stretching out in the sun with me. I'm relaxed and fall asleep. Adam wakes me, "Angel, do you want to check out of your room and ride back to San Francisco with me? Maybe spend a couple nights with me at my place? I don't have to be at work until about noon tomorrow and Saturday. I want to spend more time with you." He leans over me and kisses me. Not sweet and chaste how he typically kisses me. Sucking and nibbling on my lips. His tongue playing a game with mine. His desire for more obvious.

I sit up quickly, "I'm sorry. I don't mean to be a tease. It's not me at all. I'm not ready for someone new. It wouldn't be fair to you or me. I'm not over him. I don't know if I'll ever be over him." I pull my shorts on over my bikini and pick up my bag. "I think it's best if you take me back to my hotel now."

"Okay. Do you enjoy spending time with me, Angel? Do you find me attractive?"

"You're kind, attentive, and one of the hottest guys I've ever met."

"You're not attracted to me?"

"I don't know. I guess I'm still hooked on my ex. Forget me, it's not fair to you. Maybe if I get over him someday I'll call you."

Adam takes me back to my hotel, we sit and talk for a bit. "When are you driving back through San Francisco?"

"I'm not sure yet. I'm not ready to go home."

"Hopefully I'm in town, I want to see you."

I get out of his car and he gets out after me, backing me up against his car and claiming me with his mouth. His hands roaming my body and holding me tightly to him. His breath ragged, "Are you sure you don't want me, beautiful?"

In many ways I wish I did. Nothing feels the same as simply being in the same room with Rick. "I'm just not over him. I wish I was. You're a great guy." I turn and walk away into the hotel.

Adam called most days to check on me and remind me he wants to spend time with me.

I spend the rest of the time wandering beaches and

occasionally locking myself in a hotel room with an ocean view to be alone. If I'm alone, nobody knows if I cry. There's no proof and I'm not admitting anything.

At the end of three weeks, I start my drive home and take three days to do it. I stop at my favorite places and after almost a month, I find myself parking in my assigned spot at home.

My door has more delivery notices stuck to it, some of them three weeks old. I open the door to find an envelope had been slid under the door. I open the envelope and there's a handwritten letter:

Dear Sherry,

I don't know if you've gotten any of my messages. I've been texting you every day. I've left you some voicemail messages. I've sent you emails, too. I've tried reaching you on social media, but you're logged out. I know your business pages have been getting updated and it looks like you've been on a road trip, but I don't know where you are. I've been by your place to try and find you every day that I'm in San Diego, usually twice. I know I can make us better. I know we belong together. I believe that you know it, too. I know in my heart you feel the way that I do and nobody can replace you. I'm betting and hoping, nobody can replace me.

I don't want to remind you of the problem, but I want you to know the truth. Ava had a crush on me in high school and when she found out what happened with my ex, she was in my face wanting to make me feel better or at least make sure I wasn't

*alone. She was at my room waiting for me after
away games for a couple months, back when it
happened two years ago. She was never anything
other than sex and I know that wasn't fair to her, but
honestly I wasn't being the best person then. There
was more than her, I was the ultimate player at the
time. I didn't like myself and it's why I quit women.
It wasn't me. I'm not that guy and it didn't make me
feel better about my situation. I wanted things I
couldn't have and I wasn't going to get living that
life. I knew it and I stopped it. I was young and had
anything I wanted available to me. It's the plight of
the baseball player. It's why I don't want you to
think of me as a baseball player, I never want to be
that with you.*

*I want you to know I've never lied to you. I'm
always honest with you, no secrets. In Colorado,
when I found Ava in my room I kicked her out and
filed a complaint with the hotel. She wasn't naked
when I found her, she was sitting in the chair crying
about her boyfriend dumping her. I let her vent and
kicked her out. She wasn't happy about it and
thought I should help her get over it, but I wouldn't
do it. After you left me in LA, I explained to her in
detail that I never want to see her again for any
reason. I told her you're the only one for me and if
you won't have me, I won't have anyone—I mean it,
it's only you for me. I filed a complaint with the
hotel and made sure Ava knows I will file legal
charges against her if she does it again. I haven't
heard from her or seen her since. I'm sorry you found
her the way you did.*

My biggest concern right now is you. I haven't seen you or heard from you, or so much as seen proof that you're still breathing in weeks. I need to know you're okay. I know we weren't together long and we've been apart longer than we were together. I can't believe it was such a short time, it felt like the way my life is supposed to be and had always been that way—you and me together. This time apart feels like years.

I swear I haven't touched another woman since I met you and I don't want to. I didn't touch another woman for almost two years before I met you.

Please believe me. I need you. Nothing is the same without you. I'll always love you and it will always be you. I'll do anything and everything for you. Please come back to me. I want to make you happy. If there's anything I can do to bring you back to me, I want to do it.

I miss you, my queen.

Love Always,
Rick

I want to believe him. No matter how hard I try, I miss him and dream about him. I know these things are going to keep happening and my heart can't handle it. I hate that I'm making him hurt. I hate not talking to him and having no contact. It's the right thing. I've made it this far. I'll get over him.

I check the Seals schedule to see when they're in town.

He'll be by to find me and I need to be prepared or not be here.

I unpack and try to get settled in at home. I start by checking email and social media, get back in the full swing of my routine. I've done well at keeping my clients satisfied and booking trips while I was on my road trip. I've been contacted by a few of them wanting me to prepare an itinerary for them and book rooms for similar adventures. My beach adventure postings have gotten positive feedback and expanded my social media reach. I have months worth of photos to post and will be writing short blogs about certain locations. I check my email and have a new message.

From: MikeMic

Sherry,

The stage has been replaced and the last upgrade is supposed to be complete this week. Karaoke finals are scheduled for a week from Wednesday. You know the drill.

See you there!
Mike

I'm excited to have something positive to look forward to. I've been waiting for the finals.

To: MikeMic

Mike,

I can't wait. I'll be there!

Sherry

My social media pings, it's an odd sound to me because I'm logged into it for the first time in weeks. I'm not sure I want to check it. I guess I can see who it is and not respond.

RookCross: Hi Sweetheart! Surprised to see you logged in. Haven't seen you in weeks.

RookCross: I know you've been keeping to yourself and I don't expect you to reply to me. I know what happened. I believe him. I've spent a lot of time with him on the road. We've shared many hotel rooms over the last couple years. He's not that guy. He ignores women and isn't interested. He didn't invite her in or give her the key. She did that on her own and he didn't want her there. He still talks about you everyday. You're the only woman he's interested in. He's not that kind of player.

Sherry: I can't handle it. There's always going to be someone or something. It's too much for me.

RookCross: Can you handle being away from him?

RookCross: He doesn't know I'm messaging you and I won't tell him. You told him that you love him and I don't think that just goes away.

Fuck! Fuck! Fuck!

Text to Joey - Having a weak moment

Text from Joey - Are you home yet?

Text to Joey - Got home today

Text from Joey - You're strong. You'll make it.

Text to Joey - What if I don't want to?

Text from Joey - What? Spill.

Text to Joey - Maybe I believe him, he wasn't with her and he only wants me

Text from Joey - Who got to you?

Text to Joey - Cross

Text from Joey - He's too skinny for me, but has nice shoulders. Give him my number.

Text from Joey - Focus on something else and wait for a sign.

Text to Joey - He left me a letter under my door and he's been coming by to see if I'm home when the team is in town.

Text to Joey - He's still texting me everyday

Text from Joey - He's not giving up. I like that.

Text from Joey - I promise you'll get a sign that tells you what to do.

I call Sam and I know I shouldn't.

"Hello?" Sam answers.

"Hi. Sorry I didn't call sooner."

"It's about time. He's worried sick. It's killing his stats."

"I can't deal with finding a naked woman waiting for him in his room, and the same woman I watched use a room key to get in his room only a few days before. It's always going to be something. Honestly, I'm hurt and confused. I've never been this freaking emotional about anything. Is he okay?" I ask. I have to know.

"Alive and breathing, but I don't think I would classify him as okay. I thought you were stronger than this. He's not that guy. Shit happens, but it's the women not him. He's only interested in you. You need to do what's right for you and I can't tell you what to do. I want my bro happy and winning games. I know he's a great guy. When he sets his mind on something he doesn't give up and he's set on you."

"I miss him. He makes me feel like a weak girl... I've never needed anyone. I don't like how he can make me cry. I don't cry." I say quietly listening to the words as they're set free into the atmosphere.

"Sherry, you're a girl and sometimes we cry." Sam stops for a second and continues with a different tone. "For giggles. Have you taken a pregnancy test, emotional girl?" she laughs.

"No. Why would I do that?" I say, taken aback.

"You said you're hurt, confused, and have never been this and I quote freaking emotional... that's why." Sam using logic. "He loves you and isn't going to give up. Maybe you should buy a multi-pack of pregnancy tests."

"Sam, you can't tell him you joked about pregnancy tests."

"I'm not joking! But, I would never tell him. Too close to home for his heart."

"Besides, I'm on the pill."

"Oh, so you don't think the sperm of a professional athlete could potentially take down the pill. Have you tested the pill this way?"

"Uh..."

"I thought not. Multi-pack. Hide them where nobody can find them. You never want them to be discovered. Trust me, it's an uncomfortable line of questioning no matter what way it goes."

I move on from the conversation with Sam thinking *no way*, but better check. I'm concentrating on getting work caught up and the karaoke finals. If I can make it through karaoke finals in one piece and not fall apart like a blubbering idiot, then I can make a clear decision.

I start playing "Love Runs Out" by One Republic and "Ex's & Oh's" by Elle King on a repeat loop. I need some power songs to help me get through this week and they fit the requirements for the first round of the karaoke finals. I wander through my condo singing at the top of my lungs and I'm inspired to go shuffling through my closet. My karaoke outfit needs an attitude, bitch boots, tight pants, a top that shows off my cleavage and leather. Yes, definitely leather. I toss my skintight dark rinse jeggings and my soft black leather moto jacket onto the bed. I need a top that's low-cut, draped, and skims over my hips. My four inch black leather platform boots with the belts on the side for some metal will be perfect, hitting me below the knee—definition of bitch boots!

I need shopping therapy. I get dressed and drive up the

coast to the outlet mall. It never lets me down and gives me an opportunity to play loud music, belting at the top of my lungs. A new top and maybe some accessories. This may be what the doctor ordered to get me out of my funk.

I wander through every store and even treat myself to a frappe. I find a black draped plunge tank that gathers in all the right places, bares my shoulders and skims my hips perfectly. Better than what I was hoping for with the deep plunge dipping below my breasts. It makes me feel sexy when I put it on. I also pick up a black leather belt with a rhinestone covered buckle for some bling to brighten up the middle of my outfit and a three inch silver cuff bracelet. I keep shopping because I need a long necklace to accentuate the deep neckline of the top I found. When I see it shining at me from a store window, thirty-eight inches of silver dotted with red and clear crystals of varying sizes about every two inches along it's length. The cost is too much and it doesn't even matter, I'm having it!

$700 later I climb into my car to drive home and my pocket vibrates. I know who it is. I want to know he's okay, but I want to be okay, too. I get my phone with intentions of self-preservation, I'm going to delete him and block him. My life needs to keep going. I look at my phone and his message is right there in front of me with no way to avoid it:

Text from Rick - I will find a way to make you want to be my queen again. If it was my choice, I would be with you now, not on my way to Atlanta. I love you.

He's killing me. I physically can't block him, I can't delete him and I hurt for both of us. I'd be lying if I said I didn't miss him. I send him a quick reply because I can't help myself:

Text to Rick - Good luck on the road trip. Take some
time and you'll be fine without me.

My phone vibrates:

Text from Rick - I'll never be fine without you. You have
my heart.

Text from Rick - Getting a response from you makes
me happy

Text from Rick - Are you fine without me?

I drive home with the radio blasting The Killers and
Kings of Leon, trying to keep my head clear. I stop at the
drug store on my way home at Sam's request and buy a
multi-pack. But, instead of going home I drive to the beach
and sit in the warm sand watching the sunset. The beach
has always comforted me. My Mom would take me to the
beach and we'd sit on the rocks, watching the waves crash.
It makes everything okay. It centers me.

CHAPTER TWENTY-SIX

First thing in the morning, I pee on a stick and set it aside while I get caught up on work and start into my weekly updates. I go back to check the stick and take a picture of it, texting it to Sam. Getting an almost immediate reply:

Text from Sam - Sorry.

I have to know...

Text to Sam - Why are you sorry?

Text from Sam - I know it's disappointing even if it isn't something you're wanting.

Text from Sam - I know that's weird

(Note to self: When you're not already in the midst of

heartbreak and mental turmoil, ponder emotional response to negative stick.)

I take a few minutes to check in with my current travelers and follow up on the trips I'm currently planning.

I'm finishing my work and look up to see it's 4pm, almost time for the game. I haven't watched a game or done so much as check the score since I left LA. I haven't been able to look at the photos of us together. I want to see his face, but I'm afraid it will send me back weeks. I turn the game on because I'm just that stupid. I tell myself I will only watch an inning or two. Rick is in the lineup and hitting sixth. Seals are at bat in the top of the first inning, but there's no action. The guys take the field in the bottom of the first and Seno walks out of the dugout toward home plate in full gear. I should turn it off now, but it's a train wreck. It reminds me of the scene from Bull Durham when Crash gets tossed for calling the umpire a cocksucker. Rick is obviously mouthing off behind the plate and second-guessing the umpire's calls, possibly tormenting the hitters. After one call, Rick stands up, turns around, and looks the umpire in the face, saying something that gets him tossed. He rips his mask and helmet off, throws them on the ground and they show a close up of him walking off the field that I didn't need to see. Dark circles around his eyes. His eyes are red and the special glint I usually find there is missing. His sadness is evident and it's my fault. I turn the TV off.

I spend the next week, mostly at the beach when I should be cleaning and getting things done at home. I pay attention to the game schedule, so I know when he's in town. I don't go to any games or watch the games.

I get home from the beach to find a note on my door:

Sherry,

I was here. Hope you don't mind, I used the key you gave me to leave you something.

Love,
Rick

I snatch the note off the door and unlock it. I walk in and there are tropical bouquets everywhere. They're beautiful. I find a huge vase of red roses with a note.

Sherry,

One rose for each day I've known you and loved you. I'll always love you. We need to be together. Please love me.

Love,
Rick

I make myself busy with laundry and cleaning because I don't want to get caught up in it.

Two hours later my place has never been so clean and my brain won't stop. I start baking mindlessly and packaging up treats for later.

I can't stop thinking about him. I climb into bed and hide from the world.

I wake up early Tuesday and I know if he comes for me, I won't tell him no. I love him. But, I need to be strong and not go easily because I refuse to go through this again. Honestly, I don't know if I can handle this hurt again and

I'm not sure I want to risk my heart. Can it ever be the same as it was?

I stay busy and get business caught up through Wednesday, so I can take off for my afternoon primping.

I keep changing my mind about which song I want to sing for the second round, if I even get to the second round. I had decided on "The Flame" by Cheap Trick, but that was because of something Rick said and I need to be in control so that's not happening. I did "Thinking Out Loud" by Ed Sheeran really well at the bar in Colorado, but that was only great because it was emotion driven and Rick was there with me. I don't think Rick will be there tomorrow night. I don't know when or if I'll see him again. A tear rolls down my face and I know I need to pick something power driven to keep my attitude up. The Killers? Maybe "Mr. Brightside"? "Come Home" by OneRepublic, could be bad to do two songs by the same artist and could be good because they're male vocals, not really power driven. Maybe something 80's? I never sang my Lita Ford song for 80's Rock Ladies Night. I wish I knew what the wild card will be, then again it doesn't really matter. Karaoke finals can be a distraction, but when it's over, win or lose... I've already lost.

My phone rings as I'm getting ready for bed and there's no caller ID, "Hello?"

"Hi. I want you to know I'm sorry. I'm willing to start over from the beginning. I'll do whatever it takes to get you to go out with me again. I just want to see you again. Good luck at your karaoke finals tomorrow night, though you don't need it—it's yours for sure. Thank you for listening to me," he speaks slowly and slightly slurred, so I'm guessing he's drunk.

"Rick, please be safe. Who's with you?" my concern showing.

"I'm with Cross. I love you..."

I interrupt him, "Give Cross the phone please," I ask and know he'll do it because he's out of it.

"Hey Sherry," Chase says upbeat.

"Are you taking care of him? He sounds absolutely wasted out of his mind!"

"It's better than him walking around mad at the world, yelling, and throwing shit. This is how I can handle him. I'm sharing a room with him this trip. I'm not his woman or his keeper. I thought he might actually get some sleep if I got him drunk."

"Thank you," I say softly.

"Thank you? Are you kidding me? Talk to him and figure this out! You're both crazy!" Chase is upset with me.

"I know you don't understand. Thank you for rooming with him this trip," I say as I hang up. Chase is right. The question is, what do I want? I'm waiting for the sign Joey promised me, because I know what I want and I need confirmation it's the right thing to do.

CHAPTER TWENTY-SEVEN

K araoke finals day is finally here and I'm excited! I get up, pour my coffee, and sit down to check my email. Nothing new that has to be dealt with. I hang up my outfit for tonight, and set out my boots, accessories, and other essentials. I grab a donut, okay fine... I grab a bag of heavenly chocolate-coated mini donuts and eat half of them with my coffee. The game is early this morning, but I'm not going there today.

Text from Sam - Good morning. Rick isn't in the game today because he showed up hung over, possibly still drunk from last night. Cross can't be trusted.

Text to Sam - I was afraid of that. Your brother was wasted when he called me last night.

Text from Sam - He called you last night? You talked to him? I need the deets.

I give her the run down and add:

Text to Sam - Chase thinks I should talk to Rick and figure it out, that we're both crazy. He might be right. I need to figure out what I want.

Then there is what Sam hears:

Text from Sam - So, you're saying you believe you can be fixed?

I guess anything is possible. I would love to have him with me. I just don't know if it can be the same. I'm afraid it can't be the same.

I shower, washing and conditioning my hair, and using my body scrub so I shine on the stage tonight. I leave my hair wet and take off to get a mani/pedi. I choose a dark red color called Red Hot & Blue Luv for both my toes and my fingers, and splurge on the sea salt scrub with extra leg massage. I go home and relax a few minutes before I start brushing out my hair and take the curling iron to my long layers. I lay out all of my make-up and match up some different options, but eventually go with my rock concert look: black pencil eyeliner pulled out to the crease, black mascara, dark metallic silver eye powder, Dark Cherry Pop Lipstick that I also dab to use as blush, and high-shine lip gloss. I look at myself in the mirror and it's not me. I'm playing a part and for tonight, that's probably good. It's not me to get all made up. If I can't wear my sneakers or flip flops, I probably don't want to go there. Tonight is a special occasion and I need the extra shield.

I change into my black satin string bikinis and matching bra. I pull on my tight dark rinse jeggings and some socks up over them to keep my pants down in my boots. I sit down to put my boots on and my phone rings. The caller ID says it's a car service, "Hello?"

"Yes, I'm trying to reach Sherry about her car service today," a man says.

"This is Sherry, but I didn't order a car service for today," questioning.

"That's correct. A limo was ordered to pick you up and take you to the Batter Up. I need to know what time to pick you up or what time you need to be there. I have instructions to stop anywhere you want on the way. I was told to take a photo of you and text it to somebody when I pick you up for a nice tip, apparently they want to make sure I actually pick you up or something. I'm on call to take you home tonight, too," he continues.

"Who ordered the limo?" I ask.

"I don't have that information," he says.

"What number are you sending my photo to?" I dig. He gives me the number and of course, it's Rick.

"Please pick me up just before 7pm. I need to be at the Batter Up no later than 7:45. I'll let you take my photo, but I want to pick where you take it—okay?"

"Yes, ma'am. I'll be in front of your building at 6:40 waiting for you. Bye." He hangs up.

Why not let Rick do something nice for me? He wants to support me and make me feel special for the finals. He wants to support me. He wants me to feel special. He's trying to give me space at the same time. I send him a text:

Text to Rick - Sweet of you to send a limo for me.

No response.

I go back to putting my boots on and slide my new top

over my head without messing up my hair or make-up. I check my look in the mirror and straighten out the bottom of my top. The deep plunge sits perfectly between my breasts and enhances my cleavage. I lace my new belt through my belt loops and fasten it with the rhinestone buckle showing right where the draped material of the top separates. I slide on my new silver cuff bracelet and pick through my silver rings deciding which to wear. I open the package with the necklace I had to have and carefully place it over my head, arranging it so the crystals are placed well around my neck and accent the deep plunge. The look is exactly what I want. I grab my leather jacket to take with me and fill my purse with my make-up, mints, and brush. I'll wear the jacket for the first song and take it off for the second song. I double check the mirror and start the walk out to the front of my building. The limo should be here any time.

My phone vibrates as I walk out to the limo.

Text from Rick - You'll always be my queen, but tonight you're a rock star and you should travel like one.

If anyone has the power to fix us, it's him.

The limo is waiting for me when I get there. The driver opens the door for me. "I thought the guy didn't trust me, but now I understand why he wants a picture. You look amazing. If you were mine, I wouldn't let you out alone."

"You're kind, but I'm not the one paying you and tipping you," I say laughing.

"It's a pleasure to drive a beauty like you. Where will we be stopping to take your photo?" he asks.

"I'd like you to take my photo out on the Embarcadero

South and in front of the Batter Up. Will that be okay?" I ask.

"Absolutely, whatever you want," and he takes off toward downtown.

I jump out of the limo when we get to the Embarcadero and the driver quickly snaps a few pictures. We arrive at the Batter Up a few minutes later and the driver takes my picture with the limo in front of the sports bar. My phone vibrates as I walk into the Batter Up and sign in:

Text from Rick - You're so fucking gorgeous, perfect for your finals. I miss your face.

I sign in and get the specifics for tonight. Mike with the Mic is drawing names and calling us out to sing our round one songs. There are only five of us, so round one should take less than 50 minutes. Nothing has changed because it's the finals, except a few signs and they're charging a cover at the door. We're starting about ten minutes late, so Mike has time to review the game plan with the crowd in the bar tonight.

I go to the ladies room to check my hair and make-up, make sure everything is where it belongs. Then I wait behind the curtain. A few minutes later, everything gets started.

"Good evening, guys and gals! I'm Mike with the Mic and I'll be your karaoke host tonight. Now, tonight is not just any karaoke night. We have only five competitors left in our competition and tonight are the three final rounds. The first round each contestant will be singing two songs that are both upbeat and current. One will be originally recorded as a male vocal and the other will be originally recorded as a female vocal. Only three of our finalists will advance to round two. Each finalist will sing one song for round two and it's a song of their choice. Our top two finalists will advance to the third and final round. The final round will be a wild card round. Each finalist will be given a choice of three songs after they get on stage. They have no idea what the song choices are, and I don't either. The winner tonight gets bragging rights, $1,000, free food and drinks at Batter Up for a year, their picture on the wall and a recording of your performances will be sent to record producers just for giggles. Our performers are in random order tonight. Relax and enjoy the show, we'll be starting in a few minutes."

There are only five of us waiting behind the curtain tonight. It's a bit crazy, and from the sound of it the place is packed tonight. I wait my turn.

"Let's get things rolling. Tonight we're starting with Sherry! Sherry will be singing "Ex's & Oh's" by Elle King as her song recorded as a female vocal and then "Love Runs Out" by OneRepublic as her song recorded by a male vocal. Please welcome Sherry to the stage!" The audience is into it tonight and the applause is wild.

I step up onto the new stage, feeling it sturdy beneath my feet and realize the milk crate has been replaced with an actual stair step. The stage no longer has pieced together plywood tripping hazards built into it. It's one solid piece and slightly larger than before. I take a deep breath and wait for "Ex's & Oh's" to start. I channel my inner diva and let it rip with a strut in my attitude. I can't help but to slowly shimmy my hips and swing my shoulders from side to side with the music. It's how the song should be sung and how I need to sing it if I have any hope of making it through not only to the competition finals, but with my emotions in check. I don't want to lose it, and my competitive spirit doesn't want to lose either. I listen to the bass beat roll through. I adopt the strut in my stance and in my voice. The lyrics aren't me, but they're empowering and give me the hope that I'm wanted. I want Rick to want me, I want him to come back for more. The attitude is fun and sexy, if not a bit dark and gives me a chance to show a different side of my singing.

The whole place goes crazy. "Great job, Sherry! You really owned that! Next song is "Love Runs Out" by OneRepublic and I can't wait to see what Sherry can do with it!"

I take my leather jacket off and toss it to the side of the stage, showing more skin. I scan the room while I wait for the pounding bass intro to get to the words and I see some of the Seals in the back. Then the lyrics hit and I'm on it with exact timing. I let every bit of tension I've had bottled up out in the lyrics. I'm completely taken over by the pounding rhythmic beat and hear the intense voice of Ryan Tedder in my head as I sing. Singing the lyrics, I realize I'm not giving up on us. We'll work it out and I'll take whatever I can get. I was right in the beginning to follow my heart. I'm in this until I'm beyond road rash, I'll be roadkill before I let go. Our love won't run out. The words are honest and from my soul, even if they aren't mine. The heat, desire, devotion of the song, it all beats in my heart and drives me to sing with power.

The crowd is wild, clapping and hooting. Mike starts in, "Sherry just raised the bar for this competition, ladies and gentlemen. Sherry, please wait for the other contestants to perform backstage. I have a feeling you've made it to round two!"

I go backstage, noticing it hadn't been upgraded like

Mike had hoped and wait impatiently for the other four singers to do their thing. I check my messages:

> Text from Mom – Good luck tonight sweetheart. Have fun at your singing thing.

> Text from Sam – Good luck tonight! I know you'll rock it!

> Text from Rick - You're amazing. You continue to shock me.

> Text to Rick - How do you know?

> Text from Rick - I'm with the guys in the back. I'm staying out of sight. I don't want to make you uncomfortable. I know you don't want to talk to me and I'm trying to give you time, but I couldn't miss this. It's too important to you. If you want me to, I'll leave.

> Text to Rick - You should stay. So, you're really here?

> Text from Rick - Yes. I'm staying. You're absolutely gorgeous and your attitude on stage is unbelievable. Maybe we can talk after?

> Text to Rick - Maybe

I'm a strong independent woman. I don't need a man, I just want one. A specific man that fills the catcher position on a professional baseball team... Damn it!

I need to be ready to tell Mike what my round two song is if I advance. I want to send a message with the song, kind of my invitation to fix us. I can't believe he's here. I get some hot tea to keep my voice warm and try to relax, but my nerves are on end. I don't know if I can manage this multiple round thing. Who am I kidding? The truth is it's his presence in the building making me feel so raw. I want him. The last contestant walks back behind the curtain. Nobody got applause like I did and I wait anxiously for Mike to announce who will advance, but mostly for the opportunity to see Rick's face.

"What do you think of our finalists tonight?" Mike asks the crowd and gets a loud cheer in return. "I'm going to call out the names of our top three finalists and they will join me on stage. Our first finalist is Sherry!" and I have no idea what he said after that. It was a complete blur as I heard the team start chanting Sherry, Sherry, Sherry, Sherry.

"Sherry will be singing first in the second round. Sherry what is your song choice?"

""Come Home" by OneRepublic," I tell Mike with the Mic. I need my Rick to come home.

As he gets the song queued up and the music starts, "This is for Rick and you don't need to be hiding back there." Rick shows himself, and I feel his bright blue eyes on me. I can't believe I'm doing this. Karaoke sure, but my heart taking over my brain, needing someone, needing a man, needing my man, needing Rick Seno. Then I draw on my emotions and make the words my own with a clear, strong voice as I make eye contact across the room. It's easy when you're singing the truth and I maintain my emotion in the second verse by simply having eye contact with my Rick. I don't want to know why. I don't want to explain or have to prove anything to anyone. I just want Rick. The chorus comes out like a request at first, but turns into begging by the end of the song. I want him to come home and I'm his home.

Rick looks at me and smiles. He wants to come to me. Come home. I can't help but lock eyes with him while the music plays out to the end of the song.

The whole place loves it. "Sherry just keeps getting better! I can't wait to see what she does with the wild card! Man, that Rick guy is a lucky dog. Thank you, Sherry," Mike does his thing.

I wait back stage for the other two singers to perform their songs. It takes forever. I want to go to him. I'm listening now to hear how the other two do. Only one of us will be eliminated and I know I'll make it through. They finish singing and Mike calls all three of us to the stage.

"Ladies and gentlemen, here are our top three. One of them is done right now and the other two will be going to the final round and wild card karaoke." Mike goes on.

I made it to the final! I hear cheering in the back and I know it's Rick and the team. My heart beats hard. He's here for me, when I gave up on him and couldn't trust him.

"Okay, Sherry you're first. Here are your three song choices for wild card karaoke:

"Promises, Promises" by Naked Eyes

"Mr. Brightside" by The Killers

"Thinking Out Loud" by Ed Sheeran

Which one will it be, Sherry? You have thirty seconds to decide."

More cheering in the back and Rick yells out, "Yes! "Thinking Out Loud"."

I know immediately, "Mike, I want to sing "Thinking Out Loud" by Ed Sheeran." Whatever Rick asks for, I'll give him.

"This could be a risky choice for Sherry to go out on the

final song with something mellow. Do you want to change your mind, Sherry?" Mike asks.

"That's my final decision, Mike," in the vein of Who Wants to be a Millionaire. "Singers should always listen to the audience and take requests. I think we all heard the answer called out from the back." Mike gives me a nod and loads up the song.

"That sounded like more than a request. I'm going to guess it came from someone special," Mike with the Mic always has to get his two cents in.

"Thank you to everybody here to support me tonight." The music starts, I take a deep breath because this is risky to put it out there. My emotions have been trying to get the best of me all night. He wants to support me, he wants me to feel special. I left him because he makes me act like a girl, I gave up on him, pushed him away, and he's not giving up on me. What's wrong with acting like a girl? I believe him. I'm such a fucking idiot! I've never lived my life scared of anything. I start to sing and there's a shake in my voice. I look for Rick and make eye contact. I need his strength. I need his love. I point at him and place my hand over my heart as I sing the meaningful lyrics and let my raw emotions out. I watch him slowly stand, emotion all over his face as he walks to the front of the stage and stands on the floor right in front of me. I reach for him and touch the side of his face while I'm singing. He brings my hand to his mouth and kisses it tenderly, like I'm a queen, his queen. I'm on stage, but in my own world, our world. I somehow manage to finish the song strong and as the crowd cheers, Rick reaches up to the stage and brings me down to him. He holds me tight to his chest and buries his face in my hair, happy having me in his arms.

PLAYLIST

"Yesterday" by the Beatles
"All Right Now" by Free
"My Songs Know What You Did in the Dark" by Fall
Out Boy
"Uprising" by Muse
"Oh Sherrie" by Steve Perry
"Seek and Destroy" by Metallica
"Need You Tonight" by INXS
"Never Tear Us Apart" by INXS
"Jessie's Girl" (Beach Version) by Rick Springfield
"Funkytown" by Pseudoecho
"When You Close Your Eyes (Do You Dream About Me?)"
by Night Ranger
"Somewhere Over the Rainbow" by Israel
Kamakawiwoʻole
"Promises Promises" by Naked Eyes
"Voices Carry" by Til Tuesday
"Shadows of the Night" by Pat Benatar
"Alone" by Heart

"The Warrior" by Scandal
"Kiss Me Deadly" by Lita Ford
"Thinking Out Loud" by Ed Sheeran
"Love Runs Out" by One Republic
"Ex's & Oh's" by Elle King
"Can I Be Him" (acoustic) by James Arthur
"Come Home" by One Republic

KING OF DIAMONDS

AN ALL ABOUT THE DIAMOND ROMANCE BOOK 2

CHAPTER ONE

In the last couple months, my life has gone from being totally in control and an independent, self-sufficient entrepreneur to having my fantasy baseball boyfriend become real. Yes, a professional baseball player loves and wants me. And, it's not just any player, it's the catcher I've been fantasizing about for years, my boyfriend in my head. It's utter insanity! I'm seven years older than him and he has women waiting for him in his room on road trips. I've seen it firsthand on more than one occasion. He can be with anybody he wants and he's not interested in those women he finds waiting for him. No, he only wants me. Until it got all fucked up. Indirectly and accidentally, but fucked up nonetheless. We broke us and I'm not sure if we can ever be the same. When you break something fragile it shatters and there's no putting it back together. When you break your favorite coffee mug you can glue it back together, but it'll never be the same. It might still hold your coffee, but you can see and feel the cracks. It's broken and you're simply refusing to let it go.

I'm STANDING on the stage at the Batter Up. I just finished singing my final song in the karaoke competition and I'm overcome with emotion. The wild card round and I chose "Thinking Out Loud". What was I thinking? That's our song and he's been in my head everyday since I left him in LA. It was less than two months ago, but it feels like forever. I wasn't thinking. I was simply doing what he wanted. No matter what, I want to make him happy. Our song was one of the three options Mike at the Mic gave me and before I could consider the options, Rick was in the back of the room yelling out "Thinking Out Loud". I had already decided I wanted him back, well, that may have been him helping me there, too. I can't believe the things he does for me even though I left him, refused to talk to him, didn't reply to his texts, and avoided him and everyone he knows for most of two months. I even avoided watching the games, except for my stupid moment when I had to see his face and wished I didn't as I watched him get kicked out of a game. He was persistent with daily texts and voicemails, along with sending me flowers and having a limo service pick me up for the finals tonight. I pushed him away. I get it, now. He didn't give up on me. I need to embrace my girliness that's been driving me crazy and trust in him. It's not weakness, it's risking my heart. But, after being without him—I'll give him my heart completely. Honestly, I'll give him about anything he wants and be happy doing it. Anything to be with him. I didn't expect him to be here tonight. I wasn't sure when or if I'd ever see him again, other than in his catcher's gear behind the plate. Now, I'm in a private hazy world with Rick pulling me down off the stage to him and I hope he never let's me go...

Rick holds me tightly to his chest, breathing me into him as the music plays out. I missed him. His arms around me, his warm breath at my ear, and his words that cut straight through to my heart. "The only thing that matters is that I have you near me," he whispers in my ear.

Mike with the Mic starts in, "Another outstanding performance from Sherry. She really has ruled this contest from the beginning."

Rick whispers in my ear, "I don't want to let you go," as he sets me back down on the stage. I don't want him to let me go.

I'm directed to go backstage and the rookie, Chase Cross, drags Rick back to the table with the team.

I'm backstage and I don't care about the contest. I want to be with Rick. He needs me. Maybe, I need him. We all have our personal issues. I need to remember who he is and what has happened in his life. We don't want to hurt each other. We need to trust each other. I didn't think a text from Joey would be a big deal and he didn't invite Ava to his room. If he needs to go for a run, so he can clear his head, well at least he told me and didn't disappear into the night. He did come back and want answers, he didn't leave and it was over. No, that's what I did. Just like me. Drill it down to the base of the problem and not be able to get over it or around it or focus on anything but it. Damn it! Why is this taking so long?

Mike with the Mic pops backstage looking for me, "Sherry? I've called you out three times. What're you doing back here?" He stares at me oddly and crooks his head to a questioning angle. "Never mind, you did great. Can you come out on stage now, please?"

Mike leaves and I follow him out, stepping up onto the stage. "Thank you everybody for coming out tonight. The crew here at Batter Up and I appreciate your patronage during this contest. We know some of it has been hard to listen to, while other contestants like these two standing here made up for it in spades. The bartenders have surveyed the crowd and put the votes together." A waitress walks up and hands Mike a napkin. He turns to us and says, "One of you got 55 of the 60 votes. Amazing results. Congratulations, Sherry! You've been the one to beat since week one."

I'm speechless. I manage to mutter out, "Thank you." Not concerned about the competition at all. It's not important right now.

"It's okay sweetie, go do what you need to do," Mike encourages me to do what's in my heart.

I search for Rick, and he's back at the table with the other Seals. I go to him, but Cross stops me before I get there, "I'm not letting you get any closer to him unless this is a good thing. Are you going to fix this?" Chase questions.

"I'm going to him and not running away, so we can fix us. He's not alone in this," I tell Chase.

"You better be sure about that because his ideas for fixing it are crazy," Cross warns.

"I like crazy," I smile at him, and like the troll under the bridge he lets me pass.

I approach Rick slowly, gazing into his eyes and hoping to find our connection. "Hi. Do you want to get out of here?"

He stands up, "I'll go wherever you are," his eyes on me heavily.

My eyes start to tear up and I'm getting all girly again. I need to keep some of my wits about me to get through this and not lose it. I reach out for his hand and he takes mine. I lead him out of the Batter Up and retrace our steps to the bleachers at the Embarcadero. A peaceful place with a great memory and a beautiful night sky. A place where we can be alone. We walk silently. It gives me time to consider what I want and what I want to say to him.

We climb up the stairs of the bleachers and sit down together. He starts to talk, but I stop him. "I need to start. You didn't trust me when I've given you more of me than I've ever given anyone else. I trust you more than anyone else and it hurt because of it. Everything I've done that I'd never do screamed at me internally. You didn't trust me, and finding her in your room—It was too much. I needed to get away. It hit home with me because I don't trust people, but it was never a question with you. You never saw that part of me. I trusted you from the moment I saw you step on the baseball field for the first time. You have history, it was evident pretty quick that relationships haven't gone your way. I learned how bad women have treated you. I saw the hurt on your face then and I heard it in your voice when you called me drunk. When I told you there's only you, I meant it. I need you to trust me. I'll never hurt you intentionally." I wait for a response to my ramble, with more to say.

Rick takes a deep breath, "I have to know if you believe me." He stops and searches my eyes. "I need you to know you're the only one for me. Ava is nothing and I've never given any other woman my room key, only you. I'll never cheat on you."

"I have to. You're not one of those players." I gaze up at him and smile, while my eyes fill with tears. "I don't know if I can handle the life of a professional baseball player, it's why I ran. You didn't trust me and it weakened my heart. I couldn't see what was happening right in front of me. I couldn't trust my heart and believe in you." I look down and taste my salty tears as they fall across my lips. "I've never needed anyone." I gaze up at Rick, letting him see my tears, "I love you and I need you."

He immediately put his arms around me, holding me tight, his face in my hair, "I love you, my queen. Always you. Only you." He pulls me into his lap and we sit on the bleachers together quietly, needing to be together. I didn't know how much I needed him until I felt my heart start beating, deprived of the ability for weeks. He places his hands on my cheeks and presses his lips to mine softly.

"I'm sorry. I'll do my best to never hurt you. You haven't done a thing to make me not trust you. You've given yourself to me freely. That's all me and I know it. I've thought about it a lot and I trust you with everything, breaking all my rules. I've never been this possessive. I've never cared this much or felt this way. The first sign of another man made me boil." His face turns red simply saying the words. "Nothing is the same without you. I only want to be with you. I need my queen back."

"I freak out when I start acting and feeling all girly, and you make me girly. My whole life I've thought it was a weakness to be girly, but now I'm learning maybe it isn't. It's my happy tears and the fluttering in the pit of my stomach and needing someone else—needing you. Many things I'd never considered were all of the sudden things I might want. I come with baggage and you'll have to deal with it," I'm shaking at my honesty.

Rick pulls me tight to his chest, "I love you and your girly moments. None of the rest matters."

The girly part of me takes over and I don't let my brain talk me out of it. I need him to know I'm his. I need to know it can be the same. I need to feel that he still loves me and show him how much I love him. I need to remove this protective shield I've built around myself tonight and bare my heart to him. I lean in and whisper in his ear, "I still belong to you. I'll always be yours. I'm sorry I freaked out."

He tightens his embrace, "I overreacted. It's not all you. I love you. Please say you'll never leave me again."

"I promise I'll never leave you again," my heart tries to leap out of my chest as I gaze into his eyes.

He kisses me and his body relaxes, "I was afraid I'd never hold you again. I need you."

Why would I ever leave this man? How did I let this happen? "Please take me home and hold me all night, every night, my king."

"Anything for you, my queen. You're all I want and all I need," he smiles against my lips and kisses me senseless. His heart warms and beats against mine.

I message the limo to pick us up and gaze up into Rick's blue eyes, hoping the sadness will disappear. My new goal: before I sleep, my man will be happy again.

He holds my hand, not letting go as we walk out of the park and the limo pulls up. The driver opens the door and Rick instructs him to take us home. The driver puts the privacy glass up and Rick sits with his arms around me, just looking at me.

"I want you to know I belong to you. I'm yours. Please make me yours again. Make love to me." I need him. I search his eyes and see his brain is getting in the way of his heart and heat. What do I do? I don't want him to think I'm pushing him for sex. He needs to know it's more.

Rick gives the driver a destination change. This man always has a plan. A few minutes later we pull up to an apartment building and the driver opens the door. Rick pulls me out of the limo along with him. We walk in and get to the elevator, my body is on fire with elevator memories and I can't help but wonder how he'll handle this. He presses the button for the third floor and the growing tension in his hand is evident. "We're on the elevator," I point out simply and that's all it takes. His hands are all over me and he's holding me against the wall with his body. "Pull the elevator stop." I feel him get hard against me.

"No," he says as he takes a deep breath to gain control and the elevator door opens. "I promise I'll make love with you all night. Please work with me here. There are a couple things that need to happen before I'm out of control, and Sherry—you make me forget what control is." He leads me to an apartment and unlocks the door. "I told you I would take you to my place." Rick claims me with his mouth while we stand in the hallway and I put my arms around his neck. His need and desire shoot through me. He picks me up and continues to kiss me as he walks through the door and kicks the door shut behind him. He leans his forehead to mine. "This is my place and I've wanted to carry my woman through the door for years. I've never brought a woman here. None of this furniture is mine. I rent it furnished and with maid service. It's not home. It's the place I keep my stuff. I haven't been living my life. Living started when I first touched your lips at the Locale. You're everything to me."

"Come home with me and never leave," I offer my home and my heart. The brightness starts to come back to his eyes. "I want to go on road trips with you. I want to be at every game, behind home plate cheering for you, supporting you."

He smiles at me and I have hope for us, "Is there anything else you want, my queen?"

"You, my king. Please take me home."

Rick pulls me close, running his hands up and down my sides and searching my eyes. I feel like he's looking for something, but I don't know what.

He locks up and we head back to the limo. His lips on me from the time the elevator door closes until we get home. I want him inside me. I want him to come home. I need us to be the same. His kiss is more heated on the elevator up to my place and I run my hand along his hard length. I pull the elevator stop and drop to my knees, unbuttoning his pants and freeing his hard love. He grabs my arm and pulls my mouth to his, kissing me with need and holding me against the elevator wall with his body while he pulls my belt off hastily and slides his hand into my pants. He gets harder at the touch of my wet heat. I'm entranced by his kiss and don't even notice he puts himself away. The elevator starts moving and he picks me up to take me with him, not taking his lips from mine as he carries me home. Rick unlocks the door and kisses me, repeating what he did at his apartment and carrying me through the door. "This feels right, our home," he says as he walks into our bedroom and lays me down on our bed.

I sit up to take my boots off and he watches me. I continue to undress, removing my socks, taking off my jewelry, pulling off my pants, and slipping my top off, leaving me in my matching black satin string bikinis and bra. I move to the bathroom, to wash off my face and brush out my hair, so I can be me and bare for him.

I go back to the bedroom and Rick is lying in our bed, naked. I step out of my panties and unhook my bra, letting it fall to the floor. I climb in bed, needing him and wanting him urgently. I want to climb on top of him and mount his hard length, but he stops me. I'm so frustrated and needy. I want him inside me. "What the fuck!" Pent up tears start to run down my face. "Why won't you let me have you inside me? I need you. I need to have you. I need to feel you love me like it was before I fucked everything up!" There it is. Everything in my head out where he can hear and see my girl crazy. "I told you I have girl baggage! Damn it!" I move away needing to hide my emotions in the shower, but he grabs me and pulls me close.

"I don't know what's going on, but I'm not letting you leave this bed. Now, baby, let me love you," he says as he holds me. His hands hot on my skin as they caress my breasts and he licks from my neck down to my sex. His beard tickles my heat as he licks my sensitive nub. He moves down burying his face in my hot wet sex, licking my wetness with his tongue and slowly caressing my clit.

"Oh my god!" I cry out. Rick stops and pulls away. Leaving me wanting more.

He glares at me with an evil grin and says, "Who am I?"

"My king. Rick, my king!" I answer quickly, needing his attention.

"Tell me more. Tell me what you want," Rick tortures me.

"I want you inside me, my king. Only you." He goes back to licking my needy center, over and over, sucking and nibbling all around it until he dives back into my wet folds. Taking his tongue as deep as he can and driving me crazy. "Please can I have you inside me?" I beg and he slides a finger in me. "Please, my king. I need you. I want to feel you. I need your love inside me. Only you my king. Love me. Please love me. I want to feel you push into me. I need to feel you come inside me. Please, my king—make me your queen."

He sucks and licks knowing exactly what to do to set me off, but won't do it. He climbs my body and claims my mouth with his. His hard length rubbing between my legs, he reaches down and rubs my clit hard while he strokes my tongue with his. I'm out of control. "Rick, I love you." He slides his hard cock into me slowly and I'm done. I see the fireworks I've been missing as he strokes into me deep and deliberate while he kisses me.

His kiss slows, he lightly sucks on my lip as he moves his kiss to my neck and whispers in my ear with his low sexy voice that drives me crazy, "I love you, baby. Only you, my queen. Tell me it's only me. Tell me you want me. Tell me everything in your pretty head."

"I'm only yours. No one else will ever have me, only you. I want you always. I never want to be without you. I want to be with you forever. I love you. I want to..." I catch myself before I say something crazy, something I wasn't aware I wanted.

Rick pounds into me harder and faster. He's almost there. "You can tell me anything, baby. I'll never leave." He's getting harder and stretching me slowly with his thick length.

"I love you, baby." I claim his mouth with mine. Trying to tell him things I can't say in words with my actions. With my tongue on his and my hands on his body. I dig my fingers into his strong upper arms and cry out his name uncontrollably. My orgasm pulling at him and drawing him as he pushes in hard and holds himself at my deepest point feeling me squeeze him over the edge.

Rick wraps his loving arms around me and holds me tight to his chest. "I missed you, baby. I'm never letting go."

All I can do is smile. I didn't break us.

CHAPTER TWO

The smell of coffee came earlier than I wanted it to on Thursday morning. My alarm had already gone off and I turned it off, thanking it for waking me to the gorgeous love of my life wrapped around me. I need a remote to turn the coffee smell off. The aroma wins and I start to get up for coffee, but I'm grabbed and pulled back into bed.

"I don't think so," and he puts his lips on mine tenderly, rolling me under him and taking me with his hard length. "Good morning, my queen," he says with a huge smile on his face. "I missed being with you, but I missed your sweet talk when you're asleep the most. I need to wake up with you in my arms every day."

I can't believe I'm saying this and moving this quickly, but I'm all in. "We can make that happen. Are you moving in with me today? Sounds like a good thing to do on your off day," I suggest. I really need to figure out what I say in my sleep. Suddenly he renders me speechless with his motions and all I can do is feel. His hot breath on my ear, describing what he's doing to me slowly as he does it sends me over the edge quicker than it should and I'm calling out his name.

"Yes, my queen. Now, you're going to come for me again, with me when I'm ready. Feel me push into you and rub you with my love, then take it away, over and over, feel the friction, our heat. Feel me push all the way into you, harder, faster. Touch my cock and feel me entering you, sliding in and out. Feel my length get harder for you because you feel so damn good around me. Yes, that's all you Sherry. Only you do this to me." Rick pushes on my magic buttons. "Okay love, for me now..." and we both go off like shooting stars. He has so much control over me, I don't understand—but I love it.

Rick pulls me on top of him and holds me to his chest. Quietly he tells me, "I want to move in with you. Do you want me and my stuff here? Do you want this to be my home? I don't want to push you. It's a big change and we have challenges."

"I want this to be our home. I want you here with me," I say with a huge smile on my face.

"That's what I want, too," so happy and relaxed.

"It's date night and if you're moving in today, I'll make dinner here for your first night home. Is that okay? Date night is usually your thing."

"That's perfect. I'll shower and get Chase to come get me, so I can make him help carry. I have errands to take care of, too. That should leave you enough time to get your work done." He gets his phone and gives Chase the address. "Chase says I'm crazy. He's right, I'm crazy in love with you. I have my keys."

I pull on shorts and a tank top, then check the kitchen for supplies as I make up my dinner menu and start in on work while Rick gets ready to go. I handle a few business emails and check my messages. I have a couple of texts:

Text from Sam – I haven't heard from my brother.
Please tell me he's with you.

Text from Mom – How are you doing? How did your singing thing go last night?

Text to Sam - He's here. Neither one of us are leaving. I'll tell him to call you.

I walk into the bathroom to talk to Rick while he's in the shower and get distracted by the view. Damn! I need to write things down before I walk into a room where he's naked.

"Babe, Sam sent me a text and I told her you'll call her. Also, um, my Mom needs to meet you," I say as an afterthought.

"Can you go to lunch Saturday? Maybe you can invite your Mom down and then you two can have some time together between lunch and the game. I can get you an extra ticket for Mom if she wants to go to the game." Why doesn't he freak out about meeting parents?

"We aren't playing LA, she's not going to want to go to the game," I hang my head in shame yet again.

"Tell her I want her to go to the game and we can get dessert after or get her a room for the night," he suggests and I know what I need to do, I know what makes my Mom tick.

I shouldn't put it off any longer, I call Mom.

"Hello?" she answers.

"Hi, Mom. Would you like to drive down to have lunch

Saturday and maybe stay for the baseball game? I know we aren't playing LA."

"I'd love to meet you for lunch, but I'm not interested in a Seals Game," she says.

"I'd like you to go. Rick wants you to go to the game, too."

"No, I don't think so," difficult mother.

Rick takes the phone from me, "Hi ma'am, I want to take you and your daughter out to lunch and I'd love it if you'd go to my game. It would mean a lot to me and I'm sure Sherry would enjoy spending the afternoon shopping with you or going to the spa or something. Maybe both if you'd like to stay the night Saturday. I'm happy to get you a room." He continues, "I love your daughter, she's the best thing that ever happened to me and I'm not letting her go." He listens, "I can't wait to meet you. Sherry will get everything set up and get you the details. Thank you, ma'am," and he hangs up leaving me in awe.

"Please book a room for your Mom for Saturday night, some place nice that she'll like. She wants to go shopping after we have lunch and loved the idea of spa day on Sunday with her daughter. She agreed to go to the game, so I'm going to get you two tickets behind home plate. Lunch downtown or somewhere else and you can drop me off at the stadium?"

"You're amazing. Lunch somewhere else." I say knowing where Mom will want to go shopping.

"Perfect. Then you can take my car and park in my spot when you get to the stadium," Rick says nonchalantly.

"What? I can't park in the players lot," minor freak-out.

"It's fine. It'll impress your Mom and you might as well get used to it because I'm moving in, so you get a stadium access pass," he continues like it's everyday business.

I repeat, "What? You're killing me with all this."

"Get used to it, babe. Life of the baseball player. Not part of what you imagined? I wondered about your fantasy. Maybe add that to date night tonight?" he says laughing. He plants one of his no-way-you-can-forget-me kisses on me and says, "I love you, Sherry. I'll be home later."

What did I get myself into? I'm in it and I'm not giving it up. Baseball player craziness is better than being without him. I never want to be without him.

I TAKE a quick drive to the public market to pick up a couple of dry aged steaks from the butcher, some baby potatoes, broccoli and cauliflower from the produce girl, a wedge of parmesan from the cheese guy and a quart of Kahlua ice cream from the creamery. The ice cream is for me, not for dinner.

I get home and unload my groceries. I mix up some brownie batter adding the coffee I didn't drink this morning instead of other liquid and let the batter rest while I preheat the oven.

I have a couple of hours to get some work done, book a room for Mom, book spa time for Sunday and get the brownies baked, then I need to clean up, set the table, and cook dinner. Date night needs to be perfect.

I drop chocolate and peanut butter bits on top of my brownie batter as I place the pan of chocolate deliciousness in the oven to bake and set the timer for 30 minutes.

I book a room for Mom and spa time for both of us at the Brighton. I know she's always wanted to go to the spa there. The spa is on the roof, it features a covered pool and a tasty spa menu. Plus, it's not too far from the stadium and it'll be easy to take her there after the game.

I hear my door open, no knock or anything, "Hey babe, Chase is with me. Unloading my stuff from his truck." He walks over and gives me a quick kiss.

Total girl moment. Rick came in like he lives here, because he does. No knock. No hesitation. It's his home.

Chase adds on, "Hey babe, you baking something for me? Smells good." He walks over and gives me a peck on the cheek.

(Note to self: Need to be prepared for multiple baseball players at all times.)

Rick gives Cross the evil eye. "My woman."

"I know, but I'm being nice if she bakes," Chase says.

"Chase sweetie, I'm baking brownies and they're almost done," adding to Rick's torment.

The guys make a few trips up unloading while I take the brownies out to cool and finish up my last few work items for the day. I look at his clothes and boxes of stuff in my place, correction—our place, and consider how I can clear some space for him in the closet.

They take off to handle a few things and I shower before I start dinner preparations. I put on a short trop-ical print sundress with ties over each shoulder, made of a silky material and one of my favorites I bought in Hawaii. I work my way into the kitchen to start prep for dinner. I find my apron and pull the ties around to the front. I set the steaks out to get to room temperature and gather my veggies, cheese, herbs and spices. I wash all the veggies, toss the baby potatoes in olive oil, black pepper, garlic salt, marjoram and thyme, and set them aside on a baking sheet. I chop the broccoli and cauliflower into bite-size pieces, bagging up the stems to make a broth later. I grate up some of the parmesan and preheat the oven. It's date night and I want it to be special. I set the table simply with a candle and the frame I bought in Colorado with my favorite selfie of us together. It puts me in a romantic mood and I consider which playlist to go with. I need to make a new one that includes "Thinking Out Loud," "Come Home," "Never Tear Us Apart," "All Right Now." I want to invoke memories of everything good. I place the potatoes in the oven to start baking and watch for when they start to soften, and cut out a few brownies about three inches square. It's warm in the kitchen, so I tie my hair up on the top of my head leaving my neck and shoulders bare. I take the potatoes out of the oven and squish them with another pan on top of them, making the skins crack and exposing the soft white inside. I dust them with parmesan cheese and consider eating all of the brownies and ice cream while I wait for Rick to get home.

Rick gets home a while later and finds me at the closet. I've already moved my clothes around and started hanging up his, and added his books to my bookshelf. He puts his arms around me and smiles contently, "Chase is back, he followed me up mumbling about brownies." He kisses me like he's been gone for weeks and leaves me heated.

I smile up at him, "I've got Chase covered." He follows me to the kitchen and I have two brownies on a napkin waiting for Chase. Rick's very interested in my short dress, apron, available neck, and bare feet. "Chase sweetie, come on into the kitchen. I've got something for you," I call out.

Chase was there instantly, who knew he'd be easy to control with baked goods? Rick was standing behind me, his hands appreciating my hips. "Dude, I don't need to see that. But, I'd like a brownie, make it two brownies."

I hand him the brownies and thank him for helping Rick move in. "I'll remember and bake extra next time."

"No problem. You two need to get a room, but you're already in it. Awkward. I'm out of here. See you tomorrow, dude," and Cross was gone with brownie in mouth.

"You want to get cleaned up and I'll finish dinner?" I ask Rick thinking he just moved all his stuff and it's a hot day.

"I'd rather start with dessert," he says as he runs his hands over my body and claims me with his mouth.

I see the heat in his eyes and untie my apron "No, you should leave that on," he says as he goes for my neck, kissing, nibbling and sucking. He gets hard against me and I rub against him with my hips, driving him hotter with my sway and the feel of my body in his hands. He reaches under my short dress to find me going commando. "Fuck me." He drops to his knees putting his mouth on me, sucking hard at my sex while holding me to him with both hands on my ass. The immediate heat and intensity of his mouth and hands on me have me out of control, at his mercy.

"Oh Rick! More! Please more!" I call out to him and it drives him further. Sucking harder and sliding a finger inside me until I convulse in pleasure calling out his name.

Rick bends me over and thrusts his hard cock into me from behind, holding me up with his arm around my waist. "Baby, you're perfect. So tight around me, you were made for me." He's moving fast and the friction keeps my orgasm rolling. His need for me showing in his wild abandon. He's so hard and completely in the moment. I can't help myself and I begin pushing back against him, meeting his strokes and intensity until he grabs my hips and takes full control. Pounding me on him hard and fast, digging his fingers into my hips and not letting go until he cries out a guttural moan, biting down on my neck as he comes hard and takes me into oblivion with him. We should've ended up on the floor. Rick somehow had me leaning against him, my back to his front—both of us gasping for air. "I love you, my queen. It's only like this with you. I've always been in control, but something about you makes me lose it and drives me fucking wild. I don't just want you, I need to have you, I need to touch you, and I need to have you wrapped around me."

I turn to him unable to put words together and kiss him deeply, claiming him as my own. I feel his body sigh in relief and he puts his arms around me, holding me close.

After my recovery, I send him to shower and work on dinner. I toss the veggies with the potatoes, adding a bit of olive oil and salt. I place the tray back in the oven and turn the broiler on. I place the steaks on the broiler tray and make sure I have my tongs ready. I turn on my new playlist and place the steaks in the broiler for a few minutes, then flip them over for a few minutes more. I pull the broiler tray and cover the steaks with foil. I check the veggies and move them around the tray, leaving them to cook longer.

Rick comes out of the shower dressed in a snug fitting black T-shirt and board shorts. The damnedest things make me lose it. I feel the drool building up and preparing to drip down my face. It's unbelievable, luckily Rick is hungry. "It smells good in here. Can I help with anything?"

"Nope, everything is about ready. Have a seat." I point to the table.

He inspects the table, glaring at it unacceptably. He moves the chairs so they are on the same side, next to each other. He lights the candle and picks up the framed photo. "This is perfect," he says looking at the photo, "Crowns for the king and queen." Rick adjusts the place settings to satisfy the new seating configuration before I get there to serve dinner. What was I thinking? It will always be this way.

I put the steak on his plate and dish the veggies next to it, adding more parmesan to the veggies once they're plated.

We sit down to eat together, in our home, where we live together. Leaning on each other and making googly-eyed faces at each other like teenagers.

I clear the plates and stick them in the dishwasher. Rick sets "Thinking Out Loud" on repeat. He comes to me in the kitchen and puts his arms around my waist, "Dance with me." He holds me close and we sway in each other's arms. This may be the best thing ever, his strong arms around me, my head leaning on his chest, his smile against my cheek and our hearts beating together. I love this man.

I make a dessert plate with brownies, Kahlua ice cream, chocolate sauce and whipped cream with only one spoon, and we stand in our kitchen feeding each other, licking whipped cream from each other's lips, sucking chocolate sauce off each other's fingers and kissing until I find myself being carried to bed.

CHAPTER THREE

W e lie next to each other in bed and he says, "I'm ready to hear about your fantasy."

"I don't think you really want to hear about my fantasy. You didn't even want to be a baseball player with me and that's where my fantasy begins," I wait for denial.

"I want to hear it from you. I want to know everything about you. I don't want us to have any secrets. Nobody else matters, only us," he says as serious as a heart attack.

It's silly, but I can't get the secret I'm keeping out of my head. Sam said hide it and she probably knows best. But, I need to stick with honesty and I refuse to risk this by keeping a secret from him. I can do this. "Okay. I'll tell you about my fantasy, but first I need to confess a secret. I'm not going to say it's something silly or it doesn't matter, so I didn't think I needed to tell you. It's not bad and it's not good, it just is."

"Tell me and get it out there," he says slightly unsure.

I made too big of a deal about it because it's been

hanging out in my mind. I had no idea what affect it was going to have on me. "I have a pack of pregnancy tests hiding in the cabinet and it's Sam's fault. So, don't freak out."

"Is there anything else you want to share about that? Like, why? Or, how my sister fits in this?" he questions maintaining calm, but I can see his level of relaxation has changed.

"Uh, yea. Sam told me to buy a multi-pack and take a test, because I was being extremely emotional and the pill isn't 100% effective. She actually suggested the pill might not be able to handle the sperm of a professional athlete," I share the whole reasoning behind it.

He smiles, "Well, it's true professional athletes like myself might as well be super heroes."

I watch his train of thought change, "Did you do a test?"

"Yes, I did a test on Monday," I take a deep breath because I haven't said it out loud and I know how I feel about it will show. I hate being a fucking girl that shows her emotions even when she doesn't want to. "It was negative." My eyes start to well up and I do my best to somehow suck it back in without Rick noticing.

Rick pulls me to him and holds me against his chest. A few minutes of silence pass and he speaks in the most sincere tone, "Thank you for telling me. Please don't keep anything from me."

"I promise. I won't keep secrets from you. I have always and will always be honest with you." I take a deep breath, "I didn't know I wanted it until I was sad when it was negative and I didn't tell anybody. Well, Sam knows it was negative. I sent her a picture." A single tear rolls down my face.

Damn it! This girly stuff! "Sorry, I didn't mean to lay all of that on you."

Rick's hold on me tightens and he takes a deep breath as he kisses my forehead sweetly. "Someday, baby."

"Tell me about your happy fantasy, my queen," trying to steer our conversation into a different direction, and I oblige.

We snuggle under the sheets together and I tell him about my fantasy. "I've had a fantasy baseball boyfriend ever since you made it to the majors. I didn't look at you and consciously choose my fantasy. I'd never had one before. It just happened. I started having dreams about the fantasy. What he'd feel like to touch, from his hair to his hard body. What his beard would feel like when he kissed me. How his lips would taste and his salty neck after we'd worked up a sweat. How it would feel to have his hands on my skin. Would they leave a heated path or goosebumps? The feel of his tongue against mine, his mouth claiming me, taking my body as his and having his way with me, driving me out of control. Waking up in the morning, imagining it was real and checking in the bed next to me to find I was alone. I never spoke to him, but I was at every home game cheering for him more than the rest of the team and wearing only his jersey. I wanted his autograph, but I refused to single him out and specifically go after him and only him. I was waiting for my opportunity at a fanfest or autograph signing, and it'd been years without happening. I was afraid he wouldn't be anything near what I imagined, or I'd speechlessly lose my marbles when I got close to him. I avoided one of the things I wanted most, him. Men would ask me out and I even went on a handful of dates, but they were all compared to the fantasy and reality was tossed aside. I learned that fantasy is what you believe you want, and there was no reason why I should settle for anything less, other than it didn't really exist.

"One night after a winning game I felt froggy and saw an opportunity to get a couple autographs, so I went for it. I had a drive to complete my collection and was only missing a few of the current players. I cut through the seats to the dugout while the team was celebrating on the field and hung out a few minutes. I always love to watch the on field interviews after a winning game, and this was the perfect location for it. The rookie walked up to me, I got his autograph and he started talking to me, but I had no idea what he said. I was completely oblivious. I'm pretty sure he saw me drool as I focused on my fantasy who was standing only twenty feet away. I swear I could smell his manly, rustic scent in the air. I tried to recover, told him I needed the autograph for my collection and that he'd been doing a great job this season. I stood there getting my wits about me, while I watched the interviews. My fantasy completely ignored me and walked right passed me to the locker room. I was devastated because both of my fears had come true within a few minutes—my fantasy ignored me, making me consider he might not be who I thought he was and I became a blithering idiot. I gave up. My heart sank. I turned from the field and started for home. Then somebody yelled for a blonde in a Seno jersey and I thought to myself 'Huh, I'm a blonde in a Seno jersey... I should turn around, but they can't be yelling at me' and I turned to look anyway. The rookie was standing there looking straight at me. I walked back to the dugout, he handed me a note and was gone. I remember reading the note and thinking 'I can't date a ball player.' I had mixed emotions about meeting a man at a bar at midnight. But, none of it mattered because it was my fantasy and if I didn't go I would regret it more than any dumb thing I might do with a guy I met at the bar. It was my fantasy, rules had to be forgotten. This was one of those nights that could define your life. I'd make the most of the night and enjoy it, because it was only going to be one night. That's what baseball players do, right? Especially, when you're invited to a bar at midnight? It's a one night stand and I don't do that, but for my fantasy I'd see the night through and follow his lead or I'd always wonder 'what if.'"

Rick caresses my skin as I speak, "The interesting thing is that I learned something. I was wrong. Reality is better than the fantasy in every way."

"Proof we are meant to be together, baby," he says and claims my lips showing me his emotions. He keeps his arms wrapped around me and I fall asleep in his arms.

I WAKE up at about 3:30 and can't sleep. I get up quietly and go in the other room to do some work. I know Friday is going to be a full day and Saturday isn't going to have time left to make up for it. I check my email, social media, and to-dos for the day, update some photos on my social media and price out options for a few new trip requests I've received. I go back to the trip Rick asked me to plan for us and review the details, updating the airfare to first class and adding an oceanside couple massage. I'm fidgety and can't make myself sit still. I hit the pan of brownies, picking at the bits and crumbs around the edges. I'm awake and I don't want to be. I want to be sleeping and wrapped in my gorgeous man's arms. But my brain and body aren't agreeing with me. I finally take the time to get my Instagram started and post a few photos my customers have sent to me. I sit and read my new Hawaii magazine from cover to cover. Still not sleepy. What the fuck? I've never had trouble sleeping. What am I freaking out about? Time for a recap: I wanted my hunky boyfriend to move in and he did. All secrets have been shared. Great date night. Ate more brownies than I should have. All caught up on work. Had amazing sex. Okay. It must be that Mom is meeting Rick tomorrow or, oh shit! Sam told me to do another test. Nerves anyone? I don't want to do another test. It made me sad and I don't want to reinforce sadness. Maybe next week or if I'm late or something. Why am I worried about Rick meeting my Mom? He was great with her on the phone and even got her to do what he wanted, when I couldn't.

"Babe." I hear called from the bedroom.

Shit! I don't want him waking up alone or getting any strange ideas. I get up and walk into the bedroom to find him sitting up and squinting at me. "Hey. I couldn't sleep."

He reaches out and grabs my hand, pulling me to him. "I can fix that." He puts his lips on mine and pulls me over to lay on top of him while he kisses me and kisses me and kisses me. He caresses the curve of my back and runs his other hand through my hair. Touching me possessively, lovingly. Then he starts to tell me a story, "There was once a king who was lonely and sad, but hid it from everyone around him. His court lacked loyalty and had lied to him. His army was his family and they always backed him up, constantly looking out for him—especially the newest and youngest soldier. His castle was empty and the only maidens who wished to visit his royal mattress were merely in search of a conquest or royal title or treasure. The king focused on his kingdom and ruling his army. Ignoring the loneliness which nagged at him, the parts of him which seemed to be dead and his worry about having a royal heir.

He went into battle almost daily with his army, calling the shots from the battlefield and being an active participant. Unafraid. But, hid himself away from his personal world inside the castle and maintained special armor protecting himself from his disloyal court and the greedy maidens. Always in need of a woman who loved him and trusted him. A woman to make his queen, for only him to worship. To be his only one and give him an heir. One day after battle, his newest and youngest soldier came to him saying he had found the woman for his bed. The king chastised his young soldier for being focused on pleasure and sowing his oats, but the soldier insisted the king had been sheltered too long and must attempt to remove the armor. The king agreed to send for the maiden his trusted soldier spoke of and from the moment he touched her hand he felt he was under a spell. He left her in his sitting room to consider his battle plan, and when he returned he could do nothing but kiss her. He wondered what this spell was, what potion this woman had with her. Oddly, she tried to break the spell, seeming afraid of it. When the king saw her walk he had to have her. He had to touch her. He had to know her intimately. He needed this witch to want him and need him. He needed her to be unlike the other maidens. He would leave for battle and be unable to concentrate on the war. Her kiss mesmerized him and her body had left him addicted. He wanted her in his castle and he wanted her to rule beside him, but the intensity of the spell had caught them both off guard. The king had become enraged, questioning, and she fled in the night. The king was miserable and needed to have her. He needed her to be safe and protected. He wanted to do things he'd never done before and would send his servants to do nice things for her since she didn't want to be in the presence of the king or talk to the king. The amazing woman finally allowed the king in her presence and was accepting, but had demands. They would live together in the castle and if the king was going to war, she would be at the battlefield. This spell-casting woman did not demand treasure, she did not care about title even when I referred to her as my queen. She was not after the royal seed. Yet the king could not help himself. The king had to have her in his bed repeatedly." Rick kissed me tenderly. "I love you my queen, may I worship you now? I promise to grant all of your wishes in time. I just want to pleasure you." He pulled the blanket up over us and took me to a new world, worshiping me until I could no longer stay awake and my brain gave up.

CHAPTER FOUR

I woke up in my favorite place Friday morning before my alarm went off and before the coffee was brewing, there was a man holding me tight and talking. Does he tell me the same things I say in my sleep when he thinks I'm sleeping? I wonder. I'll probably never get to know. It doesn't matter, he's here with me. Though, this morning he's having a quiet conversation with himself while I sleep. "My sweet, beautiful, Sherry. I hope I deserve you. I hope I give myself to you as freely as you give yourself to me. I want to know everything your heart desires. I want to take care of you and give you everything. I've only ever loved you and I don't know what I'd do if you weren't with me. I never want to experience it again. My happiness, my love, my life." I absorb his words and the soft whisper he says them in, enjoying his possessive arms around me. He fills me with the love and confidence I need to be part of his world.

The damn alarm goes off and I smack the snooze button, but it'll only give me nine minutes. I pretend it never went off. Rick squeezes me and kisses my neck, then whispers in my ear, "Good morning, my queen. I love being here with you."

I roll toward him, squishing my naked breasts against his chest and put my arms around his neck. "Good morning, my king. I love you being here with me." I draw a line down his throat with my kisses. I feel his hard length on my leg. I reach for the alarm and turn it off. I grasp him and lightly stroke him with my hand, receiving a very happy response. I slide under the sheet and continue to run my hand up and down his length. I lick his tip, tasting the moisture there. I trail my tongue along his thickness and swirl around the tip as I suck him into my mouth. I take him all the way in my mouth, pulling my lips and tongue along his shaft.

"Babe, come to me so we can come together. I want to love you," he says as he sits up and pulls my lips to his. I grab his hard cock and slide it inside me. He's exquisite, filling me and stretching me. "I love the way you take control of my dick like it's yours. It is yours."

He moves inside me, pressing up into me. His arms holding my body to his and his lips claiming mine possessively. I feel the whisker burn on my face as we move together, slowly stroking and building the heat. His tongue hurried as it moves against mine. He needs this and he's trying to hold back. I run my fingers down his back and bite his neck hard right at the collarbone. "My body's yours, baby. Don't hold back."

He searches me with flames in his eyes, seeking permission. He lays me back on the bed as he begins to pound into me with need. Harder and harder, he slams into me over and over. Hard and fast and fucking amazing. Driving me to my own orgasm without any other contact, simply his hard love filling me again and again. I tighten around him, squeezing him and he continues with a few last hard strokes as he sends himself into oblivion with me. His face is red and he has perspiration on his temples. I reach for his mouth with mine and kiss him thoroughly as we both come down.

I smell the coffee brew and apparently so does he, "Want to walk over to the Yolk for breakfast with me before I go to the stadium?"

"For sure," I say as we both get out of bed and get dressed.

We walk to the Yolk and have a tasty breakfast with easy conversation. I love how he always holds my hand when we walk together and always sits on the same side of the table with me.

Walking back from the Yolk, Rick starts giving me information, "I need to be at the stadium by noon today. That's early for a Friday because I need to get a full work out in and I have some things to take care of at the stadium. I'd like you to be at the stadium in time for batting practice today. I had the membership team hold your seat for you, but I prefer when you sit behind home plate and I can hear you throughout the game. Can I bribe you because I know you have friends in your section you want to hang out with? I can get you all passes for early entry today, so you can all be in the park near the dugout for batting practice. Then you can hangout with them in the member lounge pregame before you come sit behind home plate. Also, any tips about your mom before I make reservations for lunch tomorrow?"

"You don't need to bribe me, my king. I'll be there for you and cheer for you. I promise, I'll be there yelling for you. But, Batting Practice might be cool and I'm sure my section peeps would appreciate it. They might forgive me for ditching them. Mom is pretty basic when it comes to food, she likes any place with salad options. Am I riding home from the game with you tonight?"

"Whatever you want, babe. You can drop me off and drive my car, so you can use my parking spot. There will be an envelope for you at will call."

I message all of my section peeps about meeting for early BP and try to get some work done, while Rick starts to unpack.

Rick walks up to me ready to go to the stadium, "Are you ready?"

"No, go and I'll meet you there before BP," I suggest, realizing I should've been paying attention to the time.

Rick puts his arms around me, "Okay, but be early for BP," as he gives me one of his unbelievable you-can-never-forget-me kisses. I reciprocate diving into his mouth with my tongue and moaning into his mouth with need. I don't want him to forget me and I want him punch drunk, exactly how he leaves me.

About 20 minutes later I get a text message from Rick.

Text from Rick - You drive me crazy. I'm walking into the clubhouse with a hard-on and I had sex pregame. I love you, my queen.

I love that I'm able to do that to him. I'm sure the team will enjoy some fun at Rick's expense over the hard-on.

Text to Rick - I love you, too. See you this afternoon, but can't wait to come home with you.

My phone rings and the caller ID says it's the stadium, "Hello?"

"Hi, this is Carter from the Seals. I'm looking for Sherry."

"This is Sherry. Is everything okay?" wondering what's up.

"Everything is fine. I'm a clubhouse assistant and Seno has given me some things to take care of for him today. I need some details from you, would that be okay?"

"Sure thing. What can I do?" wondering what he's up to now.

"I'm supposed to have a jersey made for your mom and need to know what size. While I'm at it, what size jersey do you wear and do you have a preference on cap styles? I also need your date of birth for your access card and do you know how many people will be joining you for BP today?" he rattles off questions.

"Mom wears a women's extra large. I wear women's large in jerseys and usually get a men's jersey. I prefer adjustable caps and don't mind snap-backs. My birthday is May 3 and give me a minute to get you a head count," I say trying to figure out who's going. I check through my messages to find out who can meet early for BP. "Ten people will be joining me," I tell him. He thanks me and asks me to have will call contact him when I get to the stadium. Rick really put him to work.

Since I already have the phone in my hand, I decide to dial up Mom and give her the plan for the weekend. "Hello?" Mom answers the phone.

"Hi, Mom! Thought I'd give you a call with the info for this weekend. How are you today?"

"Everything seems to be fine today. Is Rick the guy who was carrying you over his shoulder in that internet picture?" she asks.

"Yes, Mom. Rick is the only baseball player and the

only man in my life. You have a room at the Brighton for Saturday night and we have a reservation at the spa Sunday morning."

"I guess I do need to meet this guy. He said he loves you and he's not letting you go," Mom recounts.

"I know, Mom. I was there listening when you went along with him after telling me no." I point out the part of the conversation that irritated me.

"Okay, so what's the plan?" Mom asks.

"When you drive down tomorrow go straight to the Brighton. They'll let you check-in and park your vehicle there. Your reservation has an early check in for Saturday and a late check-out on Sunday. Everything is already paid for including valet parking. We will pick you up to go to lunch." I give her instructions and hope she listens.

"Where are we going to lunch?"

"No idea. Rick is handling that part himself. When he says he wants to take you out, he means it. He picks the place and everything. He does the same thing on date nights," I say and giggle. I like how he plans it all out and I'm along for the ride.

"That worries me. He's controlling," Mom frets.

"He's not controlling, but he has certain things that are just him. It's kind of nice to get in the car and let him have everything planned. You have to meet him," I say gushing.

"I thought you were giving it time or something? What's the current standing?" she wants details.

"You need to meet him, Mom. I love him. I'll give you the details in person tomorrow. Rick said he's getting a reservation for 11:30 lunch, so we'll pick you up about 11:10." I can hear her deciding she should back out, so I get off the phone quickly.

"I don't know..." and I cut her off.

"I've got to pick up another call that's coming in. See you in the morning," and I hang up.

I get ready for the game, and head to the trolley station feeling like a million bucks. Happy to be treating my baseball peeps to early BP and amazed at the man who's making the unnecessary bribe happen. I love how he wants me there early and behind the plate for the game, for him. I should be upset he's choosing my seat, but it's all about supporting him, and it's like being at the game with him. He wants me there. I never thought this would happen. He wants me there. He wants me cheering for him. He needs me.

The trolley gives me too much time to myself. Yes it's public transportation, smells like pee and/or barf at any given moment, could have transients wandering through, and it's still the best way to get to the stadium. It evokes baseball for me. It's part of my game process. It's all part of the event. Getting to the park. Getting stadium food. Getting to my seat in time to watch my guys warm up. Today I'm trying to enjoy the ride and take in the beautiful San Diego coast route on the green line. It's changed so much over the years. The Wyland artwork on the building near Little Italy is still there, but you can't see it with the new building built next to it blocking the way. The juxtaposition of the Tuscan accented apartments followed by the contemporary art and then the Spanish details of the Santa Fe Depot, it's San Diego defined. The trolley stops have been refurbished and even the lines have changed to be more accommodating. New public park areas have popped up a few places along the green line. No matter how I try to distract myself, my head is filled with my team and the way it's being stripped naked of the players we all cheer for. It's an annual thing, the trade deadline. And, it's bittersweet. Sad to watch deals that get our favorites traded, but I always look forward to the rookies coming up. Most years that's in September when its time for the expanded roster and the teams bring up guys to give them a taste of the big leagues. This year, it's happening in July. Because, well... trades gutted us. It's the right thing in the long run. There's no telling how the next three seasons go. Games could be a disaster. It's horrible! Everything's in my head as I walk up to the stadium and the organist is playing "Yesterday" by the Beatles. Couldn't be more right on. Trade Seno and it could gut me, too.

I walk up to the will call window and ask them to let Carter know I'm here. After a few minutes, a short bald man walks up to me with his hands full.

"Hi, Sherry? I'm Carter," he introduces himself.

"Hi! You need help," I observe.

"Only when one of the guys assigns me on a mission and today it was Seno," he laughs. "Okay, so here's your access card. It doesn't give you free rein of the stadium, but it does give you access when employees have access and it does allow you access to the players parking lot when you're driving the registered vehicle, Rick's Challenger."

The photo on the access card is cropped from one of the selfie pictures Rick took in Colorado. He kept them with him. It makes my heart warm. I'm such a freaking girl. I'm never going to understand how he has this effect on me. I've never gotten gooey over any man.

Carter continues, "This is your Mom's jersey for tomorrow." He holds up the extra large women's jersey already personalized with SENO and the big 6. The regular team uniform the team will be wearing tomorrow. "This is your full set of jerseys. Seno wanted you to have the jersey to match the team for every game, so here is the regular team jersey, the alternate jersey, the Sunday jersey, the away jersey and the matching caps." He trades me the jersey and cap I have on for the alternate jersey and matching cap. Everything of course with the big 6 and SENO emboldened across it.

"Are you kidding me?" I'm ecstatically happy. My fandom is showing.

Carter smiles at me, "You really are a fan. You two are a perfect match. I do see a wardrobe problem. I'll get that fixed and leave everything in Seno's car. You're early for BP, do you have names? I can leave passes for your guests at will call."

I give Carter the names and send them all a quick text. He gives a note to somebody at the will call booth and directs me to follow him into the stadium. He takes me into the belly of the stadium to a room with all kinds of uniforms and things the team wear. He pulls out the matching hoodies for each jersey, handing me the one for tonight's game. Oh my god! I'm spoiled! I'm having a hard time maintaining myself.

"Let me take you to Seno and he'll escort you to BP."

Is this really happening right now? Trying to maintain myself and not let my total fan freak-out show. Carter is leading me through the stadium, up to the field and into the dugout. He yells into the clubhouse, "Seno!"

A few seconds later Rick comes walking up the stairs into the dugout and he's heading straight for me with a purpose. The only people in sight are the grounds crew setting up for BP. Then it happened, a repeat of our first kiss in the corner of the booth at the Locale. No words, his lips on mine. Claiming me all the way to my toes with his intent and lighting me up like an erupting volcano. Damn!

As much as I don't like how he makes me girly, I hope this never stops.

The team starts to come out for BP and Cross starts in, "Dude, you better stop that shit. I know she's hot and spunky, but you'll be hitting BP with a hard-on and I've already seen too much of your dick today," laughing under his breath. Martin follows close behind him making smooching sounds at us.

Rick gives him a dirty look and realizes BP is starting. He walks me to my acceptable viewing area behind the dugout and introduces himself to all my peeps before he gets to work. Carter hooked my peeps up with caps that have Seno and the number 6 on them. Everybody loved it! Cross came up and gave autographs with Seno after BP. It was great!

After BP, my peeps and I all go to the lounge for $5 beer and free popcorn. Six "thank you" beers is too many, but I take them and drink them all. My baseball peeps are the best.

I find my seat behind home plate in time for the guys to come out and warm up. I'm in row two directly behind home plate tonight. I'm loopy from the beer. Rick waves at me and smiles when he comes out early to warm up our starting pitcher. Lots of hoopla going on pregame tonight and I'm not into it in my current state. I may need another beer. Luckily this section has seat service and I'm riding home with my boyfriend. Then it hits me, this is my first game back after leaving LA. The last couple of days have been amazing and so much has happened so quickly. What the fuck am I doing? Am I dating, no, living with a baseball player who I left only weeks ago? And, he's meeting my Mom tomorrow! What am I thinking? This has disaster written all over it. This whirlwind of craziness is getting the best of me and I need to take control. No more following my girliness allowed! My brain is trying to take over and I can't let that happen. This isn't a brain situation. It's a heart situation and I'm learning that's ruled by my girliness. It may be the most illogical thing I've ever done in my life, but it makes me happy and I'm risking my heart, not my brain. Maybe I shouldn't have any more beer.

A large choir walks onto the field and sings the National Anthem. The next thing I know Rick is standing at the net in front of me, smiling at me, and making motions at me like I'm drunk. I might be. I wave, smile, and do the sign language "I love you" back at him. Yelling, "Make it a win, babe!" He laughs and shakes his head as he turns around to get down to business.

The lineup is familiar other than they've squeezed Mason in. We're playing the hated San Francisco Sissy's this weekend. We need to get some wins and a sweep would be a great thing. Our ace is pitching tonight, so the game will probably go quick. The first five innings go by with no score for either team. Two of our players have been hit by a pitch, both Rock and Mason. The team is acting restless and defensive. They want to retaliate and are trying to keep a collective cool. Skip doesn't allow that crap in his dugout. Top of the sixth inning with two outs and our pitcher, Grace the Ace, lets one rip that gets away from him high and inside, skimming the edge of the hitter's helmet brim. The San Francisco dugout empties onto the field after our pitcher. Rick runs to get ahead of it and guard his pitcher. The rest of the guys on the field are there almost instantly as back up and the Seals dugout empties. Cross is at Rick's back with Mason ready to go. It's a rumble, except only hot muscular ball players are allowed to participate. Half of them know they're not supposed to fight while the other half are hooligans who don't care and want to fight—the San Francisco half. Rick has his game face on and takes control of the situation. A couple of the San Francisco guys go at him with fists ready to go, but he calmly says something I can't hear. The umpires take forever to get out there and do anything.

The hitter takes his base, daring Grace to throw at him again. "Throw at me again, meat, and I'm coming for you."

The umpire gives both teams a warning, and the next guy up strikes out. Bottom of the sixth was uneventful, we got a couple of hits but nobody scored. Bottom of the eighth, still no score with one out and Mason hits a home run bringing in Cross. Martin strikes out and Rock pops out. Top of the ninth, San Francisco responds with a homer and two hits. The runners attempt to steal and Rick picks the runner off trying to steal second base, ending the game with a 2-1 win for the Seals.

Hannah is on the field ready to do her thing. She grabs Mason and Seno for her post-game interviews. Seno tells her it's all the new rookie Mason and backs off, not wanting to get into an interview about the potential fight and what he did to avoid it.

Rick walks up to the net behind home plate and I hop over the seats into the first row to meet him. He puts his hands on the net and I reach mine up to his, holding hands through the net. "I'll be ready in about twenty minutes." I smile and nod as he takes off for the locker room. I wait for the crowd to clear and go to the elevator, using my card to get to the garage. I find Rick's car and climb into the front seat. The bench seat is comfortable and I'm buzzed. Rick finds me sleeping in his front seat and he's annoyed. "I couldn't find you and you're asleep in my car. I looked out here and didn't see you." I say something though I have no clue what came out of my mouth. "Never mind, let's go home buzzed girl." He climbs into the car and I use him as my pillow for the ride home.

I wake up and I'm being carried over Rick's shoulder into the elevator. "You can put me down in the elevator," he might want some elevator action.

"No. I'm not putting you down until we're home," he says in a tone I'm not familiar with.

"Are you okay?" I ask unsure.

"I am now. I couldn't find you and it reminded me that you know how to hide from me." His brain is playing games with his heart.

"I'm right here and I'm not going anywhere. Remember? You moved into my place and made it our place. You don't need to worry. If you want to worry about something, it'd be how to get rid of me."

"Don't even joke. I don't want you to ever leave," he says seriously and sets me down so he can put his arms around me and kiss me senseless. We get home and he unlocks the door, locks it behind us and takes me to bed.

Rick holds me close, whispering in my ear, "I love you, Sherry. You're my only. Never leave me." He kisses me softly, then again tenderly, but not stopping. His lips on mine sweetly, sucking and nibbling at me like I'm his favorite dessert. He keeps kissing me while I kick off my sneakers and he pushes my jeans off. He can't help himself. I know what he's feeling now. He needs to feel me and know I'm here, we're here together. I reach to help him with his pants, but they're already gone. He continues kissing me with need and takes me as his slowly. Pushing into me all the way, his body relaxes when he's finally home. He lays his head on my pillow next to mine, his weight delicious on top of me.

I put my arms around him, "I'm yours, Rick. I'm not going anywhere, unless I'm going there with you. There's no one else for me. I love you, my king," in the sweetest voice I've ever heard come out of me. Still don't have a clue where it came from.

He turns to me, with the biggest grin ever and his lips are back on mine while he makes love to me for hours, never taking his lips off of me and sending me to unknown places more than once.

CHAPTER FIVE

I wake up early, nervous about the two most important people in my life meeting and go for the always soothing frosted chocolate mini donuts. I inhale almost half a bag of the heavenly bites and climb back in bed quietly hoping I wasn't missed.

Rick reaches for me, "Where'd you go?" as he pulls me to him and puts his lips on mine. He licks my lips and sucks my tongue into his mouth with a low groan. "Were you eating chocolate?"

"Mini frosted chocolate donuts," I confess. "Do you want one?" I offer as I pick up the bag I had dropped at the side of the bed for easy access. He takes three from the bag and I pop another one in my mouth before they all disappear.

"Why are you up so early?" he says with his mouth full.

"Not sure. Maybe I'm nervous about you meeting Mom," I say knowing that's exactly the problem.

"No reason to worry. Your Mom will love me. I promise. Mom's always like me." He says with confidence.

"You don't know my Mom."

"All your Mom wants is for you to be happy and if that means there's a man involved, he better treat you right. I already told her I love you and I'm not letting you go." He stops. He looks at me seriously, gazing into my eyes. "I mean it. I love you and I'm never letting you go," he says realizing I may need to hear it. He kisses me and makes me feel like the only woman in the world.

I smell the coffee calling me, get two cups and take them back to bed with me, along with my laptop. Rick looks at me appreciatively and frowns, "Laptop in bed?"

"I want to do a quick email and social media check. Same as almost every other day, but I want to stay in bed with you, too," I smile and gesture to my still mostly naked body. "I have to keep up on business and I did share my donuts with you." Rick groans at me. "You'd prefer I did it somewhere else? I can take it in the other room."

"No," as he puts his hand around my ass and snuggles up against me. "You don't need to worry about that stuff. I'll cover everything for you. I want to take care of you."

I ignore him because I don't work that way. I need to be able to take care of myself. I'm independent and don't want to answer to anyone about what I do with my money.

I check my messages, email and social media. I have a few texts, some emails and a new social media post. One of my customers posted pictures of the trip they're on right now on my page and tagged all their friends—I love it! I read my texts:

Text from Sam – Tell me everything is okay. Rick didn't call me.

Text from Adam - I'm in San Diego for work this week-end. I'm hoping you've gotten over your boyfriend and would like to spend some time with me.

Text from Mom – I packed my bag and I'm getting ready to leave. Not sure about this, but I want to see you. I'll be at the hotel waiting when you get there.

Oh, crap! A text from Adam. I thought, okay, maybe hoped he'd given up on me. I can't hide it. No secrets. "You didn't call Sam!" I tell Rick and hand him his phone.

Text to Mom - See you soon, Mom! You'll see every-thing is perfect. Love you!

Text to Adam - Sorry, I'm back with my boyfriend. He's the only one for me.

I debate with myself, remembering what my Mom taught me about keeping things to myself that just hurt people. When another text pops through.

Text from Adam - I'd never hurt you like he did. Give me a chance, my Angel.

Text to Adam - Goodbye.

I immediately block Adam, so the messages don't continue and he doesn't decide to call. It would be bad and escalate quickly.

The spam meter on my email is going crazy this morn-ing, so I take a minute to go through and delete the junk mail.

I turn to Rick, take his phone and dial Sam because he hasn't managed to do it yet. She answers, "It's about time baby brother!"

"Hi, Sam," I say with a giggle. "I told him to call and I handed him his phone and he still didn't do it. So, you've got me instead. I can hand him the phone if you want."

Rick closes his eyes and shakes his head, "Why did I introduce you two?"

"I can hear him in the background and that verifies he's alive. I did watch the game last night and I could see he's back in playing form. That's good enough. But, I'd like to know what's going on there," Sam says still worried.

I'm not the one who should tell her he moved in with me. I mouth a question at him silently, "Are you going to tell her you moved in with me?"

"You tell her," he says out load where Sam could hear him.

"I've been directed to tell you that your bro moved in with me and we're together and I love him. And, if I'm the one who's going to talk to you then I'm waiting until he isn't here watching and listening to me do it." Rick takes his phone from me.

"Hey Sam," Rick says apparently not approving of the direction I was taking the call. "I'm meeting her Mom today and it's a busy day. I'm good, actually I'm better than good. I'll call you soon," and he hangs up wanting to use the time we have left this morning in a specific way. But, I stop him because I need to tell him about Adam.

Here I am needing to tell him something I thought wasn't going to matter. Maybe I should've told him about Adam before he moved in or when we were telling secrets. I don't know. But, I need to tell him before he finds out on his own. I didn't think it mattered. I'm not ever going to see the guy again. Honestly, I thought he was gone. He hasn't texted me in days and he has a busy schedule. Hot as he is, why would he waste time with a girl who's hung up on another man?

"Um, I need to talk to you about something."

Rick stops and stares at me, unsure of my tone. "Okay. What kind of something?" He already doesn't like the conversation.

"It's not bad, just filling you in on details you missed while we were apart." Realizing this is almost the worst possible timing, but it can't wait.

"Sherry, I don't think I like where this is going."

"I'm sure you won't, but listen to me for a minute. I met a guy when I was drunk in a bar in LA. I didn't have sex with him or anything. We had dinner at a cafe. We danced together at the bar and he kissed me, but I left. I didn't give him my number and he doesn't even know my name. I was extremely upset at the time, honestly hating men."

"Yea. Keep going." Rick is not happy and trying to stay calm.

"He got my number from Joey when he saw him at the bar the next night and started texting me, calling me daily while I was on my road trip. He kept telling me he wanted to spend time with me and I kept telling him I wasn't interested, that I was still getting over my boyfriend. I know you don't want to hear that, and I found I couldn't get over you. He was in San Francisco when I was driving through there and met me for dinner. He told me it wasn't a date, but it was like a date. We didn't kiss or anything. It was only dinner and I kept going on my trip." I stop trying to read his reaction.

"Is there more?"

"He drove up the coast and met me at my hotel one

morning. He took me to breakfast and explored a beach area with me one day. He asked for more. He asked me to spend the weekend with him at his place in San Francisco. He kissed me. I turned him down and he dropped me off at my hotel. That's it other than a couple calls and texts while I was driving home. I told him somebody else has my heart."

"But? Why are you telling me this now?"

"He texted me this morning and he's in San Diego for work and asked me out. I told him I'm with my boyfriend and I blocked him. I can show you the texts. I'm not interested in him at all. I thought I needed to get over you. I thought you were with Ava. He was a distraction." I pull up the texts on my phone and show Rick before he can say he wants to see it or not. I don't want him having any questions. "He never meant anything to me. I've only ever loved you, my king. I don't want to hide it from you. I figure it's better to tell you about a text from a guy than to let you find it."

He takes a deep breath. "Thank you for telling me. We were both hurting and I know you were confused. Shit, Ava was naked in our room. I don't like it. I hate the thought of another man touching you, kissing you, wanting you," his anger showing.

"None of it matters. We're here together now and we'll always be together. I didn't want him. I only want you. Believe me, trust me. I thought we were over."

Rick pulls me close, his voice low and shaky, "I know, my queen. I was afraid we were over, too. I didn't know what to do without you. I couldn't find you. I needed to know you were safe. I was worried about you being on the road trip alone and I didn't know where you were. I wanted to leave the team to go search for you. A part of me was missing. I couldn't sleep. All I could do was think about you. I hate how this guy was persistent and he's still trying. Where is he? Give me his number."

"I've already handled it. I have no idea where he is and I've already blocked him. I'm sure that's the end of it. I'm sorry. He's nothing."

Rick grins, trying hard to get over it quick, "Now, where were we…"

Text from Sam - You horndogs!

But, I can't respond because Rick has his arms around me and is claiming me with his lips. I'm not complaining. It's amazing and much better than him dwelling on Adam. Win-win. I wrap my legs around him as he carries me with him to the shower. He turns on the shower and turns his back to the cold water, keeping me warm. Slowly kissing me. I taste the chocolate and coffee on his lips. I run my fingers through his hair and feel his hard body against mine. His muscles holding me up like I'm nothing. I want him badly. His abs against me and the occasional bump of his penis near my sex increase my desire. His hands roam my body and his touch draws me into his world. I hear words around me and don't recognize that they're coming from my own mouth. "I need you. I've always loved you. I'll always be yours. Please take me now. I need your love. I need you to need me." I kiss every part of him I can reach and dig my fingers into his muscled shoulders. It's happening and I don't know where it's coming from. My need has taken control of my actions. My words affecting him.

"I'm crazy for you. I take good care of things that are mine," he says as he slides me down his body and leans me on the shower wall. He spreads my legs with his and drops to his catcher's squat. He puts his hands on my hips and runs them down my thighs as he moves closer, kissing my legs, and up my thighs. He feels my wet heat and touches my folds with his fingers, sliding one in. He latches onto my clit with his mouth, sucking and licking me until I move my hips. He has to have me. He stands up and lifts me to his body, sliding me onto his hard length exquisitely while he holds me tight to his wet body. "You're mine," he says as he repeatedly slides in and out of me. His body quivering as he pushes hard up into me and I scream out his name. The feel of him inside me, touching me, is beyond sensational. I close my eyes and see fireworks. All I can hear is our heartbeats. It hits me all at once like a rocket. I shudder and shake uncontrollably, calling out his name over and over. He follows almost immediately and presses tightly against me. We stay there pressed together against the wall, not wanting to separate and making this time together last as long as it can.

Eventually the day must get started. We have plans today. We use the shower for what its intended and get dressed for lunch. I pull on my jeans and my "Talk Baseball To Me" top, prepared to put my jersey on over it for the game. Rick dresses in jeans and he looks so good, I want to eat him up! Can I keep him like this and always have him walking around in jeans and no shirt please? He pulls on a gray long sleeved button up shirt with bright blue flecks in the material from the closet and rolls the sleeves up. The flecks make his eyes shine. The only thing sexier is when he's in full catcher's gear and his eyes pierce through his mask.

"You're beautiful, babe. Are you ready to go?" He asks smiling.

"Almost," I finish brushing out my hair and grab my game bag, so I'm ready. He locks the door behind me as we make our way to the elevator.

Rick and I hop into his car to go pick up Mom and I remember I'll be driving his car around this afternoon. I pay attention in case there's something quirky. He pulls me over next to him and rests his hand on my knee when he isn't shifting. I'm starting to understand the attraction of the bench seats. We drive to the hotel and pull up in front to find Mom sitting on the bench outside. She won't recognize the car, so I get out of the car to meet her.

"Hi, Mom!" as I give her a big hug. I turn to lead her back to the car, but Rick followed me and he's standing right behind me. I turn to him and he sees my nerves. He slides his arm around me and gives me a peck on the cheek. "Mom, this is Rick Seno."

Rick reaches for her hand, "It's a pleasure to meet you, ma'am. Your daughter is wonderful."

"Its good to meet you, too," Mom is unsure about Rick. "You didn't have to go to this trouble for me, sweetie. This place is too nice," as she looks at me.

"Rick said to pick some place you'd like and he covered everything," I look at him and smile proudly.

"Ladies, please allow me to take you out to lunch," he gestures to his car. I climb in the front seat and scoot to the middle, leaving room for Mom. Rick holds the door until we are both set before he walks around and climbs into the driver's seat. He pulls out of the Brighton and drives down Harbor, passing the Maritime Museum and turning toward the airport on the way to Shelter Island. We park at a Polynesian building and he walks around to open the car door for Mom and I. He chose another tropical themed restaurant with a view. He grasps my hand and entwines our fingers as we walk to the restaurant. "I think you ladies will like this place. They have a great salad menu and a mini buffet. It's all Hawaiian inspired." He smiles at me as he says Hawaiian. We walk into the restaurant and they seat us immediately at the table with the best view of the bay. Rick sitting next to me as always.

"This is a nice view. I've never been here," Mom trying to make small talk and not successfully, but I appreciate the attempt.

We order and I comment, "I love the Hawaiian thing they have going on here and the buffet looks so tropical. I want to try everything." Rick gives me a squeeze.

"I appreciate you driving down, ma'am. It means a lot to me that you're willing to go to my game tonight. I know you're not a Seals fan and I'd like to eventually convert you to the Seals from LA," Rick hopes to get Mom talking.

"I always take advantage of time with Sherry and if she's spending time with you, then I need to meet you," Mom lays it out there. She's been negative about men for as long as I can remember. I've always assumed it's because my dad ditched us, but she's never said anything about it.

"Mom, I love Rick and he's moving in with me. He's not like the other guys and he's not what you think when you think baseball player. He's a fabulous catcher on the field and only my man off the field."

Mom stops and looks at me, then at Rick. "You both look happy. I'm happy if my daughter is happy. I don't want Sherry hurt. What do you mean when you say you're not letting her go?" Mom says glaring at Rick.

Rick gets a big grin and says, "I mean that I want to be with her always, I hope someday she'll allow me the privilege of making her mine. I'll do whatever it takes to make her happy and keep her that way. I never want to be away from her again." He looks to Mom for her reaction to his honesty.

"This all seems so fast to me and I know Sherry needed time. I'm not sure what to think," Mom shows her concern.

"I was wrong and shouldn't have left him in LA. I freaked out..." and Rick cuts me off.

"We both handled the situation poorly and the time we were apart taught both of us how much we want to be together," Rick refuses for it to be my fault.

"True," I chime in.

"Rick, please call me Shar. My daughter can be difficult. I'll be happy to go to your game tonight and we'll see from there."

"Thank you, Shar," Rick keeps a positive conversation going.

We eat and overall I'm maintaining myself, no freakouts. Though I was in my own world there for a bit when Rick was telling Mom what he meant by not letting me go. I'm not complaining in any way, shape or form, but what a time to be smacked in the face with a huge reality check. Does he really want us to be permanent? Partners? ... Married? He's moving in with me and we're sharing a closet and an address, not just a bed. Is this my life? How did this happen? I don't chase baseball players! Then again, he didn't want to be a baseball player with me and I made it okay for him to be a baseball player. Talk about fucking confusing! People think women are crazy and mixed up, they should try a big league baseball player sometime. Warrior on the field of battle. Calling the shots on the field. Doesn't want to be that person unless he's on the field. Needs me. (Okay, rant within a rant... He needs me? It makes me so happy that he needs me, but really? He needs me? I'm seven years older than him. I'm not always easy to deal with. I'm independent. He wants to pay my way for everything, he doesn't think its necessary for me to work, and I can't imagine allowing anyone to pay my way and not being in control of my own everything, well except sex maybe. Yes, definitely sex. He is the king, that's not just a cute pet name. And, he needs me! More than that, he loves me.) With me, he wants to be that person. For me, he wants to be that person. My personal warrior. My professional baseball player. My king. Focus Sherry!

"I need to get to work, ladies." He pays and we take his car to the stadium. He pulls into the player's garage and parks the car. Rick gets out of the car and pulls me out the driver side with him, handing me his car keys and pressing his lips to mine, lightly sucking on my lower lip in the process. He whispers in my ear, "I love you, baby. I wanted my hands on you all through lunch and it's killing me. I know that's silly, I was sitting right next to you." He claims me with his mouth, sending electrical shocks through my body. "Go, your Mom's in the car. Her jersey is in the back-seat. Have fun with your Mom and I'll see you pregame, my queen." He plants one of his there-is-no-way-you-can-ever-forget-me kisses on me and waves as he disappears into the stadium. I get into the driver's seat and start up the car.

"Are you sure you should drive after that?" Mom says laughing. "Seriously, you look like you're in a daze, flushed."

I laugh, "He always leaves me punch drunk. He's so sweet though, Mom. The words that man whispers in my ear, I can't even explain. I don't know how to handle his request to take care of me. I've always taken care of myself."

We take off out of the garage and head out shopping for a couple of hours. I'm enjoying his Challenger, the stick and the rumble of the engine. Very much like him.

Mom and I have pleasant conversation all afternoon. She actually offers helpful advice and tells me I'm an adult and need to do what's right for me.

"So, to recap, he lets you drive his custom car, he wants to cover all of your expenses, he wants to live with you at your place, he's not interested in other women at all, he's a big league baseball player, kisses like sin and probably does other things just as well or better, and he's solid muscle. Not to mention he wants to keep you and I believe him when he says he loves you. It's written all over his face."

"Does that mean you'll wear a Seno jersey tonight? He had jerseys made for both of us to match the uniform the team is wearing tonight."

"Absolutely, but I'm still an LA fan," Mom smiles.

"Fair enough, for now!" We pull up to the stadium and I flash my access card, so I can park in the player's garage. We park and I get our jerseys and my game bag out of the car. We enter the stadium and walk to the section behind home plate where our seats are.

Text from Rick - Order whatever you want, your seat is permanently set up to charge my account. Love you, babe!

Text to Rick - You don't need to do that. I can handle my own. Mom agreed to wear your jersey. Make it a win! Love you, too... My king!

Text from Rick - I don't need to, I want to. I know you can take care of yourself, but you shouldn't have to. I want to take care of you, my queen.

Text from Rick - Buy your Mom some popcorn and a beer or something.

My mind goes dirty and I reply.

Text to Rick - What else do you want? Exactly how do you want it?

But, no reply and he walks out onto the field.

"There's Rick, Mom." I say pointing to the hottest man ever in full catcher's gear. "How do you like the seats?"

"He moves with a different attitude on the field, doesn't he?" witnessing his intensity. "These seats are nice, but too expensive. Is this where you usually sit?"

"My normal seat is over there, field level down the first base line. Rick gets me a seat behind home plate because he likes to hear me cheering for him and he can make faces at me from this distance. He's serious out there. He wants to make it a win every game, less than that is unacceptable."

"I can see that. He makes his mind up and does it. Determined. Good qualities," Mom shares her insight.

CHAPTER SIX

The team is out stretching and warming up. A marching band marches across the field and plays the National Anthem, and it's time to play ball! Rick walks out and gets in position behind home plate, throwing the ball to the pitcher a few times and around the infield as San Francisco's first hitter swings a bat in the on deck circle.

The Seals score first in the bottom of the third inning with Mason hitting a home run. Bottom of the fourth the score is still 1-0 Seals with two outs and runners on first and second. Seno is up to bat and the runners are Cross and Martin. Martin has a huge lead off of first base and nobody is holding Cross at second base. The first pitch to Seno and the runners go on the pitcher's release, a called ball that's probably a strike. Both runners safe at second and third. I yell out, "That's it boys! Steal'm! Wooooo!" and Rick glances at me. "Let's go Seno! Yeah baby! Knock it out! Wooooo! Bring those boys in!" Pitch two is called a strike. This umpire is making bad calls at the plate. Pitch three Seno swings because who knows what the umpire will call it, he connects and breaks his bat. There's a loud crack. Rick runs and the ball chops through the infield over the head of the first baseman all the way to the corner where it rattles around long enough for Rick to get to third, and Cross and Martin to score! 3-0 Seals. Rick is celebrating at third clapping his hands in a manly way. The next hitter comes up and pops out, leaving Seno at third.

The game is going smooth and is still a shut out at the end of the sixth inning. I make a quick run to the bathroom before the seventh inning stretch, and get back to my seat in time to stand up and sing "Take Me Out To The Ballgame" with Mom, swaying together and singing out. I love that Mom is a baseball fan, even if she does root for the wrong team.

The rest of the game was fairly uneventful. Our pitcher in good form, followed Rick's calls and pitched a complete game. Rick and Martin both got base hits, but nobody pushed them around to score. Final score was 3-0 Seals.

Hannah grabbed the pitcher for the on field interview and they talked about pitching a complete game. The pitcher tonight was brought up a couple weeks ago and this was his first start. We will be seeing more of Rhett Clay, he isn't going anywhere.

Rick turns to me, "I'll be at the car in twenty." He winks at me and takes off into the dugout.

"He's a hoot." My Mom turns to me, "Very attentive and doesn't seem to notice other women at all."

"Yeah, in Colorado he called me down to the dugout after the win and pulled me into the dugout to kiss me. He can be crazy!" I tell Mom as I remember his mother's words from later that evening.

"It's fun. I understand what you mean about needing to

meet him. You've both gotten lucky finding each other." Slightly shocked at my Mom's words, I smile and she hugs me with approval.

The crowd clears and I lead Mom to the elevator, using my access card to get to the player's garage. We slide into the front seat of Rick's Challenger and watch as a few of the other players walk out to their cars. Rick wears more gear as catcher and always takes a few minutes longer. We chat about going to breakfast before the spa and how early it'll need to be. Rick walks up to the car and sits down in the driver seat. He leans in and kisses me on the cheek, then looks to Mom "I hope you enjoyed the game, Shar."

My Mom actually smiles at Rick, "Very much. The seats were great. Thank you. You call a good game, Rick. Of course, I always like to see San Francisco lose."

I'm a bit shook, sitting between them and listening to the conversation go on around me. This is my Mom, right? While I sit in shock, they decide we should call it a night and start early the next morning. Rick pulls up to the Brighton and hops out of the car to open the door for Mom. "I appreciate you. I wouldn't have Sherry without you. Thank you." Rick hugs my Mom and she hugs him back. This isn't my Mom. When was she replaced with a look-alike?

"I can see you are good to her and you both love each other." Again, I can't say this enough... Who kidnapped my Mom and replaced her with this sweet woman that looks like her? Why isn't she freaking out about us moving in together? Shacking up? Him being controlling or some-thing? Going off about carrying me through a hotel lobby over his shoulder? She leans down to look in the car, "I'll meet you in the morning, Sherry," and she walks off into the hotel.

Rick gets back into the car and immediately puts his arm around me, pulling me close and kissing me like a fool. His hand moving up my thigh. He rolls the windows up and whispers in my ear, "This was a good day, but it's driving me crazy not having you around me right now. Let's go home, my queen."

Rick strokes my thigh the whole drive home and I sit against him with my head on his shoulder. It's amazing how much this man loves me and needs me. I have no doubt.

We park at our complex and Rick kisses me sweetly on the lips like when he's going to offer me a hand out of the car, but the kiss pushes him further. He's on top of me and we're making out on the front bench seat of his car. His thigh rubs against my happy places as he let's out a hot heavy sigh at my ear, stopping to kiss and nibble there. He's back to my mouth, sucking on my lower lip, biting and tugging at it gently. He slides his tongue into my mouth to dance with mine and I suck on it until he moans, as our bodies continue to rub on each other. "We could take this to the bedroom, my king," I suggest aware the chances we make it from the elevator are minimal.

He focuses, "Yeah, you're right." It takes him a few moments to clear his head enough to move on.

We get in the elevator and I simply say, "We're on the elevator. Anything you want to do here, on the elevator, my king?" Using my sweet, sexy, seductive voice. Rick lets out a groan that sounds more like a lion's roar, I pull the elevator stop and I'm instantly pinned to the elevator wall by his hard muscled body. "Oh yeah, my king. Show me what you want." He unbuttons his jeans and releases his hard wanting desire. He pulls my pants completely off of me and holds me up so my lips can touch his. I wrap my legs around him drawing another roar as he slides me slowly down his hard body onto his rock solid cock. I cry out as he slides in and fills me lusciously. I climb him with my arms around his neck, unable to help myself I bite at his neck and collarbone as I move on him, stroking him with my hot wet sex.

"Oh fuck, you're perfect, my queen." We move together, meeting each other's effort.

I hold on to him tight and lick his neck, kissing and sucking. I hear sexy little noises and realize the needy whimper is coming from me. I want more of him. I want all of him. I whisper in his ear, "Don't you want to bend me over? Take me hard? Fuck me senseless? My king should get what he wants."

A growl comes from within Rick and he strokes up into me hard, biting at any part of me he can reach. He lifts me up over him and licks at my hot folds, biting and sucking at my sensitive nub until I shake with pleasure. He slides me down his body and flips my back to him, holding me tightly against him. His pulse racing, his heart beating, and his cock wanting attention. Rick whispers in my ear, "Let's play a game, my queen. Every time I say something, you say "Yes, please, my king." How does that sound?"

"Yes, please, my king," I respond instantly and he gets harder.

"Good girl. Would you like me to bend you over and fuck you hard, my queen?"

This could get interesting, "Yes, please, my king." Rick bends me over quickly, holding his dick in his right hand and placing his left hand at the curve of my ass. He slides in hard and fast. Pounding into me repeatedly.

"Harder, my queen?"

"Yes, please, my king." I hear his low groan at my response.

"Do you want more, my queen?"

"Yes, please, my king." He's fucking amazing and I can hardly speak.

Rick leans over me and gathers my hair in his hand gently to pull my head back to him. He breathes heavy and hot at my ear, nibbling at my lobe. The solid muscles of his body against me, rubbing against my ass as he strokes into me. He kisses my neck and his whole attitude changes. "Nobody has ever felt like you, my queen. Do you only want me, my queen?"

"Yes, please, my king," I should answer differently, but I don't know where he's going with this and this game came with instructions.

"Never be with anyone else, my queen."

"Yes, please, my king."

"May I love you forever, my queen?"

"Yes, please, my king."

"Never leave me, my queen."

"Yes, please, my king."

"I will make you mine someday, my queen."

"Yes, please, my king." I hear a noise and I'm reminded we're still in the elevator. "My king, we're on the elevator," wondering if he's lost track.

"Do you want me to grab you by your seductive hips, and finish inside you?"

"Yes, please, my king." He does exactly that. He grips my hips and digs his fingers in like he doesn't plan to let go.

Rick leans against the carpeted elevator wall and pulls me back against him. Smacking my ass against him hard with every stroke. "Is this want you want, my queen?"

"Yes, please, my king. Harder." I break the rules.

Rick slams me harder, "That's breaking the rules. Do you deserve to be spanked?"

"Yes, please, my king." He stiffens and raises his hand, but he lightly pats my ass and squeezes my cheeks. He'd never hurt me. "I love you, my king. It'll always only be you. Hold me, love me, kiss me, fuck me. Only your hands will touch me. Only your cock will have me. I know how much you love me and the pleasure you give me is unlike any other." My words go straight to his heart. He caresses my body lovingly, then grabs hold of my hips and slams into me over and over and over, sending us both over the edge.

He reaches around my waist and pulls me back to him, his lips at my ear, "I will love you forever, my queen. Now, pull your pants on so we can go home and I can love you properly."

"Yes, please, my king."

CHAPTER SEVEN

I wake up the next morning with Rick wrapped around me, the same way I fell asleep. I'm loved, cherished and protected. The alarm hasn't buzzed yet and I don't smell any coffee brewing. It's an early morning for both of us since I'm meeting Mom for breakfast before our spa time and Rick has early practice before the 1:40 game today. I lay in silence and enjoy his arms around me, but my head is anything but quiet.

The last few days, the last week... let's face it, in the last two months my life, my whole world has been turned upside down. I guess that's not quite right. My world has been shaken loose and invaded, but somehow that's a good thing. I need to admit the truth to myself and accept it because anything else, well it just isn't going to work. Getting what you wish for isn't always a smooth transition. Fantasies aren't supposed to be real and in reality the fantasy isn't real, even this time since Rick Seno is even better than I imagined he'd be. Fuck me, because he's better than I imagined possible. He's like finding out what a ten on the scale of one to ten really is, when what you thought was a ten turned out to be only a five. I've heard of whirlwind romances and love at first sight, but I didn't believe they were real and I never in a million years thought it could possibly happen to me. I'm an independent woman with a stable head on her shoulders. I'm self-sufficient and I don't need anyone to take care of me. Okay, well, at least I was until a few weeks ago. That's the final straw that broke us when I left Rick in LA—my own insecurities. But, I've learned I can be with my Rick and still be me. Granted, the definition of me has slightly changed. I still support myself with my own business and I can keep my head straight most of the time, but this girliness that takes me over really throws me for a loop and I hate to say it, but I kind of like it. Technically, I'm still self-sufficient and don't need anyone to take care of me—but, this is where it gets sticky because I love it when Rick takes care of me (especially the sticky times). And, I want things I've never wanted before. Things I've never considered as possibilities before. What stable headed, independent, self-sufficient woman all of the sudden wants to get married after only two months? This is utter insanity! For craps sake, I was upset about the negative pregnancy test result! Why on earth would any woman in her right mind be upset about a negative pregnancy test when they've known the guy for less than two months? I should've been more upset about having to pee on the stick in the first place! But now, huh, now I don't want to see another negative because it totally bummed me out. On the plus side, I do get to go to more baseball games and I do get to travel to away games, which I still need to figure out expenses on—It doesn't matter, Rick will take care of it. Damn it! I need to be able to cover my own.

Rick pulls me tighter to him and kisses behind my ear,

"Please stop worrying. We want the same things. We need some time to get there, my queen. I promise, baby. I promise." His words are calming, quiet, and sincere. "You always say such sweet things to me in the morning. It makes me happy to know you want the same things I do, and you want them with me. It couldn't be more perfect. I love you, my queen." He snuggles his face into my hair and kisses the back of my neck, while I wonder which parts I said out loud. I've got to get a handle on that. I need to figure out what I say in my sleep and when I change from inner monologue to actually speaking out loud.

The alarm goes off and we both get ready for the day quickly. Rick drops me off at the Brighton on his way to the stadium. I meet Mom in the lobby and we walk out the back of the hotel to the marina, where we find a nice place to sit and have breakfast. We make our way up to the roof and the Spa at the Brighton. It's a very relaxing morning lying around the pool and absorbing the sunshine, while the spa attendants provide snacks, refreshing drinks, manicures, pedicures, massages, facials, and body wraps. She has nothing bad to say about Rick, so I don't prod her and I let it go accepting that she somewhat approves. I leave my Mom and head for the stadium a few minutes after 1pm. I get to my seat in time for Rick to see I'm there for him. He walks back to the net, "You make me feel like a king." He winks at me and turns away to work with his pitcher. His words fill my heart and my worries have vanished.

I yell out, "Make it a win, babe!" and relax in my seat, prepared for a warm afternoon in the sun. I get my hat out of my game bag and put it on, tying my hair up in a knot through the back. I take off my jersey and slather on sunscreen. The sun is warm on my skin, and after the morning at the spa I could take a nap right here. I kick my feet up on the wall in front of me, since I'm in the first row today and I'm ready to enjoy the game.

Tommy's pitching today and he connects with Rick, so it should be a good game. But we're still playing the Sissy's, so anything can happen. The Sissy's fans are probably the worst in the league. They take over half the stadium when they're in town and they're simply obnoxious. Typically, this is a game I'd look forward to tormenting the visiting fans at, well, if I was in my normal seat and not up front for Rick. I'd bring a big bag of peanuts in the shell and shells would be flying at the Sissy's fans, like it was a game! Meli and Samantha would be throwing shells, too. Sandy's wife would be keeping score on all of our hits. We would fake an innocent look if anyone turned around. I can't do that when I'm front and center for Rick, I don't want to cause a problem and I'm not hidden in the sea of people in the seats. If we win today, we sweep the series and the Sissy's aren't happy about it. They've got Billy the Bulldog pitching today, I call him Bitchy Billy because he seems whiny and always has a comment about the umpire's calls. The San Francisco dugout is definitely heated and the game hasn't even started. Rick walks to his position behind the plate with the intensity of a warrior that I love and "You're going to see nothing today, Seno. You're going down!" comes from the Sissy's dugout. Rick ignores them, but his head shakes as he gets to work.

"You got this, my king! Let's go Seals!" I call out, unable to help myself and wanting to defend my man.

But, maybe I shouldn't have because the first Sissy at bat focuses on me as he walks up to the plate, "Hey baby... Angel?" He nods his head at me and blows me a kiss.

Oh, fuck! Adam's a Sissy. How was I not aware Adam is a player? For the Sissy's of all teams! What alternate universe am I in? Two professional baseball players want me? This is nuts. I'm hoping Rick didn't notice, but I know better. Hopefully he ignores it. He doesn't look like the sweet Adam that drove to spend the day with me—a total dick in his uniform. Tommy struck him out on three pitches, all inside and definitely sending a message to back off. He walks the next hitter and we get out of the first inning unscathed. The Sissy's are on the field, and apparently Adam is their new first baseman. This isn't good. This can't go well. Fuck it, this is bad, bad, bad. Shit, shit, shit. Bottom of the second, 0-0, and Rick is at bat for the first time. Don't get a base hit. Please don't get a base hit. What am I wishing for? "Home run, baby!" Rock is on first, Martin is on third and feeling froggy—he wants to steal home and the signs flash around the field. First pitch is low and inside, hitting Rick on the foot and he takes his base, pushing Rock to second. I immediately jump out of my seat to watch him and make sure he's not limping. He appears to be fine. A ball to the foot is nothing compared to all the pitches he takes to the body. I'm glad I told Rick about Adam. He doesn't like it, but at least he's aware and didn't find out when he walked to first. They're chatting it up at first base. I can't hear them, but Rick's body language isn't good. Bravo is at bat, he hits into a double play and the second inning ends, still 0-0.

Top of the third, Rick comes out of the dugout still putting his equipment on and looks at me mouthing "Adam? He's a baseball player." More questioning than making a statement, he's pissed.

I nod and mouth back "I didn't know."

Adam is first at bat and this time he walks straight up to me at the net while the team is throwing the ball around the field, "Hey, Angel. You don't look like the typical baseball skank. I liked that. I thought you were better than that. But, a skank you must be if you're sitting here. I bet Seno is poking you whenever he wants. It's okay, I still want you, baby. Come out with me after the game and I'll show you a better time. I'm sure you remember what its like to spend time with me." He turns toward my Rick, to make sure he hears every word he says, but I already know he's hearing all of it just from his stance. "I remember the feel of your sweet body when I held it against me and your soft lips when I kissed them, how sweet you tasted on my tongue. I didn't push you, you felt like you were worth it. Now I know you're just another baseball skank." His voice gets quiet, "But I still want to fuck you and fuck you hard." He touches my foot that's still resting on the wall in front of me and I wish I could kick him in the nuts.

"Fuck off, asshole!" I say too loudly. Rick turns and grins at me, trusting that I can take care of myself and trying to let me. Especially since there's a net between us. I end up smiling at the realization Rick trusts me and knows I got this.

Adam the asshole walks up to the plate. Rick's loud and laughing for my benefit, "That's my woman. Isn't she beautiful? Don't even think about looking at her again." Laughing turned dead pan. I detect the unspoken "I'll fuck you up if you say anything to her or just look at her again," in his tone. Actually, it was probably "I'll put you on the DL permanently" in Rick's head. It turns me on when he defends me. I wish it wasn't like this. I wish this wasn't happening on the field.

"You got this guy, Tommy. He doesn't have a bat or balls! He's an out!" I yell out and see Rick look at the ground laughing.

"Yep. Love my woman behind home plate. She's my

own personal cheering section." There's some additional conversation at the plate, but its quiet and the volume change is on purpose.

Three pitches, all inside again and the asshole is out. Rick turns to me and gives me a sexy grin with a thumbs up. Tomorrows an off day and it's a good thing because it's going to be a late night, in a very good way.

Bottom of the fourth inning, Rick's first up to bat and the score is tied 1-1. Bitchy Billy has been wandering around the pitcher's mound like he's waiting for directions, but he hasn't pitched a bad game. It doesn't make any sense. First pitch to Rick is way inside, off the plate, and Rick has to step back to avoid getting hit. He shakes it off, swings his bat a few times and steps back into the batter's box. The guys in both dugouts are watching closely, since it appeared Billy threw at Rick—possibly for the second time this game. Billy communicates silently with Adam at first base. From there on everything happens so fast, it's hard to keep up. The next pitch blows across the edge of Ricks helmet, 2 balls. The tension in the stadium is thick and I'm pissed— they're throwing at my man. "Back off meat!" I yell at the pitcher. Third pitch is obviously intentional and hits Rick. The sound is horrible and my Rick drops to the ground instantly. I'm not sure where he got hit. In the arm? Shoulder? Maybe the elbow? I'm out of my seat trying to get through the net to him, but my fear disappears when he pops right up and walks with a purpose toward the pitcher's mound. The catcher for the Sissy's right behind him and the asshole from first running to the pitcher's mound ahead of him.

Oh, fuck. Should I call out to him or cover my eyes?

Skip calls out from the dugout, "Don't do it!" and his teammates join him on the field as both dugouts empty.

Rick doesn't wait for the rest of the team, he yells at Billy, "What the fuck? Do you want to take me on right here?" Billy simply glances at the asshole and Rick hits Adam square in the jaw with his tight fist, knocking his ass to the ground. "Next time you come get me yourself instead of sending a teammate to call me out. And, don't you ever talk to my girl. Don't even look at her again, you fucking asshole!" Rick turns to his team, "Get back where you belong, I've got this." Then he stares at the Sissy's as they all head back to the dugout. "Good, you guys stay out of this unless you want a piece of me." Skip walks out to Rick and escorts him into the clubhouse, while Saben takes his place on first base. He's out of the game and may be injured, but not too bad. I send Rick a text:

Text to Rick - Changing to my old seat for the rest of the game. Text me and let me know you're okay. I'll meet you at your car as soon as you are ready.

Text to Rick - Sorry, I should've kept my mouth shut.

Text to Rick - I didn't know he was a ball player.

Text to Rick - I'm sorry. I never meant to put you in that situation.

Text to Rick - He's a real asshole! I want to kick him in the nuts, but he probably doesn't have any!

Before Rick had a chance to get my texts, Carter is out searching for me. He catches me as I'm standing up to leave my seat, "Rick asked me to come get you. Will you come with me?"

"Of course, is there something wrong? He looked okay." I say concerned as we walk up the steps to the concourse.

Carter isn't answering me and it's starting to make me worry. He leads me to the elevator and down toward the clubhouse offices. As we get off the elevator, he says, "Rick will be fine, he's more worried about you being there by yourself with the San Francisco assholes. He asked me to have you come down and hang out in my office. I have the game on closed caption and I can get you whatever you want. They're treating him right now."

"Can I see him? I need to know he's okay." I didn't have to try to use the concerned girlfriend voice, it was real.

"He's only a couple of rooms away, but I can't take you past my office during game time. Clubhouse rules." Seriously? Rules suck.

I lean out of Carter's office and most of the doors are open. "Rick, are you okay?" I call out down the hall. Going for it. He wants to know I'm here, too.

I get a response almost immediately, "I'll be fine."

I'm happy to watch the game from Carter's office. It's air-conditioned and it was getting warm outside. Sunday afternoon games can get hot, especially during summer. "Hey, Carter. I'm sorry about this. It's probably my fault."

Carter stops and glares at me funny. "It's not your fault they threw at Seno. That's a bad attitude and poor sportsmanship. They used you as a way to get to him and that's interesting because Seno has a reputation of not being able to shake him."

"This was definitely a unique situation." I don't need to give Carter the details about my history with Adam. "He called me a skank and touched my foot through the net."

Suddenly from the other room, "Next time something like this happens and another man touches you, you break his fingers or stomp his hand if you can't kick him in the groin. No one touches you." So, apparently, Rick can hear very well, he's closer than I think, or these walls are paper thin.

"I don't think it'll be an issue and I doubt Adam ever does this again. I'm betting you dislocated his jaw." I do love how he's my protector, but not that he had to do this on the field. He'll probably get fined and could be suspended. Then again, it might be fun to have him to myself for a few days. I may need a cute little nurse outfit.

Text to Sam - Don't worry, he'll be fine. No details yet.

Text from Sam - He looked like he's okay. Not so sure about the other guy. What was that about?

Text to Sam - He called me baby and blew me a kiss.

Do I tell Sam I kind of dated Adam? I'll let it go with what everybody already knows.

Text from Sam - Oh

Text to Sam - He called me a baseball skank.

Text from Sam - He didn't!

Text to Sam - He offered to show me a better time than Seno.

Text from Sam - Ouch!

Text to Sam - He touched my foot through the net.

Text from Sam - Lucky he isn't dead.

Text to Sam - I may have defended myself verbally and loudly.

Text from Sam - LOL

Text to Sam - More info when I have it. He's 2 rooms away from me and they won't let me any deeper into the clubhouse. He did yell at me down the hall and said he'll be fine.

Text from Sam - So, are you 2 doing okay now?

Text to Sam - Yes

I review the team schedule on Carter's desk and realize we have away games coming up soon—Seattle, Chicago and LA again. But, I'm in limbo for pretty much everything until I find out what's wrong with him and if he's going to be suspended. I'm not looking forward to LA. I need to research Seattle and Chicago for travel purposes, and find out what hotels we're staying at.

I try to distract myself, but I want my Rick. I need him to be okay. I haven't heard anything from him in at least twenty minutes. The silence is deafening and I don't care about the game. Huh, I don't think I've ever said I don't care about the game. Fine, I did miss a bunch of games when I left him in LA and I missed the game when I was flying to Colorado to see him. It makes sense, he's more important to me than the game itself, but nobody else ever has been. Somehow over the last two months, Rick has become the most important thing in my life. It's an odd feeling when you've never had it before. I lean out of Carter's office and the door is closed now. "Carter, will you please go see what's going on?"

"Sure, let me try to get an update." Carter leaves the room and wanders the halls. Knocking on a few doors, but there's no talking.

I move to the hallway and stand by the door to the office, just looking around to see what's going on overall and notice player's popping into the clubhouse for things. I text Chase and go for luck.

> Text to Chase - Hey! I'm in Carter's office and they won't let me see Seno. Can you let me know if you find out anything, please? I know you probably don't have your phone, but I'm going for it. They said he's two rooms over. He was talking to me from there but now the door is closed and he hasn't said anything in awhile.

Carter comes back with nothing. I like the guy, but he's useless. I should've gone for it when he left me alone. Chase hasn't responded to me and it's been about fifteen minutes. I try him again.

> Text to Chase - Do you remember my brownies? I also bake cookies and cake. I need to know my Rick is okay. What kind is your favorite?

I get an immediate response.

> Text from Chase - I'll check on him as soon as I can. Have to wait until next inning, only one out left. Choco-late Chip Cookie Bars.

I knew it. Easily controlled by baked goods.

I concentrate on the game and attempt to wait patiently. Why is this taking so long, if he's fine? Why am I sitting around worrying about a guy? Since when do I wait around like this? This is crap! I'll check on him myself! "Hey Carter, can I get some ice cream in one of those mini helmets or some popcorn or something?" Sending Carter on a mission and getting him out of the way. Carter nods and goes to fetch. As soon as he's gone I stand up and walk in the hallway a bit, pretending to be stretching my legs and checking to see if there's anybody around.

I run smack into Chase, "Sherry, what are you... never mind, follow my lead and be ready to peek in the door." Chase gets Rick's phone from his locker and walks through the clubhouse quickly checking in the different rooms, he gives a quick knock and opens the door to the treatment room Rick is in. He leaves the door open wide so I can sneak a peek in and gives Rick his phone, "Thought you might want to see what it looked like. It's all over the internet." Somehow communicating with Rick that it's a ruse to let me see he's okay. Rick looks at me and grins. Chase leaves the door open when he leaves the room, but it gets shut again. Chase gives me a quick thumbs up and trots back off to the dugout. At least I saw him and know he's alive.

Text from Rick - Don't worry. I'll be fine.

Text to Rick - Where's your injury?

Text from Rick - They're checking my elbow, my hand, and my foot. Nothing is broken.

Text to Rick - I'm sure your foot is bruised and elbows hurt like a son of a bitch.

Text to Rick - What's wrong with your hand?

Text from Rick - Cuts on my knuckles from hitting that asshole. Not sure if it's from his teeth or just impact. May need a tetanus shot, he probably has rabies or something.

Text to Rick - I'm sorry. Are you in pain?

Text from Rick - Nothing worse than any other day catching. I should've controlled myself better. I don't have much control when it comes to you. I don't know how long this is going to take. You can take my car and go home, or whatever you want.

Text to Rick - You can't get rid of me that easy. I'm staying here with you, my king.

Text to Rick - <3

A few minutes later the door opens and Rick comes walking out, his elbow supported by a sling and his hand has bandages over two of the knuckles. No limping or anything. He tosses me his keys left-handed, "You have to drive home. My hand is numb." I felt myself go white and he must've seen it. "It's okay. It'll wear off, it's from the local anesthetic they used and I'm not supposed to drive with the sling."

"Whatever you want, baby." I focus on the sling and how closely he's holding his arm to his body.

"Don't worry. It's precautionary. My elbow is bruised and swollen, they want to make sure it's not a sprained ligament. I have to wear this thing for support so I don't make it worse." He rolls his eyes. "It's a bruise. I'm fine."

"Let me check with Skip to see what the damage is and we can get out of here." Rick turns to walk away, but Carter stops him.

"Skip says he doesn't want to see your face for five days. Still waiting on the official suspension and he'll let you know. Billy should be suspended for intentionally throwing at you, too. You need to get your elbow re-evaluated in a few days, call me first. So, get out of here." Carter provides the necessary details.

Rick grabs my hand with his right hand, his numb hand, and makes a funny face at me. "I'm holding your hand, but I can't feel it." I move in close to him so he can put his arm around me instead and he smiles.

We walk out to his car, leaving the stadium before the game is over. I've never done that before. I never would've thought dating a professional baseball player would make me watch less baseball, leave games early, not pay attention to the score—I must be ill. Huh, lovesick? Chemically imbalanced? Lethal combination of pheromones and desire, sounds right.

I'm torn in many directions. He's okay overall, but I'm concerned about his elbow and knuckles. I'm guilt stricken, because this altercation was my fault. He was defending me. Honestly, he probably wanted to punch the guy because—well, the fact he had my number was probably enough for Rick to want to take him out and it went way beyond that. It might be nice to have him to myself for a few days. I wonder how he's going to react to not playing for five days. Will he be grumpy? Will he embrace the time off? Will he blame me? Will we be watching baseball together or does he even watch games? Will there be an Adam conversation?

We get in the Challenger, I lean over and give Rick a quick kiss, "Sorry about all this."

"That guy's a jerk and I should've kept my cool, not let him get to me. You, I want to protect you and keep you safe. You didn't do anything on purpose. You didn't know he's a player. You make me crazy sometimes. I needed to defend you."

"Then we can be crazy together, my king." A little lost with the idea of having five days. We never get more than a day without a baseball game.

I'm suddenly in my head, lost in thought about my Rick. What would've been different if we weren't bound by everything baseball, his training schedule, his game schedule and away travel? Maybe I can take advantage of this time and do things that haven't been possible?

"Do you want to go home to relax and watch the rest of the game or can we make a stop?" It's Sunday and I want to cook. I need to get groceries now that he's moved in and especially since he'll be home for at least the next five days.

"What are you thinking?"

"I want to make you a special dinner tonight and stock up the kitchen. I can get everything for dinner at the public market. I can take you home first."

"You don't need to do anything special for me." Rick turns to me, today has been hard on him.

"I don't need to, I want to," I smile as I throw his own words back at him. "I'll take you home first." He doesn't say anything and it worries me. He's in more pain than he's letting on, or in his head about Adam. "Are you okay?"

He's looking out the passenger window away from me

when he answers, "I'm fine, babe." But, I can hear the truth in his voice.

"Never mind. Let's go home, so I can take care of you, my king." I reach for him, resting my hand on his thigh. He doesn't argue.

I pull into our complex and take it slow over the speed bumps. I know what it's like to be in pain and then hit the speed bumps full on, getting shook all around. I park and go to open his door, since his right hand and left elbow are both injured. He opens the door before I can get there and curses under his breath. I'm sure he's a bit sore all over after taking the dive at the plate. There's blood seeping through the bandage on his right hand as he gets out of his car. "How can I help, my king?"

"I'm fine." Louder. Obstinate.

"Let's get you upstairs and make you comfortable." I want to take care of him and he's irritated. I don't blame him. Right hand and left elbow at the same time is a bad combo.

He stares at me in disgust, "I said, I'm fine."

I don't want to make it worse, "My king, you are fine from your gorgeous blue eyes down to your strong, masculine legs. I especially love your Grade A Prime fine ass." I say laughingly and smile at him, trying to disarm his mood.

Rick rolls his eyes at me and I don't even get a smile. We get in the elevator and I consider attempting to put him in a better mood, but I'm not sure where the boundaries are with this mood he's in. I decide to wait and see what he does. Vodka might be helpful, for both of us.

We walk into our apartment and Rick goes into the bathroom, shutting the door behind him. I let him be and go search the kitchen for the magic meal I'm going to cook up for him tonight. I wanted to make steaks and baked potatoes, but there are no steaks or potatoes in the house. The pantry has Arborio rice, pastas, broths, instant gelatin mix, stewed tomatoes, pasta sauce, baking mix, cookies, donuts, and everything needed to bake sweets. I've got basics in the refrigerator, but really only the makings for a good breakfast. The freezer has a couple packs of frozen vegetables, sausage, ice cream, cheesecake cups, yogurt cups, popsicles, vodka, a couple individual frozen meals, and three things I bagged up and froze so long ago that I don't know what they are and can't figure it out through their frost bitten state. Pasta with sausage it is, or we could have breakfast for dinner. Biscuits with country gravy, eggs and sausage. Fresh biscuits will be the magic, breakfast it is.

I walk through the apartment to check on Rick, but he's still shut in the bathroom and it's been at least twenty minutes. Okay, time to check on him. I knock on the bathroom door, "My king, are you okay? I don't want to bother you. I know you've had a bad day and I'm sure you hurt." Nothing. "I just want to take care of you. I love how protective of me you are." Still nothing. There's no water running, so he can hear me. I walk away to change my clothes, but now I'm worried and it makes it hard to be sweet and understanding. I try to maintain myself, but my girliness takes over. "Rick Seno! Say something or I'm coming in there!" I wait, each second becoming more concerned. I turn the door knob and it's not locked. I open the door to find Rick looking at his blood soaked bandages as they lye on the bathroom counter because he took them off. Okay, so I need to stay calm and Rick's an adult. He can take care of himself and he wants to be left alone. He's still bleeding, so I take control. "I know you don't want help, but you can't bandage yourself up with one hand, and that hand is attached to an elbow in a sling. You're still bleeding. I want to help you. I want to take care of you. I'm taking control of this situation. No more of this crap!" I find myself yelling. "We're a team! We don't run and we don't hide from each other! We fix problems together!" Rick stares at me like I've lost my marbles and maybe I have. "Don't look at me like I'm crazy! You basically sat there and told my Mom you want to marry me yesterday, but today I can't be there for you? You know the whole in sickness and in health, in good times and in bad? It's a partnership and it goes both ways!" I go from worried and shaking mad to completely controlled in a heartbeat. I take his hand and pull the bandage the rest of the way off. I grab a clean kitchen towel and a bag of frozen peas. "Bed or couch?" He wobbles his head, but doesn't answer. "Hasn't anybody ever taken care of you? I have a hard time believing your mother didn't baby you. Sometimes you have to let somebody else take care of you. That means me and nobody else, got it?" I lead him to the couch with his hand wrapped in the towel and get him sat down. I press the cold peas to his hand and sit next to him holding it there to apply pressure, hoping to stop the bleeding and take away some of the pain. He isn't talking to me and I don't know why. He's in his head and probably mad at me. "Is the cold helping it feel better?"

"Yes." He speaks!

"Talking is good. Now, how about telling me why you don't want to talk to me?"

"I'm pissed that I let them get to me while I was on the field. That's all."

Let me read between those lines—I'm a weakness. If I wasn't there, he wouldn't be suspended. "We've had an emotional few days. I'm sure you'll keep everything in check from now on. We all have our moments." I stop and take a deep breath. "Or, I can quit going to the games."

Rick gapes at me in shock. "You always go to the games. You love baseball. The Seals are your team."

"All true, but baseball is a game and you're more important to me. I can always watch it on TV." He stares at me funny again. "Don't you get it? You're not a baseball player to me. You're my king, my love, my boyfriend, my lover, my partner, my friend, and my soul mate. Baseball or not, we still have us. I'll cheer for you no matter what you do." I watch him waiting for something, finally the gleam is back in his eyes.

"I want you at every game with me. I won't let it happen again." Rick smiles at me, the first time I've seen him light up since we got home. "Soul mate, huh? Do you believe in that? And love at first sight and shit like that?"

"I didn't until I met you." My answer pops out without thinking. He leans in and kisses me sweetly, but he's frustrated because he can't use his hands to touch me. I check his hand and he's no longer bleeding. I set his hand in his lap with the frozen peas on it while I gather supplies. I kneel in front of him and take his hand to wrap it back up. I place a gauze pad over the wound and wrap it up tightly. I put the peas back in the freezer and grab another frozen bag for Rick to put around his elbow. "Better?"

"Yes, my queen." He says smiling.

"Good. What would you like for dinner? Pasta, breakfast or pizza?"

"Pizza." He'll always pick pizza. It makes my life easier tonight and I can focus on helping him relax.

I mix up a couple of extra large Screwdrivers and give one to Rick. "This should help you relax and numb you a little." He smiles and takes a drink. I kneel on the floor in front of him to take off his shoes, carefully to not hurt the foot that got hit by a pitch. I pull off his socks. I unbutton his pants and pull them off. Rick just watches me. I take a drink of my Screwdriver and reach my hand around his cock to stroke him. I'm watching him carefully because I don't want to hurt him and he has almost finished his Screwdriver that had five shots of vodka in it. I slam half of mine and set it to the side. I kiss his tip and suck it into my mouth, licking him all over as I stroke him with my lips. I feel his body stretch, wanting more and he's starting to relax. I stroke him with my hand while I continue to suck and lick him. He runs his fingers through my hair with his right hand and feels my head as I move on him. His pleasure drives me to suck harder, move faster until there's no turning back. I hum and take him completely in my mouth while I caress his body with my hands, pushing him over the edge.

He comes hard and lays his head back in ecstasy as he cries out, "Oh Sherry, I love you." I stroke him until he makes me stop. "Please come here to me, baby." He's only partially with me, more on the drunk side.

"I don't want to hurt you, my king."

"On me, please. Please, Sherry." I reach for my drink, but it's gone. No wonder he's wasted! I make another drink and pound it. "Baby please, I want you to get off wrapped around me."

I don't argue with him, since I want the same thing. I carefully straddle him, trying not to shake his elbow or cause him more pain. I slip his tip into me and slide down his hard length until he's completely buried inside me. I hold onto the couch behind him for support and he manages to get my breast into his mouth. Suddenly sucking hard and stretching it, refusing to let go as I move on him. Biting, kissing, and licking every part of me he can reach. He starts moving as I'm almost to the edge and all I can do is scream out his name as we both go together. I can't stop myself as I move on him wildly and needy. We both cry out and I don't want to stop, he's so amazing. Rick finally touches my shoulder and guides my mouth to his, soothing me with his soft lips and tender caress. Both of us taste like orange juice and vodka. We stay together as I sit straddling him for hours while we make out.

We never ordered pizza. The vodka is gone. I don't remember going to bed. This is what it's like to be with Rick when he doesn't have to worry about baseball. Carefree and reckless. I wake up in bed with Rick holding my hand and it's only 3am. I'm guessing it's the only way he can sleep, otherwise he'd be wrapped around me. He's talking in his sleep, so I listen.

"I love you so much, Sherry. Don't be mad. I want to be with you forever. I want you with me always. Soon we'll make all of our dreams come true. We can do anything together. Don't ever give up on me. I want to protect you and take care of you. Only you, my queen. There is only you." He still sounds buzzed.

I move closer to him and lean my head on his right shoulder, so I can whisper in his ear, "I love you, too, Rick. You're my soul mate. Never shut me out. I'll always be here for you. I have a hard time believing we're real. I dreamt about you for years and you're better than any of my dreams. We'll make our dreams come true. We can do anything together, my king." I watch the smile appear on his face and fall back to sleep.

CHAPTER EIGHT

I wake up smelling coffee before my alarm goes off, so I turn it off and let Rick sleep. I get up and get prepped to make breakfast. I mix up some biscuit dough and brown the crumbled sausage in a pan. I cut out biscuits and put them in the oven. I add flour and milk to my sausage slowly, and stir it in until I get it to the right consistency and the raw flour flavor has cooked out. I crack some eggs into a bowl, add salt and pepper and whisk them up. I heat another pan and melt a little bit of butter in it before I dump the eggs in to cook. I swirl the pan around and scramble the eggs with my spatula. I get a couple plates and coffee mugs, so I'm ready. The biscuits are smelling delicious. I check on them and they're golden brown, so I take them out of the oven. Rick walks into the kitchen with pain showing on his face.

"I thought I smelled you cooking breakfast. It looks great. I'm hungry." He says as he tries to smile.

"I figured you'd be hungry. We never ate last night. I don't remember going to bed. The vodka is gone." I laugh.

"We should probably get more, it helped me sleep last night. That and the special treatment from my woman." He wiggles his brows at me dirtily.

I dish up breakfast and keep the conversation going, "Do you want to stay in today and relax? I have a couple of errands to do, so I won't be gone long. I can put them off until tomorrow if you'd rather."

"I'd like to get out."

It hits me, "How about we go to the beach and relax on the warm sand for a while, then do the errands?"

"Sounds good, as long as you'll help me shower later."

"Anything for you, my king."

"I like the sound of that. Anything for me. That might get you into trouble."

I'm in a teasing mood, "I look forward to it."

We finish breakfast and get ready for the beach. I put on my black bikini, pulling on denim shorts and a black tank top over it. I brush my hair out and pull it back into a ponytail. I find Rick sitting on the edge of the bed in board shorts, frustrated and trying to take his sling off. I kiss him sweetly and gaze into his eyes, "I love you, my king. Let me help you." I take the sling off and search through his clothes. I find a Property of the Seals T-shirt with the sleeves cut off, leaving it with large armholes and help Rick put it on starting with the left arm to keep it easy on his elbow.

"I'm not going to break." He says sternly and glares at me with his piercing eyes.

"I know you're made of iron, but I don't want to make it worse. I want you to heal quickly, so you can get back on the field." He softens a bit and doesn't argue with me. I help him get the shirt pulled all the way on and put the sling back on with only a slight wince. I grab a couple beach towels and my beach blanket as we head out the door.

It's Monday, the beach is empty this early in the day. I lead Rick to my favorite part of the beach, over toward lifeguard stand five, and find a patch of soft warm sand. I spread out my beach blanket and sit watching the waves crash. I love the breeze off of the ocean, the sun on my skin, and the warm sand beneath me. The world around me melts away, except for my king sitting next to me as he touches my hand, caressing each knuckle and finger. I turn to him and he's in the same place that I am. The beach is magic. I take off my tank top and shimmy out of my shorts. I fold up my towel and use it as a pillow. I lie back and close my eyes, absorbing everything around me.

"Babe, is this what you always do? I appreciate the view, but it's not safe for you to lay out here in your bikini alone." Rick is already back in protective mode.

"Don't worry, my king. I pay attention to my surroundings and layout close to the lifeguard stand when I'm alone. Thank you for looking out for me. Relax." I choose my words carefully. I can feel his eyes on me and I reach for his hand, wanting to hold it.

"You shouldn't come out here by yourself."

Deep breath. "I'm a big girl and I can take care of myself. I've always taken care of myself. I'm not going to stop living my life. It's always been just me. I've always lived alone and paid my own way. I don't need a keeper. I'm not a child." Can you say DOTM? His grip on my hand tightens. Fuck! Filter on the beach near lifeguard stand five, please?

Before I can speak again, "It's not just you anymore. I want to take care of you. You told me last night that we're a team and took care of me." He looks down, as if he's inspecting the sand. His tone gets quiet and gravelly. "I need you safe. I can't be without you again. Please, Sherry."

I consider the short time we've known each other. All the choices we've made. We both have a learning curve. I never realized how set in my ways I am. "I have to have a life, but I promise to be safe and not do anything stupid. I love how protective you are of me, but we both have different adjustments to make if this is going to work." I heard the "if" as soon as I said it.

"You don't believe we'll make it? I should've known. You gave up on me and started dating. I thought you wanted this as much as I do. I guess it's better to find out now before..."

I cut him off. "Rick, stop. I love you. I want everything with you and I've never wanted anything with anyone else. I'm not always going to say the right thing. I'm still learning how to be in a relationship. I know how to take care of you. I need to learn how to let you take care of me. Sometimes I wonder if we're only a good team when we're naked."

Rick laughs, "We're a perfect team. I like to make you happy. You like to cook for me. You love baseball and I play baseball. You even want to go to all of my games, none of the baseball wives do that or even cheer like you do. You love my sister even though she's crazy. We've made life-changing decisions together. And, of course, the sex is amazing." He has a dirty grin at the end of his rant. I'm good as long as he isn't going down the bad road.

I sit up and kiss him. "We'll get there, my king." I jump up, "Stay here, I'll be right back." I run for the ocean and wade out until I can't touch the bottom. I float, diving into the waves one by one as they pass through, the ocean sharing its energy and playing with me. I wait for my wave and ride it to shore. I walk out of the water feeling like a new woman. Refreshed, I twist my hair and look up to see my man waiting for me with a towel.

Rick holds my towel up for me and I wrap up, "You're so beautiful, even soaking wet." He kisses me on the nose, "And salty."

I lead him back to the blanket, so I can layout and dry off. He sits next to me, watching me. "Lay down, so I can talk to you." He does as I ask and lies on his side, facing me. "Do you remember the last time we were on the beach?" I realize this could take me down a bad road because that was the night that ended with a horrible morning in LA, but that's not my focus.

"I remember Malibu." Flames instantly fill his eyes.

"I'll never forget it. I love the way you plan date nights. You picked me up at the airport in the convertible Porsche and kissed me like we hadn't seen each other in days. You drove us to that Hawaiian themed restaurant on the water in Malibu because they have a dessert you know I'd love, but we never got to dessert. We left the restaurant and ended up on the beach, unable to keep our hands off each other. I stripped down for a swim, but you wouldn't go with me and I ended up underneath you on the sand, then on top of you. I'll never forget how raw it was, you were shaking for me. You needed me. I needed you." I started speaking in my sweet sexy seductive voice, but by the end I had myself breathing hard at the memory.

"I still need you." His eyes and his tone give me goose-bumps. "I've never needed anyone, the way I need you." This man does crazy things to me. He can fry my brain with his words. His voice changes, he sounds unsure, "Sherry, do you still need me?"

"I need you more than ever before, my love. Everyday, I need you more." It's the truth. I always speak the truth, but sometimes I surprise myself with the words I say. Huh, I really need to record myself when I'm sleeping. "I wanted to beat the shit out of that pitcher yesterday for throwing at you, and Adam better hope he never sees me on the street or he's going to sound like he's been sucking helium. He'll wish he didn't have balls." I take a deep breath, "I heard the ball hit you and I watched you fall, but I couldn't get to you. I watched you get up and go at the mound like someone was getting the beat down. I saw you dislocate that asshole's jaw with one punch and get escorted off the field. I heard the voice of a worried girlfriend come out of my mouth when I wasn't allowed to see you. All I wanted to do was take care of you and take the pain away. I, I don't know what it is, but it's never been more present in my life than it is when I'm with you now—love, need, our connection, all of it together." I feel tears running down my face and I didn't know I was crying. I was so focused on Rick yesterday, I didn't allow my emotions to affect me. I simply took control of the situation. He needed me to. He was bleeding.

Rick smiles at me, "You really did take care of me last night. I didn't realize how much until you said it. You stopped my bleeding. You made my hand not hurt. You got me wasted, so I would relax and to dull my pain. You made it look easy."

"It's easy, when you want to take care of someone like I want to take care of you."

Rick reaches for my hand and brings it back to his lips, kissing each finger and each knuckle. "I love you, baby. How about you let me take you to lunch? Then we can go home."

I don't want him to overdo it today and hurt. I nod, "I know just the place." We dust off and I pull on my clothes.

I take Rick to the public market, so I can get food to cook for dinner while we wait for our lunch. He'd never been there and we end up with all kinds of stuff that wasn't on my list. I stop and run into the grocery store on the way home to get vodka, orange juice and a couple of other things. I want to make sure Rick isn't too sore to sleep tonight.

I get everything put away. I mix up some jello shots and put them in the refrigerator to set up. Orange and grape flavors, both made with vodka. I shower quickly and take Rick to bed with me for a nap. I'm worn out and he needs a break, too.

CHAPTER NINE

I wake up a couple hours later and Rick is sacked out. My nap didn't help. I kept replaying my man getting hit and going down. Every way it could've played out, I played it in my head. Everything from him not going down, to him not getting up. Every time I couldn't get to him. Every time they wouldn't let me see him. Visions continue to run through my head of things that didn't happen. The 92 mile per hour fastball hitting him in the head and cracking his helmet. The ball smashing into his handsome face. The full bone-breaking sound of the impact of the ball colliding into him and the ground when he falls to it uncontrollably. His blood soaking his uniform and streaming from his temple. Knocked out cold. Lying there lifeless. The images and sounds invade my head and won't leave me. Torturing me with horrible things that didn't happen, but now I'm realizing they could. He wants me safe because he never wants to be without me again. I get it now, but he's not going to quit playing baseball. We're going to keep living. Life has risks unless you quit living it.

I whisper quietly to Rick, "You rest baby, I'll be in the other room if you need me. I love you." I kiss his forehead and close the bedroom door as I leave the room. He needs rest. I need a distraction to get my head in the right place.

I was a bad girl today, completely skipping work. Just because the team has an off day and Rick is suspended for five days, doesn't mean I get to vacation. I quickly get my work caught up and handle all of my messages. But, what I want to do is bake. I take a suggestion from Chase, mix up some chocolate chip cookie bars and get them baking. I scrub the baking potatoes I bought for dinner and toss them in a bowl with olive oil, sea salt, and black pepper. I take the steaks out of the refrigerator to bring them to room temperature. I decide to make a compound butter and split the leftover biscuits to toast with garlic. I set a stick of butter out to soften in a bowl and add thyme, marjoram, basil, and some of the soft gooey cheese we bought on a whim at the public market. I smell the chocolate chip cookie bars and check on them, but they need a few more minutes to be GBD (golden brown and delicious). I split the biscuits and spread them with a light layer of butter, then sprinkle them with garlic salt. I pull the cookies out and set them on the stovetop to cool. I place the potatoes directly on the oven rack and turn the oven up to 400, they'll take some time to cook. The butter has softened, so I mix it together thoroughly with the herbs and cheese. I get a piece of plastic wrap and place the butter in the middle, wrapping it up tightly, twisting the ends, and put it in the refrigerator to solidify. I find myself singing "We Belong" by Pat Benatar as I work in the kitchen. I cut up the cookie bars, packaging a few for Cross and find myself scouring the cabinets for something else to make.

I need to keep busy and out of my head because I can't

shake the visions of my Rick. The worst of them keep coming back to me and I'm being silly because he's here, in bed sleeping. It's in slow motion over and over. He goes down in the batter's box and he's not moving. I'm watching him for any movement, just to see he's breathing. I can't get to him. I can't be there to hold his head and comfort him. I can't talk to him, so he hears I'm there with him. I need him to know I'm there for him and I need confirmation he'll be okay.

When did I turn into the worrying, needy girlfriend who can't control her emotions? What the fuck is wrong with me? I can't go on the field. The players get the best possible medical attention. Damn it! It truly is a battle on the field and they don't love him the way I do. I hate the Sissy's and that asshole and their stupid ass whiny pitcher. They did this to me. They made me an emotional wreck! I stop and listen to my internal rant and I'm placing blame. The truth is, I opened my heart and Rick filled it. I wouldn't have it any other way.

I open the bedroom door quietly to check on him, but end up climbing in bed with him like a moth to a flame. I wrap my arms around him and kiss him repeatedly. "How are you feeling, my king?"

He smiles at me, like he could be woken up by my kiss whenever I want. "I'm stiff and sore. What smells good? I'm hungry."

"I've been in the kitchen. I've got a plan to help with the stiff and sore. I'll go finish dinner and you come to the kitchen when you're ready?" I move to get out of bed, but he grabs me pulling me back to him and kissing me passionately. "I love you, my king. Let's work on the sore and then the stiff." I laugh, but more than anything I don't want him in pain. He runs his hand over my body and lights me up, trying to get me to change my plan. It's working, but I manage to slide out of bed and scamper back to the kitchen.

"Come back," Rick yells from the bedroom.

"Can't hear you, cooking." But, I could hear him just fine and it wasn't the sound of a man needing help, it was the sound of my man wanting me. I love his desire for me.

I check the potatoes and they're almost done, so I finish the rest of dinner. I season the steaks on both sides with salt and pepper and slide them into the broiler. I place the tray of split garlic biscuits in the oven and find myself singing again, apparently Pat Benatar has possessed me with "We Belong" for the time being.

I hear him get up and he slowly makes his way to the kitchen, still wearing the clothes from the beach. I find something about it sexy. The laid back style with his hair a mess. He stands behind me, kisses my neck, and reaches his right arm around me to pull me back to him. I feel what he wants against my ass and it's an impressive need.

I pull the biscuits out of the oven and flip the steaks over. I hear Rick's stomach growl and the smell of the food is distracting him until after we eat. I retrieve the compound butter from the refrigerator and cut open the baked potatoes, pushing the ends in to make them open better. He eyeballs the chocolate chip cookie bars I have packaged for Cross and starts to open the package, "Stop it, those are for Chase. We have the rest of the pan." I point to the pan and he immediately breaks off a small piece, shoving it into his mouth.

I place the steaks on the plates and set a slice of the compound butter on each steak. I add the baked potato and a toasted garlic biscuit to the plate. I take the plates to the table where the two chairs now sit next to each other permanently. Then I grab the sour cream, butter and compound butter for the table. I sit next to Rick, ready to eat dinner and his brain is working as he inspects me.

"You've been busy this afternoon. Everything looks perfect and smells good." It's not the end of what he wants to say. He kisses me sweetly on the lips, sucking lightly on my lower lip as he pulls away. He gazes deep into my eyes and connects with my heart, I want to melt into him.

I smile, "Sometimes I need to be in the kitchen." I look at him and realize he's going to be challenged to cut his steak, so I take his plate and slice it up for him. He shakes his head with a frustrated grin and eats his dinner. I sit and watch him. I put my arm around him and lean on his shoulder, simply needing him here next to me.

"Are you okay? You aren't eating."

"I will be. I just need to know you're here with me."

"I'll always be here with you, my queen. You keep cooking like this and there may be more of me." He laughs. I get lucky and he doesn't ask any more questions.

We finish dinner and I clear the table. "Orange or grape?" I ask ready to start the relaxing process I have in mind.

"I like both." Ha! I take two of each flavor jello shots to the table.

"Ever done jello shots?" I peer at Rick mischievously. I pick up an orange jello shot, run my tongue all the way around it inside the small cup and suck it down. His eyes heat and I'm guessing it's the tongue action or maybe the sucking action that's doing it for him.

Rick copies me, sliding his tongue into the cup and running it all the way around the shot, then sucking it down. Holy fuck Batman! I get wet just watching him. We both pick up a grape one and watch each other closely as we do the shots. Fuck me! Fuck me! Fuck me! I didn't say it out loud, but it was like I did. My panties and shorts are off in mere seconds, his lips are on mine needy, licking and sucking. I push his shorts down, releasing and stroking his willing cock. I turn around, pressing my ass to his hard cock and his guttural groan shakes me. I bend over and he slides his dick against my ass while he explores my hot wetness with his fingers. His length gets even harder and I whimper with need. His right hand moves to my hip, gliding over me as I move, wanting him. He grasps his cock and slides the tip into me. I want all of him and I want him now. I push back against him and take all of him at once. He moans with appreciation. His hand on the small of my back is warm and guiding. I slide on and off of him, rubbing on him, wrapped around him, the slow friction driving me to the edge.

"Oh, my queen. How are you so perfect? You make me... I just want... I love you wrapped around me," Unable to finish his thoughts he reaches around my waist and bends over me, kissing my back and neck. He's limited without his left arm, but creatively making it work. His hand at my sex, he circles my sensitive center slowly, building my need and I'm a grenade on countdown to explosion. I move against him faster and harder. I can't control myself, I want more and I want it now.

I scream out his name, "More, baby! Please! Rick! Oh, my king!" As I explode and he goes with me. Exploding at the same time, we both cry out at the intensity. He wraps his arm around me tightly and pulls out. I want him inside me, but he pulls me back up to him and kisses my neck.

He turns me to him and devours my mouth with his as he drags me to the bedroom. He takes us both down on the bed and immediately pushes into me. "I need more of you.

You're my world." He moves quickly getting faster as he pounds into me, driving me crazy with every movement.

I shudder almost instantly, "You're amazing! I'm yours!"

"Always, baby. You'll always be mine. When you squeeze me like this, it just feels... fuck. I need you with me." Rick slams into me a few times, throwing himself over the edge and shaking in pleasure. He rolls to the side and pulls me back against him. His whole body heaving with every breath as he regains control. His hot breath at my ear, "It's always us. We'll always be together. You'll always be the queen to my king. I promise I'll make you mine. I want nothing more than to make all of your wishes come true."

They're only words, but I believe every single one of them and feel them to my soul. I fall asleep content using his chest as my pillow with his arm holding me to him.

CHAPTER TEN

"Sherry. It's okay. I'm right here. Sherry, wake up. Sherry!" Rick startles me, trying to wake me up. He searches my eyes. "Are you awake now? Do you see me?" He takes my hand and holds it to his heart, so I feel it beating.

"I see you. I like how you're holding my hand to your heart. Are you okay?" I speak calmly, wondering what's going on.

"You were screaming and calling out my name. You kept saying you were right here and asking why I wasn't moving. You kept saying you love me and telling me not to leave. It sounded like you wanted to get to me, but couldn't. You were hysterical and I don't want you to be. I love you, Sherry. Were you dreaming?" His voice going from concerned to calming.

I wasn't dreaming. I was having the repeated nightmare that's been keeping me awake. I don't want to tell him about it. "I'll be okay."

"Tell me, Sherry. I need to know what's going on. Remember, we don't have secrets."

I take a deep breath, "It's silly. I'm freaking out and need to get over it. I'll be fine." The chance this is an acceptable response is about zero.

"Whatever it is, it'll be okay. Just tell me."

"I started having nightmares when I was napping with you this afternoon. That's why I got up and found something to keep me busy. I couldn't get them out of my head. Different versions of you getting hit by the ball and falling to the ground. Mostly the worst one and I don't want to talk about it." I come to an abrupt stop because there's no way I tell him how I'm seeing him get hit, fall, and lay there lifeless.

He holds me tight, "I know things can be scary sometimes. It's hard when the team rules make you wait for hours to see that I'm fine. But, the thing that matters most is that I'm here with you right now and I love you." He's right. I kiss him, distracting myself and proving to myself he's right here with me alive and breathing. I reach for his cock and find him to be ever-ready. I climb on top of him, mounting him, and lie down on his chest. Rick lifts the arm in the sling and rests it on my back, holding me to him. I move slightly as I appreciate him inside me, but mostly I lie with my head on his heart. I want to listen to it beat and feel how strong he is.

"I love you, Rick. Can I stay right here, just like this?" I sound needy, like I want to be taken care of. And I do.

He kisses the top of my head. "Whatever I can do to help, my love. I always want to hold you." I fall asleep on him, soothed and protected.

Early Tuesday morning I'm woken by a ringing phone and I don't recognize the ring. I'm still on Rick and he stirs beneath me. He holds me to him and doesn't seem to care that his phone's ringing. "Let me get the phone for you." I say groggily.

"The phone will be there when I'm ready. Right now, I want to be with you." I completely melt at his sweet words and sleepy tone.

"Wow. Say more things like that." I giggle happily.

"We should sleep with you on me every night. It helped both of us relax. You're still on me..." He pushed into me with his morning wood. "The phone can definitely wait." He moves slowly, in and out while he continues to talk to me. "What do you think?"

"Oh," I try to find my voice, but all I can do is appreciate my warm, sexy man, "Phone can wait. Oh, Rick."

"Oh, Rick... huh? Oh, Rick what?" He's in his sexy, horny, teasing mood—I love it!

"Oh, god," sleepy groggy sex is the best. I'm not completely awake and he makes me where I can't think. "You, oh Rick, you just... you make me forget where I am." He pushes into me harder, appreciating my words and the sexy sounds escaping my lips. I move with him and dig my fingers into his hair. "You make everything disappear. It's only you and me."

"Do I really do that for you?" This hot sexy man questioning his abilities.

"Oh, yes! Yes." All I can do is feel him moving, filling me, stretching me. I cry out his name uncontrollably.

"I'm the only one who does this for you, always. Nobody else can have you, my Sherry."

"It's only ever been you. Nobody has ever taken me the places you do." His slow pace continuing, driving me crazy and holding me back from the edge.

Rick growls like he's not only my king, but the king of

the jungle and I see the proud look on his face. I kiss his neck, drawing out another low groan. "Not yet, baby." Rick slides out from under me and out of bed.

I'm left confused and abandoned. But not for long, he grabs my ankle and pulls me to the edge of the bed with my legs hanging off. Immediately burying his face in my sex, licking my wet folds and fucking me with his tongue. I'm on sensory overload. He sucks at my sex and I scream out his name. He slides two fingers into me and tongues my clit, lapping, sucking, teasing me until he bites down on me hard and sucks like his life depends on it, sending me into a flying spiral. I hear the sounds coming from me and I'm not in control. It drives him further. Everything goes dark and now he's plunging into me. He's huge, filling me repeatedly, "Oh, fuck me. So, fucking perfect."

"Not yet, please more..." I hear myself selfishly beg him to hold back.

He smiles, my request is an honor he'll happily accept. He takes my breast in his mouth, sucking and nibbling at my nipple, and I'm lost again. Rick strokes into me faster and faster, pushing me over the edge, drawing out my orgasm while he meets me there. He slams into me hard a few times and collapses on me with his lips at my ear, "I love you, Sherry." He kisses my neck and wraps his right arm around me, holding me to him.

I sometimes wonder how I deserve this, him. There are many women out there who would do anything to have someone take care of them, cover all of their expenses, give them great sex, and I mean even if they didn't love them. Yet here I am with my perfect man, my better than any fantasy I ever had baseball boyfriend who worships me as much as I worship him, but I don't want to be kept or have someone else pay my way. Okay, fine, I want the out of this world sex. Only a foolish woman wouldn't. I know he loves me when he kisses me, touches me, slides inside me or, honestly, just holds my hand. I feel it in his eyes when he looks at me. My seat for every game. Traveling to away games. His planned date nights. My stadium access card and Seals wardrobe. His sweet, meaningful, words and gestures. How he always sits next to me at the table. Even his quirks, like elevators, that I admit I love. It has required some adjustment, but no hardship. The horror of having a professional baseball player in my bed every night, what will I ever do? I just don't know.

Rick's phone rings again as we're dozing back off to sleep. He sighs and reaches for his phone to find the stadium calling. He'd rather be home with me and doesn't want to deal with work. "Hello?"

"Hey Seno, Skip wants you to come in this morning and get your elbow checked. Are you having any pain?" Carter calling to take care of team business and I can hear him through the phone.

"Not really, slight soreness and mostly stiff I think from the sling. I'll be there this morning." All business.

"Billy got a five day suspension for throwing at you. The first baseman is on the DL for an undetermined amount of time. Remind me never to make you mad. Also, Seals called up the catcher that's been hot on the farm team to cover while you're out. Saben can't handle four games on his own." I see the shit look cross his face.

I smell coffee brewing and it's almost time for my alarm to go off. I get up and leave the bedroom to go thank my coffeemaker while Rick finishes his conversation. His eyes on me as I pull his dirty T-shirt on and leave the room bottomless.

I take advantage of the time to check what I need to do

for work today, check the baseball schedule, turn the shower on to warm, and make a mental list of things I need to discuss with him. I've been thinking about it and since he's moved in and wants to pay, it'll be better to talk about it and have it decided than to wait until he thinks he's just going to pay. I give Rick a cup of coffee on my way to the shower and toss his T-shirt on the bed on my way out of the room.

I turn on some music to listen to while I'm in the shower. Who am I kidding? I put on my *Singing in the Shower* playlist, turn up the volume and close the bathroom door. "Love is a Battlefield" by Pat Benatar takes over my bathroom and I take advantage of the acoustics in my shower as I sing along with her. I love this playlist, it empowers me with strong female vocalists. I dance around the shower singing as I wash my hair and turn to the corner for the best vocal effect on "Million Reasons" by Lady Gaga. I enjoy the water falling over me as 'Til Tuesday's "Voices Carry" comes on and I sing into the water with my eyes closed, feeling the music. I kick it up a notch when "Never" by Heart comes on and I'm ready to get out of the shower when Pat Benatar is back with "We Belong," but it sucks me in and I close my eyes as I sing. I open my eyes and leave the water on for my Rick. I turn to step out of the shower and find him leaning in the doorway watching me with a smile on his face. "I left the water on for you," I grin at him from my eyes and cheeks. "How's your elbow? Can I help you wash your hair or anything?"

"You already do so much for me. I was in a shitty mood after that phone call, but I heard you in the shower and watching you made everything better. I love the way you connect with me and music, you give both of us everything you have."

My cheeks warm and I know I'm blushing. "Let me wash your hair." I open the shower door for him and invite him in. Helping him take his sling off without it getting soaked. I reach my arms around his neck and stretch to kiss him, pushing him into the spray of water with my lips. I love his naked body against mine and the reaction I get from his body tells me he feels the same way. My happy place gets excited and his cock gets hard against me. I shampoo his hair, rubbing his scalp all over and rinse it out. I rub conditioner into his hair and leave it while I soap up his body, rubbing my hands all over him and trapping his cock between my thighs. I rinse his hair, running my fingers through it and pushing my breasts against his chest. I rinse the soap off of both of us and when I drop to my knees to wash his legs, he groans at my release of his cock. I soap up his legs and rinse them off, running my hands up and down both of his legs. I have some fun and soap up his hard cock, stroking it repeatedly and more than necessary before I rinse it off. As soon as I get all the soap off, I kiss his tip and slide my lips over his hard length. I grasp him at his hips with each of my hands, digging my fingers into his deliciously hard ass. It's times like these I truly appreciate his catcher's body, his strong legs and muscular ass. What is a girl supposed to do other than love, pleasure, and worship a man like this? The thought makes me do something I shouldn't. Something that would really piss off my Rick. I close my eyes and blow him like the professional athlete he is, like he's a baseball player and not my man. I take him deep with every stroke and suck hard with every pull, moving on him quickly and with a purpose. Rick leans back against the wall and spreads his feet for balance. He touches my face, caressing my cheek. My eyes are closed, but he must be watching me.

"That's not you, baby. I only want you. I'm still a man, but I don't know. Something is different. I don't expect you to do this for me, my queen." I stop, sit back and gaze up at him. He has a look of confusion. Eyes open and on him, I kiss him from base to tip and swirl my tongue around him, lightly sucking. "That's my baby loving me. It's only ever you wanting to, my queen." I stroke him with my lips and hum to vibrate him. I put my hand around him and stroke while I suck. He gets harder and all I want is him inside me. I stand up and kiss him passionately, demanding. I suck on his tongue and lower lip as I pull away. I turn around and lean against him as I bend over and slide back on to his hard cock. "Oh, fuck. You feel so good wrapped around me." We push and pull together slowly, feeling each other and enjoying the moment. "There's nothing better than you, my queen. I swear you're perfect. We were made for each other. I want you every day. You're my forever, Sherry." I can't even form words, only he does this to me. Suddenly he pulls out of me and takes control, turning me around, he wraps his right arm around my waist and lifts me to him, sliding me down onto his cock and guiding me to wrap my legs around him and hold on. He fucking surprises me with what he can do, and with one arm no less. He claims my mouth with his and I know why. He needs me, he wants to communicate more with me without words. He loves me and he needs me to know, he wants to know I feel the same. It sounds silly because I'm right here with him, but he needs to know I'm here with him, for him, and it's real. Sex is almost a moment of weakness and insecurity we need to surpass, to prove our love. Sometimes I swear he wants it to be more than sex, almost like he has a specific purpose in mind. Other times, like where he's taking us now, he simply wants to love me and everything is in his kiss. He wants a deeper connection and I'm not talking about his dick. His kiss drives the mood and our need. He licks my lips, tasting me with need while he pushes into me. I move on him, stroking him the best I can while I hang onto him. The intensity is getting the best of me quickly. Rick breathing heavy whispers in my ear, "I love you, baby. Can you feel it?" His tone tells me he's not talking about his cock.

"Yes, my love. All over, especially in my heart. I know you love me. I couldn't have a better king." This man just kills me sometimes and I don't know what to say. "Can you feel that I love you?" I wonder if he asked because he doesn't feel it. Tears roll down my face.

Rick presses his lips to mine, over and over. Open-mouthed he slides his tongue into my mouth to dance with mine. His right hand firmly on my back and holding me to his chest, his cock rubbing against my clit with every stroke. He's using his kiss to drive me to orgasm, sucking on my tongue. He moves to my neck, kissing at the perfect spot and when he knows I'm on the edge he sucks hard sending me down the rabbit hole. He leans back against the wall and slides down to the floor. I have no idea what happened. I go dark and I'm surrounded by the firework show with stars and pink bursts. I hear music and I'm relaxed with no worries. Rick kisses me, "Sherry, are you with me?"

I open my eyes and gaze straight into his. He's holding me in his lap. "Why are we on the floor?"

"You let go all of the sudden and I didn't want you to fall, so I leaned back to keep you from falling and slid down to the floor. It was the best I could do with one arm. Are you okay?"

"I'm better than okay. Sometimes you rock my world

and I don't know where I go. You should see the fireworks. This time there was music."

"You were singing, my queen." I sing a line from the music I heard and Rick says, "That's what you were singing." I need to get control of this talking and now singing when I'm not conscious. Apparently, "We Belong" is still possessing me.

We get up off the ground, rinse off and get out of the shower. Rick towel dries his hair and pulls on shorts, while I find panties, denim shorts and a Seals tank top. He sits on the edge of our bed and pulls me over to sit next to him. "I know you love me everyday when I wake up feeling like a king. It's all you, your sweet words, how you make me feel. You make me warm all over and I can't control my smile when I'm with you. I meant it before when I told you I wasn't living. Your love gives me life." He kisses me sweetly and slowly, then pulls back while keeping eye contact. "Someday I'll ask because I want to be with you forever, but I'm already committed to you. You're more than my girlfriend."

"It'll always be us, my king." I hug him warmly with my cheek to his.

"So, do you want to watch the game tonight?" I ask wondering how this will play out. I want to watch the game and we haven't watched a game together.

"Yes. I need to go to the stadium this morning to get my elbow checked. Drive me? I don't want to show up without the sling on."

"Anything for you, my king." He pulls a T-shirt on by himself, but he did put it on his left arm first. I help him get the sling back on and can't wait until I get both arms around me again. I pack my work bag, so I can get some work done while I wait for him at the stadium. He won't be staying there, since he's suspended. I brush out my hair, find my sandals and grab Chase's chocolate chip cookie bars, so I can leave them for him. I cut one out of the pan to eat it with my last drink of coffee, and its obvious Rick has been picking at them. I yell through our home, "I'm ready whenever you are." Rick walks out and hands me his keys.

I drive Rick's Challenger into the player's garage and park. I follow him in and check with Carter to find out where my boundaries are today. He checks the clubhouse and let's me leave my special package for Chase in his locker. Since I'm allowed to wander the seating bowl and concourse, I decide to sit in my season ticket seat and enjoy the view while I get some work done.

Text to Rick - I'm sitting in my old section. Let me know when you're done.

Text to Cross - I left you a present in your locker :)

Text from Rick - Okay. I'll find you.

Text from Cross - I hope it's sweet and baked! Thanks!

Something about my seat always seems right, it welcomes me. I miss my view of the field. I sit field level, but I'm up about halfway and it gives me a view of almost the whole field. The field is a beautiful thing, green, fresh, and perfectly manicured. I can hear the bats connecting with the pitches, the hum of the crowd, the peanut vendor wandering through. In reality, the field is empty other than a few guys playing catch and running around the field like a track. It simply makes me happy. This is the perfect place to work. I open my laptop and work on updating my social media. I add some new photos, update travel specials, and post a picture of my current view to Instagram asking who's interested in a stadium vacation. I check my email and reply to the customers I'm working with. I review my customer's social media accounts for travel posts and photos, anything I might be able to use or comment on for exposure. I prepare an email about planning for winter trips to Hawaii with the suggestion to book early for better rates and give yourself something to look forward to, and send it out to my customer base. I tweet about a stadium vacation using #baseball #SanDiegoSeals #vacation, thinking my fellow fans who follow me might be interested. I review the vacation plans I started for Rick and I, updating them with the best prices, and getting everything set. It makes me excited just thinking about it. I can't wait to spend two weeks in Hawaii with my Rick.

I change gears and review my budget, as well as the away games coming up and check airfare for Chicago and Seattle. As I review the schedule I'm reminded the trade deadline is almost here and it hits me, they brought up the new hot catcher. Rick doesn't want to get traded and the way they've been trading, nobody's safe. I check for the lineup, but it's too early. We'll definitely be watching the game tonight.

Rick sits down next to me. "I see why you like it here. I never see the field like this. It's gorgeous." Spoken like a true baseball fan. "Plus, it's foul ball territory, the seats are angled toward the field perfectly and you've got a clear view."

"I've been sitting in this seat for years. I've never changed. Great view of all the action, total fan section and close to my favorite concessions." I stop abruptly. I may have just had a DOTM moment and I need to make up for it. "But, I love sitting behind home plate. I've been cheering for you for years from out here and you didn't even know it. Now you have no doubt when I cheer for you, I'm closer to you, and I have an awesome view of your ass!" I laugh hysterically because I'm so funny, well at least I think I'm funny.

Rick shakes his head, "My queen, everybody knows when you cheer for me and I love it. It's better than when the whole stadium goes crazy over a home run or even a grand slam. I don't have to be great for you to cheer for me. You cheer for me before I do anything and get me pumped up, and when I do something great you're louder than everybody else. I can always hear you and it feeds my ego every time." Rick leans over and kisses me sweetly, "I didn't know what I was missing."

I notice he's not wearing the sling, "How's your elbow?"

"I'm okay. I need to pay attention for any pain, otherwise I should be able to play after my suspension." He puts both arms around me and kisses me silly, showing me he's fine.

I still feel guilty about his suspension. But, I do get him to myself for the rest of his suspension.

I put my work away and hand Rick his keys. We walk out to the garage and Rick gets in the driver's seat. I slide in the passenger side and scoot over next to Rick, so I can lean against him and rest my hand on his thigh. It's what he likes me to do and wants me to do, it's not just me.

We stop at the Yolk for brunch on the way home and I take the opportunity to handle business, considering I can't concentrate when we get home and will most likely end up naked. "Can we talk about some roommate things over lunch?"

Rick glares at me like I'm crazy, "Roommate?"

Bad choice of words, "Let me try again. Can we discuss a few things? I want to have a plan when it comes to money and traveling." I'm not sure that was any better.

"I told you, I'll pay for everything. Don't worry about it."

"That's what we need to talk about. I don't work like that." I'm struck with a vision of the future and suddenly I know in the future it'll be different. We're partners and it won't be like he's paying for everything. It might not be that bad to be taken care of. "I mean right now. I know it could be different in the future."

"Okay." We find a table at the Yolk and sit down on the same side of the table as always. He puts his arm around me and we order our usual. "What's on the agenda?"

I turn and glare at him because he's picking on me for planning. "Traveling for away games and household expenses. I understand that you have enough money to pay for everything and want to cover it. I appreciate that you want to do that for me, but it'll make me feel like I have to answer to you about how I use my money and I don't want to."

"Okay, keep going."

"My airfare for the away games could be a challenge for me when there are multiple away series during a month. I can't afford the tickets where you want me to sit and I've come to terms with that. Going to the game is kind of us being on a date. Sounds crazy, but it really is like being on a date with you. I spend the whole time with you, right there watching the game and cheering for you and sharing the whole thing with you."

"In my heart, what's mine is yours. I want you to have anything and everything you want."

I put my hand on his thigh, appreciating him and not wanting to get off track. "When I was waiting for you in Carter's office, he was complaining about travel arrangements for the team. I want to offer him my services and handle travel for him. I can do it all for the same cost and make a profit. It should cover the expense of my airfare and make me some extra spending money. If it works out I can offer my services to other teams and make new contacts for doing stadium tours in the future. I don't want to do anything you're not comfortable with. What do you think?" He starts to talk and I add quickly, "I know you don't think I need to work and think it will stop soon, but it's not going to and it doesn't take me that much time. Working with travel is fun for me. I like having my own thing. It's not like I work for somebody else, on their schedule and can't travel with you. I can do all of it."

Diffused, "I don't expect you to give up your business. I know you enjoy it. If you want to approach Carter, you should. Just tell me if you need money. I'm an expensive boyfriend."

"That's the other part, food is definitely more expensive traveling and feeding you at home. I figure the shared expenses are the mortgage, association fees, utilities, and food. I'm happy to keep paying all of it and I can afford it, since you pay when we go out to eat. But, you want to pay for everything, so how about we split the mortgage, I'll pay association fees and utilities, and you cover food."

"Does that make me paying less than half?"

"I'm not sure how much food will be. You're probably paying more than half, but I figure it's easier since all the utilities and everything are already in my name."

"Mortgage? You aren't renting there?"

"No. It's my place. Does that make a difference?"

"No, I love it there." He leans in close to my ear and speaks quietly, "We'll want more room in the future, Elle will need her own room." My whole body shivers and he holds me close, rubbing my arm. "Just thinking of the future, my queen. You said you wanted to have a plan." He throws me off and I've lost focus. Luckily, our food shows up and I have time to recover while we eat.

Rick turns to me, "What if we pay it off?"

"No."

"I know you like to save money and it would save a bunch of money that's getting spent on interest."

"No."

"Why not?"

"It's my place and I've done it by myself." I really need to check my filter, it might need cleaning or something.

Rick runs his hand over his face and takes a deep breath, "This conversation would be a lot easier if we were naked."

"I chose to have it here on purpose. I want to be coherent and not distracted."

"I live there, too. It's our place. Don't you want me there?"

"Yes! I want you there with me. It's just... I don't know how to explain this to you without you deciding I'm crazy." I stop and breathe, "I managed to buy it on my own and that's a big deal to me."

Rick smiles, "I love that about you, my queen. The problem is you're not on your own anymore. It's not only you. I'm here and I don't care how you want to say it, there's a we or an us or partners or team—there are two of us. Two of us doing everything together and to quote a wonderful woman I know 'we're a team'." Son of a bitch! That's twice today he's used my own words against me.

"I'd like to change my definite 'No' to 'Not Yet'. Better?"

"It's progress. Do you have an idea when?"

Pushy bastard. How do I tell him when we're permanent without him being pressured, feeling like he needs to propose? Or thinking I don't have faith in us? Then the tears start rolling again. Damn it! My mouth takes over and I need to get a filter replacement. "What if you get tired of me? Or, realize I have my own special brand of crazy? What if you meet someone you want more? Maybe you'd rather have someone easy. Someone who lets you pay for everything and take care of them? I mean there are..."

Rick cuts me off. "Sherry..." He stops, drops cash on the table and drags me out of the Yolk. He stops in the middle of the parking lot, "You make me crazy," and pulls me to him, plastering my body to his while he kisses me passionately. He pulls back, holding my face so that I have to look at him and listen to him. "The only one of those things that's even remotely true is that I want to take care of you and pay for things for you. I don't want to do that for anybody else, only you. You're the one who makes me crazy and makes me lose control. You're the one who made me need you when all I'd done was touch your hand. You're the only one who's ever made it okay for me to be a baseball player. You want me and love me for all of the right reasons, and none of the wrong ones. Can't you see that we belong together?"

"Say that last bit again. Please."

"We belong together."

I don't know why, but the words straight from the song that's been possessing me strike me and I smile uncontrollably. Is it a sign I've been waiting for or simply my music connection getting the best of me? I can't help myself, I sing the song right there in the parking lot and Rick holds my hands smiling at me like a fool. He picks me up and twirls me around. He's mine. We belong together.

Rick drives us home and pulls me out the driver's side with him. He tosses me over his shoulder and he's mumbling to himself, though I can't make out the words. He carries me across the parking lot with his hand on my ass. We get into the elevator, "Fuck!" Rick yells out and pulls the elevator stop. He slides me down his body and already has his hard cock out and ready to go. He sets me down and presses his lips to mine, demanding, claiming, needing. Sucking on my lips and tongue. Kissing my neck, breathing in my ear, as he unbuttons my shorts and pushes them off, quickly making me naked from the waist down. He keeps kissing me as he discovers how wet I am for him, "Fuck it!" I love Rick in an elevator. He turns me away from him, bends me over and gets inside me as fast as he can. "Ggggrrrrrr..."

I know what he wants, "How do you want it in the elevator, my king? Hard? Fast?" All I get in response is a manly groan. "Oh, you want to take me like I belong to you. Like you just got me back to your cave, caveman style?" I actually feel him get harder at my words and decide to go further. "Oh, I see. You want to fuck me so hard that I can't stand. You want to fuck me into submission, so I'll do whatever you want?" He starts moving quicker. He likes my words. Maybe he needs a challenge. "Do you think you can actually do that? Conquer me? Go for it. Give me everything, fuck me as hard as you want, maybe harder." He slows down and slams me hard over and over and over. I had no idea he'd been holding back. I bend over farther and shake my ass at him. He's fucking me so hard that I have to brace myself, yet, "If you fuck me good enough, I'll do whatever you want."

"Huh," I actually hear a real thought go through his head and he fucks me harder, and harder. He takes my hands behind my back and holds them. He backs to the elevator wall, taking me with him and digs his fingers into my hips. Pulling me back on his cock hard and slamming into me at the same time. He pulls me up to him and, "I'm going to push you over further, so you can watch my hard cock while I fuck you. Every stroke slamming into you. I want you to see how huge I am slamming into your tight hole. I want you to tell me what you see and listen when I talk to you. Nod that you understand." I nod and bend over, but he pushes me farther so my head is between my ankles and I can see him inside me. He pulls out and pushes in, he's exquisite. "I'm going to pull out and you're going to watch carefully. Say yes."

"Yes."

He slides out a couple inches and then a couple inches more. "How many inches do you see?"

"Maybe five and your tip is still in me."

"Good girl. How long do you think I am right now?"

"Maybe seven."

"Keep watching, baby." He slides another inch out. "Oh, you feel good. Keep watching, I need back in for a minute." He slides all the way back into me with no effort at all. He strokes in and out, as I watch him move and see how solid and thick he is. "Do you see how hard I am? How you're pulled tight around me?"

"Yes, my king." I start to cry out.

"No." He slams into me hard five, six, seven, eight, nine, ten times. "Now I'm doing that again harder." And he did, I don't know where it came from and he didn't stop at ten,

"You feel so fucking good right now and I don't think I've ever been this big and hard." Fifteen, sixteen, seventeen... "Time to watch again, baby." He nestles in tight, our bodies mashed together and starts to slide out slowly. I watch as he keeps sliding out. "Tell me what you see, my queen."

"At least eight and you're still inside me."

"Yes I am. I'm going to pull out all the way and I want you to reach for my tip with your mouth and suck on it hard. I want to feel how big I am before I slam back into you." He pulls out further until his tip pops out and I reach for him as directed, latching on to his tip and sucking hard. He's big and bulbous at the end of his long thick shaft. He groans, "Oh, fuck... almost there, baby." He pulls out of my mouth. "Tell me you're watching. I want you to see me slam into you. I fucking need you so bad all the time. Fuck me."

"Watching, my king." He lines his tip up and slams hard, all the way in and he's mashed against me again. Stroking over and over, in and out. I start to sway and he grabs me around the waist.

"I've got you, my queen. But, I'm not done until you're ready to give me whatever I want." I don't respond. He keeps fucking me, harder and harder. "Harder, my queen?"

"Yes, harder please, my king."

"Oh, fuck me, fuck me."

My body is out of my control and I'm completely his. I cry out his name with every stroke. He's the only reason I'm still up, I couldn't hold myself up if I wanted to. Where did this come from? Is this off-season Rick? Bad Boy suspended Rick? "Tell me what you want, my king. Whatever you want, anything. I'm yours."

"That's all I want. You, anyway I can get you, my queen." He holds me to him, stroking in and out, and I shake in pleasure. He follows me immediately, as if my orgasm is the final straw pulling him with me. He goes to put himself away and button up, when he realizes he can't let me go. "Babe? Can you stand and pull your shorts up?"

"No and yes."

"It's okay, I've got you. I'll always have you, my queen."

I pull up my shorts and he scoops me up in his arms before I can fasten them. Kissing me immediately. It's like he gets elevator fog and then the fog clears. He gets us home, locks the door behind us and takes me to bed. He stops suddenly and inspects me, "Did I hurt you? I never want to hurt you."

"No, I'll be fine. You literally fucked me until I can't walk. Where did that come from? Just the elevator?"

"I'm suspended. I don't have to be prepared to play baseball. So, you get all of my energy."

Well fuck me. "So, that's off season sex?"

"I guess, yea."

"You were sure demanding."

"I think that was the elevator and you asked for it. You pushed with your words and that always does it for me. Whatever I want after our talk earlier, sounded good. But, Sherry, I want you the way you are. I don't want you to change, then you wouldn't be you." He looks into space, contemplating something, "Did you like it?" His voice quiet and dirty.

"Yes. Seeing how long and thick you are, watching you slide in and out of me. Fucking insane seeing and feeling it." I watch him and see his eyes glaze. "Baby, do you need more?" Next thing I know I'm naked from the waist down again and his face is buried in my sensitive sex. I never thought I'd be wishing for the off season.

CHAPTER ELEVEN

Rick's alarm goes off in time for the game and he kisses me. "Game is on in thirty minutes. I'm going to order pizza and get the game turned on. Do you want to watch with me?"

"I've been waiting for a chance to watch a game with you. I'll be out there in a minute. I like to watch the pre-game and review the lineup. Oh, no anchovies and if you want veggies on your pizza order your own separately."

"Baseball with my woman and she knows her baseball. I like it. Mushrooms aren't veggies in your book are they?"

"Of course not! Mushrooms are delicious fungus. Tell them to bring red chili flakes. Oh, we have jello shots left for tonight, too!" It's going to be a good night. I pull my panties on with my Seals tank top and grab a blanket to picnic with pizza in front of the TV. I get myself settled in front of the TV and research the lineup on Twitter while I wait for the pre-game show to start. "The lineup is pretty normal, just missing you."

"Who's catching?"

"Stray is catching and hitting fifth, Cross is in center and leading off, followed by Mason and Martin. Are you watching as a fan or to breakdown the catcher or what?"

"What are you talking about?"

"The tone of the game. Business or pleasure? Maybe we should go ahead and get started on the jello shots?"

"Might as well. I need to get back to training on Thursday." I line up the remaining jello shots on a tray and bring them to the living room. I grab a grape one, wait for Rick to be watching me and lick around the inside of the cup to release the shot, then suck it down. I want him to be relaxed and have fun while he's suspended, not stress about the game. Rick's eyes go dark as he watches me suck the jello shot and he pulls me to his lips, kissing me with need. I giggle like a school girl and grab another shot, repeating the process. I hand one to Rick, but he's watching the game. I get it. I want to watch the game like I always do, but I don't want my man focusing on a new catcher who is potentially his replacement. Besides, you should never waste jello shots. The doorbell rings and Rick hops up to get the door, "Stay down in front of the couch, the pizza guy doesn't need to see you in your underwear."

"Isn't that how you're supposed to tip them?" I laugh because, well, I'm buzzed on three shots.

"Sherry." Rick scolds me. He doesn't have a sense of humor when it comes to me.

I push it, "What? You never flashed somebody to get free food or maybe beer when you were too young or something? Maybe it's a girl thing."

Rick shakes his head. "Please tell me you don't tip with your tits."

"Sometimes you're no fun. Of course I don't! Relax and have a jello shot."

Rick shakes his head and gets the pizza from the delivery guy. He sits down on the blanket with me and opens this huge pizza with pepperoni, sausage, sliced meatballs, mushrooms, bacon, and ham. The cheese is oozing off of it and the smell is making me hungry. It's hot, so I do another jello shot. I'm not paying attention to the game, but I'm watching it. Mostly, I'm gaging it by Rick's responses and there hasn't been any. There's no score yet and it's uneventful. We're playing a three game series against Houston, and they aren't a big rival or anything. The games will be pretty tame other than the game action itself, and the stadium won't be overrun with fans from Texas.

Seals are at bat, Chase swings at the first pitch and connects with a double to the left field wall. I yell out, "Wooo! Go Chase!"

Rick turns and glares at me, "You know he can't hear you, right?"

"I can cheer for my team if I want!" He shakes his head. "I talked to you through the TV when I would watch games from home. Sometimes I encourage the pitchers with positive words. I also tell the other team they suck."

"What did you say to me through the TV?"

"That depends on what you were doing and when it was." He glares at me strange again. "Always encouraging and positive."

"Why do I feel like you're holding back? Tell me." Joking, now he's in a better mood.

"Well, I've said a lot of things: You're so fucking hot! Tag'm out, baby! He's going, throw to second! Knock him on his ass!"

"That's it? I expected more."

"I changed it up after the Locale, but I haven't watched many games on TV since then. I'm always at the stadium with you. You know exactly what I say at the stadium, you hear every word!" I laugh out loud. "You know more of what I say than I do. I still don't have a clue what I say in my sleep. You should probably tell me."

"No. That's private." He smirks.

"How can it be private if I'm the one saying it?"

"I think it's just for me. If you wanted you to know, you'd remember." I smack him with a throw pillow and he takes it away from me, grabs my hands and holds them up while he searches the depths of my eyes like he's trying to read my soul. His eyes are serious, dark and heavy. "You tell me what you want. You tell me what you're scared of. Sometimes they're the same thing. Some mornings you tell me about your dreams." He turns away and then back up at me, "I love all of it. I love you. I want to give you what you want more than anything." He takes a deep breath and quietly continues, "I want it, too."

Shit. I do a couple more jello shots and lean back to watch the game. Rick reaches for my hand and entangles his fingers with mine as he pulls me closer to him. I'm wasted and do my best to keep my mouth shut. At least I'm getting to watch the game and hold hands with my man.

CHAPTER TWELVE

I wake up to the smell of coffee brewing. It's morning and I don't remember going to bed last night or the end of the game, but I'm in my bed and I'm naked. Rick is next to me sleeping and I remember the conversation we had about what I say in my sleep, but nothing in between other than jello shots and holding his hand. It gives me an idea. I snuggle against him and keep my eyes closed.

"I don't remember coming to bed last night." I say into the room and wonder if the man I'm sleeping next to will respond.

"I carried you to bed." He says in a sleepy voice.

"What do I want?" Pushing my luck, but asking before I get him talking too much.

"You want to give me things. You love me."

"What am I scared of?" I need details.

"Your feelings and wanting to give me things." It's the same as what he said last night, I tell him what I want and I'm scared of what I want.

"What things do I want to give you?"

"You know."

"I want to give you a lot of things. What things do I tell you I want to give you?"

Rick wraps his arms around me and holds me as tightly against him as he can. Wide-eyed and obviously awake, he'd been going along with my ruse. "Maybe you're right. Maybe you need to know. I'm going to tell you, but I'm going to hold you and not let go. You will want to get out of bed and go for coffee or use something as a distraction to ignore it, run from it. I'm not going to let you. You run when you're scared. You've said things when we're having sex, but I think that's almost the same as in your sleep. You want to fill the soft spot in my heart where I've been hurt. You're what I've needed my whole life, you Sherry." He stops talking, possibly reconsidering this whole conversation or maybe trying to put together the best words. "Do you still want to know? You want me to say it?"

"Yes." I need to know.

"You tell me you want me to get you pregnant, so we can have Elle. You tell me you never wanted that and you only want it with me." He tightens his grip and he's right, my flight instinct is trying to kick in. "You know that's a sensitive subject for me and I think that's why you don't say it when you're awake, you don't want to hurt me." He stops again, assessing my reaction. "Then you tell me you're scared of getting pregnant." He stops and waits, like I should say something.

Without thinking, words come out of my mouth and I hear them for the first time as I say them, "It's true, and I want it more than I'm scared of it. The most important thing is that I'm with you." My whole body relaxes and I don't want to run. I guess I just needed to say it.

Rick's eyes light up, "Sherry, tell me what you want while you're awake and coherent. I want to know it's real. I want to read it in your eyes."

I gaze at him and smile, "I want to be with you forever. I want you to get me pregnant, so we can have Elle together. I'm not running. I love you, Rick, and I only want it with you."

He kisses me, like he's breathing me in and I'm his air. "It's even better when you're awake." He rests his forehead against mine. "I want us to have our time together and we'll get to everything else. It makes me so happy to hear you say the words. I have plans for us, my queen."

"Like what?"

"You'll see." He grins at me like a fool. "Can you book our vacation today? And, your away game airfare?"

"I'll book our vacation, but are you sure I should book the away game airfare?"

"Do you mean because I could get traded?"

"Yes. I don't want you to get traded. You've always been a Seal and should stay one. I'll go with you, if you get traded."

"I know you're a fan and know all about trades, but I didn't think about talking with you about it. I guess, I haven't had anyone like you in my life that mattered." He laughs, "You were funny watching the game last night. Naked girl sitting there and second-guessing the coaching on both teams. You were drunk, but you know your baseball." He stops and gazes at me, "You'd really go with me?"

"Of course, think of it as a long road trip." My mind goes dirty. "Think of the silver lining. Do you know how many elevators there are out there, just waiting for us?" I start to laugh, but Rick's eyes go dark and needy. He kisses me with intent and my belly starts to flutter. His hands flat on my back as he holds me to him. His lips warm and soft on mine, while his beard brushes against my face. He holds me and kisses me for the longest time. "I really do love you. I'll do anything for you, my king."

"The game starts at 12:40 today. Want to go get breakfast?" Rick must be hungry.

"How about I cook breakfast for you?"

"Even better." He gives me a quick kiss and we get out of bed. I beeline for the coffee and check what I have to work with in the kitchen.

"Omelette, biscuits and gravy, or my magic waffles?" I call out to Rick.

"Magic waffles?"

"Waffles it is!" He wants to know what makes them magic, but he said waffles and that's enough for me. I grab the bacon, buttermilk, eggs and butter from the refrigerator, and I retrieve my custom waffle mix. Yes, I have my own waffle mix that I put together myself. It's so much better than the box. I melt some butter in the microwave while I beat up some eggs with buttermilk. I add my special dry mix and stir until it's almost incorporated, then add melted butter until I get it to the right consistency. I set the batter aside and warm up my waffle iron. I toss precooked bacon pieces into a pan and toast them up a bit, making sure they're crispy and bringing out some of the bacon grease. When the waffle iron is ready, I brush it with butter, add some batter and drop in some bacon. I close the waffle iron and flip it over repeating the process, but this time I add chocolate bits and bacon. I flip the waffle maker back over and wait for the light to go off, keeping an eye on the steam to make sure they don't overcook. I pull the first waffle and repeat the process again, brushing the iron and refilling it with batter and bacon. I make six waffles total, half bacon and half bacon with chocolate. Rick walks into the kitchen while I'm in the process of making the waffles and he catches me pulling them to pieces and eating them as I make them—a quarter of a bacon waffle, then a quarter of a bacon waffle with chocolate, and he wants to know what makes them magic! Ha!

Rick takes a piece of waffle and gets a mouthful with bacon. He groans in pleasure, as if he's submitting to the food coma. I hand him a piece with the chocolate and he stares at me stunned. "I didn't think it could get better than bacon. This is delicious."

"Wait until next time. If you're good, I'll make banana and chocolate."

"You're a fantastic cook, my queen. How did I get so lucky?" He smiles at me with waffle shoved in his mouth.

I smile because his words mean so much to me. "I'm going to bake something to take to Carter when I present him my offer."

"Why don't you bake enough for the whole clubhouse when I go back after my suspension?"

"I'm happy to. What do you want me to bake?"

"Cross wants more of those chocolate chip cookie bars. He's been texting me."

"I can do that. What do you want?"

Rick turns me to face him and holds my eyes with his, "I have everything I could ever want." He kisses me and we go back to eating waffles. Tell me again how it is that I deserve this man?

"Do you have any plans tonight?" He smiles.

"Well, there's this guy I've been spending all my time with. But, I might be able to get away. What do you have in mind?"

Rick shakes his head at me, "Date night. I want to take you out, my queen. Can you be ready at 6pm?"

"Yes. I can't wait." I really can't because I love that he plans date night and I'm along for whatever he has in store.

"Tonight is fun, not fancy. It's a jeans night. I'm going to take a run before the game. Please book our vacation." He hands me his credit card. "And, keep the credit card info for booking your away game flights. I want you there with me and I'm paying for it." He looks me in the eye like he's looking a runner back to third and he means business, I'm not making a run for home. He disappears into the other room and I quickly clean up the kitchen, before getting to work. Rick walks up behind me in his running shorts and T-shirt, wraps his arms around me and turns me so he can apply his patented you-won't-forget-me-kiss. He takes off on his run, leaving me punch drunk yet again.

CHAPTER THIRTEEN

I spend the rest of the morning checking my messages and working on our vacation reservations. I get lost in the vacation plans. I can't help but daydream about spending two perfect weeks on the beach with my Rick. I look at the cottage we'll be staying in and the beautiful view of the clear green blue ocean. I scan through the photo gallery of the resort, dreaming about all of the gorgeous sunsets and perusing the updates that have been made since my last visit. I close my eyes and I hear the ocean, I feel the tropical sun on my skin, I smell the fresh pineapple and coconut oil, and I taste the passion orange juice. I imagine us wandering the North Shore exploring together, but mostly it's us lying on the beach together and having plenty of alone time. I envision Rick in his board shorts and no shirt, and me in my bikini snuggled into the crook of his arm. Both of us getting a tropical tan as we nap together on our lanai. The ultimate relaxing vacation and somehow I get to enjoy it with my not-a-fantasy-anymore-baseball-boyfriend.

I feel Rick's warm hand on me and I reach up to put my arms around him. "Hey, baby," I start talking sleepily.

"I'm just letting you know I'm home." I open my eyes and look at him. Happy to see him, not happy to be home and not on the beach in Hawaii. "Sounds like Hawaii is going to be perfect." He has a dirty grin on his face and who knows what I said. Well, he does and he probably won't tell me.

Rick takes off for a quick shower before the game and I attempt to get some more work done, but in reality all I do is turn on the pregame and check the lineup. Rick gets out of the shower and I call out, "Saben is catching today." That should make this an easier game to watch than last night. There are only three more games including today until Rick is back in the clubhouse.

Rick joins me on the couch to watch the game and this time I'll actually be watching the game, so he'll experience what it's really like to watch a game with me. The game starts and Rick's picking everything apart.

"Saben doesn't have the skills that Stray has." Rick starts in, analyzing everything.

"Not near, but Stray is a righty like you and Saben is a lefty." Rick turns and looks at me, as if he's waiting for more. "You have a more determined attitude on the field than either one of them. Saben always feels more laid back, but Stray is definitely trying to prove himself—but, he's still a baby. Also, you're catlike behind the plate and instinctual. Saben isn't. Stray's getting ahead of himself, he'll probably be great in a year or so."

"Anything else, my baseball queen?" He grins and laughs, but doesn't disagree with me.

"Actually yes, pay attention to Rhett. I bet he can be an ace if he's given the right support." Rick shakes his head and we continue to watch the game. No action yet, and the team has been defending well.

I've intrigued my king with my baseball opinions, "What else do you see when you're watching the team?"

I look at him unsure and not wanting to say something I shouldn't, but spill it anyway, "I'm starting with a disclaimer. I love my team. Cross should be in centerfield every game, he has the range and isn't afraid to dive for it. Mason feels better to me when he's in left and I'd love to see him get tried at shortstop. Rock belongs in right field, he's solid, he's senior, and he's earned it. Bubbles needs to get benched and used strictly as a designated hitter, he doesn't care about the game as much as he does other things any more. Martin is as good at first base as you are at catcher and it'll be years before somebody takes that spot from him, nothing matters more to him than the game when he's on the field. Lucky's good wherever he gets played and I know that's his job as a utility player, but he'd be a bigger benefit for the team if he played the same position every game and I like him best at third base. Second base is a revolving door, nobody is sticking there and we need somebody new there. The back-up outfielders are what they are and do fine when they're needed, but I can never even remember the guy's name who's been playing third. He isn't impressive at all. The relievers have been doing a great job, but not getting as many innings of work this year. The starters are strong and going deep into games." I stop my ramble and watch Rick processing.

"I get a different view from my vantage point behind home plate. But, I'm going to watch for what you're seeing."

"I'm not playing. I'm not paying attention to signs, balls and bats getting thrown all around me or players running toward me ready to knock me out of their way to score. I envision it more as a big puzzle with moving pieces. I'm sure you have a better idea than I do, I'm just a fan." I smile at him, happy to have a real baseball conversation.

Rick leans in, "You're much more than a fan to me." He presses his lips to mine, sending his electricity through my body and pulls me over to sit against him with his arm around me while we watch the game. He gets an odd look on his face, "I've never sat like this and watched a game with a woman before." I pull my feet up onto the couch and snuggle into him, enjoying the moment and the game.

Time for the seventh inning stretch, so I get up and toss a bag of microwave popcorn in to pop and run for a bathroom break before the popcorn burns. I grab the hot bag from the microwave and a couple sodas, then back to my spot on the couch. The score is 4-1 Seals and those rookies in the outfield have been killing it, generating all four RBIs. The rest of the game isn't very eventful and my king seems to be more interested in me. Who am I to argue?

Rick starts to rub my arm and hold me tighter to him. I catch him looking at me and not his usual glare while he shakes his head thinking I'm off the deep end or intense when he's serious. He's just looking at me. He pushes my hair out of my face, running his fingers through it and cups my head bringing my lips to his. He releases me, "You make me so happy." His eyes tell me that he loves me and wants me. "I have a couple errands to take care of and I'll be back to get you at 6pm for our date night, okay my queen?"

"I'll be ready." I smile at him, happy to have time to get ready. It's a jeans night not a fancy night and those are my favorite, more my style and I can play with my outfit. I already know it's going to be a fun night. Rick disappears into the bedroom for a few minutes and returns wearing his perfect fitting jeans, a black T-shirt that's stretched enticingly across his chest and tennis shoes. He grabs me, kissing me passionately before he winks at me and walks out the door. That man drives me crazy! I want to look good for him tonight, but not be overdressed so I follow his example and pull out my best jeans. I look through my shoes for my cutest tennis shoes and my red metallic Chucks jump out at me. I know exactly what I want to wear! I turn on some music and listen to my *Fun* playlist while I get ready, it starts off with The Go-Go's "We Got the Beat." I strip down to nothing and start over with red satin panties and a matching push-up bra. I pull on my jeans and my sparkly Chucks. I want to wear my black sleeveless deep V-neck that says POP STAR in red foil letters across my breasts. Before I pull it on, I brush my hair out and try a few different things, finally taking my curling iron to it and going fluffy. I have time to get it all curled and it'll make me feel like I'm dressed for a date even though I'm basically wearing jeans and a T-shirt. I pull my shirt on and look in the mirror as "One Way or Another" by Blondie comes on. I put on smoky silver eye shadow, black eyeliner, black mascara, a touch of blush and cherry flavored fire engine red lip gloss. I look in the mirror again and I love all of the red. I'm pumped up, dancing around the house and singing to "Lola" by the Kinks with the volume turned up.

I scream out startled when someone touches me. Rick got back and I didn't hear him come in. "Sorry, my queen. I knocked because it's date night, but you couldn't hear me over the music." He looks me up and down, "Those are some red lips."

"They're cherry flavored just for you." His body reacts, he wants to taste.

"I can't kiss you. I'll mess you up before we ever get out of the house."

I giggle, "It's just lip gloss and I have more."

"Before you distract me, I want to take you out tomorrow for a late night picnic. Interested?" He waits to see how I respond and he has a bag in his hand.

"Anything with you, my king." I smile wondering what he's up to.

"I thought you could put together the food, seems right up your alley." He pulls a backpack out of the bag, "Everything we need will have to fit in here and I'm driving, so no alcohol. Think midnight snack or something like that."

The backpack is made for picnics. It has a section that keeps things cold, a place for a blanket, and everything else you might need. I see a trip to the public market on my to do list for tomorrow. "Challenge accepted!"

He puts his arms around my waist and pulls me in for a taste of my cherry lips. "The cherry is fun, but you taste sweet all by yourself." Enjoying my playfulness and making sure I know he loves me the way I am, without anything extra added.

"We're walking tonight. Are you ready to go?" I put on my moto jacket, adding my ID and lip gloss to the pocket. I smile at him and he takes my hand as we walk out the door.

We casually stroll and talk on our way to wherever we're going. "I've really enjoyed having more time with you the last few days. I've been rewarded, not suspended." His words make me warm all over because I feel the same way. At first I felt guilty because it never would've happened if I wasn't there, or I simply managed to keep my mouth to myself. But, getting to help him with things like getting his hand to stop bleeding and reducing his pain, well, somehow it burrowed him deeper into my heart and brought us closer together. The effects of real life, pushing us together rather than pulling us apart like they do to so many people. I'm thankful his injuries weren't worse and the last few days of his suspension have been time for us.

We walk up to the Locale and Rick opens the door for me, "I thought it would be fun to go back to where it started." He guides me through the door with his hand on the small of my back and gets a nod from the hostess. This has obviously been set up ahead of time. Rick leads me to the table in the back corner where I found him that night a couple months ago and I slide into the corner with him next to me. There's a bouquet of tropical flowers on the table and a small white gift box with a purple bow stuck on top of it. I look at him and he nods at me to open the box. There's a long gold beaded style necklace with a key pendant on it engraved with "You have the key to my heart" on one side and R+S on the other.

"I love it!" I kiss him leaving a lip print on his cheek and he blushes. I wrap the chain around my neck three times and wear it like a choker, arranging the key to hang down a couple inches in the center front. I hug him and whisper in his ear, "I don't know how I got so lucky. I don't deserve you. I'll always be yours, my king." His arm pulls me closer to him, sitting hip to hip.

"You deserve everything, my queen." He smiles at me. "How about dinner and then we actually play some pool?" We order drinks and dinner and more drinks. This is one of the rare times he drinks while we're out, probably because we could walk. We laugh together and talk the whole evening. We even play pool after he shows me how to handle the stick, which turned a bit dirty. We had to take a break in the parking lot after he was rubbing up against me from behind. The juke box was playing and when the music stopped, Rick went over and got it playing again. The first song he plays is "Oh Sherrie" by Steve Perry. Then he's at my ear, "Oh Sherry, I'm in love." He's got the lyrics wrong, but that's typical for this song and I appreciate his effort. His version is better. We continue to play pool sloppily and I dance around to the music playing. "Thinking Out Loud" comes on and he grabs me, holding me close and dancing with me. It's a special moment when I feel his heart beat with mine, our eyes connect and he whispers the last line of the song in my ear, "We found love..." I've never heard anything more sincere.

We keep tossing back the drinks, I order shots to challenge him. I'm having so much fun and Rick is, too. Touching each other. Kissing each other. In a happy haze together. Teasing him by swaying my hips, shaking my butt in front of him when I bend over to shoot, and making sure he has a view down my top when I lean over the table. Rubbing against him at every opportunity. To say we're buzzed is an understatement. We aren't paying attention to anyone around us. We don't care. We're just out having fun together. I walk up to him and put my hands on his chest. His shirt pulled snug across his pecks has had my attention all evening, I finally give in and touch with both hands, fingers spread. He draws my lips to his and I move my hands, now gripping his fine ass. He pushes against me, telling me how much he wants me. We dance around together playfully, comfortable together. Our server keeps bringing us shots of Jack. I gaze into his eyes and claim his mouth right there, climbing him and wrapping my legs around him. His hands hot on my back and the need in his pants evident, hard against me. Rick walks to our table, I pick up my flowers and he walks home in the late night with me wrapped around him, kissing him everywhere I can reach.

It's a short walk and we're home, Rick steps into the elevator and I can't help myself, "We're in the elevator."

"I know, baby. That's not what I want. I don't want to be a bonehead caveman. I want to love you." We get home and Rick locks the door behind us. He slides me down his body, and I put my flowers in water while he puts on some music. Apparently, he has a few playlists as well and starts his *Lovin' Time* playlist. It starts with "Thinking Out Loud" and he puts his arms around me to dance around our place. He leads me to bed and I pull his T-shirt off over his head, focused on his chest that's had my attention all night long. I can't help myself, I kiss his chest all over, dragging my tongue and nibbling a bit as I go. He's so fucking sexy. I run my hands up and down his upper arms, exploring his muscles. I kick my shoes off and he pulls my shirt off, finding my red push up bra. He kisses the tops of my breasts and unbuttons my jeans while I unbutton his. He's not wasting any time. He hooks his fingers on my panties and pulls them off with my jeans. His jeans disappear and he leans over me kissing me as he slides into home, "I love you, my queen. I'll always love you. Tell me you want to be mine."

Rick's unbelievable sliding in and out of me slowly, methodically. "I'm already yours, my king. I want to give you everything I can, to show you how much I love you. It'll always be you. I want nothing more than to be yours forever. You're my only man, my only love." He holds me tight, claiming my mouth with his while he continues to push and pull, driving me out of my mind with his lips on me and his hard love inside me. His heart beating strong, his pulse racing, his breathing goes ragged and uneven, enjoying the weight of his body on mine. I feel how much he loves me and I give myself to him completely.

He strokes into me deliciously and repeatedly, bringing me to climax multiple times. Each time telling me, "I love you, my queen. I'm only for you, Sherry. You're my happiness."

CHAPTER FOURTEEN

I wake up early Thursday morning with Rick holding me possessively and our legs entangled. My alarm hasn't buzzed yet. I don't smell coffee brewing. It's early, I'm awake, the playlist from last night is still playing on repeat and I'm in bed naked with my man. I'm a happy girl. "Won't Stop" by OneRepublic is playing and it hits me that he made this playlist for me. I didn't pick up on it in my drunken state last night, but I should've since it started with our song. Its like he made me a mix tape.

I'm anxious for our late night picnic and lay in bed considering options for the backpack. I want to bake something. I want something sweet and something savory. Maybe a cheese sampling, fruit, crackers, and some dry deli meat. I need to inspect the backpack and see exactly how much room I have. I also need non-alcoholic beverages. I admit I'm curious about where we're going, but the anticipation makes it fun and I have no idea what he has in mind.

I roll over and snuggle into Rick's chest, wrapping my arms around him, running my hands up and down his back, and kissing his chest after having flashbacks of last night. The vision of him in that tight T-shirt is permanently imprinted on my brain, and did I mention he's sexy as fuck? But, the way he loved me last night—He made me shake with pleasure and emotion, and I know he was showing me our future. It's almost as if this strong man feels like he needs to prove himself to me. He doesn't need to, but I'm not complaining.

Rick runs his hands down my body and rolls me underneath him. "I may not need to, but I want to and I'm going to again," he says as he pushes into me. He moves slowly and doesn't seem completely awake. He gets a big grin and groans in pleasure as he moves, "So, you think I'm sexy as fuck, huh?"

Damn it! I was talking out loud again! I can play this. "Yes! Have you looked in the mirror?"

"You're my version of sexy, my queen. Everything about you is perfect. The way you make me feel—oh fuck me." He strokes into me harder and faster, with need taking him over. He grabs my nipple with his teeth and sucks my breast into his mouth, tugging at me like a direct line to my orgasm. Everything crashes in on me at once and I scream out his name as he pushes me head first over the edge and goes with me, releasing his pleasure with a manly guttural groan. Can I start everyday this way? Rick lays his head down on the pillow next to mine and I fall back to sleep in his arms.

THE ALARM WAKES me a couple hours later and I smell the coffee brewing. I stretch and Rick whispers in my ear, "Good morning, Sherry. I love you, my queen."

I turn to him and kiss him, "There's no one else like you, my king. I love you, Rick. I'll always be yours." I say this looking straight into his eyes, so he knows I'm awake and not just saying sleepy things. He hugs me tight and I feel his happiness radiate off of him.

"Do I get any other details on our late night picnic?" I'm curious.

"You need to wear long pants, preferably good jeans, and good closed toed shoes. We'll be outside, so don't worry about your hair and make-up —I like you without it."

Interesting. "Okay, then I have a few errands to run today before work."

"I need to run and work out, so I'm ready for the field on Saturday. Game is at 7:05 tonight. Afternoon nap between my work out and the game. We'll take off on our adventure after the game. Okay, my queen?"

"I can't wait." I kiss him and get up quickly, my mind racing with ideas for the backpack. I hear Rick on the phone with Chase, planning to go work out together. I pour coffee for both of us and peruse the refrigerator and pantry.

"I'm going to breakfast with Cross and we're going to work out. He's picking me up and I'll be back later, my queen." He disappears into the shower quickly and there's a knock at the door before he comes back out. I check the peep hole and see Chase looking back at me.

I open the door, "Good morning, honey!"

Chase hugs me, "Hey, sweetheart."

"Come on in. He's still in the shower. Want some coffee?" I offer up being a good hostess.

"No thanks. Got any cookies?"

I pull the reserve from my last batch from the freezer and pop them in the microwave for thirty seconds. I hand them over to Chase with a glass of milk.

His eyes get big, he's such a big kid. "Thank you," and he's a happy camper.

Rick comes out ready to go. He shakes his head when he finds me hanging out with a cookie eating Cross. He kisses me, leaving me punch drunk and drags Cross off on their work out. I happily eat the last two cookies with my coffee and get my day started.

I go to my closet and pull out my good pair of old school regular jeans and tennis shoes that are good for hiking, not just looking cute. I thumb through my closet in search of a top that's better than a plain T-shirt, something to add some style to my jeans. I find a fitted ribbed black long-sleeved shirt with laces at the chest and immediately trade my tennis shoes for my black combat boots.

I find where Rick left the backpack and realize he already had it stored somewhere. I wonder what else he has hiding. The backpack has a pouch for a blanket at the bottom, two tube shaped spots for wine bottles, an area that can be kept cool and open space for room temperature food, utensils, napkins, etc. It has quite a bit of room, considering it's not very big. I decide to make my chocolate chip banana bread and baseball sugar cookies for my sweet. I've been considering my savory options and I keep changing my mind. Maybe I'll make up some Italian Sand-wiches on Focaccia, and maybe some grapes or sliced up fruit, possibly some popcorn. I toss my beach blanket into the wash, and go to the store.

I wander the store picking up bananas that are a little over ripe, a tube of red icing, a fresh loaf of Focaccia, a variety of Italian meats and cheeses from the deli, a bunch of grapes and a take and bake pizza. I pick up some throw away plastic containers, so it'll be easy to pack and nothing will get squished.

I get home and immediately mix up my sugar cookie dough. It needs time to chill before I slice it up and bake it. I turn the oven on to preheat. I mash up my bananas and mix up my banana bread batter, adding the chocolate chips last and pour it into a buttered loaf pan. I put the chocolate chip banana bread in the oven and wash the grapes, putting them in a container ready for the backpack. I move my beach blanket to the dryer and cut the Focaccia, seasoning the inside with garlic salt, basil, oregano, black pepper, and a drizzle of olive oil on both sides. I cover the bottom with provolone cheese, followed by layers of thinly sliced ham, pepperoni, and hot capicola. Then I top it with another layer of cheese and put the top on. I cut the sandwich into finger sandwiches and load them into plasticware. I really want something salty and I'm inspired to make some popcorn. I get a pot with a lid, put it on the flame and add some popcorn kernels along with some butter and olive oil. I put the lid on it and swirl it around until it starts to pop. I keep shaking it around and listen for the popping to stop, hoping I don't burn it. I turn off the stove, and I give it a peek and a taste. I add some more olive oil, salt, some fine crushed red chili flakes and some grated parmesan cheese. I put the lid back on and give it a good shake, trying to get everything coated evenly. I give it a taste and I'm satisfied, so I package it up for the backpack. I check on my banana bread and it's almost done, it needs a few more minutes. I get my sugar cookie dough out and slice thin round medallions, dip them in sugar and arrange them on my parchment lined baking sheet. I pull my banana bread out of the oven and slide my cookies in. I take the bread out of the pan to cool and it smells delicious, so I have a piece. I need to get some work done before Rick gets back. I can't neglect my work because I'm having fun playing house with Rick Seno.

Interesting. Am I playing house with Rick Seno? Sometimes reality just slaps you in the face. First of all, I'm dating, no, I'm living with Rick Seno. Holy hell! I've gone from having a fantasy baseball boyfriend and dirty dreams to Rick Seno living with me and in my bed every night. Not only that, but he takes me out on date nights. We have fun together, the sex is amazing and he says he loves me. I know it's true. I don't understand why. He must be off his rocker. I worry that my unique brand of crazy will send him running away, but he's broken, too. That might be what keeps him with me. Honestly, after the last few days I believe he really does need me. Before I thought he'd move on and date a woman his own age or maybe one of those hotties who are always hanging around the field. Somebody who would succumb to his desire to take care of them and pay their way. Not any more. He needs someone who can stand up to him and be his equal, it's why he wants to take care of me and pay my way. We're learning to be a team. Though, I admit, the beginning of this week was probably the hardest day of my life. I'm embracing my girliness, and even though I don't want him to take care of me—I need him and I need him to be okay. I'd never felt things, said things, considered things that ran through my head on replay. Hearing my own voice and knowing it was me, I was the worried girlfriend. I don't do those things! I'm independent! I'm self-sufficient! I don't need a man or anyone else to take care of me. And I still don't, but I want one. Only one. Only Rick Seno. The funny thing, or maybe not so funny thing is that I'm not playing. This is my life. This is what I want. It's what Rick wants right now and I hope it stays that way. He's my soul mate.

Distracted by my own thoughts, I suddenly smell cookies and pull them out just in time. I move the cookies to the cooling rack and let them cool completely before the next step. I slice up some thick pieces of the chocolate chip banana bread and put it in plasticware, ready for the backpack.

I move on to my work, checking my email and social media. I reply to a few emails, but not much going on really. So, I take the opportunity to write up my proposal for Carter and the Seals. Illustrating how it will save them money by freeing up time for Carter to do other things. I put together a portfolio of group trips I've planned to use as a resume accompanying my proposal. I go over it multiple times, trying to make it perfect. I'm ready, and I plan to drop in on him at his office when I bring in cookies for the whole clubhouse.

I fold up my dry beach blanket and pack it in the backpack along with the popcorn, banana bread, and napkins. I put a couple bottles of water in the freezer and move on to my baseball cookies. I knead the tube of red icing and snip off the tip, then I carefully pipe baseball stitching onto my cookies. I love them!

I have some free time and take advantage. I change into my bikini and lie out on my lounge chair to enjoy some sun on my private balcony, face down with no top. It's a warm, lazy afternoon and I'm falling asleep, so I go inside and lay down on my bed... The warmth of the sand and the breeze as it blows over my body are relaxing, leaving me to focus on the sound of the ocean and the tender touch of a hand and lips on my body. The palm trees swaying and the sea turtles surfing. The tropical sun zapping all of my energy, I sleep while my man's hands protect me... I'm dreaming, but those hands are real. Rick whispers in my ear, "I'm home, my queen," and his hands wander my body, exploring me like he needs to have me. He moves his hands from my belly to my breasts to my ass and finally my hips, and he rocks against me. "I love you, my queen. I missed you. I need to have you."

I roll to him and gaze into his eyes, "I love you, too." He was only gone part of the day and I missed him, too. It's getting worse. I'm fucked. "I missed you, too, my king." I kiss him and he pulls me on top of him, straddling him while I kiss him. His need reaching for me, I slide back onto his hard cock, dragging my kisses from his mouth down his neck to his strong chest. His chest is solid muscle and I want to touch it, lick it, kiss it, bite it, suck on it—I want to leave a mark with my teeth. He grabs my ass appreciatively and strokes into me deep, taking control and driving me to call out his name. Sometimes his touch is all it takes to drive me out of control.

He rolls us over, taking me underneath him and I whimper as he pushes into me all the way, holding his solid length there while he talks to me, "I need you. I need this. We fit perfect together. I only want you. I only love you." I feel his heat. I reach around his neck and pull my mouth to his, claiming him while he strokes into me. He feels amazing and I know this isn't going to be a marathon because he's already breathing unevenly. This is him needing to have me. This is one of those times he needs to know I'm here and I'm his. It's part of how he's broken, what other women have done to him. I hate that they've made him feel like this, but I'm happy to be the one he needs. I cry out at his every stroke and it adds to his drive. He tries to pull back, but I don't let him. I hold his head and kiss his neck, sucking and nibbling, driving his intensity and pushing him closer to release. He pulls away and takes my mouth with his quickly, roughly, letting me know I'm his. As he pulls away I kiss his chest and bite there, sucking as he strokes into me hard, sending me farther over the edge than before and I cry out into his chest as I bite him and bring him with me.

I wake up to Rick worshiping between my legs a few hours later. It has to be the best way to get woken up. Better than breakfast in bed. Once he knows I'm awake he slides two fingers into me while he licks at my sensitive nub and sets me off almost instantly. Fuck me. He takes me in his arms as he climbs me and slides into me deliciously. He kisses me and he has something else in mind. He pulls out and drags me to the edge of the bed where he takes me from behind, slamming into me hard. I may be his playground this afternoon. I'm not complaining. He leans over me and nibbles at the back of my neck while he circles my magic button. I scream out at the connection and he pushes it farther. "Tell me you want all of me. Tell me you always want me in you." His voice raspy and giving away that he's on the edge.

"I want all of you that I can get. Every inch of you. I always want you inside me. Nobody makes me feel like you do. Nobody else can ever have me."

"Fuck me fuck me fuck me." His release is hard and pulsating. He pushes into me hard and takes me with him.

A few minutes later he pulls out and I roll over. He has a huge grin on his face and kisses me. He wraps his arms around me and picks me up. I put my legs around his waist and he slides right back into me, like it's where he belongs. He carries me to the bathroom and turns on the shower. Kissing me and holding us under the warm shower spray.

CHAPTER FIFTEEN

Rick and I miss the pregame, ending up in front of the TV in time for the second inning to start. I preheat the oven and put the take and bake pizza in to bake between innings. We're comfy in sweats and T-shirts, snuggled together on the couch to watch the game. Stray is behind the plate tonight with Tommy pitching. There's no score after the third inning, but in the bottom of the fourth Cross hits a home run with Mason and Tommy on base. Martin hits a double. Stray hits a double, bringing Martin around. Lucky gets a single, pushing Stray to third. Rock hits a home run bringing in Stray and Lucky Lucine. We could do no wrong in the fourth inning, it was a continuous line of hitters taking turns getting hits and RBIs. The end of the fourth inning and the score is 9-0 Seals. I worry about games like this because of the false sense of security. There are still five innings left and anything can happen. Nobody scored in the fifth inning. Nobody scored in the sixth inning. Top of the seventh and Houston had a run like our fourth, scoring eight and taking the score to 9-8 Seals. Bottom of the seventh and the Seals respond with thunder, Martin hits a grand slam and Rock hits a double bringing in Stray. Lucine gets tagged out at home and Tommy hits into a double play. Score at the end of seven 14-8 Seals. It's insane! We never play high scoring games! Top of the eighth, Houston scores two more. Bottom of the eighth, bases loaded and we can't score to save our life. Top of the ninth, bases loaded and Houston gets a grand slam. The game is tied at 14 and we go to the bottom of the ninth hoping for a walk off win. It doesn't happen. The game goes into extra innings and as much as I love baseball, let me be clear, I'm anxious for our late night picnic adventure and we aren't going until the game is over. This game needs to hurry up already! The game is still tied at 14 and going into the fourteenth inning, current game time is 4 hours 50 minutes and it's almost midnight. The players are tired, the silly mistakes start to happen and I hope Houston loses it first. Bottom of the fourteenth inning, Kris Martin hits a solo homer off Houston's seventh pitcher of the game and we get the walk off win 15-14 Seals. I cheer out loud and Rick shakes his head.

"Should we get ready for our picnic adventure?" I ask ready to find out what he has planned.

"It's later than I thought. We can do it another night." He sees my frown, "Actually later might make it better. Go get ready."

"Yay!" I smile and start a fresh pot of coffee to put in the backpack. I take off for the bedroom to get ready. I change into my jeans and put on my black combat boots with thick socks. I brush out my hair and put a hair tie around my wrist. I pull on my long sleeved black top that laces up at the neckline and leave the laces loose. I look in the mirror and I'm happy. I pour the coffee into a thermos and pack it in the backpack. I pack the sandwiches and grapes, and package up the baseball cookies. Everything fits into the backpack easily and I pull the frozen water bottles from the freezer, dropping them into the wine bottle spot in the backpack. Rick walks out, ready to go. He's wearing jeans, black combat boots and a black long sleeve waffle-knit shirt that's stretched deliciously across his chest. We kinda match. I hand Rick the backpack, proud of the spread I've put together.

"Are you ready to go, my queen?"

"Yes, I just need to grab my jacket."

"You don't need a jacket. I've got that covered."

"Okay." I glare at him funny, pretty sure I'm going to freeze my ass off.

"Just you, you don't need money or keys or anything else." He smiles and now I really want to know what we're doing. Rick locks the door and we walk out to his car. He pops open the trunk, but rather than putting the backpack in the trunk he starts pulling things out. He pulls out a lime green leather jacket with a black stripe and white reflective trim and he hands it to me. "Put this on." He pulls out another jacket that's exactly the same, but larger from the trunk and puts it on. It fits him like a glove. He reaches for me and zips mine up, it's snug in all the right places. "So, have you ever been on a motorcycle?" He hands me a matte black helmet with custom lime green paint on the back at the neck that reads "My Queen". I look around and see there's a motorcycle parked in front of Rick's Challenger, sharing the parking space. It's a cool looking matte gray Yamaha motorcycle with lime green wheels. It looks fast.

"Yes. I rode dirt bikes when I was a kid and I've ridden with friends before."

"Are you up for this adventure?"

"Anything with you, my king." I smile at him knowing he has a plan. "Um, how many women have you called your queen?"

Rick laughs, "Only you, Sherry. I bought the helmet and had it done custom for you. I had it linked to mine, so we can talk and listen to the same music while we're riding." He shows me his helmet matches and has custom lime green paint just like mine, but his says "Catch Me".

I smile at him, custom car, probably custom bike, custom matching helmets and matching leather jackets. I'm his queen. "My queen. I love being your queen." How was I not aware my fantasy baseball player boyfriend rode a motorcycle? This seems like something I would've heard about on an interview or something. Then again, it's Rick Seno and he's one of the most private players there is. Well, until he started carrying me through lobbies and dragging me into dugouts and kissing me at the field wall and holding my hand at the net. "So, do you have any other secrets?"

He looks at me caught off guard. "This isn't a secret. I have a garage I rent to keep my bike, sporting goods, accessories and stuff like that I use, but takes up too much space. Mostly, it belongs in a garage and not inside."

"What else should I know about you?"

"That I'll do anything for you. I'll never hurt you. And, I want to make all of your dreams come true." Rick leans in and kisses me with intent. "Are you ready?"

I nod with enthusiasm and he pulls his bike out into the open. I put on my helmet and he straps it on tight, making sure it fits right. He puts on his helmet, fastens the strap and starts talking to me through the helmet. "Can you hear me? I haven't tested this yet."

Cool! "Yes. Can you hear me?"

"Yes. Let's try the music." He turns on music and it's old school Metallica "Seek and Destroy," his walk up song.

"Bike ride appropriate. I love the old Metallica." Helmets appear to be functioning correctly. We're wearing our matching jackets and helmets. Time to get on the road. Rick puts the backpack on backwards, wearing it on his front and climbs on the bike. He starts it up and stands over it, letting it warm up. He offers me his hand for help on and I hop on the back like it's nothing.

"Put your arms around me, my queen. Hold on tight." I reach around him and slide my hand into the front of his jeans. "How about not on your first ride?"

"Oh, my hand was cold." I laugh trying to pretend I wasn't getting into his pants. I'm giddy on the back of his bike with my arms wrapped around him, plastered to his back and the bike rumbling between my legs.

"Ready?"

"Yes! Let's go!" He slowly takes us through the complex to the street, cruising the surface streets to Shelter Island and sticking close to the shoreline. It's a nice ride with a beautiful view, but nothing crazy. He takes Harbor past the airport, around the curve and past the Maritime Museum. He takes us out to the roundabout at the Embarcadero North and then over to the Coronado Bridge where he picks up speed and I remember what I love about motorcycles. He has control of everything. I knew he would, he doesn't do anything without being the best at it and knowing everything about it. He takes us up and down the Silver Strand a few times, truly a breathtaking view and it's high tide.

He pulls off into the parking lot at Glorietta Bay, (now I know when to find parking) turns off the bike, and I hop off. He gets off the bike and sets the backpack on it. We take our helmets off. He unzips both of our jackets and pulls me close. He gives me a quick kiss. "What do you think, my queen? Are you having fun?" He's happy, relaxed, and all smiles.

"I like it. It's fun." Very matter of fact.

"Okay. What else? I can see you have more to say."

"Um." I don't want to lead him to trouble. "Faster would be better. Forget the view, I want speed." He basically attacks me, tongue in my mouth, fingers digging into my body. He pulls back and a glint shines in his eyes. I have a feeling it's time to experience how he really rides.

"Promise to tell me if I go too fast?" He searches my eyes for my answer.

"You can't go too fast. Show me what you got." I know better than to taunt him, but I can't help myself. I kiss him, rubbing my body against his, and put my helmet back on.

He grins, zips me back up, and looks at me in a way that tells me this night is going to end well. I hope I don't have anything I need to do on Friday. Fuck it! Even if I do, it's my last day with Rick on suspension. He gets ready and climbs back on his bike, starting it up, and I hop on. I wrap my arms around him, "I'm ready for take off, my king."

"Hold on tight." "Caught Up In You" by .38 Special starts to play as we take off on the Silver Strand at a faster speed. The music is loud and upbeat, perfect for a ride. We get to the freeway and Rick takes us Northbound on the 5 to the 15, the freeway with the highest speed limit. "The Stroke" by Billy Squier comes on. He kicks it into a higher gear and when he hits sixth we're blowing past the other cars on the freeway like they're standing still. He takes us into the fast lane, there aren't many cars on the freeway once we get out of downtown. I hold on tight, loving the adrenaline as we fly up the 15. The music gets louder as we go faster. "Fell in Love With a Girl" by The White Stripes fills my helmet and I totally love that song. This is obviously Rick's riding playlist, fast, pushing, loud. I sing along to myself in my helmet and the music stops suddenly, "Are you okay? Did you say something?" So, apparently he could hear me singing along.

"I'm fine. I was singing along. Love the playlist." I spread my hands and fingers across his abs in appreciation.

"Are you staying warm?"

"Yes, my king. I'm fine."

"Do you need anything?"

"I have you in my arms. I don't need anything else."

"You're so fucking perfect. I love you." I can hear his grin.

I lean my head against his back and The White Stripes come back. He cuts West into a canyon near San Marcos, leaning into the curves and I squeal with joy. "Blow Me Away" by Breaking Benjamin comes on and the driving force in the music keeps going throughout the playlist. He makes a couple of turns and we're at the East end of Batiquitos Lagoon.

The music stops, "Freeway or coast?"

"It's your adventure. I'm along for the ride." I couldn't decide. I love the view of the beach, but not much beats the adrenaline from the speed. He takes us back onto the freeway at La Costa and we're Southbound on the 5 at full speed in no time with Foreigner blaring "Feels Like the First Time." He takes us from the 5 to the 805 to the 163 and off the freeway at downtown. We ride around the stadium and out to the Embarcadero South, stopping at the end of the parking lot.

He turns off the bike and holds it steady for my dismount. I take my helmet off as he gets off the bike and takes off the backpack. He takes his helmet off and claims my lips with his immediately, sending a warmth through my body. My hands go to his waist possessively, standing there and kissing him. He locks the helmets to the bike, gets the backpack and leads me to a grassy area near the bay. We take the blanket out of the backpack and lay it out on the dewy grass. We stretch out next to each other and I lean on him affectionately. The lights from Coronado reflect on the bay romantically, like Van Gogh's Starlight Over the Rhone. The sound of the bay lapping against the rocks is relaxing. The night sky is dark and glittered with stars sparkling like faceted diamonds. There's nobody out here, but us. There's no place I'd rather be.

I have no idea what time it is and it's refreshing to be out with no phone or anything. I'm wondering why this was a late night adventure. Maybe Rick likes to ride at night? Or when there are less cars on the road? Embarcadero South has kind of become a significant place for us, so I get the picnic location and besides you can't get a better view. I feel so close to him, I don't want to forget this moment. "Do you have your phone?"

"Yes." He responds with a questioning tone.

"Be the selfie master and take pictures of us here together." I look at him imploringly. He pulls out his phone and starts taking photos of me, making me laugh and continuing to take more pictures. "No, I mean of us together."

"I know what you meant. I want some of you." My heart is lost completely to this man. He pulls me close and clicks away, kissing me, making faces, putting up bunny ears, kissing me more, gazing at me, lost in each others' eyes and claiming me completely. He drops his phone and focuses on me, like he doesn't have a choice. His lips worship mine. His hands on my back, hold me to him. He stops and looks at me like he wants to say something, but doesn't.

"Are you okay?"

In his low raspy voice, "I'm better than okay."

"Me, too." I'm done letting my head get in the way of my heart. I press my lips to his, nibbling and sucking on his lower lip. I want him so bad right now, I rub my hand against his crotch and his change in breathing tells me he wants me, too. I push my luck and slide my hand into his pants, waiting for him to make me stop. He doesn't, instead he pushes me further with his greedy kisses. I wrap my hand around his cock and stroke him while we kiss, but I want more and I unbutton his jeans. There's nobody out here, right? It's the wee hours of the morning.

"You can't do that, baby." Obviously wanting it and trying to control the situation. Rick doesn't do anything to make me stop, yet keeps kissing me and sucking on my tongue.

"I know you don't want me to stop." He responds by flexing his hips. I lay my head in his lap and unzip him. Rick pulls the blanket up around us and I find him with my mouth, licking him and sucking him in.

"We're in the park, my queen."

I respond with a positive, "Mmmmhhmmm," with my lips wrapped around him. Again, he does nothing to make me stop and encourages me with his actions as he runs his fingers through my hair, feeling my head move as I pleasure him.

"Fuck me. We can't do this." He's so hard I couldn't put him away if I wanted to, and I don't want to. "My queen. Fuck."

"I'm not stopping, my king. I'm taking care of you."

"I need you, Sherry. I love you. I, you fuckin' make me crazy." He's still in his head and not saying words that want to come out, but at least I have his other head in control of the moment. I continue licking and sucking on him. "Need you, Sherry. In you." I stroke him with my lips, truly loving on him and worshiping him. "Please. Please. In you." He begs with need and I glance at him to find his eyes are closed, he's lost in the moment. I take control of the blanket and wriggle my pants off of one leg. Blanket wrapped around us, I straddle him and take just his tip inside me.

"You want this?"

"Yes."

"You want this now, here, in the park."

"Yes." He gets a hit of reality trying to sneak through. "Oh, fuck me. I'm so fucked." He puts his arms around me and holds me while he pushes into me with need. He's hard and fills me instantly. I take his mouth with mine and lose control at the heat of our connection.

I wrap my legs around him and whisper in his ear, "Better, my king?"

"Yes, my love. Everything is better when I'm in you." He loses his words and gets absorbed in the moment. He starts rambling and he isn't with me... "I need her. She needs to be mine. She needs to be mine always. I can't control myself around her. She's so fucking perfect. I need to make her mine. I need her to say yes. I need her to love me forever. Fuck me! I can't keep being a caveman. Shit!"

I'm not sure if I should say something or let it go. He isn't talking to me, but I hope he's talking about me. He can't be talking about another girl. Can he? No, there's no way. Don't even go there, Sherry. No backwards slides. "I'll always say yes to anything you want that's legal, and apparently sometimes things that are illegal." I say as I consider the charges for indecent exposure and fornicating in public. "We should go home."

"No. It's not time yet. I want to watch the sunrise with you." That's why it was a late night adventure!

"I was just thinking if we go home, we might not get arrested."

Something in his eyes change, "Why did you say you'll always say yes?"

"Seemed like the thing to say. It's the truth." His face changes. "I guess the 'her' you referred to could've been someone else."

"I was talking?"

"Yes."

"What did I say?"

"First, am I the 'her' and 'she' you kept talking about?"

"I don't know what I said."

"Then I think it was private and just for me." I laugh, enjoying the opportunity to use his own words against him. "How many 'hers' and 'shes' are you thinking about in there?"

Rick rubs his hand over his face in frustration. "You, Sam and my Mom, in that order. What did I say?"

"Something about wanting me to say yes and needing me. Nothing big." I kiss him before he can get out of hand. "Now, how about we finish this when we get home and enjoy our picnic?" I smile at him, he always wants food. He nods at me, still lost in his head. I stand up quickly and get my pants back on while I wonder what's going on in his head. I've learned my head needs to stay out of it when it comes to us. I sit back down next to him with the blanket wrapped around us and his jeans are still undone. I unpack the backpack, setting out the different containers and opening them. I pull out the thermos of coffee and bottles of water, realizing I didn't bring cups for the coffee and that's okay because we can share. "Okay, my king. We have Italian Sandwiches, seasoned popcorn, grapes, chocolate chip banana nut bread, baseball sugar cookies, coffee, and water." I take a drink of the coffee and it's still warm. We sit together grazing and talking for a long time. Our conversation flows organically and he likes everything I brought to eat.

Sometimes I catch myself staring at Rick and trying to determine if I'm dreaming. I've dreamt about him so many times. Even the first time I woke with him, it felt like a dream. If this is a dream, I don't want to wake up.

I look up and Rick's smiling at me, "I'm real. This isn't a dream." Damn it! I did it again. I must be getting tired.

I wonder if this is a way for him to make sure we spend time together without having sex. If it is, it didn't work. He gets the weirdest ideas sometimes. I get it. We need to have more between us than physical attraction, even if the physical attraction is off the charts and so far off the charts it's in a completely different galaxy. We're growing everyday. Becoming a team, true partners. Honestly, I don't think our need to be close and our physical connection could be nearly as strong as it is if it was just sex. I know it's been fast and a lot has happened, but I wouldn't change it. I can honestly say I would do anything for him.

"I want to spend time with you. I want to do everything with you. Everything is better with you." His words melt me.

The stars start to fade and the lights on the Coronado Bridge shut off as daylight breaks. Rick holds me close, "I wanted to watch the sunrise with you. You brought me back to the living and you show me you love me everyday. Your heart, your love is everything to me." Tears fall down my cheeks as he holds me tight and I listen to his words. We sit quietly and watch the sunrise.

I've never watched the sunrise. Sunsets many times, but this is different. The way the sunlight outlines the white fluffy clouds, giving them a glow. The fresh light making everything new. The dandelions and wild flowers opening to greet the sun, like they've been woken up and need to stretch. The cottontails sitting still like statues observing the beginning of the new day and casting shadows before they hop off into the bushes. The trees that were somewhat ominous, now filtering the light and allowing it to speckle the ground. Everything gets to try again, hope has been granted by the new day.

I have a new strength and I'm not afraid of the love in my heart. I grab ahold of Rick's hand, squeezing and entangling our fingers. I think about the desperation he's been hiding in his head and how I never want to play games with his heart. The warmth of the sunlight reaches my face and I caress his cheek with my thumb as I lean in to kiss him tenderly. I pull back and gaze into his eyes, unable to control my happiness. "It's only been a short time and you might think I'm crazy, but I'm already yours." I giggle and a tear rolls down my face. "There will never be anyone else. I promise you, I'll say yes. And, for the record, I love your caveman moves." I smile at the shine in his eyes, "Now, please get out of your head because that's not what we're about, with us it's all heart."

"How about I get into you?"

"Yes, but not until we get home."

"Do you have any plans today?"

"Yes."

"What are they?"

"I'm spending the day in bed with you."

"I like those plans. When does that start?"

"As soon as you take me home."

Rick claims my mouth and I shiver at his touch. "Home it is." We quickly toss everything into the backpack and shove the blanket back into the pouch. We zip up and Rick gets our helmets off the bike. He gets on the bike and starts it up, holding it steady for me to climb on. "Hold onto me for a second before you put your helmet on." I happily wrap my arms around him and reach to kiss his neck. He has his phone out and he's taking selfies of us on his motor-cycle together. I reach around and stroke his beard. We put our helmets on and he's still doing his selfie thing. He starts some music and slides his phone back into his pocket. We take off for home as "Kashmir" by Led Zeppelin plays.

We get home and strip as we walk through the door, leaving a trail of boots, jeans, jackets, helmets, shirts, and undergarments on the way to our bedroom. We climb into bed together and nestle in under the warm blankets. Rick holds me close to him, our bodies against each other and his lips on mine with need. Lying on our sides and facing each other, I wrap my upper leg around him and invite him in. "Please, my king."

He slides into me with desire. "Is this for me, my queen?" He groans in pleasure.

"Only for you." We lie together making out while we move slowly, knowing we have all day to ourselves.

CHAPTER SIXTEEN

I t's Friday, the last day of Rick's suspension. I wake up in the middle of the afternoon with his left arm around my waist, his right arm under my pillow and his warm breath at my neck. He's completely out and I'm wide awake. I move his left arm and attempt to get out of bed without waking him, but my attempt is unsuccessful.

Rick wraps his arms around me, pulls me to him and says, "No," without ever opening his eyes. This would've been really sweet and made me giddy, if I didn't have to pee.

I try again, this time whispering, "I gotta pee," before I make quick action. He still doesn't open his eyes, but he must've got the message. I run to the bathroom and close the door behind me.

I don't live by myself anymore. There's a man's razor and deodorant on my bathroom counter next to my tropical soaps and personal items. The mosaic sea glass cup that holds my toothbrush, now holds two. He moved in with me. Makes sense, since I asked him to. We've spent most of the last week together, most of it here at home. But, somehow seeing his razor and toothbrush—he lives here with me! I wonder what other people think when they see me making choices, committing to things and then realizing what I did a week later. I asked him to live with me. I put his books on my shelf. I made space for him in the closet. I've been cooking for two. I gave him a key. What have I done? I start to freak out and wander through my, no, our home in search of other signs he lives here and the sight of our riding gear strewn across the house smacks me in the face with memories of our late night adventure. The blanket that has taken up residence on my love seat, where we use it to snuggle and picnic in front of the TV when we watch the game. The small picture frame with the crowns on it sparkles in the sunlight, featuring our photo from Rick's first selfie session and reminding me we're here together. I catch my reflection in the mirror and I look different. My face is thinner. My skin is glowing. My eyes are shining. I have a bounce in my step. I look up to discover Rick standing there looking at me and my smile lights up. I stare at him through the reflection in the mirror, "Did you know your toothbrush is in the cup with mine, and your razor and stuff is on the bathroom counter? You live here now." I say it and it's more for my benefit than for his. I turn to him. Freaking the fuck out. I sink into his eyes and feel his arms wrap around me. My freak-out instantly fades away and my heart wins.

"Yes, this is home. A king usually lives with his queen, sharing their castle together." He is all it takes to make everything right. "I thought you were coming right back to bed, but it's been over an hour. Everything okay?"

I lost an hour catching up with my own life? Or, I guess it's our life. How is that possible? "I'm fine now. I was just looking around. We made a mess. I don't remember this place ever looking so lived in." I glance around me. "I don't know where the hour went, I was going back to be with you and I ended up here with you behind me. Did you know you live here now?"

Rick strokes my hair and hugs his cheek to my head, helping me calm down. "It's a big step for us. We made it a whole week, and we were tested this week with my suspension, my injury, and my temper. I love how you took care of me when I needed it and didn't take my shit. What would I have done if I weren't here with you?" Rick pulls back to search my eyes and smiles, "I live with you. Where doesn't matter as long as we're together."

I was freaking out and maybe I blacked out or something from the emotional trauma. "You make everything better."

Rick kisses me sweetly on the forehead and holds me to him, "Good, because I'm not letting you go." I feel his worry in the way he holds me. He means it when he says he's not letting me go. He doesn't want me to leave him again.

I lead Rick to the love seat and wrap the blanket around us. "I was freaking out, but that doesn't mean I'm leaving. My head is catching up with my heart. You have your own version of it. You start to say something and then stop or edit your words before they come out. You tell me more with your touch and kiss than words could ever say. I know what you want. I know how you feel about me. I know your dreams." I take his face in my hands and lock eyes with him, "I want everything you want and I only want to have it all with you. I've never wanted any of it before, never even thought about it."

"You left me in LA. You packed your stuff and left me, ran from me. I know you were hurt. You pulled away from me and wouldn't listen to what I was saying. You hid from me and wouldn't answer my texts when I couldn't find you. You wouldn't even respond to Sam. You didn't come home for days and when you did, you packed and disappeared for weeks. We can't do that, we need to go to each other for answers—not run. When you freak out, it makes me worry that you'll do it again. I'm not leaving you alone. Now I know that asshole was after you, when you were weak and needing me, but wouldn't admit it. I did my best not to get pissed about you dating Adam, and I still hate it. Sherry, we need each other. Stupid shit happens, but together we make it okay. I don't blame you. I know what it looked like. You're what's important to me, none of the rest matters. Honestly, I suck at the rest without you."

"We can't be together every minute of every day. You have to trust me."

"Stop! I do trust you. But, you have these moments like today when something clicks in your head about me living here and I don't want a moment to make your flight instinct kick in. Shit! With you, you could be on a plane in thirty minutes and on your way to Hawaii."

"That's not going to happen. I'm not going anywhere without you." Rick shakes his head unsure. "You have to trust me. Stop letting your head get in the way, believe in your heart." I take a deep breath, "Do you want me to tell you the crazy thing I've been thinking about doing? I guess I may have already told you in my sleep. What can I do to help you understand and believe I'm with you, never leaving you?"

Rick stares at me, his wheels turning.

"You know I have days where I'm waiting for you to take off with one of the young baseball hotties, right? I'm older than you. You can have any of those girls you want. I know they're perkier and tighter all over. They'd be easier, do whatever you want and let you take care of them. Not insist on paying their own way, not difficult in any way. You have girls waiting in your room on road trips! Damn it! I'm already 35. You want a family. I've never worried about any biological clock before, but I have limited time to give you the family you want and your mother already thinks I'm too old for you. Fuck! And, that crazy doesn't even include the crazy thing I've been thinking about doing! So, we might as well put all our insecurities and crazy out there."

Fuck! Fuck! Fuck! The tears start rolling down my face. My tone turned to yelling as I ranted insanely. He's already concerned about me having moments that could make me want to run away and I'm showing him how fucking crazy insecure I am about him.

"I only want you. You want me for me. None of those girls out there care who I am. They all want a baseball player. I don't care how old you are. I love being with you and if it's always just me and you, well I'd rather have you than anyone else." He closes his eyes, "Tell me the crazy thing you've been thinking about doing. Might as well get it out there."

I'm quiet for a few minutes while my thoughts twirl about. I can't tell him what I'm thinking about doing. I just need to do it, crazy or not. I don't know why I want to give him everything and maybe it will make some of our insecurities disappear. I gaze at him with a quivering smile and take his hand. "I'm done thinking about it. I know what I want. I'm ready to stop taking my daily pill for you. You tell me when. I promise this isn't a trap. I want to give you everything and I'm not pressuring you. I'll keep taking my pill until you say when." We've talked about someday, but I made someday real.

Rick's whole attitude changes, his body language loosens up. "Do you mean that?"

"I wouldn't say it if I didn't mean it. I'll never hurt you intentionally and I know it's a soft spot for you."

His smile reaches his eyes and his cheeks, "I love you. I don't want to rush it. I want us to have time together. Please don't take this the wrong way, because I want it with you more than you know." He stops. "Maybe when we get back from Hawaii," he says quietly.

I need him, I turn to him with sexy eyes, "Is there anything else I can do to help eliminate your worries?"

"Please book your air travel for all the away games for the rest of the season and use my credit card. I want to know you're going to be with me."

"I'll do that right now." It's a little thing to help make him happy. "The game is on soon."

"I only want to be with you tonight. No game. I'll be back at the stadium tomorrow." His eyes are shiny, "Sherry, you make me happier than I've ever been. Nobody has ever offered me anything that means so much to me. We'll talk about it together closer to the right time. Joint effort, my queen. We're a team." He holds me close and I feel his heart beating.

I turn on the radio and open my laptop to schedule my flights. The sexy sultry sound of "Let's Hurt Tonight" by OneRepublic fills the room and Rick's at my back watching me schedule my air travel. He's listening to the music and wraps his arms around me as he kisses my neck. The lyrics are on the nose for the conversation we're having.

"Let's stay in tonight," he whispers in my ear.

I can't think of anything better, "Perfect." I smile at him. "I'll make dinner."

"No, let's order in. I want you and no distractions

tonight. I need to be at the stadium early tomorrow. It's the last night."

"It's not the last night, my king. I'll be with you every night, wherever you are, baseball or not. I can't wait to get out there and cheer for you tomorrow. I'll drop you off and come back early for batting practice in your car, so I'll be in the garage waiting for you to drive me home after the game."

"How are you so perfect?" He keeps kissing my neck.

I giggle, "I'm excited to get to go to the different stadiums. We're going to be on an adventure together."

"It's work for me."

"I know you have to be at practice and work out and play games, but maybe I can make it more fun."

"It'll definitely be better with you. I like quiet time between games, holding you will make that better."

"I was thinking about all the elevators." I bite my lower lip and grin deviously. "I'm going to start a travel diary with a map, so I can keep track of the elevators you pull the stop on and the elevators we have sex on and the elevators that don't see any action. Maybe a special section for sex outdoors. You know, on the beach or in the park."

Rick's gaze is heated, "...and in the car."

"Maybe we should start a selfie collection. Pictures of us together in every city we visit or in the shower of every hotel room we stay in, or maybe the bed." I grin at him suggestively.

"Are you done booking your flights?"

"Yes. Emailing you my confirmations, so you have my flight info." I turn to him and he's looking at his phone. "Are you checking my work? Did I spend too much?"

Rick rolls his eyes, "I'm not looking at my email. I don't

care how much you spent." He seems distracted. "I'm looking at the selfies from this morning."

"Oh! Send them all to me, selfie master."

"All of them? I took quite a few."

"All of them." My phone starts vibrating with pictures coming in. I hear it buzzing wherever I left it last night and go searching for it, following the sound. I find my phone and it finally stops vibrating with messages.

"Check out this video I have." Rick calls out to me.

I find him sitting on the love seat and stand behind him to watch over his shoulder. He plays the video of him kissing me at the first base wall the day I went to tell him I love him, but it's so much more. Somebody has edited it together with me on the big screen when he sent me his bag with his glove and him watching me, him kissing me when it was on the big screen in Colorado when Hannah was interviewing him, him pointing at me from the field a handful of times, him carrying me through the hotel lobby, us holding hands through the net, us kissing in the dugout, us walking across the field to the bull pen holding hands—all set to "Thinking Out Loud." It's absolutely perfect. Rick looks back at me, "Are you okay? Come here, baby." I realize I'm crying as I sit in his lap and he embraces me.

"I'm fine," I say as I wipe my tears away. "Its perfect." I'll do a test in the morning to check because I'm so emotional, I think to myself as I hear Sam in my head. "Who made that?"

"I don't know. Cross sent it to me. He's missing me this week." Rick chuckles and kisses my cheek. "He might be jealous."

"Tough luck for him because he can't have you!" I laugh and claim Rick's mouth as I change my position and press my naked breasts against him, straddling his lap. Rick groans appreciatively and takes control, lifting me with him as he stands. I wrap my legs around him while he kisses me. "I need you, my king."

"I need you, too. We're in the same place and want the same things, so no more freaking out, okay?" He puts his forehead to mine and gazes into my eyes, while he carries me to the bedroom.

"I can't promise to not freak out, but I can promise not to leave." I say, knowing I have no control.

"I'll take it." Rick takes a deep breath, "How about we keep everything the way it is right now until the end of the season? I need to work on keeping my head straight and not getting suspended. Me and you in a monogamous relationship, living together, spending time together, traveling together, and sharing expenses until you let me pay for everything. Big decisions and next steps all on hold. Two months or so of status quo."

"Okay," I kind of smile.

He looks at me as if he's reading my mind, "Don't go getting in your head and reading anything into it. You know I want more. I want the same things as you and I want them with you. I need to manage to get through the season and bring my stats up."

"I understand. You might need to remind me that I want my team to win and that means you need to be behind the plate." I grin happily, laughing at myself.

I wrap my arms around him and he takes the bed on all fours with me hanging on him. He puts my head on the pillow and rests his body on mine, sharing the pillow with me and pulling the blankets up over us. His hands touch me tenderly with desire. He kisses my lips softly, sweetly, tasting me. He moves his mouth to my neck where I feel his hot breath and he whispers, "I love you, baby," in my ear as he pushes into me. His whisper so sincere, I feel how much he loves me. He moves slowly and he's in another world, needing to love me. He moves, making noises under his breath with every slow stroke.

I wrap my legs around him tight and my whole body needs him, more of him. "I love you, my king. Please give me more. Not harder. Not faster. All of you, deeper." He sits back on his knees and pushes all the way into me, and I cry out in need. My cry pushes him forward and he hooks my knees with his arms as he comes back down to me. Pressing his lips to mine, his tongue dancing with mine as he pushes into me further and holds my knees spread at my chest. Pushing in more with each slow stroke until he's all the way in and driving me crazy with need. "Oh, Rick. I need you, baby."

"I'm right here, baby. You're so tight, I don't want to go too fast." He stops moving and leans into my ear, "That's me buried all the way in you, Sherry. Do you remember how big I am? Do you remember watching me slide in and out of you? Do you remember how far I can slide out and still be in you? Do you remember how thick and hard I was, when you were watching me stretch your tight hole? That's what you have again right now. All of me, baby. All of me and only for you. Nobody else will ever have me. You're the only lock for my key." He grinds against me while he remains buried deep and I cry out his name. He does it again and I scream out. "How about some more." He says more as a statement than a question and keeps grinding against me at our connection. My heat builds instantly and I can't help but squeeze him. "Fuck me. Sherry, tell me you want more. Tell me to take you. Give me permission. Something. Oh fuck. Please Sherry. Please. You're so fucking tight, I..."

"Take me, my king. However you want. I'm yours." I know he wants it hard and fast. I know he wants to pound into me in this position. He doesn't move. "I need you to slam into me hard and fast, and I need you to not stop. I need you to spread my legs wide and hold my feet at my ears. I need you as deep as you can get, hard on every stroke and I need you now. You can still love me, while you send us over the edge." He smiles and does what I ask. He didn't need permission, he needed to know he was still loving me. "That's perfect. I love you, baby." He's amazing and it doesn't take much to send us both into ecstasy together, as we cry out in unison and reach for each other, needing to hold each other close while we come down. Our physical and emotional connection together are crazy. He claims my mouth, kissing me while we keep our connection and I'm in heaven.

I WAKE up starving at around 4am and go to the kitchen to find food. I make an Italian Sandwich, and I grab the left-over cookies and banana bread. I take it all back to bed with me, he'll be hungry and awake when I get back to bed.

"Where'd you go, baby?" He says sleepily.

"Grabbed us something to eat. I know you're hungry."

Rick sits up groggily, "How are you so perfect, my queen?" Happily inhaling part of the sandwich. He's not fully awake and that's okay. I close up the banana bread and cookies, leaving them sitting on the floor at my bedside. I lie back down in bed and Rick immediately rolls me underneath him as he slides back into me, stroking in and out slowly until he has a smile on his face.

I WAKE up to the smell of coffee brewing. It's Saturday morning. Rick is off suspension and back to playing baseball today. Right now he has me lying on top of him and his arm holding me there. "Good morning, my king. It's a 5:40 game day, what time do you want to be at the stadium? Do you want breakfast? Shower?"

Rick groans at the thought of morning, "Earlier is better today. How long to make breakfast?"

"I can have an omelette and coffee ready for you in less than fifteen minutes."

"Okay. Breakfast, please. I'll shower and be ready to eat in under fifteen." He sits up with his eyes still closed and I pull the blankets away to find his naked cock in need.

I lean down and kiss him on his tip. "Do you have an extra five minutes for me?" I ask as I slide my lips over his cock, licking and sucking.

"Oh, yeah." He doesn't have anymore words.

He gets harder in my mouth as I stroke him with my hand and my mouth. He's in the moment and half asleep, so this isn't going to take long. I suck and lick as I pull him with my lips. He grabs me, pulling me on top of him and I slide on to his hard length, drawing a growl from him. He flips us over and pushes into me hard and fast, setting me on edge and pushing me over rubbing my magic button. I fall hard and crashing, pulling him with me uncontrollably.

"I love you, my king." The alarm clock goes off and it's almost 9am.

"One snooze and then we get up, my queen." I hit the snooze button and enjoy Rick wrapped around me for nine more minutes before the real world invades our private world once again.

CHAPTER SEVENTEEN

The alarm goes off. I want to support him and make the rest of the season as easy as I can. I'll be at every game for the remainder of the season and I'll be cheering for him like nobody else can. I jump out of bed and get dressed quickly, pulling on some black bikinis, denim shorts, a black bra, and a black strapped camisole tank with lace edging. I put a fresh towel in the bathroom and turn on the shower for Rick. I turn on some music and go with my *Good Morning* Playlist. I hit shuffle and "Shape of You" by Ed Sheeran comes on making me want to dance, so I set it on repeat and hear Rick get in the shower as I make my way to the kitchen. I quickly gather what I need for breakfast and switch up my normal omelette a bit, using provolone, my leftover Italian sandwich meat, mushrooms, basil, thyme, and a shake of garlic salt. I toast up the last couple pieces of bread to go with the eggs and meet Rick at the table as he walks out in his gym shorts, running shoes and "Property of the Seals" T-shirt. I grab my phone and take a picture of him because he's fucking hot.

"Really?"

"Shouldn't you be more appreciative of a woman who woke you with a blow job and made you breakfast?" I say jokingly, I want him in a good mood.

He smiles and shakes his head, "Take as many photos as you like." He laughs and sits down to eat his omelette. "This is really good. Italian style?"

"Sure. Using up the leftovers, since there wasn't enough left for another sandwich. You can put the eggs on the toast and make it a sandwich if you want." I clean up the kitchen real quick while he's eating and make sure I have everything for making cookie bars. I pour coffee into two travel cups and package up a few baseball cookies with a piece of chocolate chip banana bread for Chase. I give Rick one of the coffees and start to nurse the other. "When do you want to leave for the stadium?"

"Cross is picking me up in a few minutes. Thought it would make it easier on you since he's going early today, too."

"I'm happy either way. Tell him to come up and get you because I have something for him." A few minutes later Chase is knocking on the door. I open the door and hug him, "Good morning, sweetheart." Rick gives me the eye.

"Hey lovey, heard you have something for me and I'm hoping its chocolate chip."

I hand him the bag of baked goods and tell him what they are. "Let me know what you think."

"You two don't need to talk. Remember, my woman." Rick grabs me and claims me excessively before he walks out the door, leaving me boneless and needing to recover before I can continue.

Chase smiles at me, "Thank you." He laughs and follows Rick out the door.

I have things to get done today and a limited amount of time.

Text from Sam - Good morning! My bro is back playing today, right?

The message from Sam reminds me the first thing I need to do is pee on a stick. I decide to include Sam because I need moral support. I don't want to be sad, I need to keep it together and be happy to support Rick through the season. No freaking out.

Text to Sam - Yes. He just left for the stadium. I know he was on suspension, but I had the most wonderful week with him.

Text to Sam - Really emotional again last night and missing him like crazy even though he just left. Doing a test. Cross your fingers.

Text from Sam - Cross my fingers?

Text from Sam - Uummm... Do we want it to be positive or negative?

Text to Sam - I don't want to talk about that.

Text from Sam - You should definitely pee on a stick. Go now. Send me the results.

I work myself up on the short walk to the bathroom and

pee on a stick with intentions of walking away from it and getting some work done, but that doesn't happen. I stand there and watch it for ten minutes. Confused and freaking out with tears running down my face. This makes no sense at all.

> Text from Sam - Remember a negative isn't bad, it
> means not yet and you have time to practice. ;)

What the fuck is wrong with me? Sam's right. I'm on the pill and that means it should be negative. I look back to the test and sure enough, negative. I send Sam a picture of the test.

> Text from Sam - It's okay. Probably better not to come
> up positive during the season anyway. You know how
> possessive he is, who knows how that would
> affect him.

> Text to Sam – True.

> Text from Sam - I know how you really feel, trying to
> find the silver lining. It just means not right now.

> Text to Sam - I know.

> Text from Sam - Get rid of that test, so you don't have
> to see it and nobody else does.

> Text to Sam – Okay.

I toss the evidence down the trash chute and clean up a

bit. I start some laundry and mix together a huge batch of chocolate chip cookie dough. I set it aside to rest in the refrigerator and turn the oven on to preheat, while I sort out a couple more loads of laundry. I sit down to drink my coffee, check email, and social media. I missed a text from Rick, crap.

Text from Rick - I miss you.

Text from Rick - BP is at 2:30.

Text from Rick - ?

Text to Rick - Sorry, hands were in cookie dough.

Text to Rick - I've been thinking about you ever since you left.

Text from Rick - What are you thinking?

Text to Rick - How I can't wait to be in your arms with you inside me...

Text to Rick - Is that bad?

Text from Rick - I want to be close to you, too.

Text from Rick - Maybe you can get here early and we can steal a few minutes somewhere before BP.

Text from Rick - I need a mid-day visit. I feel like I'm addicted and went cold turkey.

I laugh at the mere idea that a professional athlete could be addicted to me, but get warm all over at how much my king needs me.

Text to Rick - I'll be there before batting practice.

Text to Rick - I love you, my king.

Text from Rick - :)

Text from Rick - I don't remember what it was like without you. I love you, too.

He can make my heart thump with a text. I pick up my pace, so I can get to the stadium early. I take my cookie dough out of the refrigerator and press it into three cookie sheets. I put them all in the oven and set the timer.

I want to be sexy for Rick, and appropriate for Carter, when I get to the stadium with cookies and my proposal to assist with travel plans. I peruse my closet for the right thing to wear that'll easily change over to game attire. It's a warm day and a 5:40 game, great day for a skirt. I toss my denim mini skirt on the bed and put my Seals leggings in my game bag. I pull the jersey for today's game from the closet, it's the navy with white jersey. I hate wearing white tops, so I search my closet for navy blue options. I get the matching hoodie and cap, adding those to my game bag. I go with my navy sleeveless V-neck that gathers on the sides and then change my mind, choosing a basic navy camisole. I brush out my hair and smell cookies baking, so I check on them and the timer goes off as I open the oven. They're perfect, so I take them out of the oven and let them cool before I cut them into squares. I turn the shower on to warm up and tie my hair up in a tight bun. I bring up my playlists, wanting something different than my normal *Steamy* playlist and see a playlist I don't remember *Sherry*. I go for it and hit shuffle. "Oh Sherrie" by Steve Perry starts playing as I make my way to the shower. I stand in the shower with the hot water beating down on me, taking a few minutes to relax and let everything go. "If I Lose Myself" by OneRepublic comes on next. Tears start falling and I wonder what's wrong with me. When did I become a girl who cries for no apparent reason? There must be a reason. Maybe it's the big changes. I'm living with my fantasy baseball boyfriend, he's real, and my life has definitely changed. Shit! What I want in life has changed. I turn to the water and close my eyes, feeling the water on my face. I focus and finish my shower, so I can go see my man. I dry off, then cut up and package the chocolate chip cookie bars before I get dressed. I let my hair down and give it a shake, hoping for a bit of wave. I get dressed, get my things together, and check the mirror. I put on my baseball bracelet and my key necklace. I text Rick on my way to his car.

Text to Rick - Leaving for the stadium now :) See you soon!

I get in the Challenger and start her up. The muscle car reminds me of the man she belongs to—powerful, rumbling, sexy, and fast.

I arrive at the stadium in no time and park in the player's garage. I take the cookies and my proposal, and I make my way to Carter's office. I knock on his open door and Carter smiles at me, inviting me in.

"Hey Sherry, what are you doing here?"

"I'd like to talk to you for a minute and I brought you some cookies." I hand him the smaller bag of chocolate chip cookie bars and wait for his response.

"Thank you." He looks at them and feels they're still warm. "What's up?"

I hand him my proposal. "You mentioned that you don't like dealing with the travel arrangements and you may not know this, but I'm a travel agent. Planning travel is what I do and I enjoy it. So, I'm offering you my services."

Carter stares at me unsure, "I don't have a budget to pay you with. It's part of my job."

"I understand. I've done the research and I believe I can take the duty from you with the cost staying the same. Allowing you to have more time for other things, essentially adding to your value with the organization and saving the organization money with whatever extra duty you take on—and I'll make a profit." I stop because I don't want to go too far and I don't want to be pushy. "This proposal gives you some of my background and illustrates why you should have me handle travel. It makes sense." I smile and shut up.

"This isn't my call, but I'll review it and run it by my supervisor. I'm not sure about this and Seno."

"This has nothing to do with Seno. This is all me. Let me help you handle the part of your job you don't like to do."

"I'll check it out."

"Thank you." I turn to get out of his office. "Do you happen to know where Seno is?"

Carter under his breath, "Stray is catching tonight."

"So, where does he go when he wants to be a dick?"

"He's probably running the warning track. Hold on..." He calls out, "Seno?"

Of course, he would be running somewhere. That's what he does when he gets pissed and pouty.

"Not in here." I recognize the voice.

"Chase?" I call out and he comes walking in.

"Hey lovey, twice in one day!" He smiles while he talks to me.

I hand him the cookie bars, "Rick said you wanted more of these and asked me to make enough for the whole club-house. Please share and they're compliments of Seno. Do you know where he is?"

"Nope." I send him on his way.

Text to Rick - Elevator?

"Thank you, Carter. I'll get out of your way."

I walk out to the concourse looking for him on the field while I wait for his reply. I see him look at his phone and reply.

Text from Rick - Been working out hard. I'm not in the lineup.

Text to Rick - I know. That's why I suggested the elevator and not your car. Did I mention I'm wearing a short skirt and no panties?

Okay fine, I lied. But, he needed to be persuaded and I can take them off before I get to him.

Text to Rick - I bet you're all hot and sweaty. You're not starting, why not have some of me?

Text from Rick - You're a bad girl.

Text to Rick - I'm your bad girl.

Text from Rick - Elevator

Yes! Fuck! I'm as bad as him! I quickly run into the ladies room and pull off my panties, shoving them into my purse. I go to the elevator and he's there waiting for me when the door opens. Rick presses the button for the top floor and pulls the stop before we get there.

"Nice skirt." The only words that come out of his mouth before he presses me up against the elevator wall, passionately claiming me with his lips. He runs his hands all over my body, feeling for the edge of my skirt and reaching under it to find out if I'm going commando. He finds my wet folds and slides a finger into me, groaning appreciatively at how wet I am. He strokes me while he continues to kiss me, and slides a second finger in. He drops to his catcher's crouch and pushes my skirt up around my hips as he licks and sucks at my wet sex. His tongue is fucking amazing as it glides along my wet heat and dips into me. His big warm hands on my bare ass, holding me to him. He goes back to stroking me with his fingers and moves his mouth to my clit, sucking on me hard. He can feel me start to go over the edge...

"No. Don't come. No yet, my queen."

"But... Please... I can't help it..."

"No. Bad girls have to wait."

I whine uncontrollably and he squeezes my ass. Rick stands up and turns me away from him, bending me over in front of him with his hands spread across my hips and ass. I can't help myself and I shake my ass in front of him. He slides into me hard, fast, and deep, all at once and his body mashed up against mine.

"Fuck me. You can come now, baby." He says as he pounds into me repeatedly. He reaches around me and circles my sensitive nub, feeling how wet and ready I am. "You want it harder?"

"Yes. Bad girls deserve to get fucked hard."

"Yea, and you're my bad girl. Do bad girls deserve to get spanked?"

"Bad girls have to do whatever their man wants them to." I say breathlessly.

"Oh, fuck me. Then you have to watch." He bends me over further, so I can see him fucking me and holds me up with his arm around my waist. "Do you like that?"

"I like whatever you want, my king."

"Fuck! Fuck! Fuck!" He grabs my hips hard and pulls me back onto him, using my body to stroke himself. Sliding me on and off of his hard cock, harder and harder, faster and faster. He sends me soaring and doesn't stop. "A few more strokes, baby." He groans and I feel his pulsating release. He pulls me back upright and leans me against him where he talks in my ear from behind me, "You make me fucking insane."

"You're a baseball player for me, right?" I say out of breath.

"Yes, my queen."

"I'm going to be there to watch batting practice and I want you to knock it out of the park. I want you to get yourself in the game today. You work Skip and you make it a win for me. Can you do that?"

"I'll work it, my queen."

"My team can't win without you. They need you behind the plate. I'll be cheering for you and I'll be in your car waiting for you after the game. You look like a warrior going into battle when you step behind the plate and it's the hottest thing I've ever seen." His eyes start to heat up again.

"I love you, baby. I'm taking this elevator down to the clubhouse before I need to have you again. I'll see you at BP." He turns me to him and kisses me until the elevator doors open and he leaves me there without another word.

CHAPTER EIGHTEEN

I was early getting to the stadium and have some extra time before batting practice. I wander out of the stadium and across the street to sit at the bar and have some carne asada fries. How can you go wrong with fries made up like nachos?

I keep track of the time and get situated behind the home dugout before its time for batting practice to start. It feels good being back in the stadium after missing a week. It's my happy place, especially on a sunny day like today with a clear blue sky and a high of 75 degrees. I take my jersey off, put my cap on and slather myself in sunscreen. The coconut scent makes me happier. A cool breeze blows through and I realize I should've put my panties back on, but there's no time for that right now. The team is starting to wander out onto the field and the field is set up for practice. The seating bowl isn't open yet, so I'm the only one sitting in the stands. I see the new catcher, Stray, as well as Mason, Lucky, Kris, Rock and Chase with bats in their hands. Cross looks up, noticing me in the stands as he swings a bat and heads my direction.

Cross walks up to me in the stands in his happy-go-lucky way, "What did you do to Seno?"

"What do you mean? Is he okay?" Elevator injury?

"He's not hurt. He was happy to be back this morning. Then he was pissed when he found out Stray is catching today, and I was avoiding him because he was being so pissy. Now he's walking around with his chest puffed out, like he's the king again and he won't leave Skip alone. He says he needs to play today."

Yes! I look straight at Chase, "He's going to put on a hitting display during BP, too."

"I believe it because you said it. Those cookie bars were still warm, and delicious by the way."

"They should be. I made them fresh this morning. Did you like the stuff I gave you this morning?"

"The baseball cookies were cute and good. The banana bread was yummy, you should add nuts."

"I'll remember that for next time. So, where is Seno?"

"He's probably still working Skip."

He needs to get his ass out here and show off his bat. "Seno!" I yell out, thinking I might get a response. I know, not only did I give him instructions, I want it done my way. Damn! I'm bossy today. Maybe he just needs it today to get through.

"You still didn't tell me what you did to him." Cross stares directly at me.

"Let's just say it was the cookies," I smile innocently.

My Rick comes walking out of the dugout, he looks up at me in the stands and smiles. He quickly makes his way to me. He glares at Cross, "My woman, go."

Chase mutters as he walks back to the field, "Shit dude, you've got it bad. I'm the one who found her."

Rick pulls me out of my seat, puts his arms around me and dips me while he kisses me, getting catcalls from the team. He's in a much better mood. He brings me back up and makes close eye contact with me. "You give me strength and point me in the right direction when I've lost my focus. That's proof we're more than physical." He gets a big smile, "I'm not starting, but Skip says he'll put me in."

I clap loudly, "Go show me your bat, big boy!" I swat him on the ass as he turns back to the field. Both of us laughing as he gets to work.

The team as a whole is hitting well today. My Rick gets his first turn to hit and sends the second ball to the Right Field Upper Deck, home run. The third ball straight out and over the wall in Center Field. He broke his bat on the fourth ball, sending a grounder up the first base line. He walks to the dugout for a new bat and looks at me for affirmation. I blow him a kiss and yell, "Perfect, baby!" He continues to hit them out of the park on each turn at batting practice.

Text to Rick - You have an awesome bat.

Text to Rick - Yes, I'm referring to both kinds of wood ;)

Text to Rick - Since I'm already here, should I scout the other team for you?

Text from Rick - I'm glad you like my wood. I'll give you a demonstration with it later.

Text from Rick - Stay behind the home dugout while
you're scouting and be quiet. Very interested in what
you see.

Text to Rick - Yes, sir!

Text from Rick - You are the baseball queen.

Wow! There's no way he values my baseball opinion.
He does this for a living and I'm merely a spectator.
Though he didn't argue with me when I gave him my views
during the games. His suspension was a gift. When would
we ever have been able to sit and watch a game together?
Baseball is something we have in common. Rick has obviously been thinking about that, trying to find proof we're
solid together and not just sex. It was a glimpse into
spending the off-season together.

The visiting team comes out for batting practice and I
don't even pay attention to who we're playing. We're
playing LA and that means the stadium is going to get
rowdy. LA is a rival team and the fans flood the stadium
whenever they play here. They aren't obnoxious like the
Sissy's and their fans though. I check their website to see
who they have on their current roster and who is on the
lineup for tonight's game. I figure out who is in the outfield
catching balls, and who is hitting. I watch for anomalies,
unsure footing, bad hitting, anything odd and see if it
repeats.

Text to Rick - Their lead off hitter can't connect with
the ball to save his life

Text to Rick - Check out Kragen when you come out.
Lineup says he's hitting fourth and playing Left Field. I
think he's favoring his right leg. See what you think.

Text from Rick - Are you serious?

Text to Rick - Yes! This is baseball!

Text from Rick - Anything else?

Text to Rick - I'm still watching. Outfielders aren't
paying attention, but that's probably because it's BP.
There are a couple of them out there in a deep conversation. Can't see who they are.

Text from Rick - Any observations from Seals BP?

Interesting that he'd ask.

Text to Rick - Stray seems a bit full of himself for a guy
who's been up less than a week. Probably makes him
a liability behind the plate.

Text to Rick - Mason, Cross and Martin are on point.
Rock looks tired. Bravo is favoring his hip. Nothing
else stood out to me except your big bat.

Anybody who watches batting practice can see these
things. You'd think somebody from the team would be
watching everyday.

Text from Rick - Thanks. Tell me if you notice anything
else.

Text from Rick - My bat and I miss you.

Text to Rick - I'll show you how to handle your bat later.

Text to Rick - Did everybody like the cookies?

Text from Rick - Mason requested peanut butter cookies, Martin requested brownies, and Rock said more please and thank you.

Text from Rick - I thought I owed you a batting lesson.

Text to Rick - Either way I get to touch your bat.

Batting practice is over, so I check my phone to find out which seat I'm in tonight and I'm behind home plate where Rick wants me to be. I check the schedule, Monday is an off day and we're in Seattle on Tuesday. I need to do laundry. I've been too busy or I should be honest—I've been neglecting household chores and opting to spend time with my Rick. Like there's really any choice to consider, it's a no-brainer. I run up to the bathroom and pull on my panties, as well as my leggings. I stop by the member lounge to pick up $5 beer and free popcorn on my way back to my seat, and I'm a happy girl.

The pregame hoopla gets started and since Rick isn't starting, he catches the ceremonial first pitches. Which is nice because I get a glimpse of my favorite view and he's not wearing full catcher's gear. He turns to me and smiles before he heads back into the dugout. He's focused and ready to play.

Stray gets set behind the plate and I wonder about his

name as I read his jersey. Stray like a stray cat? Stray because he's not loyal? He doesn't follow rules? A wanderer maybe? It doesn't matter, probably just his name and means nothing.

The game is moving slowly, like it always does when Rick isn't behind the plate. It's the top of the fourth inning, there's no score, and Skip hasn't put my Rick in to catch yet. Young catchers always keep a slower paced game and that's bad because a) it bores me out of my mind, so I eat or drink more and most likely end up wasted and b) everything becomes transparent to the opposing team when you don't keep them on their toes. I don't know why I have an urge to numb my brain when I'm already bored, like putting myself out of my misery I guess.

I text Rick, knowing he probably can't see it.

Text to Rick - Stray needs to pick up the pace. LA can see right through him and he's boring me.

Text to Rick - I'll be sleeping in your car or possibly passed out from the quantity of alcohol I'm going to require to get through this slow ass game.

Text to Rick - I know you won't see these during the game.

Middle of the fourth inning and I need time to make two beer runs if I'm going to make it through this game. I stand up and stretch. I turn to walk up to the concessions stand and hear, "Hey, blondie! Where do you think you're going?" It's my favorite voice. I turn around and my Rick is standing in the on deck circle swinging his bat. His grin burns through me and I go back to my seat.

I yell at the top of my lungs, "Let's Go Seno! Woooooooooooo!" There's a new electricity in the stadium, at least there is for me.

Rick's replacing Stray in the seven spot, so he'll be catching the rest of the game. First pitch is outside. Second pitch is low. 2-0 count, and the third pitch is on fire straight down the middle. Rick connects and let's the fastball do all the work, launching it over the Center Field wall. The horn sounds and the fireworks fly. Home run. Rick runs the bases at a quick pace and he makes eye contact with me as he approaches home plate. He kisses two of his fingers and points them at me as he steps on the plate. "Yeah, baby! Wooooo! Seno!" I yell for him and he can hear me. The next hitter pops out and the pitcher is up in the nine spot. Tommy is pitching tonight and he's not a great hitter. He sees an opportunity to bunt and ends up half hitting it down the third base line, somehow legging it out and making it to first base safe. Mason is in the lead off spot and hacks at the first pitch, sending the ball over the first base-men's head into the Right Field corner. Mason safe at first and Tommy on second. Cross is hitting second, "Wooooo! Cross! Smack it!" 2-2 count and he breaks his bat, knocking the ball straight up the center of the field and sending wood shards toward the pitcher and short stop. The ball choppers through the infield and right over the short stop's head. Bases are loaded for Kris Martin and he's swinging his bat like it's the at bat he's been waiting for his whole life. First pitch, hit foul into the stands off first base. Second pitch, smacked hard foul and only a few feet from being a home run in Right Field. Third pitch, 0-2 count, is a ball high and outside—they're trying to get him to chase, but Kris isn't falling for it. 1-2 count, and the fourth pitch is outside away again. 2-2, fifth pitch is hit foul into the Seals dugout. Sixth pitch and I hear a clean ringing noise, I stand up and watch to see if it has the distance. The ball hits the outfield wall, missing a grand slam by about 9 inches. Tommy scores, Mason scores on his heels and so does Cross only a few feet behind him. Kris is safe at second base. Score is 4-0 Seals, still the bottom of the fourth and one out. Lucky hits a ground ruled double, bringing in Kris. Rock steps up to the plate and gets walked intentionally. Bravo covering third base tonight, steps up to the plate and hits into a double play. Of course, running slow with his hip obviously bothering him is pretty much a give away for LA. Ending the fourth inning at 5-0 Seals.

The team comes running out of the dugout to their positions for the fifth inning and the last one out is my Rick dressed in all of his catcher's gear, ready for war and sexy as hell. "Looking damn sexy, Seno! Wooo!" I stop myself and reset, "Take these guys out! 1, 2, 3, Tommy!" Rick turns to me and shakes his head.

The next few innings are quick and all three outs in a row except Cross getting a double and knocked in during the seventh inning. My Rick catching makes all the difference in the world. Okay, I may be biased, but the game is going quicker and I no longer feel the need to kill anyone or be intoxicated. Seno always keeps the game on track and in motion.

Top of the ninth inning and the score is 6-0 Seals. Tommy's still pitching and LA comes out ready to eat him alive. Four consecutive solo home runs, taking the score to 6-4 Seals. Skip pulls Tommy and brings in Houck since it's now a save situation. I watch Houck throw a few to Rick and something's off. This doesn't look like Houck's normal stuff. Rick's catching him fine and they're in sync. I can't place what's different. No outs and nobody on base. Houck throws and it's away, and I mean away like I could've caught that pitch if I was still sitting at the bar across the street. Seno manages to grab it and not let it get by him, arm straight out to reach it. Next pitch is away, but not as far. Third pitch is just outside and high. At least he's getting closer, but the count is 3-0 and it might as well be a lead off walk—always a bad thing. Houck manages to get some control and takes the count to 3-2, and ends up walking him anyway. The tying run is at the plate and I'm on the edge of my seat, "Get this guy out!" The pitch isn't where Rick is set up, I knew Houck was off! I hear the bat connect, "Oh fuck!" The ball is out of the park and it's a tied game. Skip pulls Houck and Rhett comes running in from the bull pen. Interesting move. I watch him toss to Rick a few times and he's on point. Rick claps a few times and makes eye contact around the field, I can almost hear him saying "Let's do this!" It's a whole new game. We need to get three outs and then come up to bat and score. Rhett fires in three in a row and strikes out the next hitter before he knew what hit him. Next hitter is their DH. Rhett and Rick are playing a game with him, each pitch located at a different spot around the plate, they almost circle it. The hitter gets a piece of a few of the pitches and pops out. The lead off guy is up and Rick glances back at me, then turns back to Rhett. I told him he couldn't connect to save his life and he hasn't connected all night. They literally play catch with him at the plate, pitches at about 78 miles per hour. Rick didn't even get all the way down into his crouch— strike three and the third out. That was a bit of a ballsy thing to do. Doesn't matter, on to the bottom of the ninth.

Bottom of the ninth inning and we're starting with Chase. Cross hits a double. Martin strikes out, caught look-ing. One out and one on when Lucky walks, taking the empty space at first base. Rock gets a base hit and every-body moves up one. Bases loaded and we only need one to win. Bravo is at the plate and Seno is swinging a bat in the on deck circle. Bravo strikes out swinging. Rick turns to me and grins. "All we need is a base hit! Let's finish this, baby!" He nods and walks to the plate, pointing at me before he turns his attention to the ball. "Go Seno!" The coaches are flashing signs, and Rick has made eye contact with his teammates on base. I don't think they're going to stick to the script. I hope they don't get crazy, we need Cross to score. The first pitch is low and inside. The second pitch is a fast-ball straight down the pipe. Rick swings and connects. It's beautiful and almost an exact copy of his home run from his first at bat in the game, except this time it's a grand slam! The horn blows. The fireworks go crazy. The big screen is my Rick running the bases with comic book word bubbles, pow, pop, wow, boom, wham, smack, bursting around him. Cross scores, Lucky scores, Rock scores and Rick slows as he approaches the plate, jumping on home plate as his team mobs him. I'm out of my seat, jumping up and down, clap-ping and dancing like a wild woman. "That's my man! Woooooo!" Walk off win, 10-6 Seals. The celebration on the field is insane and Gatorade is flying everywhere.

Hannah grabs Cross and nods to Rick for an interview. She starts with Cross and Rick walks over to the net, "The team wants to go out and celebrate, but I want to celebrate with you."

"We can celebrate together later. I'll be waiting for you."

Rick nods, "Or, you could go with us."

What? I can go celebrate with the team? Oh, I mean, I can go celebrate with the team! "I don't want to impose on your fun time with the guys."

"It'll be better with you there. My girl sitting on my lap will just make me happier." He smiles at me and takes off to do his interview with Hannah. I watch the interview, he's absolutely beaming and as always not taking credit for anything.

Hannah focuses on him, "This was a great return from your five day suspension. The days away didn't hurt your game at all. Do you regret your actions on the field last Sunday?" Uh oh.

Rick stops before he speaks, "I regret that I didn't have enough self-control to keep it off the field. It was evident they were throwing at me intentionally. I allowed them to get under my skin, personally, and that won't happen again." A reasonable and politically correct answer for the fan base. He looks at me and the truth is he'd do it again in a second. He'll always protect me and defend me.

Text from Sam - Bullshit! He'd do it again in a heart-beat. Guys shouldn't fuck with you if they want to live.

Text to Sam - Ha ha! I was just thinking he'd do it again in a second!

Text to Sam - He's taking me out to celebrate with the team tonight.

Text from Sam - That's new. Remember he needs to be the man around the team and have fun!

Sam's right, I need to make sure I don't embarrass him around the team.

Text from Rick - Let's meet up with the team, but not stay too long. I want some alone time and tomorrow is an early game.

Text to Rick - Alone = naked with me?

Text from Rick - YES

My body shivers in anticipation. You'd think we didn't spend most of the last week together and we haven't been naked at every opportunity we've had. It doesn't get old. I always want more. I always want to be with him. I can't believe it's only been a couple months. It feels like it's always been this way, it's how it's supposed to be.

Text to Rick - I can't wait.

Text from Rick - Meet me at the clubhouse level elevator and we can walk over to the Batter Up together. I'll be there in 15 minutes.

I take the elevator down to the garage and drop off my bag in the Challenger, keeping my ID in my pocket. I walk back to the elevator as Rick is walking up to it.

"Did I tell you how amazing you were tonight?" I throw my arms around his neck and he lifts me, so I wrap my legs around him. "I love that you're only a baseball player for me. Let's go celebrate with the guys, so we can go home and talk about your big bat." I kiss him, sucking on his lower lip while I run my fingers through his hair, rubbing his head.

"Maybe we should skip it and go home." His eyes hooded with serious sexual need.

"You should hang out with the team. You're just back from suspension."

Rick agrees with me and we walk to the Batter Up. We find the guys at the table in the back where they always hang out. Rick walks around the table shaking hands and offering high-fives. He has me in tow and introduces me to the guys I haven't met yet. Chase gives me a hug and gets reminded I'm Rick's woman. I get Kris to pose for me and text the picture to Sam. We get settled at the end of the table where there's enough room for me to be planted on his lap, and he holds me there possessively with his arm around my waist.

Mike with the Mic walks up, "Sherry? I'm about to start open mic night. How about you get us started tonight instead of my tired Bon Jovi tune?"

I look at Rick and he nods. "I'd love to!" I kiss Rick on the cheek, hop off his lap and walk across the bar with Mike. "What am I singing?"

"I was thinking Pat Benatar "Shadows of the Night" or Elle King "Ex's and Oh's." You rock both of those. You can do both."

"Let's do both." I smile and Mike goes to the stage.

"Welcome to the Batter Up! I'm Mike with the Mic and it's time for karaoke! We have a special treat tonight! Our contest winner, Sherry, will be opening for us tonight with a couple of her best." He hands me the mic and gets the music queued up, starting with Elle King. I love to sing this one and its even more fun when I'm not competing. I'm not dressed the part, but I still have the strut and attitude in my voice. Rick's watching me and there's a crowd of women that have swarmed the table. A couple of them standing by my Rick and taking pictures with him in the background, but he doesn't even know they're there. The crowd claps while Mike starts the next song, the wrong song. Instead of "Shadows of the Night," "We Belong" starts to play. I'd be irritated if it was any other song, but this one has invaded my head over the last week and there must be a reason. Mike looks at me and mouths "oops," giving me a self-deprecating smile. I give him an accepting nod and let it rip. I'm trying not to watch the team's table while I sing the lyrics off the screen. I know Rick isn't interested in that drama. I finish the song and there's cheering from the crowd, but I honestly don't even remember singing.

I walk back to the table slowly, watching the team interact and the swarm try to infiltrate. The women touching them and, for the most part, not being acknowledged. Just as I'm walking up to the table a woman walks up to Rick and puts her hand on his shoulder, smiling at him like she's offering him everything. I pick her hand up off of my man and stare at her directly in the eyes with a look that could kill, "He's taken, honey. Hands off."

"I don't see a ring." She says glibly and puts her hand back on Rick. Chase is watching, suspecting there could be blood. Why is he letting her touch him!

I turn to Rick for direction because I keep hearing Sam say not to embarrass him with the guys. "I'm so taken. I'm fuckin' addicted to you, my queen." Rick's eyes are heated and focused on me. He pulls me into his lap and I put my arms around his neck, ignoring the player chaser as he claims my mouth with his. I wanted to flip her the bird as she walked away, but my hands were busy in Rick's hair and that's more important. Rick moves to whisper in my ear, "How about we get rings to wear, so we can avoid this crap?"

I'm not sure what to think, but I don't want a ring that

doesn't mean anything. I don't care if I ever get a ring, as long as I have him. I whisper in his ear, "I'm not after a ring, my king. Just you."

He whispers back to me quietly, "You have me. What if I want you to have a ring? A pretty one with diamonds that means I love you and I want to be with you for the rest of my life."

Tears are building at the thought and I'm struck with the reality of never wanting this until now. Never wanting to get married, but Rick makes me want things. What happened to keeping things the way they are and not talking about taking things further until the season is over? I kiss him passionately and speak breathlessly, "I'll never say no to you."

Rick stands and picks me up with him, throwing me over his shoulder. "Good game today, guys. Have a good night, gentlemen. I'm going to leave you now to handle some personal business." I wave as we leave and he carries me all the way back to the stadium parking garage. I can't wait to see this on the internet.

CHAPTER NINETEEN

I snuggle up to Rick for the drive home and he wakes me up taking me out of the car. I admit I'm tired and it's been a long day, following an emotional week. My head is spinning at a different speed than the world around me. I need to pack for away games, make sure work is caught up, and all kinds of other things, but all I can think about is the player chaser at the bar and a ring with diamonds that means he loves me. I'm tired. My brain isn't functioning. I nestle against Rick's strong chest and hold on with my arms around his neck, letting him carry me in. He kisses my forehead while we ride up on the elevator, "You're being quiet and that worries me. What's going on in there?"

"I didn't like that girl touching you."

"I know, you took her hand off of me and claimed me like a cavewoman." Rick chuckles.

"But, when she did it again then I didn't know what to do. I didn't want to overstep my boundaries, especially with the guys there."

"What did you want to do?" Rick unlocks the door, and takes us to the bedroom where we continue our conversation.

Tell her to get the fuck away from my man and knock her on her ass, oh wait, I can't say that. "I don't know. It made me possessive and I wondered why you were letting her touch you." Which is also true.

"Its like that a lot. I pretend they aren't there and they usually go away."

"Usually?"

"If I don't give them any attention they move on to another player. I'm only interested in you, my queen."

"What happened to keeping things the way they are until the season is over? Not making any relationship decisions."

"As soon as I suggested rings, I knew it came out wrong. I heard myself say it and thought 'what an asshole,' rings aren't to make chicks stay away. One special ring is for the one special woman in my life, because I love her and only her forever." Rick stops, "Don't worry about the team being there, just be you. It makes me happy you won't say no."

I grin at him and roll my eyes, feeling like a fool.

"It's late, come here my queen." He holds me and we fall asleep in each others' arms.

Early in the morning, Rick whispers in my ear, "Come here, baby. I need to have you." He pulls me up on top of him and pulls my panties off while he kisses me, needing me. I don't know where this comes from in the middle of the night, but I'll never get tired of it. It's hot, needy, and quick while we're half asleep. He holds me on top of him. I sleep there with my head resting on his chest, and his cock still inside me. I'm his home.

THE ALARM GOES off and I smell the coffee brewing. I'm still lying on him. "Good morning, my king."

"I love you, my queen. I'm so happy you're going on the road with me. I hate empty hotel rooms and every hotel room without you in it is empty. I hug his chest as I appreciate his words and I don't want to get up, I want to stay right here.

CHAPTER TWENTY

I must've known my world was about to become a
whirlwind. I should've stayed in bed longer. In fact, I
should've stayed right there on my Rick's chest for as
long as I could.

Suddenly, I find myself living the life of a professional
baseball player. Well, that runs a travel business, too. From
the moment I step foot out of the house on Sunday morning, the world only seems to stop when I'm *alone* with Rick.
If we're home, I'm doing laundry, cleaning, baking (because
I need cookies on the road), or at the game. If we're away,
I'm working, trying to find time to explore, sleeping, or at
the game. Either way, my nights and some of my mornings
are spent with my man. My he-used-to-be-just-a-fantasy-
baseball-boyfriend that turned out to be better than I
could've ever imagined, real life, breathing, hot and sexy,
we need each other more than air, professional athlete who
worships me. I'm still not sure I deserve him, us.

The Seals have been playing well. The trade rumors

have been hard, especially since the team kept Stray up a week longer than they needed to cover Seno. But, he didn't talk about it and we made it through the trade deadline without getting traded. In fact, the Seals have made it clear they intend to offer him a long-term contract, but that's something that'll get handled in the off-season.

I've made a point of making Rick get out to see the places we travel to for away games, even if it's only one thing and not always the tourist spot associated with the location.

In Seattle, we had a late night dinner at the top of the Space Needle. That's over 600 feet up in an elevator. I know, totally touristy, but the elevator sealed the deal and it had to happen. It was pitch black out and the lights across the city shone with a haze from the marine layer. On our free morning we explored Pike's Place Market, enjoying breakfast together with a beautiful view of the Puget Sound. Seattle's elevator action was unparalleled. We had a late night reservation and I made sure we'd have the elevator to ourselves for the ride up. We lost the series 2-1, but they didn't sweep us and Rick was a double hitting machine with two in each game. Unfortunately, none of his teammates were able to bring him around to score even once.

Chicago was crazy! We were on a pizza-testing mission. Every day we tried pizza from a different place, including Chicago style—which we agreed was good, but not what we want from pizza. Pizza shouldn't require a fork, there should be no cornmeal and the toppings are called toppings because they belong on top. The stadium there is in the middle of a neighborhood with no parking. It was interesting to see everybody come out of the woodwork, watch from their rooftops and fill the old stadium, maintaining traditions. We won the series, taking two of the three games. Cross was on point for the whole series, hitting two home runs and making a diving catch that had the internet world photoshopping a cape on his back like a superhero. Rick was a single shy of a cycle in game three, but we all agree that we'd much rather have the two homers he hit that pushed three of his teammates across home plate to score.

LA was hard. First, we got swept. Second, it resurrected bad memories. I could see and feel Rick watching me, almost waiting for me to leave him there. He took me back to the Hawaiian Themed restaurant in Malibu, this time he insisted we start with dessert. We spent all of our time at the hotel, and when I say he needed me, I mean I required help to stand at one point and nearly missed a game due to soreness. It was because we were in LA. Every insecurity we have was right there in front of us, taunting us, and we didn't say a word about it. There weren't many words between us at all, LA was more about not having anything between us. I'm not sure if I've ever felt how much he loves me like when we were in LA. I hate to say it, but Rick was distracted and it was reflected in his game. He didn't call the games with the same confident positivity. The whole team combined only got six hits total over the three games, scoring only once.

San Francisco was a fun trip. Rick got me a ticket in the friends and family section, so I was sitting with the wives. He didn't want me to be alone in the stands and he didn't want to worry about the Sissy's pulling crap like they did the last time they were in San Diego. The truth is, he didn't want Adam to know I was there. He was hiding me in the crowd. I understood, and knew he still thought about Adam touching me. He hates him, luckily he wasn't in the lineup. I don't know if he got sent back to the minors, or if he's still on the DL and it doesn't matter either way. He's not in the stadium and that's a good thing. The players' wives were mostly welcoming. I cheered louder and made sure Rick could hear me. I don't understand the friends and family box. They clap and occasionally call out, but there isn't much excitement or cheering really. I felt slightly judged for my decibel level, but continued anyway. I haven't heard any comments from their dugout and Rick keeps looking for me behind home plate even though he knows I'm not there. It's a habit at this point. We wandered the wharf one morning, checking out the sea life and taking in the scenery. I managed to find a chocolate shop where I bought my weight in high end flavored chocolates, and wandered a jewelry store that only had items from estates, so nothing new and trendy, only cool pieces and some one of a kinds. We took the series 2-1 and made the hitting slump a thing of the past with ten hits or more in each of the three games. The outfielders were really working for it and held it together until game three when the Sissy's took the win. Rick hit a grand slam in game two and a homer in game three, but it wasn't enough.

The freeway series against the Orange County Characters was only two games and was bookended by off days, so Rick indulged me and took me to Disneyland. Walking through the amusement park while holding hands with my guy, having his arms around me on the rides, buying silly hats and matching T-shirts that point at each other with a character's cartoon hand saying "I'm with her" and "I'm with him"—I was in heaven. We split the series, and the whirlwind continued.

The home games were refreshing. I missed my stadium.

I missed our private penthouse. I missed my bed and my kitchen. None of it mattered or even came close to how important it was for me to be with him wherever he was playing. Not just for him, but for us.

CHAPTER TWENTY-ONE

It's September and we're finally home for more than a week. I finally have time to get the laundry caught up, change the bed sheets, clean out the refrigerator, and catch up on some email I've been putting off. Mike with the Mic has emailed me numerous times for different things. He wants me to host karaoke at the Batter Up, so he can add another location to his list and still get a day off. He wants me to cover him, so he can go on vacation. He wants me to judge the qualifying round for the next competition. He wants me to lead eighth inning karaoke for the Seals. What? Hold on, I better read that one...

From: MikeMic

I got a special request from the San Diego Seals. Are
you interested in going on field and leading eighth
inning karaoke? They want to feature you because you
won the contest and they'd like to do it this Saturday
night. They said something about it being part of fan
appreciation week. Let me know ASAP!

Mike with the Mic

I turn to Rick and show him the email. "That's cool!
You should do it and invite your Mom. Show all your baseball peeps and your Mom how good you are."

I think about it for a few minutes. It's an opportunity to
show my Mom my "singing thing" and a chance to sing on
the field. It could lead to singing the National Anthem.
That's it. I'm doing it! I send a message back to Mike.

To: MikeMic

I'm in. What song am I leading? Since I'll be on field, is
my baseball jersey acceptable?

So cool!

Thank you,
Sherry

From: MikeMic

Baseball attire is preferred as long as it's Seals. They're
going to let the fans vote on which song you sing, but
will only give them choices from the songs you sang in
the finals and semifinals. I have already sent them a list
of those songs. Will call has a ticket waiting for you.

Mike with the Mic

To: MikeMic

I already have a ticket to the game. I'm sitting behind
home plate if you need to find me.

Sherry

I check the schedule and the game starts at 5:40 on
Saturday.

Today is an off day and it's nice to have a day at home
alone together. Rick turns on the music and his arms are
around me instantly. He's holding me close and we're
dancing to "Thinking Out Loud." There is nowhere I'd
rather be and nothing else matters, it can all wait. Twenty
minutes later we're still dancing and he has the song on
repeat. We aren't talking. We aren't kissing. He's holding
me close while we move together. He pulls back and gazes
into my eyes. I don't know what he sees, but it makes him
happy and I feel a change in his body. No words pass
between us. He turns the volume up loud, picks me up, and
takes me to bed in the middle of the afternoon. He's
different this afternoon, its good different and I didn't think
that was possible. I mean, how could he possibly get better?
We lie on the bed together and he starts to kiss me tenderly.
He rolls me underneath him and kisses my neck. He cups

my head, holding me where he wants to kiss me and slowly pushes into me, burying himself a little at a time. He feels amazing.

He gazes into my eyes as he strokes into me deeply and deliberately. "Do you know how much I love you, my queen?" He already has me rendered speechless with his movements. "I love you more than anyone else in the world. I truly would do anything for you. I want to make you happy and I want to make your life easy. I want to be with you every minute of every day. I want to give you everything. I can't imagine my life without you in it, and I don't want to." Still moving at a steady, even pace, and driving me out of my mind. "When I look at you, I see forever."

I whimper as tears roll down my face and I'm unable to put words together. I pull his face to mine, so I can kiss him because it's the only way I can respond to his words right now. I rub his head and play with his hair lovingly. I do my best to convey my feelings for him without words and he gets it. His heart is pounding and it's not from exertion, since he continues his slow deliberate pace. The friction building is driving me out of my mind. Our connection is strong and growing as we become more familiar. It's only been a few months, but it feels like it's always been us together, somehow, and the world would end if we were torn apart. Well, the world might not end, but my world would end. When he loves me its special, I feel it in every bone and in every muscle. I wrap my legs around him, encouraging him for more. He strokes just a little harder and a little faster, but I suddenly feel like I've been hit by a truck, slammed into a brick wall. My body tenses up and he comes hard, "I love you, baby. Always you, Sherry." He holds me tight against him. "Are you okay?" Concern in his voice as he goes back to his slow, steady strokes. I can't answer him. He kisses me and reaches to play with my magic button. I simply keep eye contact with him and when he sends me over the edge I cry out his name in ecstasy. His eyes lock on mine, reading me and seeing it's more than usual. He stops moving and lays down next to me, pulling me back to him so he can hold me and comfort me. "I've got you, my queen. I'll never let you go."

CHAPTER TWENTY-TWO

I t's Thursday and it's an off day, which usually means date night. But, it's already late in the afternoon and Rick hasn't said a word. "Since we're home, how about I make dinner for you tonight?"

"I was thinking it should be date night, but I just want to stay home and have a romantic evening with you." I totally get it. All of the travel during the season wears on you and I only did it for half of the season. I've never heard him say the word romantic, I'm intrigued.

"Romantic, huh?" I giggle.

"Yep. I'm going to romance your socks off you."

I look at my feet, "I'm already barefoot." The words come out and I immediately hear "and pregnant" in my head, which I'm not. I see his grin and know he's thinking we can practice for the "and pregnant" part.

His bright blue eyes soften. He reaches for my hand, bringing it to his lips and he kisses every knuckle of every finger. Tenderly spending time with each one. "You're beautiful, inside and out. Nobody has ever made me feel as loved as you do. I know you love me completely." He leans his forehead to mine while he holds my hands in his, "I hope I'm worthy of you. I hope you feel how much I love you. I promise I'll always love you and I'll never hurt you." His voice goes raspy. "I promise to give you everything you want. You're my happiness. You're my forever." I lean into his chest and he holds me as I absorb his words.

Rick wraps his arms around me and holds me tightly to his chest, "I know we said no relationship stuff until after the season is over, but the season is almost over and you're in my head." He kisses the top of my head and regroups before he continues. "I'll be the happiest man alive whenever it happens and I only want it with you." He stops again, taking a deep breath, "But, I don't want to try to make it happen yet. I want you all to myself longer, maybe another season." I feel his heart beat while he's talking.

"I'm not rushing you. You tell me when, my king." A lone girlie tear falls and I'm afraid I'm going to start bawling. I worry that maybe I'm too old for him, but try to hide the thought away. "I just want you to know I'm willing. Anything for you." Rick tries to pull back, but I don't let him. I don't want him to see the crazy girl that's trying to come out. He cups my head, running his fingers through my hair and holds me there in silence.

"I changed my mind, let's get out of the house for a bit."

"Okay. I need to get ready." I probably have a tear stained face, the shorts I'm wearing have a hole in them, and I never got anything on my top half beyond the bikini top I'm wearing.

"No, you're fine." He pulls a T-shirt on and scoops me up off the love seat, carrying me out the door. I giggle uncontrollably. "That's what I want to hear. Happy woman."

We get in his car and he drives us toward the beach, parking near dog beach and, my favorite, lifeguard stand five. He takes my hand and we walk out onto the sand. It's almost sunset and the tide is higher than normal. The wind is blowing at the tips of the waves, sending misty breezes toward the shore. Rick sits down at the top of the berm and pulls me down with him. He puts his right arm around me and I lean into him. He pulls me into his lap and we sit together watching the sunset as the waves crash and sizzle. The sky is mostly clear, the few clouds in the far off distance turning dark purple as the sun lowers. The sun blankets the sky with golden yellow hues and surfers turn to dark silhouettes on the horizon. My happy place, sitting in his lap with my back to him and his warm breath at my neck, watching the sunset. I melt into him and he kisses my cheek, "I love you, my queen." The sun disappears, the golden sky turns rusty, and the breeze turns colder. Rick stands and pulls me up with him leading me back to his car.

Rick looks at his phone, "The guys are at the Locale playing pool. Do you want to go?"

"No. But, you should. You need some time with the team. I have some baking I want to do and I'll be home when you get there." I smile at him.

"Are you sure?"

"Yes, you can continue the romance when you get home." He drives over to the Locale and parks in the lot.

He takes my face in his hands and kisses me, sliding his tongue across my lips before claiming me completely. It's one of his don't-forget-me-kisses and so much more. I slide behind the wheel as he takes off across the parking lot. I pick up take out from the deli at my favorite Mexican Food place on my way home and consider my baking options.

Text from Rick - Cross wants to know what you're baking.

Text to Rick - I haven't started yet. Picked up tamales for later on my way home.

Text to Rick - Do you or Chase have any baking requests?

Text from Rick - Cross wants you to save some for him and says he likes it when it's still warm.

Of course he does.

Text to Rick - What about you?

Text from Rick - I'm a fan of cake and whipped cream.

My body reacts to his response, low in my belly and I'm going to make a cake. I need to check the whipped cream supply.

Text to Rick - I have a couple 12 packs hiding in the cupboard if you want to bring the guys by. I'll bake up some good stuff, save the cake for us later. ;)

Text from Rick - Chill the beer just in case. You're perfect.

First thing, I put the beer into chill. I look through my

pantry trying to decide what I want to make and I decide on PB&J Thumbprints, butter cookies, brownies and, of course, cake. I mix up a batch of my butter cookie dough and a batch of my peanut butter cookie dough, putting them both in the refrigerator to chill. I turn on the oven to get it preheating and mix up some brownie batter, adding chopped walnuts and toffee bits. I butter my brownie pan, pour the brownie batter into it and slide it straight into the oven. I clean up the kitchen and get a bowl for my cake batter, but I can't decide what flavor I want to make. I pull the butter cookie dough from the refrigerator, portion out the dough onto two cookie sheets, and put them in the oven. I get the peanut butter cookie dough and portion them out evenly over two cookie sheets. I press my thumb into the middle of each one and pull the brownies out of the oven, replacing them with the peanut butter thumbprints.

> Text to Rick - What kind of cake would you like? I made brownies with walnuts and toffee bits, I have my PB&J Thumbprints baking and butter cookies are about to come out and get dipped.

It takes a few minutes for him to answer, but I finally get a response.

> Text from Rick - Be creative. I like it when you make stuff up.

> Text from Rick - Now Cross is rushing us because the brownies are warm.

Text from Cross - Seno hit me because I want
brownies and they're warm

Text to Cross - They'll be warm for awhile. The cookies
aren't done yet. Play another game of pool.

Text from Rick - Is Cross texting you?

Text to Rick - Yes. Lol.

Text from Rick - Looks like the guys are going to come
home with me. Since Cross can't shut up about
brownies now.

Text to Rick - He's such a sweet kid.

Text from Rick - You really don't need to talk to him.

Text to Rick - Gotta go, baking!

I pull the butter cookies from the oven and let them
cool. I search my kitchen for something creative to do with
cake. I see the leftover coffee from this morning, s'mores
flavored instant pudding mix, and marshmallow fluff.
Coffee makes everything better, especially chocolate. I pull
the peanut butter cookies out to cool and move the butter
cookies to the cooling rack. I mix up my cake batter starting
with a box of yellow cake mix and start adding things to
make it delicious. I replace the water with my leftover
coffee and add the instant pudding mix. I add about a cup
of milk and debate with myself about adding the marshmallow fluff in place of the eggs or dropping spoonfuls on
top, so they get toasted like at a campfire and go with toasty.

I add eggs and stir it up, adding some melted butter instead of the oil and more milk until I get to the right batter consistency. Baking is a science, but it's never been a problem for me to doctor stuff up and make it better. I taste the batter and now I can't decide if I want to cover it with mini marshmallows instead of pools of fluff. Sometimes it's hard to be me, but when baking decisions are the hardest thing you deal with—I guess I shouldn't complain. I can swirl the fluff through the cake. I can mix the marshmallows into the cake. That's it, I add mini marshmallows to my cake batter and pour the batter into my buttered cake pan. Then I drop spoonfuls of marshmallow fluff all over the cake and kind of swirl it through, which doesn't work very well and I go with it anyway. I slide the cake into the oven and cross my fingers. I melt some chocolate and chop up some pecans, and proceed to dip my butter cookies using the chocolate as the glue for the pecans. I get the grape jam from the cupboard and put a few big spoonfuls into a small bowl with a small amount of water and microwave it, stirring it repeatedly until it's the consistency I'm looking for. I move the peanut butter cookies to the cooling tray and fill my thumbprint with the grape jam mix. Both cookies are done. Brownies are done. Cake is baking. Not bad for a couple of hours. I clean up the rest of my mess, making sure I lick all of the utensils and don't let any batter go to waste. Just as I'm licking the batter off the last spatula, I hear the door open and throw the spatula into the sink quickly.

"It smells amazing in here. Where are the brownies?" I hear Chase before anybody else.

"Dude, chill." I know Rick is shaking his head at the rookie even though I can't see him. Rick calls out to me, "I'm home and the guys are with me. I walk out of the kitchen and Rick grins at me as he walks toward me. I prepare to be attacked with the team standing right there, but Rick simply laughs and licks my nose. "That's chocolate with something?"

I turn red and wonder where else I have batter on me. "That's your cake. You'll have to wait and see."

"Are you toasting marshmallows?" Chase, of course.

"Kind of, its Rick's cake." I say trying not to give away what I'm making because it's for me and Rick, it goes with the whipped cream. "My king, you want to get the guys drinks while I plate up some sweets?"

Rick walks past me in the kitchen, making sure to rub against me on his way by and kiss me on the neck. I cut up the brownies and stack them pyramid-like on a plate. I make a plate of PB&J Thumbprints and a plate of chocolate dipped butter cookies. "Chase sweetie, will you help me?" Before I finished talking he was there at my side, eyes wide. "Will you get the two plates of cookies, please?" He picks them up and follows me out to the guys in my living room.

For the record, I'm getting used to being around the team. However, when I step foot into my living room and my leading man along with Chase, Jones, Kris, Rhett, Tommy and Lucky have all made themselves at home—stretched out all over the furniture and the floor, basically filling my living room while they talk about what movie to put on or if they should play video games—I about lose it. It's too much for a fan to take. I knew Rick was bringing the guys back with him, but seven professional baseball players in my living room sets the testosterone levels in here to emergency overload.

I walk directly to my Rick and announce what I've baked, "Okay, so these are PB&J's, these are dipped butter cookies, and these are walnut and toffee brownies. Let me know what you think, so I know which ones to make for you again," I say as I look into Rick's clear blue eyes.

"Sure thing," Chase chimes in.

I laugh, "That's fine, but I was mostly talking to Rick. My man gets what he wants." I realize how it sounds after it comes out of my mouth, but decide it's true and I don't care who knows it.

"You got it, baby." Rick smiles at me and I leave them alone to their guy things.

The plates get passed around and they've come looking for more beer. Well, except Chase, and he wanted milk. Once I have a chance to absorb it, I like having them all around. The team is family. Rick is home and hanging out with the guys. I can hang with them or do my own thing, and they like my baking. Rick finds me periodically, to kiss me or touch me or whisper in my ear. I know he's buzzed, but the promises he whispers in my ear—well, fuck me. I discreetly take a picture of my living room and another of Kris, texting both of them to Sam.

Text to Sam - So, this is my living room tonight.

Text from Sam - OMG! Are you handling that okay?

Text to Sam - Yes. I like it. I freaked out a bit internally when I first saw them all, but I got over it. I'm good now.

Text from Sam - Tell Kris hi for me.

At about midnight, a couple of the guys had left and I find Rick kicking the rest out, "Game is at 7:05 tomorrow night. Go get your rest and be ready."

I heard varying responses.

"Whatever. You just want to get laid."

"Okay. Porn king."

"Can I have another brownie to go?"

"Make sure you treat that girl right."

"Thanks for the beer."

Sudden silence followed by the sound of the door latch locking, romantic music starting to play, and Rick's hands on my hips. His body against my back and rocking against me.

"Do you want to try the cake and whipped cream?"

"Will it still be good after the game tomorrow?

"Yes."

"Then, I'd rather have you right now," Rick says as he picks me up and carries me off to the bedroom. I wrap my legs around his waist and my arms around his neck. "I feel like I've been away for days and I was only out playing pool for a couple of hours." Rick strips me naked quickly and makes himself comfortable between my legs putting his mouth on me. Licking and sucking at my tender folds and clit, he slides a finger in and strokes me.

"I want all of you, my king. I want you inside me. Please make love to me, Rick." His whole tone changes and he loses his clothes. He pushes into me and grinds against me. He pulls out and strokes in with purpose, repeatedly until he comes. He slows and claims my mouth with his, sucking on my lower lip. He holds me to him while he kisses me and goes back to stroking into me with intent repeatedly until he comes again on a growl. He keeps going, pounding into me harder now. Wanting more. I lift my legs for him, trying to give him better access and he catches them with his arms, bringing my feet to my ears and spreading me open for his pleasure. He buries himself as deep as he can get and leans in to kiss me while he grinds against me. His grinding action rubs against my sensitive nub and I want more. I grind back and squeeze him, feeling how deep he is. I rock my hips and he growls as he slams into me once, and again and again and again and again until we both crash together and fall asleep in each others' arms, unable to recover.

CHAPTER TWENTY-THREE

Friday morning I wake up before the alarm and before the coffee. Rick is wrapped around me and has his hard length snugly between my thighs. "Are you awake, my queen? You were saying sweet things to me and suddenly stopped."

"I don't know. What did I say?" I respond sleepily on a yawn.

I feel him smile, "You told me how amazing I was last night and then you woke up." Sounds right. I probably said more than that and he isn't telling me. I'm beginning to wonder if there's more to why he doesn't tell me, but I guess it doesn't matter. We have no secrets and the personal things between us are out there. There's nothing to hide.

"That's true. I think you had different things running through your head last night." Rick rolls me over to face him and I feel his gaze on my face.

"Maybe I did."

"Do you want to talk about it?"

"We already did."

I wonder if I was awake for that conversation because I'm obviously not going to get any clues.

"Let's walk over to the Yolk for an early breakfast. Cross is going to pick me up early to go work out." He kisses me on each eyelid and then my lips. I can't argue with that.

It's a beautiful San Diego morning with no marine layer hindering the sun's rays and I love the warmth on my skin as we walk to breakfast. Rick holds my hand, rubbing his thumb on my hand and across my fingers while we walk the four blocks to the Yolk. I love to walk with him at my side, when he holds my hand he makes me feel like his queen.

He leads me into the Yolk and they immediately seat us in a back corner booth where he slides in next to me and puts his arm around me. The waitress doesn't even ask if we want coffee anymore, she just brings it and knows I like the flavored creamers. We sit together happily and enjoy breakfast while we pick at each other's plates. We laugh as he steals the chicken from my waffles and I eat most of his hash browns. He always has his arm around me or his hand on my thigh. I love how he's always touching me. I love the way he looks at me and I find him watching me lick the maple syrup off of my fingers. He takes my hand and sucks on my fingers, licking off the sweet syrup with his blue eyes focused on me, watching me as he's driving me crazy. I reach for his leg under the table and somehow end up with my hand around him inside his shorts. I have no idea how that could've happened.

Rick looks down and then back at me. "I thought you wanted breakfast."

"Turn about is fair play, finger sucker." Oops, where did that come from? I know better. It's a game day. I review our surroundings. We are facing the wall and nobody has a line of sight to under our table unless the waitress wanders by. I stroke him a few times. He stiffens in more ways than one. I'm being bad, but I can't help myself.

"You know it's a game day and we're sitting in a restaurant we like to go to?"

"Yes."

"You know you'll have me walking home with a raging hard-on?"

Playing innocent, "Oh, I'm sorry. Let me out so I can go wash my hands, they're all sticky. Your hands might be sticky, too. Do you need to wash up?" He slides out of the booth and I get up, glancing back at him as I walk to the bathroom swaying my hips at him.

I walk into the bathroom and look in the mirror to see I'm red, warm to the touch and my breathing is irregular with hope he'll come find me. If I stay in here long enough, he'll have to. I turn on the water to wash my hands and hear the door open, close, and lock. I see Rick's reflection in the mirror and his eyes meet mine. He walks up behind me, unties the back of my halter top freeing my breasts and slowly pours warm maple syrup all over my breasts and nipples as I watch in the mirror. He turns me and lifts me up, setting me on the edge of the counter. He pushes my short skirt up and groans in pleasure as he finds me going commando, shoving into me hard as he licks and sucks at my breasts. His mouth and tongue all over me, cleaning up the maple syrup. No words. He sucks at my nipples while he fucks me and the combination makes me want to scream out. He can feel where I'm at and claims my mouth with his to quiet me while he strokes into me as deep as he can with every pass. I shake and shudder without warning as Rick slams into me, filling me completely with his rock hard cock. I pull him with me and he pushes us through, while he kisses me roughly. He smiles at me with a dirty glint, ties the back of my halter top, pulls his shorts up, washes his hands, puts my feet back on the ground, and leaves the bathroom. Still no words. I turn back to the mirror and see the red blotches all over my chest and neck. There's no other way to say it, I look thoroughly fucked.

I do my best to quickly put myself back together and go back to the table, where Rick lets me slide into the booth to finish breakfast nonchalantly.

"You okay, my queen? You were gone for awhile." Like he doesn't know what he did.

"I'm better than okay. I'm energized for the day."

"Why is that?" He asks smugly.

I'm still feeling playful, "The hand soap scent in the bathroom is invigorating."

"Is that all?"

I lean in and kiss him, refusing to comment.

CHAPTER TWENTY-FOUR

We walk home quickly and Cross is already there waiting for Rick to go work out. I bribe him with brownies, so Rick has a few minutes to clean up.

Rick gives me a kiss on his way out the door and grins at me, unsure of the situations we can get into. "Are you going to be early for batting practice?"

"Yes, sir!"

"I'll look forward to your scouting report. Love you, my queen." He walks out the door with Chase in tow and looking at Rick like he's lost his marbles.

I'm home alone and I have hours before I need to be anywhere. This is an uncommon occurrence in my life of a professional baseball player. I have tons to do. Work to get done. Groceries to shop for. Cleaning to put off. Since I'm making bad decisions today, I run with it. I open all the windows to let the breeze and the sunshine in. I turn my music on random shuffle and kick up the volume, ready to dance around or do nothing or whatever I want. Except for one problem. I don't want to be alone, unless it's me and Rick alone. Dancing around isn't fun without him holding me close and randomly twirling me around or dipping me. Nothing is great, when he's with me. What I want is to be with Rick. I switch gears and work as quickly as I can to get everything done, so I have more time to be with him. I shower using my good scrub and the conditioner that makes my hair shine. I make sure I smell fabulous and look radiant. I take the time to blow dry and curl my hair. I even put on mascara and lip gloss. I'm getting ready to go to the game, so I take a hair tie just in case and pull on my skinny jeans with my Seno V-neck T-shirt. I shove my cap and jersey into my bag and grab my hoodie on the way out the door.

I hop into Rick's Challenger to drive to the stadium. Guys are usually protective of their cars. Their cars are their babies and they don't let their girl drive them even if the car is crappy, or maybe because the car is crappy and I'm missing the point. Rick didn't even flinch. In fact, he told me to drive and handed me the keys to his custom car with the extra power built in under the hood and the 6-speed stick-shift. He doesn't worry about his car. He wants me riding home with him and he doesn't want me on the trolley. The car doesn't matter, I do.

I pull into the player's garage with a wave from the parking attendant and find a seat to watch batting practice.

Text to Rick - Just letting you know I'm here for BP :)

Text from Rick - :)

Carter steps out of the dugout and sees me sitting in the stands. He looks at me twice and then comes up to see me.

"You look gorgeous today and I mean more than usual, you're always pretty. I had to take a second look to make sure it was you." My extra effort is going to be noticed!

"Thank you. It's nice to be home and have some time to relax."

"You're here early."

"It's becoming a habit. Rick likes me here for BP and I don't always manage BP at the away games, its easier here. Let me know if I'm in the way. I don't want to be a problem."

"No, you're fine. It makes him happy and the guys get a kick out of their tough as iron catcher being crazy over a beautiful blonde that yells at the game, bakes, sings, and from what I hear—knows her baseball. We expected to see you more when he came in and told me to get you set up with your access card. The guys don't do that if the girl's a gold digger or baseball skank, well unless they're whipped. No offense. We all know that's not you. Especially, Seno. I was surprised when he came in to request an access card for a woman."

I smile, unexpectedly flattered. "I have a pretty good understanding of the game."

"Well, you keep up the good work. Those cookies were great, by the way. I liked your proposal and I passed it on to my supervisor, but I suspect it's sitting somewhere and won't be discussed until they start talking about plans for next season." He smiles as he turns and makes his way back to the field.

I look out to see the field had been set up for batting practice while we were chatting and the team has started to make their way out to the field. My Rick comes out with a bat in his hand. I yell out, "Looking good, baby!" Cross, Martin, and Bravo all turn to look at me and start to move in my direction. They don't wave or yell hi back. No, they don't recognize me? Do I look that shitty when I come to the game or what? I edit my shout out, "Looking good, Seno!" Seno looks at me and smiles, as he notices the other three turning back away.

Rick runs up to me, "You're fucking beautiful. Glowing. Are you sure you're mine?"

"Only yours, my king." I smile uncontrollably.

"You cleaned up all nice like this for me?"

"You're the only reason I want to look good. Part of it could be the maple syrup." I giggle like a teenager and he kisses me before he runs back to the field. "Knock it out, Seno!"

I watch the guys as they wander the field, hang out around the backstop and hit, with my eyes on irregularities. I find myself concentrating on my Rick, not because he's doing anything odd. Something about the way he holds himself on the field, I can't help myself. It's always been that way for me. It's why he was my fantasy. Bravo is still favoring his hip. Mason might be limping. Rock keeps rubbing his right arm. These things are to be expected as we get close to the end of the season. 162 games is a long time to stay healthy. The roster was recently expanded and some of the minor leaguers have been invited up to the big league club. I don't know who they are yet, but I see them waiting for their turn to hit. The newbs are rambunctious, but I guess it's to be expected. Every time my Rick connects to the ball it's out of the park and I cheer him on every time, reminding him that he's the king—or at least my king.

Text from Rick - Scouting Report?

Text to Rick - Bravo is still favoring his hip, Mason looks like he might be limping, Rock's right arm is bugging him.

Text to Rick - The newbs are a little out of control. They need to be knocked down a notch or they're going to hurt someone.

Text from Rick - Interesting

Text from Rick - Has anyone ever told you that you're the most beautiful baseball scout of all time?

Text to Rick - Stop!

Text from Rick - Well, if anyone told you that they were wrong.

What? Where is he going with this?

Text from Rick - You're the most beautiful woman anywhere. <3

Huh, my extra effort really was noticed. That makes it all worth it. Since I can't help myself...

Text to Rick - You're biased because I have sex with you and cook for you.

Text from Rick - I can only tell you what I see from my eyes and my heart. Anybody that doesn't agree is blind and stupid. Cross, Martin and Bravo were going to hit on you and didn't even recognize you today. You're in demand, my queen.

Text to Rick - Exactly... Your queen.

Text to Rick - Go get ready for the game. I'll send you the visiting scout report after their BP.

Text from Rick - I love you... My queen.

I check the lineup and we're playing Colorado this weekend. They have some of the new guys brought up for their expanded roster on the lineup tonight, including a first time starting pitcher, a second baseman, and two outfielders all making their debut. I wonder if it's because they need to give their everyday guys a break due to soreness and injury, because that's not a bad idea when you're not in the running for postseason anyway.

I watch Colorado's batting practice and about halfway through a couple of their players are looking at me. I sink down into my seat, hoping they'll ignore me. "Hey sweetheart! Are you a baseball fan?"

I ignore them, seeing a flashback of Rick getting hit by a pitch and dislocating the jaw of the Sissy's first baseman, Adam.

"This is my first time in San Diego. Do you think you could give me a personal tour? I'll give you a tour of the visitor's clubhouse and a night you'll never forget." The veteran player high-fives the rookie for going for it.

Anything I say, can and will be used against me. I know

this. I learned this the hard way. I need to keep ignoring them. Or, I could play a game with him and his game will go to shit. No, don't do it. Rick will get pissed. Observe and keep your mouth shut.

> Text to Rick - I learned to keep my mouth shut, but I need to cheer for the whole team equally tonight or these guys will target you like the Sissy's. Keep your eye on 15 at third base and 77 in the outfield. The veteran was pushing the rookie to go for it and they're paying close attention to me, yelling at me from the field. Maybe I should sit in my old seat for this series?

> Text to Rick - Also their centerfielder is limping, they have four players debuting tonight, starting pitcher, second base and corner outfielders. Outfield is probably weak, centerfielder won't be able to help cover as much territory.

> Text from Rick - Good intel. I trust your judgment, but I'd rather have you behind home plate and cheering louder for me. Give me a minute.

A few minutes later Carter sits down next to me. "I happen to have the seat next to you for the game tonight. Mind if I hang out with you for the game?"

Sure you do. "Wow! Really? How long have you had it?" I look at him and he knows I'm not stupid.

"It's my solution to keep Seno happy and everybody off the DL. I'll handle any potential disasters and you can cheer the way you want. I'll call them out if they pull anything."

"I'm too much trouble for you, Carter."

"I never get to watch the game from the stands and most likely you've heard all you're going to hear about it."

"So, basically you're my babysitter?"

"No, let's say personal security."

"No, thank you. I don't need a keeper."

Text to Rick - Seriously? You sent Carter to watch me? I don't need a keeper.

Text to Rick - How about I do what I did last time and you manage your temper? I can handle myself.

Text to Rick - Damn it! I didn't get hurt last time... You did and I don't want you hurt again. I don't want you to get hurt worse or...

I'm about to lose it when I have an idea. "Carter, when you magically got the seat next to me, how many seats next to me were available?"

Text from Rick - My first instinct is to protect you, baby. Don't be mad.

"Four or five."

"Can you get them all for me? And include yours?"

"Absolutely."

"Thanks. Then I have this handled." It is Friday night after all and all my girls are here.

Text to Rick - Don't worry. Found my own solution. I will be behind home plate cheering for you and it will be more than normal. Hope you like it!

Text to Rick - I may have added some seats to your
account for tonight. Hope you don't mind.

I run up to the member's lounge and catch all my girls
in line for beer. I tell them about the problem and how I
need help, so I'm not singled out causing a problem for
Seno on the field. I don't want him on the DL or suspended
again. We all leave the member's lounge with two beers
each and head down to the seats behind home plate. We
haven't talked in so long, it's a nice departure from
watching the game and cheering by myself. I catch them all
up on traveling to the away games and of course that Seno
now lives with me and I show them my access card. They
all tell me how good I look and that the changes are definitely agreeing with me. It's great having Meli, Dina,
Sandy's wife Shan and a couple of the part-timer's, Jenn
and Rona hanging together and cheering as a team. Carter
checked on us to make sure we got seated and brought
down bags of peanuts, buckets of popcorn and some hot
dogs.

Rick was already out in the bullpen warming up our
starting pitcher, Grace the Ace, by the time we got to or
seats. I hope I didn't screw up his game. The girls and I
make a plan, so we will all yell and clap together. The beer
may be making it more fun than it really is, but what the
hell! Why not have fun at the game?

Rick walks across the field from the bullpen with Corey
and looks straight at me. He gets a weird expression on his
face and walks all the way to the net in front of me without
stopping. "Do I want to know?" Rick asks unsure.

"Probably not. There are six of me tonight." I smile at
him and I'm already buzzed.

"It's hard enough to handle one of you, my queen. And, you're all buzzing already. This is going to be a fun game."

"Hey, whatever you do, you have to do for all of us or to all of us, or this plan won't work. So, if you want to kiss me through the net, make it on the cheek and be prepared to kiss each of us on the cheek. Get it?"

"I love you, all." Rick shakes his head, turns and walks away.

We all yell in unison, "Make it a win!"

Rick turns back and looks at us, unable to keep the smile off his face.

Jenn and Rona hadn't met my Rick before, "He's really cute up close," Rona drools.

"You should check out Chase Cross. Total sweetheart, better age for you, available, and easily controlled by baked goods." I suggest as I look at her and think they'd make a cute couple.

"You mean the centerfielder?" Rona confirms.

"Yes."

No action in the top of the first inning. Chase is leading off for the Seals and walks into the on deck circle, swinging his bat with time to spare. "Chase!"

Chase looks up and walks over to the net, "How are you today my lovey? And, who are all these women?"

I smile, "There are six of me today, just avoiding a problem with the visiting team." I run through everybody introducing Chase and then I get to Rona, "And this is Rona, she gets my stamp of approval. Get it?" she smiles with a shy expression on her face.

"I get it. Do you bake, too?" Chase asks Rona. She nods and Chase gets to work.

"I don't know why I nodded. The only baking I've done is pre-made cookie dough." Rona laughs.

"I can teach you if you end up needing to learn." I laugh mostly because I probably don't need more beer, but also at the young girl that went flush talking to Chase. Kids!

We all cheer for Chase together and for Martin and of course louder for my Rick. But the game is pretty tame until the beginning of the third inning when 77 comes out on deck ready to lead off the inning and walks up to the net.

"So, do you ignore all the players or just me? Give me a chance and go out with me tonight. I promise you won't regret it."

In unison, "Sorry, you're on the wrong team. Bye-bye!" Loudly and of course Rick heard it. He hangs his head and laughs.

The game picked up after that. We may have relieved Rick of his worry so he could focus on the game. Carter shows up during the next inning with a dozen beers and he has apparently been enjoying the show.

No score and it's the top of the fifth, 15 is leading off for Colorado and walks over to us at the net, "Why are you ladies stuck on the Seals?"

In unison, "Colorado sucks!"

"You should let me show you how good I am at sucking. You'll never forget me and you'll want me again."

In unison, "Fuck off, asshole!" 15 walks up to the plate and we plot against him. As soon as he's ready to hit, we chant, "Suck, suck, suck, suck!" and laugh uncontrollably. 15 strikes out looking and Rick looks back at us giving us a thumbs up. I love that my girls are able to see what games with Rick are like for me, well sort of.

Bottom of the sixth inning, still no score. One out, Martin on second and a newb running for Mason at third base. My Rick is swinging his bat in the on deck circle and making faces at us because we're loud obnoxious drunks. As he walks up to the plate, "We love you, Rick! Knock it out, baby!" In slightly slurred unison. And he does just that on the first pitch. We all jump up and scream different, finally coming together with, "That's my man! Go Seno!" The newb scores with Martin on his heels. Rick comes around and focuses on me as he's ready to step on the plate, but plays along blowing all of us kisses as he scores. It's perfect, all of us flailing about like teenage girls and fanning each other. It was the highlight of the game, final score 3-0 Seals.

Hannah grabs Rick for her post-game interview, but he insists she talk with the newbs first. She interviews each of the newbs while Rick comes over to the net, "Thank you, ladies. I appreciate you all for going along with Sherry tonight. Sherry, are you ready to go home or are you going out with these wonderful ladies?"

I do a quick census, "We're all pretty much done. We drank enough. Good game, baby." I laugh and eat some more popcorn.

"I'll meet you at the car in about twenty." He leans in and kisses me on the cheek, and then he did the same for each of my baseball girls, winking at me as he goes to Hannah for his interview.

"All 3 runs tonight came from your bat. You've been hitting well as of late. Are you doing anything different?" Hannah questions.

"The bat feels really good when I'm swinging. I'm not doing anything different. I always put my all into the game." I like seeing him on the big screen.

"You've had your own personal cheering section behind home plate for a few months now. I think we're all aware of that. Tonight that seemed to grow. Have you been recruiting fans?"

Rick smiles and laughs under his breath, "That was all my personal cheering section. She's my only."

Hannah hangs her head to the side as if she's saying how sweet, "I heard a rumor she'll be on the field tomorrow night. Do you know anything about that?"

Rick looks at me and I nod, "Yes, she'll be leading eighth inning karaoke tomorrow night from the field. Not my doing. That's all her and her winning the Batter Up karaoke competition. She's great, everybody is going to love her." Rick smiles proudly.

My girls are still here and I hadn't told them about that. They're all excited for me and going to try to come to the game. I thank my ladies and say my goodbyes, taking a bucket of popcorn with me to Rick's car as I try to dry up my stomach.

Rick finds me sleeping on his front seat, "Again?" He shakes his head and slides into the car.

I sit up and snuggle up against him for the ride home. "It was a special party night. You have to admit my plan worked."

"What about tomorrow and Sunday?"

"Those guys have already forgotten about it and I'll try not to look so good, so they aren't interested." Rick laughs and puts his arm around me for the drive home.

We get home and Rick holds my hand as we walk into the building and get in the elevator. As the elevator doors close, he presses me up against the wall and claims my mouth while he rocks against me, causing me to rock my hips and a low groan to escape him. His hands on my hips, he nibbles at my neck, ear, and collarbone until the doors open.

I sit down on the bed to change, before I get the cake and whipped cream—and fall asleep.

After midnight, "Cake and whipped cream is no fun without, my queen. I did taste the cake and it reminds me of a campfire. Does it somehow have s'mores and coffee?" Rick's warm breath in my ear has me half awake.

"What, baby? Do you need something?" I turn to him and touch whatever part of him I can reach.

"I need you, my queen. I need you to feed me cake and whipped cream. I need to cover you in whipped cream and lick it all off. I need you wrapped around me, so I can be whole." His voice low and raspy.

I sit up and Rick sits behind me, holding me. He has the cake and whipped cream with him. He gives me a piece of the cake and fills my mouth with whipped cream so he can take it from me. The cake is delicious, but right now it's in the way. I put the cake pan on the floor, take the few remaining pieces of clothes I have on off and look at Rick, already naked and I didn't even notice. I cover his cock in whipped cream and enjoy my dirty dessert. Rick spreads my legs and covers me in whipped cream, the cold sensation intensifies with the heat of his mouth on me. We kiss, suck, and lick each other clean while we drive each other toward orgasm. Rick is close and I work him with my tongue and lips, I want to make him come for me. I want to taste him in my mouth and feel how hard he comes. "Sherry, please. I need in you. I only come in you."

"Whatever you want, my king." How do you deny a request like that? I climb on top of him and slide onto his hard cock drawing a shiver from Rick. "Is this what you want, my king?"

"Yes, my queen. Always need to be in you. Tell me you'll always be here for me."

"I belong to you. It will always be us, my love. I promise I'll never leave." He gets harder and I grind against him. I lean forward and kiss him on the lips softly, sucking on his lower lip. His hands on my hips guide me to what he wants and he takes control, wrapping his arms around me and rolling me underneath him.

"I need you, Sherry." He strokes in and out, needing me desperately even though we're one.

"I'm here, baby. I'm right here." I run my fingers through his hair and pull his lips to mine. "I love you, Rick." I lick his lips and slide my tongue into his mouth to dance with his. I suck on his tongue and he moves faster. "You're so hard right now, you feel amazing. Come hard for me, baby. It's okay." He needs to be loved and taken care of. I don't know why. It's the first time he's shown any insecurity about us in weeks. I hold him tight and whisper in his ear, "You're my forever. Nobody compares to you. I want to give you everything. Nobody makes me feel like you do." I whimper and I don't know where it comes from. Rick is completely in control and I'm simply his. He sucks on my lips, nibbling at me, and needing more of me. I feel him get harder and our bodies tense up, we hit our release together as we cry out. He tightens his grip and pounds into me harder and faster, needing more. He pulls my legs up to my chest, and slams into me deeper until he releases a low guttural groan.

"Oh, baby. You drive me crazy, my queen. Everything is perfect when I'm in you. I need you to love me."

I hold him tight and rest my head on his chest. "Always, my Rick. I'll always love you."

CHAPTER TWENTY-FIVE

Saturday morning I'm woken up by the smell of coffee brewing and find cake on the floor in the bedroom with a can of whipped cream sitting next to it. I don't feel Rick anywhere and I don't like it. "Rick?" I call out hoping he got up to use the facilities. He walks into the bedroom doorway, looking tired. "What's wrong? You didn't sleep?"

"I couldn't sleep."

"What time do you need to be at the stadium today?"

"Cross is coming to get me to go work out."

"I think you should get some sleep. Come here." Rick walks over to the bed and crawls in next to me. I pull the blankets up and wrap my arms around him, snuggling into him. "Try to relax, my king. Whatever it is that's bugging you, it'll be fine. The season is almost over and then it'll be you and me, nobody else. We can stay home, hide out, and order food delivery for weeks and never go outside if you want. I'm not going anywhere. I'm happy as long as I have you."

"Really? I'm enough to make you happy? Enough to keep you happy?"

Now we're getting somewhere. "You're more than I ever wished for. More than I thought was even possible. You make me happy everyday. I only want you." I get a smile. "I'll do anything to make you happy and keep you that way. I can't wait to nap on the beach with you and share a lounge chair every afternoon in the sun while we're in Hawaii. I want to show you my favorite places. I want to share everything with you. Nothing means as much if you're not part of it." I mean every word I say and have been driven to tears by my own words. I'm such a fuckin' girl! I can't maintain myself even when I need to, but then I see Rick's face and realize what my tears mean to him. They prove how much he means to me, that all of my words are real and not empty, meaningless words to console him. "Hold me, my king, so I can start the day with you happy." Rick holds me tightly until the alarm goes off and we agree to snooze a couple of times.

Eighteen minutes later, "I want to stay in bed with you and hold you."

"I don't know how you do this every year. The season is so long for you, yet too short for the fans. It's almost over. I can't wait to have you all to myself." I say softly and gaze into his eyes. He squeezes me and doesn't let go until the alarm goes off again. "Do you want coffee?"

"All I want is you." He presses his lips to mine and slides his tongue between my lips to dance with mine. His large hands glide down my body, stopping at my hips and I rock against him pulling a low groan from his lips. Rick sits up against the wall and pulls me with him, leaving me straddling him. He squeezes my hips while he leans in to kiss me passionately. I feel his need for me and see how desperate he is. I reach for his cock to find him huge and solid. I rise up on my knees and work myself down onto him until he fills me completely. I see the pleasure on his face as he holds me, breasts pressed to his bare chest while I rock my hips. His chest is wide and muscular, but not hard. Rick wraps his arms around my shoulders tightly, "I want to keep you right here, like this. I love you, Sherry." He gazes at me and I see things in his eyes I've never seen before, or maybe I've never looked. It's not only my reflection. It's our reflection together. The story of our life together and ready to unfold. I can see us together years from now. I can see our family. Our happiness. How much I mean to him and how my love for him effects him. His head has insecurities and is uncertain, but not his heart. He's afraid I'll leave with someone else, like I'm worried he'll realize I'm old and difficult, and go with a younger girl that does what he wants. We're both crazy, worried about the same thing. I want to comfort him and take away his fear. What if I'm wrong? What if I'm seeing what I want and not how Rick feels at all? I'd rather be wrong than have him torturing himself with worry.

"Do you know in your heart that I only want to be with you? Do you believe I love you?" I search his eyes.

"I know you love me. I can feel it every moment that I'm with you." Rick replies quietly.

"It's only been you for me, even in my dreams. It's only been you for years. That's never going to change. I'll always give you everything you want from me." I search his eyes for something, relief maybe. "I've never felt this way with anyone else. I've never told another man that I love them. It's only you, my king." His eyes relax as my heart tries to beat out of my own chest at my admission.

Rick whispers in my ear with his sexy voice, "I love you,

baby. I love how you take care of me and I wish you'd let me take care of you." I realize I haven't given in on anything real, I've only offered him more.

"You take care of me. Paying my way has nothing to do with loving me." I hear the words as they come out of my mouth and it's the truth.

Rick's eyes light up as he claims my mouth with his and rolls me underneath him. "I have other ways of taking care of you." He says as he strokes into me deeply, taking control and, yes, taking care of me. His hands on me both soothe and excite me. "We're sticky, my queen." He pulls me up to his chest, "Hold on." He carries me off to the shower and turns it on, blocking me from the cold water while it heats up. He kisses me and turns around, pressing me to the shower wall while he pushes into me.

I call out his name and he's in complete control of me. I'm on the edge and he pulls out of me. I whimper at the emptiness and he slides down my body, licking and sucking at my breasts on his way down to his catcher's crouch. His large hands move to my ass and hold me where he wants me, while he licks and sucks at my sex. My legs are shaky and he leans me against the wall, "It's okay. I've got you, my queen." I cry out instantly, flying over the edge at the flick of his tongue to my clit and he grabs me around the waist to keep me from falling to the floor. I worship his cat-like catcher's skills, even more when he's catching me. He lifts me back to his chest and slides into me deliciously. He strokes into me quickly and hard. "I love you and I'll always take care of you in any way you'll let me," he whispers in my ear as we come together and he leans against the wall, pulling my head to his shoulder.

We hear a knock at the door and Rick's body tenses. "That's probably Cross." He grabs a towel and wraps it around his waist on his way to peek through the peep hole. Rick unlocks the door, "Come in and help yourself to some coffee in the kitchen. I'll be right out."

"Dude, why aren't you ready?" Cross irritatedly questions.

Rick runs back into the bathroom and slams the door behind him as he loses his towel and gets back into the shower with me. I giggle uncontrollably and scream out as Rick wraps his arms around me, holding me under the spray of the shower and kissing me silly. He's obviously feeling better, and so am I. He turns the water off, "I need to go work out with Cross, baby. I'll see you at the stadium. I know you'll rock it tonight leading karaoke." He smiles at me as he quickly gets ready and grabs his things. I dry off and stay out of sight since Chase is here.

"Dude, seriously? Tell me you didn't have sex while I was getting coffee." Cross complains, but more likely is jealous.

I yell from the bedroom, "No, we were already done. Just finishing up the actual showering portion of the shower."

"How about I go have sex again and make you wait longer?" Rick being a smart ass looks to Cross for a response as he walks out with his gym bag, ready for their work out. Rick yells back to me in the bedroom, "I love you, my queen."

Cross yells out, "I love you, too, sweetness." Rick chastises Cross and gets laughed at in the process as they leave, locking the door behind them.

———

498

TONIGHT IS the night I lead eighth inning karaoke at the stadium. I'm excited and anxious, only a tiny bit nervous because I don't know what song I'm going to be leading. But, it'll be a song I know well. It's at the game, so I need to wear my Seals gear. It's a 5:40pm game and it's a warm September Saturday. I'll be out in the stands early for batting practice and I decide to wear my denim mini skirt with a tank top, bringing my jersey and cap with me. I blow dry my hair and curl it, then put on a touch of make-up.

I'm concerned about the visiting team giving me a hard time again, but not as concerned as I am that I look good for the game and karaoke. I refuse to go out on the field and probably be on the big screen looking like crap.

I take a few minutes to myself to enjoy my coffee and eat some of the leftover cake, while I check my email, social media, and messages. Nothing new or crazy going on, so I have some free time for a change. I handle an important errand and restock the kitchen, making sure not to forget the whipped cream. Huh, I'm not sure what part I like best —The whipped cream on me, the whipped cream on him, or the shower. I lose more of my day considering this question in a daydream than I should probably admit, and find myself eating more cake.

> Text from Sam - I feel like it's been days since I've talk
> to you or my bro. Oh wait... that's because it has been!

I read Sam's text and call her. "It's about time!" Sam exclaims.

"Hi, Sam. I'm home alone right now."

"How's things? No drama? My bro is doing okay?"

"Everything is fine. Rick is great. I'm happy it's near the end of the season."

"It's a lot of baseball, isn't it?"

"I love the baseball. Honestly, I'll probably miss it when the season is over. But, we're definitely looking forward to some time together that's not regulated by his schedule."

"What was with the women sitting with you last night? I've never seen that before."

"Those are my friends from the section my season ticket is in. The visiting team noticed me in the stands during BP and yelled at me, and I mean asking me for a personal tour of the area and offering me a night I wouldn't forget. Anyway, it was my idea to have six of me and that would avoid anyone getting suspended or having their jaw dislocated."

Sam laughs, "Seriously? I guess it worked."

"Yea, and the girls and I got toasted. It was fun, but your bro was slightly irritated with me when he found me sleeping on the front seat of his car after the game. I may have been more inebriated than I thought." I laugh remembering the time with the girls, all of us cheering together, and yelling at the jerks on the other team.

"I'm sure he got over it quick."

I wonder if it's what triggered him not to sleep. "He was amazing this morning and happy when he left to work out."

"Don't tell me my bro was amazing. I don't need to hear that."

I try again as I giggle, "Rick was fine when he left this morning, better?"

"Much."

"He's been out of the house early the last couple of days. Chase has been picking him up to work out."

"He's looking good behind he plate, especially considering how deep into the season it is." The proud sister tone in her voice shining through.

"Yeah, but I think he's in his head about me." I'm not sure I should be sharing, but Sam has been there for me since the second I met her.

"Why do you think that?"

"He couldn't sleep last night. He told me I've been in his head. We had decided no relationship stuff until after the season, but he brought it up anyway."

"And, no positive tests?"

"No, I'm still taking my pill."

"You still believe the pill can guard you from the super sperm of a professional baseball player?" Sam jokes with me, I think.

"I don't know. So far it has. I told him I'd quit taking it whenever he wants me to." F'ing DOTM!

"You what?" Sam's voice hits a higher pitch than I've ever heard.

"What?" Play dumb Sherry, maybe it will go away.

"Did you say you offered to quit taking the pill?"

"Yes."

"But, you're still taking it, right?"

"Yes. He basically said not yet and it made him happy that I offered."

"I know my bro. I'm sure it made his chest puff out and he strutted around. You can't play games with him like that. You know how much he wants it."

"I only play board games with him, and some flirty teasing sometimes."

"You know what I meant."

"Yes, I do. Don't tell him, but I was sad that he didn't want me to quit taking it."

"Sherry, it's only been a few months."

"I know and the things I want—Fuck! I've never wanted them before and it makes me crazy, Sam. I'm doing my best to keep my head straight and to support him."

"I knew you two were combustible together, but you really do love him. I've been worried."

"We belong together." I hear my voice and my heart beats faster. "I'll do better at staying in touch. I've got to get to the stadium."

"It's kind of early, don't you think?"

"Rick likes me there for BP. I've been scouting intel for him pre-game." I laugh at the thought of it.

"Okay, I'll be watching as always."

"I'm leading karaoke on the field tonight. Don't know if you'll be able to see that. Talk soon!" And I hang up as I grab my things and run out the door for the stadium.

CHAPTER TWENTY-SIX

I pull into the player's garage to park and Carter catches me walking into the stadium. "Do you have your jersey for being on field later?"

"Yes, sir! I'm ready!"

"I could get use to your new look, gorgeous." I made an effort, but I have no idea what he's talking about. Big deal! I curled my hair. "Contact me if you have any issues with the visitors. All of these guys need to be professional."

Text from Carter - Text me if you need to be discreet.

Text to Carter - Thank you, sir.

"I'll tell Seno I saw you walking into the stadium. I don't know what you do to that man, but I know I've never seen him as happy as he is when he sees you." Carter walks away into the depths of the stadium leaving me with a warm heart and a bright smile that I couldn't hide if I wanted to. Who would want to hide a Rick Seno smile anyway?

I sit behind the Seals dugout and slather on my sunscreen.

Text to Rick - Behind the dugout. Ready to watch you swing your bat. ;)

No response. I check the lineup to make sure my Rick is starting and he is. The lineup is normal.

The field gets set up for batting practice and the team starts to show up on the field. Most of the guys stretching and loosening up. Some running sprints and throwing a ball around in the outfield. No Seno. I look around to see who's out and there's no Chase. Okay, that's interesting. The rest of the team goes on about their business, nothing out of the ordinary. Kris and Mason wave at me. I observe and keep an eye out for Rick and Chase. They finally join the team about halfway through batting practice and they're all smiles, joking together. Rick runs up to see me between his turns at bat, kissing me like I'm his life source. His bat is on fire today. The knock of the ball against his bat is perfect every time. It's almost as if the ball and bat are being pulled together by a magnetic force, they can't miss each other. Bravo isn't taking batting practice today, since Skip put him on the DL. Mason is showing no sign of limping. All of the Seals look good, except Rick and he looks like a super hero.

Chase visits me after batting practice, "What did you do to him? His bat is on point and he's been picking on me all day."

"Nothing that's not normal. He didn't eat breakfast

before he left with you because we chose to stay in bed a bit longer."

Chase looks at me funny, "He said he already ate this morning."

I blush as I remember him eating me this morning in the shower and make a quick recovery, "We did have cake early this morning."

Chase nods, "I think I need a woman. I want to be getting it whenever I want and have a woman that wants to do sweet things for me, like you do for Rick."

I wonder what Rick has told him, "You might not be ready for that. You're so young still."

"What about your friend that you introduced me to last night?"

"Rona? She's nice and she's not a player chaser. But, she needs to get settled a bit. She'd be fine for dating, I think you should wait and see what happens. The season is almost over and you're going to want to go home, not the best thing when you start dating someone who lives here."

"You're probably right. I need to think about it over the off-season. Will you keep baking for me?"

"I will bake for you even when you have a girlfriend. You basically introduced me to Rick, I've got your back." I owe him everything and he's such a good kid. Chase smiles and gives me a hug, before disappearing into the dugout.

Colorado is already out doing their batting practice, so I watch for any tells and try to stay low-key. I don't want any special attention from any of the players. I don't want any trouble tonight. No extra drama. I want to stay calm and not get nervous before going on the field to lead karaoke in front of thousands of people. I'm watching Colorado and they have even more newbs brought up for the expanded roster. Carter's hanging out behind the backstop. Why do I feel like Carter has taken on the job of regulator? I guess it makes sense for the team to avoid trouble, he's not just looking out for me. Shit! He wouldn't be doing this if I wasn't here. Get out of your head, Sherry! Get back to baseball. Don't worry about Carter. I check Colorado's lineup and their shortstop is making his debut tonight, with the newb second baseman that debuted last night. Hmmmm... Lots of focus on one of the players.

Text to Rick - Colorado short stop is debuting tonight and 2B is the same guy that debuted last night. They came from different farm teams.

Text to Rick - Trainer has been paying too much attention to Martinez that's in the lineup to play 3B. Looks like his neck is stiff.

Text to Rick - Same lead off as last night, still not hitting well. But—he did actually connect to a ball.

Text to Rick - Hope Carter isn't out here watching because of me. I'm not here to cause a problem.

Carter finds me after BP, "So, tell me what you saw."

"What do you mean?"

"Seno says you're feeding him info you see at BP. What did you see today?" I share the info with Carter that I shared with Rick. "Interesting. What about the Seals?"

"They all looked good. Nobody hurting or anything that's in the lineup. Seno's bat is above average, even for him—I know I'm biased, but this has nothing to do with that. He's going to kill it tonight. Seno and Cross have been working out more and I think they're determined to end the season strong."

Carter quirks his head, "I was out here to see if I saw the same things you see. I do for the Seals, but not for the visitors and I'm not saying your wrong. I don't have your eye. Enjoy the game." Carter heads off into the dugout and I indulge in a $5 beer from the member lounge. Just one.

CHAPTER TWENTY-SEVEN

Sitting behind home plate is where I belong now. It's not just about the game, hanging out with my section peeps, gazing down upon the serene green expanse of field, and supporting my team. In fact, most importantly it's about Rick Seno. Yes, I've been following his career and yelling louder for everything he does for years. This is different. This is about the smile he flashes me when he's crouched behind home plate and a heavy hitter strikes out. This is about him pointing at me and blowing me a kiss when he steps on home plate generated by his own home run hit. This is about the way he hangs his head and laughs when he hears me yelling at the other team. This is about the way I feel his eyes pierce me when I defend him by yelling at the pitcher that's throwing at him when he's at bat. Nothing is the same without him with me. It makes him happy when he can see me here with him. Maybe nothing is the same without me.

I look up and my Rick is standing at the netting looking at me. "You okay?"

I jump up to meet him at the net, "Now I am."

"Are you ready to blow this place away in the eighth?" He says as he smiles at me.

"I'm always ready for karaoke." I give him attitude. "Just like I'm always ready for you, my king." I gaze into his eyes, willing him to know how much he means to me and my own eyes fill up with tears.

His voice drops and he reaches for my fingers at the net, "I love you, Sherry."

I smile, unable to speak and when he turns to walk out to the bull pen and warm up our pitcher I yell, "I love you, Rick!" He runs back to me and gives me a quick kiss through the net, before he kicks it into high gear and full baseball mode.

The ceremonial pregame hoopla starts and they announce I'm leading karaoke in the eighth inning. It sends a shock through me and a rush of adrenaline. I'm excited and can't wait to find out what I'm singing. The big screen says:

Vote until the end of the sixth inning for the eighth
inning karaoke song on social media using
#sealskaraoke and your pick
#LoveRunsOut #ComeHome
#ThinkingOutLoud #TheWarrior

I love it! Now I know what the options are. Which one do I want? I should vote! Leading karaoke on the field. I performed all of them in the competition. Don't freak out. I have to wait and see what the social media world decides. I wonder who votes and how that'll impact the results.

Rick is walking toward the plate and yells at me, "Get out of your head, my queen! You got this." He does that thing where he points two fingers at his eyes and then at me a couple of times, like he's telling me to focus because we got this.

"Woooooo! Make it a win, babe!"

He smiles and nods at me as the game gets underway. I knew Rick was on point with the bat, but he's also right there calling the game and moving like a cat behind the plate. Nothing will stop him tonight. He's in control of the whole game and it's moving quickly, the top half of the first done in less than five minutes. Three strike outs in a row. I should be giving some of the credit to Rhett Clay, he has come far since his debut and his arm is a live wire. Bottom of the first, Cross leads off with a double. Mason walks. Martin strikes out. Seno is hitting fourth and connects on the second pitch. The ball bounces off the right field wall and the rookie in right field can't come up with it, Rick turns it into a triple sending Cross and Mason home. 2-0 Seals. Lucky gets a single. Rock hits into a double play and onto the next inning. The next few innings are uneventful. Rick hits a ground ruled double, the ball bounced over the wall, but nobody brought him home. Colorado is still score-less in the fifth, and the Seals are giving a hitting demon-stration. The bases are loaded and they keep pushing each other around the bases with singles and doubles. Rick starts the inning with a single and I get a shiver, he's a home run away from hitting for a cycle. When he runs across home plate and smiles at me, I yell, "Get a Homer!" He glares at me funny and continues into the dugout. The merry-go-round on the bases and with two out, my Rick is back in the batter's box with bases loaded. Colorado brings in a new pitcher. Rick chokes up on his bat, turns to me and smiles before he focuses on the pitch. Strike, Rick swings and misses. Strike, right down the middle of the plate. The third pitch and I hear it smack, I jump out of my seat screaming because I know he hit it out of the park. Rick watches the ball fly out of the park as he drops his bat and turns to me as he pounds his fist into the air and runs the bases. 10-0 Seals. Lucky strikes out ending the inning.

Top of the sixth, the big screen is showing the current voting results with a few minutes left to vote for the karaoke song. It looks like the two OneRepublic songs have split their share of the vote and the other two are running close with "Thinking Out Loud" ahead by a small margin. I run up to use the ladies room before the seventh inning stretch, so I don't have to pee when I'm on field. Mike with the Mic catches me on the concourse and tells me that I'm singing "Thinking Out Loud."

Text from Rick - With you singing in the eighth, the win is a lock!

One out in the bottom of the seventh, no score change and a Seals representative escorts me from my seat to the field gate. We wait there for a few minutes and I watch Rock hit a solo home run. Colorado goes down one, two, three in the top of the eighth inning and I'm rushed onto the field near home plate as I hear Mike with the Mic over the PA, "Ladies and gentlemen, please welcome the Batter Up Karaoke competition winner Sherry to lead your eighth inning karaoke tonight. You voted on the song and chose her wild card song, the final song she sang in competition. Please sing along to 'Thinking Out Loud!'" I hear cheering from the Seals dugout and watch the karaoke start up on the big screen. I'm looking around to see where Rick is because I've never sung this song without him. I hear the crowd cheering me on from the section behind home plate and it makes me think of him, what he hears when I cheer for him. I'm singing the song and happy with myself for not freezing in front of this huge number of people. The baseball park has always been my happy place and I'm relaxed here. Rick is walking toward home plate in full gear about halfway through the song and I figure they're going to cut the song short because of the game timing. But, none of the other players are on the field. As soon as I see him, my emotions flow and I hear the song get better. My heart gets happier. I let it rip. At the last few lines of the song...

Rick kneels on home plate in full catcher's gear, takes my left hand and slides a ring on my ring finger. He searches my eyes with his mask up on the top of his head while he holds my left hand in both of his, "Please make me happy and be my wife, Sherry Seno. I promise to do everything in my power to keep you beyond happy for the rest of our lives. I will always love you."

I stand on the field with a microphone in my right hand, in shock. I can't move. It feels like hours pass, though it's only a few seconds. I don't know what the ring looks like, it doesn't matter. I love him and I want to be with him and I never want to hurt him and I've wanted to be Sherry Seno for longer than I should admit. "Yes! Please!" I have tears in my eyes.

Rick squeezes my hand and stands up, squeezing me, and kissing the daylights out of me right there in front of everybody.

EPILOGUE

I didn't realize how badly I wanted it. This man keeps making my dreams come true. My fantasy world, only better than I ever imagined, and real. How did I end up being what makes my fantasy baseball boyfriend happy in real life? This can't be happening. I must be dreaming again. Somebody pinch me or wake me up. No. Don't wake me up. I like this dream.

Text from Sam - Did I just see what I think I saw?

Text from Sam - Was that you at home plate with my brother kneeling in front of you and then kissing you?

Text from Sam - I swear that looked like a proposal.

Text from Sam - It looked like a yes.

Text from Sam - Why aren't you replying to me?

Text from Sam - I need to see the ring.

Text from Sam - Answer me already!

Text to Sam - Why are you texting me in my dream?

Text to Sam - What game are you watching?

Text from Sam - I'm watching the Seals game, just like always. The team my brother is the catcher for and you were on the field and I swear he proposed. Take a picture of your left hand and send it to me now!

Text from Sam - FYI you're not dreaming!

I look at my left hand, take a picture and send it to Sam. If this is a dream it doesn't hurt anything. Then I really look at my left hand, the ring looks like a queen's crown with a diamond solitaire at the center, surrounded by numerous smaller diamonds decorating the crown all the way around my finger. I'm his queen.

I'm not sure what to do. Is this reality? No way. We've been together less than six months and I'd never move that quickly, besides he's a professional baseball player. There's no way I fit in that equation! Fuck! It's what I want. Brain repeats—You want this. Heart celebrates—We love him! Everything Rick does is because he knows it will make me happy.

I totally miss the bottom of the eighth and the top of the ninth, realizing the game is over when the announcer says the Seals won and congrats to the Senos!

Text from Sam - You did say yes! OMG, you're going to be my sister! I can't wait!

I look up and Rick's standing at the net in front of me. I move to meet him there as fast as I can. He reaches for my hands at the net. I gaze at him, "Is this real or am I dreaming?"

"I hope it's real, because you're my dream come true. I love you, Mrs. Seno." He says happier than I've ever seen him. I'm warm all over and I don't know what to do with myself. "I'll be at the car as quick as I can." He takes off for the clubhouse.

Rick steps into the garage with his huge grin and beelines for me. He kisses me senseless. "Let's go home, my queen," as I slide over to be next to him for the drive home.

DIAMONDS IN PARADISE

AN ALL ABOUT THE DIAMOND ROMANCE BOOK 3

CHAPTER ONE

The season was over and Rick's team, the San Diego Seals, made it to the playoffs. Unfortunately, they were knocked out in the first round. I was concerned he'd be grumpy, but it was the opposite. He was content to have free time and be able to rest. He turned into a baseball fan and watched every single playoff game all the way through the end of the World Series. Granted, he's more critical of the players than the average fan and took notes about some of the players, but he's into it. He had a team he was cheering for. It's nice to finally be able to sit together watching baseball and hold hands. Some of the games were watched naked and watched may not be the right word. Let's face it: Some of the games were background noise or noise to cover my, uh, my calling out my king's name.

I was anxious for our trip to Hawaii and had already started packing. My work was caught up, our condo was clean and I'd been dreaming of white sandy beaches with beautiful glassy blue waves. I'd booked us a studio cottage on the sand at the only resort on the North Shore of Oahu for two weeks and I couldn't wait to take Rick to some of my favorite places.

I call the car service to take us to the airport, since I'm a travel agent I'm dubbed the "Vacation Commander". I pull my suitcase out of the closet, packed and ready to go. I pack light because, well, it's Hawaii. What do I really need? Swimsuits, shorts, tank tops, flip flops, tennis shoes, sundresses, panties, bras, beach cover up, my small make-up case with toothbrush, camera, and a sweater in case it gets cool in the evening or to dress up my tank top for a restaurant. I considered lingerie, but considering I won't be wearing much already, it kind of seemed redundant. Rick packed everything and I mean he needed a separate bag for his workout gear. I carry my huge purse with me, so I can keep my laptop, iPod, earbuds, book, magazine, fuzzy socks and snacks with me on the plane. Sometimes my feet get cold on the plane and fuzzy socks are the answer. I packed extra snacks, so I have enough for both of us and even got a splitter for my iPod in case Rick wants to share with me. I'm dressed in jeggings, flip flops, tank top, and my Seals hoodie with Seno and a big 6 on the back for the flight. Rick is wearing jeans, tennis shoes, a snug fitting Seals club-house T-shirt screen printed with "Property of the San Diego Seals" across the chest and a short sleeve button up shirt that's probably the closest thing he owns to an aloha shirt. I'm still stuck on the T-shirt. Sometimes Rick simply puts on a T-shirt and I'm reminded my fantasy baseball boyfriend is not only real, but loves me. The snug fit of the shirt showing off his muscles every time he moves, especially the width of his shoulders. Doesn't matter how long it's been, I still get slapped across the face with reality when he introduces me as his fiancé or leaves me something under the name Sherry Seno.

His world of professional baseball is now my world and I'm still adapting. Today as we board the plane and sit in first class for example, I would never have flown first class, but Rick told me to book first class. It's a luxury, like having the private cottage instead of a simple hotel room. It's not what I'm used to, but I'm not complaining.

We get on the plane for our 9am flight and the flight attendant is passing out Mai Tai's to everyone in first class. I realize we've traveled a lot over the last six months going to away games, but never flown together. We focus on each other as we take the drinks and each have a second one before we take off. We don't have to speak, we're in the moment together. I can't tell you much about the flight, but we laughed and kept the flight attendant busy bringing us drinks. I took the snacks out of my bag to share with my man and he shook his head at me, "What else do you have in your bag?" Rick takes my bag away from me and pulls me over to sit in his lap. He gazes into my eyes, "Hi, my queen," and smiles. I want to suggest we join the Mile High Club, but there's no way we fit in that tiny bathroom together. I snuggle into his strong chest as he kisses my forehead and holds me tightly against him. Rick leans his head down against mine and we must fall asleep because the flight attendant wakes us when it's time to land. "Hi, baby. Are you ready for our first vacation together?" Rick asks with a dirty grin and clear blue eyes that remind me of the ocean we're flying over as we come in for landing at Honolulu Airport.

"I like the sound of that. Our first vacation. It means there are many more to come." I smile at my man, unable to contain my happiness as I'm struck again with my amazing reality.

Rick gets a dirty glint in his eyes, "I'm looking forward to making you come many times on this trip." My body hums at his words and I know we're going to spend most of today in bed. Rick claims my mouth with his, taking my breath away with his intent and the flight attendant has to tap him on the shoulder to get me back into my seat for landing.

The sun is shining and the water below us is so clear you can see what's underneath it from the plane. There's a beautiful view of Diamond Head, Waikiki, and Honolulu as we fly in. The landing is easy, and Rick grabs for my hand intertwining our fingers as we disembark.

We're met immediately by a friendly Hawaiian woman who places a lei over each of our heads. Our leis are made of beautiful, fresh, purple orchids. We walk through the airport to the rental car lot and pick up our wheels. I'd reserved a Jeep Wrangler and they had it ready and waiting. I love it when things go as planned. We get our things loaded into the Jeep and climb in. Rick is driving, while I navigate from the shotgun position.

I've been playing this day in my head for weeks, imagining where we'll start and what we'll do. Rick wants to get checked into our cottage, relax and have some time to ourselves, naked. I want to give him everything he wants. I'm excited to see our cottage, I know it'll have a spectacular view. I direct Rick to the freeway, and eventually the gorgeous view of the ocean comes into sight as we drive down the hill toward Kamehameha Highway. I have him take the turn off for Haleiwa and turn right. It's a two-lane road through town and it can be crowded, but it's always worth it. The main road is lined with restaurants, shopping, galleries, shave ice, and mostly locally owned small businesses. I direct Rick to turn right into the shopping center with the general store and the Surfer Grill, then to park off to the side where it's not crowded. I hop out of the Jeep and strip down to the bikini I have on under my clothes. I take off my hoodie, slide my slippahs (I'm in Hawaii now, right?) off, pull my shorts out of my purse, and shimmy out of my jeggings right there in the parking lot. I pull my shorts on and my tank top off, while Rick is watching me the whole time, enjoying the view. My side of the Jeep is hidden to everyone enjoying the shopping center. Rick walks around to me and his eyes heat up instantly. He shakes his head at me telling me how much he's enjoying me changing clothes in public and that he doesn't like to share at the same time, which I didn't even consider being an issue or indecent in any way. But, it did it for Rick. He backs me up against the Jeep, splaying his hands across my bare skin as he presses his lips to mine tenderly, gently sucking on my lower lip as his heat, need, and desire builds. I run my fingers through his hair and my body reaches for his. I slide my tongue in his mouth and he sucks on it. He pulls away from me and feasts on me with dark hooded eyes. I get a big grin on my face and I can't control it, "Soon, my king." I give Rick a quick kiss, grab his hand and drag him into the general store to get us aloha shirts. We laugh as we thumb through the rack, trying different shirts on and finding the shirts we want. I pull him into the Surfer Grill next door, and I know the surf is going off because the service staff is at a minimum. It's a Hawaii thing. If the surf is good, the service probably isn't. Everybody takes off for the waves and leaves the guy with the short straw left at work to cover them. Especially at local places like this. What do you expect from a place that has rafters full of surfboards hanging from the ceiling and big screens playing surfing? The bar has thatching around it and the outdoor tables have thatched umbrellas covering them. The windows run down to the floor and turn open, allowing birds to wander and fly in. We get a table by the window with a view of one of the big screens and the waitress walks up with menus. The waitress is wearing Uggs with cut-off denim shorts and a tank top over her swimsuit which is obviously as wet as her hair is. She's recently back from her lunch break and she spent it surfing. Rick puts his arm around me and I do the ordering since we're in my place. I order a lava flow, a ginger beer, kalua pork fries, and a macadamia nut chicken sandwich.

"Is this how it's going to be? Are you in charge in Hawaii?" Rick grins at me jokingly.

"You started it with the 'Vacation Commander' title." I can't help myself and laugh. "This is one of my favorite places to eat, I love the atmosphere and the food. The resort is only about eight miles from here and the drive is one of the most beautiful that you'll ever experience. We'll stop and explore later in the week, but today we're going to check in and hang out together at our cottage. Unless that doesn't work for you?" I wait for his response.

Rick runs his hand up my leg and leans into my ear, his hot breath on my neck when he whispers, "I'm with you and that makes everything perfect. I love you, my queen." He gives me an open mouth kiss below my ear and it sends shivers all the way to my toes.

The waitress brings our drinks and the fries. The lava flow is served in a coconut cup with an umbrella and the fries are deliciously cheesy, better than I remember. Rick holds my hand under the table and we share the kalua pork fries. The fries are a huge serving, so we also share the sandwich when it arrives. The sandwich is a boneless skinless chicken breast coated in macadamia nuts on a wheat bun. I slurp the last bit of my lava flow and Rick is antsy. We take off for the Jeep and head out to the highway. We drive the seven miles of miracle beaches from Haleiwa to Kahuku, passing Waimea Bay, Sunset Beach, Sharks Cove, Three Tables, Goat Island, Ehukai State Beach, Banzai Pipeline, and unbelievable ocean views the whole way.

CHAPTER TWO

We arrive at the resort and pull up to the valet who greets us with shell leis. Rick and I walk into the open lobby area and get checked in quickly. We're introduced to our personal concierge, Alika, who has already loaded our bags onto a golf cart. He gives us a quick tour of the lobby, shows us where the pool is, where the restaurants are, and points out the gift shops. We get in the golf cart and our concierge drives us along a pathway through lush tropical gardens with huge palms and birds of paradise to the cottages. Alika stops at our cottage, unlocks the door for us and carries our bags into our room. The cottage is appointed with Hawaiian woods and patterns, everything is luxurious. He shows us how to work the lights and the big doors out to the beach, leaving us a number we can reach him at if we want anything. He leaves the big doors open giving us an amazing view of the waves rolling into the shore and pulls down the privacy screen, so we can take pleasure in the beauty of the ocean and each other.

Rick simply smiles at me and we're drawn together like magnets. His hands on my hips, standing a few inches apart with him gazing into my eyes, "I can't wait for you to be Sherry Seno." His low, wanting voice cuts straight through me.

"I'm yours already. Only you, Rick." We lean into each other and kiss. Our connection controlling my heartbeat, it's all consuming and nothing else exists. I need to get closer to him, I need him inside me. I unbutton his jeans and he slides my aloha shirt off of my shoulders, tossing it across the room. I push his jeans down, releasing his hard cock. He toes off his shoes and tosses his shirt aside as he leads me to the huge king bed. I sit on the edge of the bed and find my position perfect to lick his length, I swirl my tongue around his tip and taste the moisture there. I draw a manly groan from Rick and he takes over, pushing me down on the bed. He crawls up over me, laying between my legs with his weight on me and presses his lips to mine sweetly. Rick wraps his arms around me, holding me and kissing me, and kissing me, and kissing me. I feel his cock at my hot wet sex and he slides into me deliciously while he continues to kiss me. Slowly moving in and out, filling me and then taking it away. Both of us shiver at our connection. "I love you, my king. We belong together."

"Yes, my queen. We belong together." He moves his magic lips to my neck with a trail of kisses as he continues to move in and out, deliberate and slow. He moves his hands to my breasts, feeling my nipples pebble and squeezing them. I drag my fingers across his shoulders and wrap my legs around his waist as I arch into him. I need him. I need more of him. I want him to know. He lets out a low groan and moves his mouth to my breasts, sucking my nipples as he pushes in and holds himself deep inside of me.

"Oh, Rick!" I can't help but to call out to him.

"That's right, baby. I'm right here. Do you want more? Tell me what you want, my queen." He says evenly.

"More. All of you, my king. I want all of you." Rick pushes in further and I about lose my mind. "My king, oh, my king!" I buck uncontrollably and he holds me down, not willing to give up control.

"Not this time, my queen. I want it to last." He pulls out of me and kisses a trail down my body until his mouth is almost on my sex, "I'll always take care of you," he licks circles around my clit and sucks at it hard while he slides a finger into me. He feels me start to come and buries his face in my wet sex, licking and sucking me senseless.

I see nothing but darkness with bursting stars as I scream out words I don't comprehend. He continues his licking with one hand under my ass and the other spread across my bare stomach.

Rick moves back over me and slides his hard length into me, "You say the sweetest things to me, baby. I love you." Yet again, I don't know what I said. I really need to start recording myself all the time. He continues with his deliberate strokes and his cock is rock solid. He feels so good stroking me, it's incredible. He's incredible. I'm on the outside watching and listening as I hear myself start to whimper with every stroke, and call out his name. It pushes him faster than he wants and he can't help it. I meet his strokes and he moves faster. I reach for his face and pull him to me to kiss him. I press my lips to his, licking across his lips and sliding my tongue against his in time to his stroking in and out. Suddenly I'm on the edge again and he pulls me over with his loud cry muffled by my mouth as he strokes in hard a few times and collapses on top of me, still kissing me. "I love you, baby. All you need to do is tell me when." Rick puts his arms around me and rolls over, bringing me with him and keeping me on top of him.

When what? What did I say? The things I say when I'm sleeping are honestly how I feel and the truth. I wonder about what I say during sex? Do I ask my Rick what I said? Last time I asked him what I said when I was sleeping he told me that I'd tell him when I was awake within a few days. Hmmm... I wonder if I did? Maybe I have a disease and I say the things I want to say, but block myself out from them because I'm actually afraid of the words or the response I'll get to the words. I guess I'll say it coherently sometime in the next few days.

CHAPTER THREE

I wake up a couple hours later still on top of Rick with his arms around me and a blanket pulled up over us. Rick's face nuzzled into my hair. I move to get up, but he holds me to him tightly and caresses my back. It's a feeling I'll never forget, this feeling of being needed, wanted, and loved. He'll do anything for me, and I can't think of anything I've ever been more confident about in my life or anything that meant near as much to me. I touch his chest with my hands, flat palmed and kiss it. His heart beating strong gives me strength to ask. "Rick, earlier you said to tell you when. When what?"

Rick opens his eyes, "Are you serious?"

This is crazy, I shouldn't be, "Yea. I think it's like when I say sweet things to you in the morning before I wake up, which means whatever I said is the truth. But, I don't have a clue what I said." I press my lips together and roll them in, nervous for the response because Rick's body already responded and it's not happy. "Please tell me what I said."

Rick let me go and rolled to his side, so he could focus and read my eyes, "You said you want to get married here."

"And you said to tell you when?" I question him.

"Yes."

"I assumed you'd want to have a wedding in the off season next year, so we'd have time to plan it." It makes sense to me, it takes time to plan and order and reserve locations.

"I just want to be married to you, Sherry. I don't want a big wedding. I want you. This is your favorite place and the scenery is incomparable, we should get married here. If it makes you happy, it makes me happy. I want you to have everything you want. If you want to get married in Hawaii, that's what we'll do." Rick puts his heart on his sleeve for me.

"So, you're thinking maybe we should get married while we're here on vacation? Before we go home two weeks from now? Just us? No family or friends or anything? Is that too quick? We haven't been engaged very long." I ask too many questions and need to shut up. I need to control my DOTM.

Rick smiles at me from his eyes and almost giggles, "Actually, you said we should get married while we're here. It was your idea. I'm sure we can get the few people who matter here in a short amount of time. Most importantly, there's been no one else for me since I first held your hand in mine at the Locale and as far as I'm concerned you can't be Mrs. Rick Seno soon enough. There's no one else who compares to you, Sherry. It will always only be you." He leans his forehead against mine and kisses me sweetly.

I'm completely lost here. Caught off guard. No idea what to do. It seems so fast. And, I did this to myself. Then again, why make another trip to get married when we can do it now? Am I going to be Mrs. Rick Seno? I need a reality check. This can't be my life. Seven months ago the catcher for the Seals, number 6 Rick Seno was the star of my dreams, clean and dirty. He was my fantasy baseball boyfriend and I couldn't get his autograph to save my life. I loved to watch him play with an unmatched intensity on the field. I daydreamed about what it would be like to get to meet him, what I would say. I hung around after the game to watch the on field interviews and wait for my chance to get the couple of autographs I was missing. One night after the game I got lucky getting Cross' autograph and told him I needed Seno's, but went all starry-eyed when Seno was right there doing his on field interview and Cross worried something was wrong with me. Fast forward a couple hours and I'm meeting Seno at the bar, screwing everything up, being tongue tied, saying the wrong thing, lying and somehow still making out with Seno in the back corner booth. Now, I never want to be apart from him because we did that and it was heartbreaking. He's already moved in with me and my life has never been better. I turn the crown engagement ring he gave me around my finger, it shines at me as if it's the shooting star I'm waiting for to wish on. I turn to Rick, "Want to go for a sunset walk with me?"

He smiles and jumps up to change. We get unpacked and go out for a walk around the resort, hand in hand. I'm sure we're annoying to everyone around us, with our huge smiles and arms constantly around each other. The view is breathtaking, but not holding my attention that's centered on the man with his arm around me who wants to marry me and the consideration of getting married while we're in Hawaii. It's unexpected, which is out there because I was sure I'd considered everything we'd do on this trip ahead of time and getting married while we're here is apparently my idea! I'm scared, but the more I think about it, the more I want to do it. Can we do this? It's a dream come true. First my Rick and now marrying him in my favorite place? It's so spontaneous. I smile all the way into my cheeks and my face gets warm all over, happiness at the thought of marrying my Rick, my king.

We stop at the edge of the ocean facing the sunset and I'm leaning back against Rick's chest, his arms around me, holding me. There's a musician playing at the pool bar, just him with his guitar and microphone. He's a local and he's been playing mostly Hawaiian, folk, or Hawaiianized music. I feel Rick's smile at my ear while we watch the sunset's colors change to pinks and shadowed purples with the line of sunlight peaking out around the edge of the clouds. The wind is moving the clouds along, breaking them up into smaller puffs and they look like baseballs rolling across the sky. The guitarist finishes *Somewhere Over the Rainbow* by Iz and starts in on something that sounds familiar. That's it! Every sign that could possibly be thrown at me has appeared. Rick turns me to him and we dance right there on the grass at the edge of the water with the waves crashing. His eyes are locked with mine and he smiles, inspired to dance by the guitarists rendition of "Thinking Out Loud" by Ed Sheehan, our song.

I gaze into his eyes, "When," and his smile actually grows.

He picks me up and swings me around, "Let's do it, my queen. I love you. Let's get married." Rick calls the cocktail server over and asks for champagne to celebrate.

"Hawaiian style?" She asks and he nods at her with no doubt.

He kisses me and swings me around again. I'm not sure I've ever seen him this happy, and my face hurts because I can't stop smiling. This is the right thing to do, more importantly it's what we want to do. I lean my face against his chest, "I love you with all of my heart."

The cocktail server brings us two Blooming Champagne Cocktails that look fancy and exotic. It's a preserved hibiscus flower in the bottom of a champagne flute with champagne poured over it. The flower appears to be blooming and the red tone makes the petals look like flames. Perfect. Rick clinks his glass to mine, "To our forever." I love the effervescence of the champagne, it tickles my nose. We both take a drink. He takes my glass away and sets them both down, freeing our hands. He takes my face in his hands, brushing my hair back and puts his lips on mine, kissing me sweetly. He moves his hands to the back of my head and the small of my back as his kiss becomes claiming, he dips me as he kisses me. The kiss is long and flutters in my gut more than any of Rick's don't-forget-me kisses. When he breaks the kiss and brings me back upright, the crowd of people watching the sunset around the pool bar cheer and clap. Rick all smiles responds to them, "We just decided to get married while we're here. I can't wait for this beautiful woman to be my wife." I blush uncontrollably, my whole body buzzing. We stand together watching the sunset and finish our champagne in silent happiness.

CHAPTER FOUR

W e walk back to our cottage and Rick orders room service for a light dinner on our lanai overlooking the ocean. The shine from the stars, moon, and resort dancing off the water's surface. The occasional sea turtle pulling itself out of the ocean onto the sand or poking it's head up out of the water like a periscope. The resort pool glowing in the distance. The time difference and long, eventful day has made us ready for an early night in. We spend the evening talking and making out like teenagers, until we go inside and close up the cottage for the night. We make love for hours with the sound of the ocean roaring in the background and fall asleep in each others arms.

I wake up the next morning confused and I don't know where I am. Something is different, similar to the feeling I had several months ago when I found I had my fantasy baseball boyfriend in bed with me. I hear the sound of the ocean and Rick's arms are wrapped around me, I remember we're on vacation. Then it hits me... We're getting married!

I roll over to snuggle my face into Rick's chest to find he's already awake. "Good morning, my queen. You make me happier than I've ever been. How do you feel about ordering breakfast in?" Rick talks into my hair.

I breathe deeply, relaxed and happy to be in my favorite place with my man, my protector, my true love. "Order macadamia nut French toast please, and coffee, and maybe some tropical juice. Ask how long until it will be here. Maybe we can get wedding stuff planned over breakfast. I want to have our vacation time, too." I read his expression, not wanting to be too pushy.

He gives me a cheeky smile, "Sounds good." He goes to order room service and I turn on the shower. "Room service will be here in thirty minutes," Rick calls out.

I walk up to Rick and take his hand, pulling him to the shower with me. We're both still naked from last night and I put my arms around him, pulling him under the shower spray with me. Water dripping over both of us, I watch the droplets build up and run over the tip of his nose once his hair is soaked. I open the small tropical shampoo the resort has supplied and squeeze some into the palm of my hand. I run my hands and fingers through Rick's hair, massaging his scalp and washing his hair. He takes the shampoo and repeats the same thing on me, his hands are magic even when they're simply rubbing my head. We stand under the shower and rinse. He shampoos his beard and I soap up his body from his neck down to his toes, it's an enjoyable journey of touching his body all over, feeling his muscles and admiring my favorite parts. I soap up from my breasts down to my thighs and rub against him, spending some extra time soaping up his now hard cock and drawing a low guttural groan from my man. Rick kisses me roughly and holds my head to his, taking control. I stroke his soapy hard length and enjoy his possessive handling. When he breaks the kiss, I whisper in his ear, "You know the problem with staying in the cottage is there's no elevator. What would you do if we were on an elevator?" His eyes flare and I turn away from him quickly, bending over in front of him. He grabs my hips without hesitation and pulls me to him. His tip is at my entrance and he stops. "That's not what you'd do if we were on an elevator. You can't keep your hands off me and you wouldn't. You'd slide your dick into me and fuck me hard. I'm so wet for you. Don't you want to fuck me?" He doesn't say a word. He slams his hard length into me all the way and pounds into me over and over, as he digs his fingers into my hips and slides me over his dick, using me to stroke himself. I love it and he's amazing. I scream out, "You're my king, baby. Take me. Take me." He continues to slam into me, in and out, in and out. I'm blindsided by my orgasm and he grabs me before I fall over from the force of it. He immediately follows me over the edge, both of us moaning in ecstasy as he slows and rides us through.

He pulls me up to him and holds me against his solid body, "You drive me crazy sometimes, fucking out of control." He turns me and kisses me, "I love you and everything about you." The water sprays over us while we have our moment, making it our own private space. There's knocking at our door and Rick quickly rinses off, grabs the hotel robe and puts it on as he makes his way to the door. I finish showering and pull on a pair of denim short shorts with a lime green camisole style tank top.

I find Rick on the lanai with breakfast and changed from the robe to a pair of board shorts with no shirt. Fuck me! He's so hot shirtless! I won't manage to get anything done today, well, other than him. His board shorts riding low on his hips. No shirt covering his eight pack of abs and his strong chest. Seeing the muscles in his chest and shoulders move distracts me, he's fucking sexy! I walk up to him on the lanai and put my hands on his chest. He smiles at me and I reach around his neck, pulling his mouth down to me so I can taste him. What is it that makes him undeniable in shorts and no shirt? Who am I kidding? He shows a bare arm and I'm ready to jump him.

Alika walks up to our lanai, "Aloha! Ho'omaika'i 'ana! That's congratulations in Hawaiian. I heard you decided to get married while you're here and thought you might want some assistance."

Rick turns to me and I wonder if Alika's a mind reader. "Yes, please! Does the resort have a minister? How do we reserve him? When is he available?" I stop before I ramble out another dozen questions.

He smiles, "We need to reserve the space at the resort and the minister. How many people will be there and do you need rooms for them?"

Rick answers, "About a dozen people. We will needs rooms. It would be great if we could book a time maybe a couple days before we are scheduled to check out." He looks to me for affirmation and I nod.

"Let me go check the schedule and availability," and he was off to the main hotel to do research for us.

I'm making a list, "We'll need to drive over to Honolulu to get a marriage license, but that's fine. I wanted to take you over to that side of the island exploring one day anyway. I need to visit my friend at the gift shop today, she'll know where to get a dress and things like that I need. Do you think Sam will be my Maid of Honor?"

"She'll love that. I'll call Cross to be my Best Man. We should book the spa and salon for you ladies, too." He tenderly runs his hands up and down my arms. "I want this to be perfect for you, for us. I don't want you worrying about spending money. I want you to have everything." His tone said it all. He wants me to have everything and he means it. I'm giddy and can't help, but to laugh like a schoolgirl. We sit together on the same lounge chair and enjoy some breakfast together. I love everything with macadamia nuts, even the coffee tastes better here.

Alika comes back and catches us making out on the lounge chair, "How about ten days from now at sunset and I can have you set up at the edge of the ocean with the sunset behind the minister?"

Rick and I lock eyes anxiously, then turn to Alika, "Yes!" at the same time. It's the perfect option.

"I'll reserve the time for you. Please get me details on how many rooms as soon as you can. We have availability then, so it shouldn't be a problem."

"Thank you, can you book the spa for my bride that day please. Everything she'll want. Also, book a second spot for her Maid of Honor to go with her." Rick looks to Alika waiting for confirmation.

"I'll do that right now, please let me know if I can help with anything else. I'll check in with you tomorrow." He walks off toward the spa.

Rick gazes at me with a happy grin and dials out on his cell phone, "Hi. Here's Sherry, she wants to talk to you." He hands me his phone.

"Hello?"

"Hey! What do you want to talk to me about?" It's Sam.

I squeal like a child, "I'm getting married in Hawaii, in ten days and I want you to be my Maid of Honor. Will you please?"

You could hear Sam scream without the phone all the way from her home in Colorado, "Yes! I'm honored and I wouldn't miss it!"

"Yay! I'll be sending you flight information later today and a boarding pass the day before the flight. I'll text you the details. Oh, don't tell your parents because he didn't call them yet."

"You two are crazy and I love it! Talk soon!" and she was gone.

Rick calls his parents, while I call my Mom. His father was happy and anxious to get to Hawaii, while his mom hemmed and hawed about us getting married so fast and not having the ceremony in a church.

"Hello? Is everything okay? Why are you calling me while you're on vacation?"

I laugh, "Everything is fine, Mom. Better than fine. I want you to come to Hawaii."

"You know I don't like to travel alone."

"Bring someone with you because I'm marrying Rick!"

"I saw the way he looked at you. I know he'll take care of you. Are you sure about this?"

"I don't need anyone to take care of me." I stop myself, "Mom, I love him and I can be me with him."

"Do it. I'll be there. I wouldn't miss it for the world."

"Thanks, Mom."

"I want you both to be happy. Now, get off the phone and go enjoy your vacation with your husband to be," she laughs.

"Aloha." My mom is ecstatic, with some trepidation about traveling by herself and she's going to find a friend who wants to join her on the trip.

CHAPTER FIVE

Rick needs to work out and call Cross, so I take the Jeep keys and drive to the North Shore Gift Shop in Haleiwa to visit my friend Malia. I love the drive from Kahuku to Haleiwa. It's green and lush, with the ocean at your side. The trees hang over parts of the two-lane highway and there's a bike path on the beach side for sections of it. Some of the beaches have parking lots, while others find people pulling onto the dirt at the side of the road and hoping they don't get stuck there. It's almost all residential and beach, with a few businesses spattered in between. No chain fast food or anything franchised, the one grocery store with a coffee place inside, the local bakery, a couple of cafes, and food trucks parked wherever they find a spot. There are a couple of places where fresh fruit stands pop up occasionally and surf, swim, snorkel equipment rentals are available in the more popular beach areas. I pass Sharks Cove and the grocery store, then Saints Peter and Paul Mission as I approach Waimea Bay. I take the curve slowly and drive the cliffside road with the panoramic view of Waimea Bay. The highway quickly turns back inland through a residential stretch until I see the Haleiwa surf sign and turn right, passing Haleiwa Beach Park as I head toward the Rainbow Bridge and the souvenir shop my friend Malia runs with her family. I've known her for years and she's part of Hawaii to me. I turn onto the side street, park and hop out of the Jeep.

I stop and look around at all the green, the overgrown grassy areas, the ocean birds, the wild chickens, the canoes, the surfers and the wannabe surfers. Hawaii is all about taking time to enjoy—the view, the ocean air, food, friends, and love. I guess Hawaii is love for me, it's the Aloha State and aloha means love, affection, compassion, mercy in Hawaiian.

I walk up to the gift shop and see Malia's sons cleaning while her daughter sits singing and playing "I'm Yours" by Jason Mraz on the ukulele. She's awesome and gets better every time I hear her, so I stop to listen. "She's getting good, huh?" Malia had walked up next to me without me noticing. I turn to her and give her a hug. "This isn't the time of year you usually visit."

"I have news." I smile uncontrollably. "I got engaged over the summer and we're getting married while we're here."

"I'm so happy for you! But, that doesn't tell me why you're here in November." Malia always wants the facts.

"My Rick is a professional baseball player and he wanted to take me on a vacation as soon as it was his off-season. Last night, we decided to get married while we're here. We flew in yesterday and we're here for two weeks."

"I like to see you happy, my friend. You deserve every happiness. Is he with you?" Malia looks around.

"I want you to meet him and this was supposed to be a

completely social visit, but I'm hoping you might be able to help me with a few things for the wedding. I left him at the cottage to do his work out. You'll know exactly what I need, will you help me?"

"Of course! What can I do?"

"I need a dress for me and for his sister, my Maid of Honor. I need flowers and leis. I need Hawaiian traditions. I need music, but I may have found it. Can your daughter play 'Thinking Out Loud?'" Wouldn't that be perfect?

"What sizes?" Pia finishes playing. "Pia play 'Thinking Out Loud' for Sherry." Malia is all business.

Text to Sam - What size dress do you wear?

As I'm texting, Pia starts playing and it's perfect. I video record her and send it to Sam.

Text from Sam - Size 9
Text from Sam - Who's that girl?
Text from Sam - She's playing your song!
Text from Sam - She's great!
Text to Sam - My friend Malia's daughter
Text to Sam - Wedding music?
Text from Sam - Yes Yes Yes
Text to Sam - Don't tell Rick

I turn to Malia, "Will she play for my wedding? It's a paying gig."

"Pia, you want a paying gig playing at Sherry's wedding?" Pia lights up and nods. "You need to have a ring blessing, Ti Leaf and Lava Rock Ceremony, leis for every-one, special leis for the wedding party, flower garland for your hair. White dress for you, tropical print for Maid of

Honor, white for the groom with a colored sash, white for the best man with a tropical print is okay. I will make sure the music is good. 'Thinking Out Loud' is your song?"

"What would I do without you? Yes, it's our song." I smile and daydream about my Rick.

Malia laughs, "You've got it bad, girl!" Don't I know it! Before I met Rick I was happy being an independent single woman. Now, I'm not happy if I'm not with him. I never imagined I'd be in this place in my life, wanting to share my life with a man and get married.

My phone vibrates.

Text from Rick - I miss you my queen.

I reply quickly.

Text to Rick - I'm in Haleiwa. I'll be back soon. I miss you, too, my king.

I've been gone a couple of hours and need to get moving. "I have to get back to the cottage. I'll bring him by to meet you tomorrow."

"I can't wait to meet him. What are your sizes? I have an idea and I'll have a couple of dresses for you to see tomorrow. I think I know exactly what you want."

I give Malia the sizes and Alika's phone number at the resort. Malia gives me a phone number to her friend who makes leis. "I want to get Pia a dress to match my Maid of Honor, too."

"Don't worry! Everything will get done. This is Hawaii, no stress. Go back to your man and bring him by to meet me tomorrow." Malia hugs my neck and sends me off.

I take off for the Jeep and wish I had something to take back to Rick, then I realize I'm taking him me.

I pull up to the valet and Alika is waiting for me with the golf cart to take me to the cottage. Malia already called him and he set up the ring blessing, the Ti Leaf and Lava Rock Ceremony and made arrangements for Pia and her ukulele. I tell him I'm a travel agent, in case he needs travel arranged for anybody.

CHAPTER SIX

I walk into the cottage and find Rick napping. Fresh from his after work out shower and wearing only a robe. I climb onto the bed and crawl up him, thinking about abusing his cock with my mouth. But, it can't be like that every time. I keep climbing and gently place my lips on his while I run my fingers through his damp hair. In no time his arms are around me and his smile is against my lips. I nuzzle my face into his neck and kiss him there. "Beach, pool, adventure or sex?" I ask at his ear.

Rick rolls me off of him and postures over me on all fours. "I let you out of the house in these shorts without me? I'm a fool!" He squeezes his hand up my shorts to feel my ass and slides his thumb into my wet folds unexpectedly. I cry out and move against him. He unbuttons my shorts and pulls them off to find my "Eat Me" panties. He pulls them off and takes their suggestion, immediately burying his face in my wet heat. Licking and sucking at my folds, he slides a finger in and moves to circle my clit with his tongue. I reach for his head to hold him there and grind against his tongue. What's come over me? I can't help myself. He sucks harder and nibbles at my folds, driving me absolutely crazy. He groans against me, adding vibration to the attack on my senses. I whimper and call out his name. Rick takes his mouth away and stays very still. "Maybe this is too much for you. I better stop." He's sitting up and watching me.

"No! Please, my king. Please, more!"

"No, you've had enough."

What the fuck? I've had enough? I have not! I want more! I'll know when I've had enough. This has to be a game. I can wait him out. Or... "You're right, I've had too much. Best to stop. Thank you for looking out for me." The expression on his face is priceless, my response was unexpected. I sit up and he pulls back. I get up and start to walk toward the bathroom with a sway to my hips, he can't resist my hips and I'm half naked.

He reaches for me, placing his hands on my hips from behind me, "Where are you going?" His large warm hands caress my hips slowly, lovingly, with heat and desire.

I don't play games with Rick because that's not what we're about and he's been played before. I'm tempted to right now, he's teasing me. I turn around to find him sitting on the edge of the bed naked and drop to my knees to worship at his hard dick, but he stops me. "That's not what I have in mind." He brings me up to my feet and wraps his arms around me as he sits back on the bed as far as he can while still being able to keep his feet on the ground. His mouth at the same level with my breasts, he pulls my top off over my head, unhooks my bra and sends it flying. I kneel on either side of him, my body plastered against his as he runs his hands down the sides of my body. I slide down his body and mount his cock, moving on him slowly as he squeezes my breasts and kisses every part of my body he can get to. The heat is palpable, I let the temptation of teasing him go and enjoy the ride. Hot, sweaty and breathing hard within seconds, I reach for his lips with mine and our connection is complete as he slides his tongue into my mouth.

Both of us on the edge, I hold his face in my hands, pull my mouth away from him and lock eyes with him. I'm emotional and feeling everything, including regret for the thought of playing with him. "You're the only one for me. My only true love. I only want to be with you for the rest of my life. I'll never play games with you. I'll always love you. I want to give you everything. I want to be your everything. I never want to be without you." Rick wraps his arms around me and leans his head against me, holding me.

He gazes up at me, "You're my happiness, my love, my everything." Tears stream down my face. He pulls my lips to his and kisses me sweetly, tenderly with his open mouth. I meet him emotionally and we make out until I start moving on him again. Sliding my body up and down on his hard length slowly. Drawing low groans and cries from him, "Oh, baby. You're so tight on me, you... ggrrrrr..." His hands move to my hips, it's a sign and he's ready. He guides me to exactly what he wants with his gentle touch, increasing the speed I'm stroking him and adding a slight grind with my hips. I know the pattern, it's what does it for him and I'm not arguing. The grind is rubbing my sensitive nub and pushing me faster. His mouth on mine moves to my neck, where he kisses and sucks lightly until I'm on the edge and he pushes up into me hard, biting my neck at the same time and sending me over the edge. He holds me up as I scream out his name and he pumps into me a few times before he follows me over the edge. He falls back onto the bed, taking me down on top of him. I lay there on him, with my head on his chest listening to his heartbeat, his pulse racing, mine matching his.

CHAPTER SEVEN

R ick falls asleep and I get up, letting him rest. We're on vacation and that's what it's for, relaxing. I take advantage of the time to quickly check on work. Everything is good, but I do have a couple emails to take care of and some airfare to book.

First, an email from Rick's dad:

Sherry,
I'd like to bring the Mrs to Hawaii a few days before the wedding. Sooner is better. We don't have to be where you are, we can join you the day before the wedding. Can you help me with this?

Thank you,
MrSeno

I send him a reply...

Mr. Seno,

I'm happy to help you with this. Here are a couple of options, please keep in mind you're wanting to do this on short notice causing the price to be higher than expected.

Option 1 $3,250
1 Week in North Shore Resort Hotel
Roundtrip airfare for 2
1 Week of Rental Car – Jeep Wrangler
Lei Greeting for 2 at the airport
Add upgrade to First Class Airfare +$780
Add Oceanside couples massage +$240
Add Surfing Lessons $200/person

Option 2 $1,885 +
3 Nights in North Shore Resort Hotel
Roundtrip airfare for 2 to Oahu
3 Days of Rental Car on Oahu - Jeep Wrangler
Lei Greeting for 2 at the airport
+++Options for Second Location+++
1. Lanai $2,100 (Quiet, Luxurious, Small Island)
4 Nights Lanai Sweetheart Rock Beach Spa Resort
Roundtrip airfare for 2 hop to Lanai
Lei Greeting for 2 at Lanai Airport
Lanai Transportation Fee for 2
Add Lanai excursion package +$200-$500
2. Maui $1,985 (Resort Area, Close to Shopping,
Tourist Island)
4 Nights Kaanapali Hotel
Island airfare hop for 2
Lei Greeting for 2 at Kahului Airport
4 Days Rental Car on Maui - Small SUV
3. Waikiki $1,100 (Beautiful beach in the city, near
shopping, party zone)
4 Nights at the Grand Village
4 Additional Days of Rental Car Oahu - Jeep
Wrangler

I'm happy to provide more options based on your
needs. I'm personally familiar with all of the locations I have offered to you. In my opinion, Waikiki
is only good for more than one visit if you want to
party it up and go dancing every night. Maui has
lots to see if you are interested in exploring. Lanai
is simple, relaxing and a unique experience.

Please let me know what you think and feel free to call me.

Aloha,
Sherry
Beach Vacations

Second, an email from Cross:

Hey Sherry,

A few of the guys on the team want to go to the wedding and we want to get there a couple days early. If you don't mind we'd like to take Seno out for kind of a last night with the boys and get him wasted. It's part of my job as Best Man and he doesn't know, so shhh! Promise no girls, it would be a waste on him anyway. If you're good with that, we want to get there two days before the wedding and stay for four nights. Can you get us rooms at the resort and airfare? We can share rooms and will need transportation to the resort. Total of eight of us, so four rooms is good. Quote us first class for the airfare.

Oh! Congrats!

Thanks,
Chase

I love how the kid wants to do what's right and take care of Rick the way a Best Man should. He deserves a Bachelor Party. I check the vacation rentals for the resort to

see if they have any villas available the days the team wants
to be here and reply to Cross.

Chase,

A Bachelor Party will be fine, but I need him to be
functioning the next day!

Roundtrip First Class Airfare to Oahu is $1,190
each (Limited availability the dates you are
traveling)

4 Nights in the North Shore Resort Hotel $1,200
per room

But, I found another option for you that may be
better. There's a villa available for the days you are
looking for with 4 bedrooms and sleeps 12 at $500
per night. Plus, it would give you room to party and
the villas have their own pool and hot tub area.

For transportation, you can rent two vehicles for a
total of $390, use a car service for about $300 or
helicopter over from the airport for about $1,600
roundtrip.

Please get back to me soon, so I can get you guys
booked quick.

Thank you for taking care of Rick.

Aloha,
Sherry
Beach Vacations

I spend some time working on airfare options for Sam and my mom. Then I make a list of things that need to happen for the wedding and make notes next to the things that are handled, or need additional follow up. Rick is standing behind me and the cottage is getting dark. "Babe, are you working?" Shit.

"Not really, I had an email from your dad about wanting to fly over early and vacation, and Cross wanted me to set up his airfare and room for him. I checked on flights for Sam and my mom. Then I started a list of things that need to get done for the wedding. Too much?"

"Why don't we go for a sunset walk, sit with our feet in the pool and you can tell me all about the wedding stuff?" He smiles at me and pulls me up out of my chair to find I'm still naked. I giggle, pull my bikini on with shorts over it and I'm ready to go. Rick had already pulled his board shorts on and pulled a T-shirt on as we walked out the door. We walk over to the pool holding hands and get beach towels from the pool hut. I fold the towels to use them as cushions on the edge of the pool and take my shorts off before I sit down. I dangle my feet in the water while Rick takes his shirt off revealing his woman melting body to the world. He sits next to me on his towel and puts his arm around me. The water is inviting, not too warm and not too cold. He kisses me sweetly, "Talk to me about our wedding and our vacation and why you were working. Most important, what do I need to do to keep you from crying? I don't like you to cry."

I need to give him a real answer, but allow myself to get

caught in the beauty of the sunset and everything that's surrounding us. Happy to be in my favorite place with the love of my life and getting married. A single tear trickles down my face and I consider jumping into the pool to hide it.

"I don't understand, my queen," Rick swipes his thumb across my cheek, wiping the tear away, "I need you to help me here. What am I doing wrong?"

"Nothing. You're perfect. I'm just happy and being a stupid girl that can't control her emotions." I gaze at him and another lone tear rolls.

"I like that you're a girl and you're not stupid. You are on the emotional side, but there's a lot going on. I get it. Tell me about tomorrow." Rick is trying to keep me distracted, and I think it's a good idea. I also think I should find a pregnancy test.

"I have a plan for us tomorrow! I want to take you to my favorite place for breakfast, then I want to take you out to Laie Point, and if the locals swap meet opens early enough I want to stop by there. After that, I want to take you to meet Malia and to Surfin' Shave Ice for a creamsicle. If we have time we can browse the galleries and do some beach hopping on the way back to the cottage. Oh! I want to stop at the grocery store on the way back to the cottage. Okay?" I gaze at him smiling with no tears in sight.

"Sounds great! So, what you're saying is you're the Vacation Commander tomorrow and I shouldn't interfere with the plan?"

"Yes!" I laugh and lean in to kiss him, taking us both into the pool instead. Rick tries to grab me underwater and I swim away before he can get me. He swims after me and we play in the pool, having fun like children. We both come up for air at the same time and he pulls me to him, kissing me with intent and then taking his mouth away.

"Tell me about the wedding stuff, my bride." Rick says while he holds me in the pool, not letting me go.

I'm distracted by the blue of his eyes. The reflection of the pool seems to add to their depth. "Wedding stuff. Alika has a couple Hawaiian customs handled for us. There will be a ring blessing and a Ti Leaf and Lava Rock Ceremony. It'll be nice to have the Hawaiian touches, since they're both positive things and we're getting married in Hawaii and it's my favorite place. Malia should have dresses for me to try on when we visit her tomorrow. We need to get you and Cross appropriate attire. I have a phone number to call about getting traditional Hawaiian Wedding Leis, leis for the wedding party and leis for the guests. We need to drive over to Honolulu to get a marriage license. I have the music handled. How about taking everyone to dinner afterwards or having cocktails at the ceremony sight immediately following the ceremony instead of having a reception?"

"You've been busy. I like it all. If it's what you want, I want it." He puts his forehead to mine and gives me a quick kiss.

I turn to Rick with a crinkle in my lip, "I'm concerned about one thing. I don't know how much everything's going to cost and I don't know if I'll have enough money."

"My queen, I love how you're thrifty and self-sufficient. Will you please not worry about the money? Let me take care of it. I want to pay for it. I want to give you everything you want. Think of it this way, there's no way it costs even half as much for our wedding here as it would for whatever we'd plan at home. I love you and I want this to be the way you want it. We're only doing this once, right?"

"No reason to do it again when you're married to the

perfect man, like I will be." I smile so big it hurts and I kiss him. The sun is almost down and the music is playing at the pool bar. We dance around together in the pool with our arms around each other. We have the pool to ourselves and romance is swirling around us. We gaze at each other and my eyes turn warm, I feel like he can see into my heart and soul. I wonder if he feels the same and his expression tells me he can. He holds my face with his hands and kisses me wantonly until I wrap my legs around him. He takes us underwater and we continue making out until we have no more air. Rick picks me up out of the water and sits me on the edge of the pool, and wraps his towel around me. He pulls himself out and sits next to me shaking the water out of his hair like a dog, making me laugh. He stands up next to me and offers me his hand to get up. When he pulls me up I'm as light as a feather and get chills as the breeze hits me. He puts his arms around me and I get goosebumps. He pulls his T-shirt over his head, picks me up and carries me all the way back to our cottage. We enter the cottage and he takes us directly to the shower, turning it on and letting it warm up while he peels my wet bikini off of me. He appreciates my hard nipples and stops what he's doing for a moment to kiss them. Rick pushes me toward the shower, "I'll be right there, baby," and disappears into the other room. I hear music come on and the volume go up until the bathroom is filled with Hawaiian music. A minute or so later Rick walks in, strips and joins me in the shower. He holds me to him tightly with his right hand wrapped around my back to my right shoulder and his left at the small of my back. His cheek leaned against the side of my forehead. Not kissing me. Not groping me. Not wanting sex. Simply holding me and loving me. I've never felt so loved and cherished. No words, only a slight sway with the music as the warm shower falls over us.

The water starts to cool and Rick turns off the shower. He gets the robes and wraps me in one, then puts the other on. He has candles lit around the room, especially by the couch facing out to the ocean and blankets sprawled on the couch. He leads me there and gets me settled on the couch, covering me with a blanket. I'm toasty all bundled up in the robe and soft quilt. Someone knocks at the door and Rick goes to handle it. He comes back with a pizza, macadamia nut cake, whipped cream, and a small box with a bow on it. He sets everything down on the coffee table and nestles in under the blanket with me. The light from the candles flicker about the room romantically. Rick holds me close as we watch the light of the night sky reflect off the ocean and listen to the thunder of the rolling waves as they crash at the shore. I'm warm and relaxed in his arms.

"I love you no matter what and I'll always take care of you." He talks into my hair, nuzzling me. "I know there's a lot of craziness going on and when I thought about it I realized I've turned your life upside down with my baseball world. None of that is as important to me as you are. I don't want you to take me the wrong way, but are you late?" Rick waits for me to answer, but I don't. I'm in my head dissecting what he's asking me. I don't pay attention, I just take my pill everyday and go about my life. I stop and try to figure out when Aunt Flo last visited, but I'm not sure. "Sherry?"

"I don't remember when I had my last one. Um, I don't keep track of it. It's never been a concern." I answer aware that my answer is unacceptable.

"How about I run over to the gift shop and buy a test, just in case you want it in the morning?"

"Okay, but I have a full day planned for us tomorrow."

Rick smiles at me as he gets up and pulls on his clothes, "I'll be right back. Do you want anything else?"

"Maybe chocolate syrup, if they have it." He shakes his head as he takes off out the door. I get my phone and call Sam.

"Hello?" she answers and sounds like I may have woken her up. Crap! Forgot about the time difference.

"Hi, sorry to wake you. Didn't remember the time difference."

"No problem. Is something wrong?"

"Just freaking out, nothing major. I've been being emotional and your brother asked me if I'm late. I actually don't know. I've never had to pay attention to that."

"Slow down, Sherry."

"I can't, he went to the gift shop to get a test and chocolate syrup and he'll be back quick. I need you to talk me through this." I'm slightly frantic while I try to maintain myself.

"You definitely need to do the test first thing in the morning. Most likely you're just stressed, but if nothing else you need to find out so the wondering doesn't add to your situation. You've been thrown head first into the professional sports world and now you're getting married while you're on vacation. I'm sure it's been a wild ride for you since you met my brother. Don't go thinking about it. The test is purely for factual purposes. Got it?" Sam gets it all out quick. Plain and simple.

"I can do that, but what about Rick? I don't want him getting hopeful and then... He's back, going to have to go pretty quick."

"Don't worry. He's a big boy. Remember it gives you two something to work on after you're married. It'll happen, you just don't know when." Sam teases me, but she's right.

"Thanks. Keep your eye out for dress pictures tomorrow."

"Goodnight," and Sam hangs up. Probably thinking I've lost my mind.

"Everything okay?" Rick asks as he comes in.

"Yeah, talking to Sam. I love your sister, can I keep her?"

"More like you're stuck with her once you marry me," Rick laughs and gives me a quick kiss as he joins me back on the couch. He digs into the pizza and I go straight for the cake. "Cake first?"

"Duh! I don't need pizza, I have cake!" I smile at him and shove a piece of macadamia nut cake into my mouth. It's delicious, sweet and crumbly.

Rick hands me the small box with the bow on it, "I saw this earlier when I was wandering around the hotel and I want you to have it."

I open the box to find a gold necklace with a tropical leaf charm hanging on it. Inside the box is a message that reads: Because you are as beautiful and unique as a tropical flower. Wear this everyday and remember what it feels like to be on vacation. It's delicate, and the leaf is organic and feminine. "I love it! Put it on me please." I hand it to Rick and he fastens it around my neck. "What do you think? Do you like it?"

"My queen, you're more beautiful than any tropical flower." Rick leans into me and kisses me tenderly. He gazes into my eyes as he leans back, "I really do love you more than anything, Sherry."

I'm not sure how I deserve this man. I turn my back to him and lean up against him while I eat cake, and he devours the pizza. I guess he's the meal and I'm the dessert. I reach for the bowl of freshly whipped cream and he takes it from me, "It's not the same as the can, but I can make it work." He dips his finger in the bowl and comes out with a dollop of cream. I reach for his finger with my mouth and suck off the whipped cream, bringing a dirty glint to his eyes. I dip a piece of cake in the whipped cream and inhale it. He smiles at me, "We should save that for later," and puts the whipped cream back on the table.

We sit together quietly in the candlelit cottage, snuggling under the blankets on the couch while we listen to the waves crashing on the shore. The shoreline is only a matter of thirty feet away, yet it's like looking out into an empty blackness and only seeing the light of the night sky bounce off of it.

We kiss and eat whipped cream out of each others mouths, sucking it from our tongues. Touching each other and simply enjoying the time together with no away games in the near future and nothing forcing us to spend time apart.

CHAPTER EIGHT

I'm woken by a chill and the sun has broken, but there's a layer of clouds. The breeze blows in again and I realize I fell asleep lying on Rick on the couch. I carefully get up and close the door most of the way as quietly as I can. It's still early, but I have to pee. I pad to the bathroom silently and close the door. I find the pregnancy test sitting there waiting for me and Sam's words echo in my head. It's for factual purposes. Negative is okay, it just gives us something to work on after we're married. No need to get worked up or be upset. Okay, those are my words and I need to remember them. I pee on the stick and set it back down on the counter where I found it. I read the box to see what the directions say and wait for the facts to be told. I could get a false reading or not be pregnant enough for the test to pick it up. I walk out to admire Rick asleep on the couch, so handsome with his trimmed beard and muscular build. I can't help but smile knowing I'll always be with him, we'll always be together. I walk back into the bathroom to check the stick and it's negative, as it should be since I'm taking the pill everyday. I look at my pills and notice they're a different color during that time of the month, starting with yesterday. I take a picture of the test and throw it out. I may need to pick up another one in a few days. Somehow, I manage not to be upset.

I walk out to the couch and crawl up Rick, pulling the blankets up over us and placing my head on his chest where I can listen to his soothing heartbeat. He immediately wraps his arms around me and nuzzles his face into my hair.

A couple hours later I wake up in bed alone and hear Rick in the bathroom. He walks up to the bed and leans over me, "Are you ready to get up and take us on the day you have planned?"

I beam at him and nod. "Breakfast is the first stop." I jump up out of bed and quickly get dressed, pulling on a short Hawaiian print sundress with big red hibiscus flowers on it over my bikini and sliding my slippahs on. I fill my big purse with my wallet, camera, water, beach towel and sunscreen. I put my Seals baseball cap on and slide my sunglasses over my eyes. Then I stop and turn to Rick, "Ready?"

He focuses on me unsure, "Is there anything we need to talk about?" He's referring to the test and is probably confused because I'm pretty together this morning.

"Not really. Test was negative, but I checked my pills and I should've started yesterday. Probably not late enough for the test to be positive if I was pregnant. I'll get another test in a few days if I'm late." I smile and reconsider his heart, "Are you okay?"

Rick laughs, "If you're good, I'm good. It doesn't have to be right now." Obviously, happy I wasn't freaking out or crying. Rick pulls on a pair of khaki cargo shorts and his aloha shirt. "Let's go."

Alika is driving by in the golf cart right when we step outside and gives us a ride to the valet, calling ahead for us so the valet has our Jeep waiting. "Where are you two off to today?"

"Breakfast at Hidden Cafe, Laie Point, Kahuku Swap Meet, and then to Haleiwa for creamsicles at Surfin' Shave Ice and to meet a friend of mine at the North Shore Gift Shop. Some beach hopping in the middle." I spout off the itinerary I have planned.

"Oh, you got this down! Don't forget the resort has hula classes and ukulele classes if you want to learn. Need help with anything else? Anything new I should know about for the wedding?" He's with it.

"Nothing new. I'll check in with you later and give you an update." I catch Alika's eyes in the rearview mirror, not wanting to tell him about the guys from the Seals who will be joining us while Rick is there.

The valet pulls up our Jeep as we get there and we take off for the Hidden Cafe. It's about a twenty minute drive, but it's worth it for the best breakfast ever. We take a left out of the resort and drive Kamehameha Highway over to Laie turning right into a residential area, then drive most of the way around a traffic circle and find parking on a residential street. We walk a couple houses back and open the screened door of the Hidden Cafe to be greeted by the server from wherever she is in the small cafe "Aloha, sit where you want and get your own water." I agree this sounds odd, but it's this place and it works. The windows are glass shutters and screens, the tables are old and mismatched, and the walls are covered in sports memorabilia—mostly autographed photos from football players from the island, neighboring Kahuku High has produced a few professional football players and this area is into football as if it were Texas. I review the menu, but I already know what I want. The waitress walks up, "Long time, no see sistah. Welcome back! You want your usual?"

I look at her not believing she remembers my order, "Yep, passion orange juice and a beef stew omelette." Rick focuses on me and I order for him, "Give him the same please." Rick shakes his head at me.

"You got it. Your guy looks familiar. He play sports?"

Rick chimes in, "I'm the catcher for the San Diego Seals."

"I thought so! You should sign our wall after you eat. I'll get you the sharpie."

"What is this place?" Rick glares at me like I brought him into the twilight zone.

"Best breakfast on the face of the Earth. This is where the locals go. You're going to love it." The server brings us our juice and the taste of it makes me happy, a taste of Hawaii. We watch the locals come in to pick up food and hangout, talk story while we wait for our breakfast. The cooks and servers are all part of somebody's family and everybody knows everything, who their mom is, who they're dating, you want the scoop you come here. You can't help but smile in this atmosphere. Then the food gets to our table and the meal I've been craving for months is sitting in front of me. You're probably thinking the same thing that Rick did, Beef Stew Omelette? Yes! It's a big bowl of rice covered with chunky pieces of stewed beef, with huge pieces of carrot that make you wonder how they grow them, big chunks of potato, and some onion with the egg part of an omelette folded up on top of it. The stew is flavored with a touch of Polynesian flair and it's one of my favorite things. I cut through the omelette with my fork and spear a piece of stew. As I place the oversized bite in my mouth, it tastes better than I remember and I'm on my way to a food coma. I watch Rick go straight for the meat before trying the combo with the egg, "Do you like it?"

"What's not to like? Stew should be on every breakfast menu."

"Good! Tomorrow we should come back and split macadamia nut pancakes and macadamia nut french toast!" I laugh, I'd eat here everyday if I had the option. "Maybe the Loco Moco the next day."

Rick shakes his head and grins from ear to ear, "Whatever you want, my queen."

After breakfast we drive a couple miles to Laie Point and I get my camera out, ready to tromp all over the sandstone terrain and get some photos. Rick meets me on my side of the Jeep, while I set up my camera. He reaches in to kiss me, standing between my legs and showing me his appreciation. He lifts me out of the Jeep. I wrap my legs and arms around him tightly, pressing my lips to his. His clear blue eyes reflect the sky and shine as he gazes at me. "Hi," he says simply.

"Hi," I say right back at him and smile coyly. I laugh nervously and I have no idea why.

"You love this place, and I mean this island. It makes you comfortable, playful. It suits you."

"I love the North Shore," I feel myself blush and I don't know why. "I've always fit in here, even though I'm a tourist. There's no place more beautiful and full of history, legends. This is Laie Point, the hole through the rock formation out there was caused by nature. Locals say it was created by one storm in one day, but there's also a legend about how the small islands got here." I give him a brain sucking kiss and slide down his body, "Watch where you walk." I take him by the hand and drag him with me all over the point taking photos like crazy. Taking advantage of a few opportunities to catch my Rick on film with the view. When I find the perfect place, I take a selfie of us together and try another using the timer on my camera. The ground is jagged and the sand can be slippery, but we manage to survive without injury. Rick parts from me while I take photos in other directions. I turn to find him and he has walked out to a cliff edge. He appears to be appreciating the wind in his face and the mist off the ocean. I take some more photos of him and realize I might enjoy taking photos of him more than I do the ocean. Wow. I walk back to the Jeep to send my pictures to the cloud and drink some water. I check out the photos with Rick and I love the selfie of us together, so I send it to him in a text with a heart emoji. Then I send it to Sam and my mom because they'll love it, too.

CHAPTER NINE

Rick hops into the Jeep, "Where to next, Vacation Commander?" He salutes me and waits for instruction.

"Kahuku Swap Meet," I direct him back to the highway and toward the resort, hoping the vendors are open. We pull up to the small group of tents and wander through checking everything out. I get two new sundresses, well one of them is more like a tube top with a skirt attached. Rick gets a pair of board shorts and an aloha shirt that matches my sundress. We watch the locals carving tikis and browse the Hawaiian wares.

We drive toward the resort and a part of me wants to make a sex stop, but there's no way we would leave the cottage for the rest of the day and we're going to see Malia this afternoon. We pass the turn for the resort and keep going. I have Rick turn off onto the dirt parking at Goat Island and park in the shade of the trees. We roll down the windows and relax, kicking our feet up on the dashboard.

The breeze blows through and the sound of the ocean soothes me.

I take a minute to check my email and make sure I'm not missing anything. I have a couple of texts and emails.

Text from Mom - You two are good together. Great picture. I can see you're having a good time and well taken care of. See you soon!
Text from Sam - You two are adorable. It's gorgeous there! I want to go!

Sherry,

Let's go with option 2 and Lanai, but make it 4 days on Oahu and 3 days on Lanai. Is that an option?

Thanks,
MrSeno

I send a quick reply:

Mr Seno,

I'm sure I can make that work. I'll work up the details when I get back to my laptop later today and get it booked for you. I'll email your itinerary.

Aloha,
Sherry
Beach Vacations

Sherry,

The guys like the idea of the villa, but are worried they'll have to share beds. If you can verify they can have eight separate beds, we want the villa. Otherwise, book us four rooms. Set us up a car service from the airport and do what you can to get us all first class on the airfare. See attachment for names and info for the guys who are coming with me.

Thanks,
Chase

I think about it and I wonder if I can come up with a better travel option for the guys since they all want to go first class.

Chase,

I'm going to do some research for you and see if I can come up with something better. I'll email you details and itinerary later today.

Aloha,
Sherry
Beach Vacations

I send out an email to Alika to find out about the number of beds in the villa and I send an email to a charter service to get pricing to charter a whole airplane.

"Are you working again?" Rick is staring at me.

"Checking email real quick. Taking care of your Dad and Cross. This beach is great for wildlife. I've seen monk seals napping here." He gives me a look that tells me my diversion isn't working. "Shave ice or Malia at the gift shop next?"

"I have a better idea," Rick reaches for me and touches the side of my face, softly running his fingers over my lips. He stretches across me and reclines my seat back as far as it will go, then reclines his own seat. This beach is almost empty other than us, and we're backed into a pretty secluded area. Rick rolls up the dark tinted windows most of the way and hangs my beach towel over the visors to block the windshield.

I'm out of breath with anticipation, "Shave Ice and Malia can wait."

Rick leans over me and claims my mouth with his greedily. Pure heat blazes in his eyes, "I need to have you, baby. Your whole attitude today turns me on."

I push him away and slide into the back seat. "Move over to the passenger seat." He glances at me funny, but goes along with my request. The passenger seat reclined to almost flat, Rick moved over effortlessly. My intent was to climb back over him and ride him, but I slide my bikini bottoms off in the backseat and admire him. I reach over him and kiss him upside down while I unbutton his cargo shorts and push them down enough to release his needy erection. I wrap my hand around him and stroke a few times, as I enjoy his lips and searching tongue. His tongue. I climb over him, running my hands over his body as I work my way down to his hard length. I lick his tip and take his cock in my mouth as he reaches up my dress to find me bare, spreading my legs and kissing me there. I suck on him gently and he tongues my sensitive center and folds, sucking and nibbling. Driving me to take him deeper in my mouth and suck on him harder, I lick his length and swirl my tongue around him. I suck on him and stroke him with my lips, dragging my tongue along his cock. His large hands are spread across my ass holding me where he wants me, driving me to the edge with his tongue buried in my sex. I grind against his tongue, but it's not what I really want, what he really wants. I slide back into the backseat and turn around. Rick slides a finger inside me as I do my best to back down his body and mount his rock solid dick. It pulls a cry out of me and Rick helps me into position. He puts the seat up part way and claims my mouth with his, each of us swallowing the others cries of passion. I ride him hard, my need matching his while he's seated as deep as he can get. I'm grinding against him and I'm out of control.

Rick reaches around me and pulls me tight to him, running his hands down my back. He whispers in my ear, "You say the sweetest things to me every morning before you even wake up. You empower me and make me truly feel like a king. You're the only person who can do that. I will do anything for you, everything if you'll only let me. I love you, Sherry. Let me take care of you." A stray tear rolls down my cheek and I don't know why. Rick wipes it away and kisses my cheek. He somehow manages to roll me underneath him and strokes into me long and slow, with his lips on mine kissing me, needing more. Suddenly I'm on the edge. I reach for Rick needing to have my hands on him. I dig my fingers into his shoulders as my orgasm hits me and all I can see are bursts of light. Rick's grasp on me tightens and he follows me over the edge. Our kiss is heated as he rides us through, both of us out of breath, hot and sweaty. He stops kissing me to catch his breath and leans his forehead to mine. "Baby, you drive me fuckin' crazy. I've never done anything like this with anyone else."

I giggle to myself, I haven't done hardly anything other than what I've done with him. I understand what he's saying, we get pulled in by sudden desire and need each other. We lose control and it doesn't matter where we are. I used to wonder if it was some type of reassurance, a need to make sure we're okay. But, it's simply sexual desire and sometimes it's a need to prove we love each other—we can't get close enough to each other.

Rick moves back to the driver's seat and buttons up his shorts. I reach in the backseat for my bikini bottoms and catch my flushed reflection in the mirror as I'm pulling them on. My hair is a mess. I dig in my bag hoping for a brush and get lucky. I brush out my hair and tie it up in a ponytail. I direct Rick towards Haleiwa, and he's the full definition of sexed up. "Ocean or beach shower?" We need to freshen up and we have extra clothes.

"I was thinking shave ice." Of course he was! He's always hungry after sex.

"Okay, beach shower it is." I direct Rick to drive to Haleiwa Beach Park. We park and I strip down to my bikini. Rick takes his shirt off. We run over to the beach showers and play, splashing each other, getting soaking wet. Then run back to the Jeep. I share my towel and we dry off as much as we can. I find my new sundress and pull it over my head. Rick puts his new shirt on and we match, even though it wasn't the plan. We're still wet and have wet spots on our clothes, but that's expected. This is the North Shore! At least we don't look and smell like sex.

CHAPTER TEN

We drive the short distance to Surfin' Shave Ice and get in the line that's wrapped around the building. I order a creamsicle which is shave ice with orange syrup and sweetened condensed milk. Rick orders a tropical which is ice with three tropical flavors of syrup, no condensed milk, no ice cream, no adzuki beans. As soon as he sees mine he knows he's made an error, so we share half and half after he promises we can come back and get another one while we are on vacation. We eat our shave ice in the parking lot, with the other patrons and the wandering wild chickens.

We get in the Jeep and drive back across the Rainbow Bridge to the gift shop, and find parking on the side street. We walk up to the shop and Malia is sitting outside relaxing with her mother.

"Hey girl! I've been waiting for you. Is this your man?" Malia makes eyes at me conveying he's a hottie. "Nice to meet you." She nods at Rick and wraps her arm around mine. "Come with me and see the dresses." She points at

Rick, "You need to stay here. You can't see the dress. Browse around the shop, maybe you'll find something you like." Malia drags me into a room behind the shop where she has a makeshift dressing room set up with mirrors and dresses hanging up, waiting for me. "Your man is a good one, he has a pure heart. I can tell. You look different today. What changed? You're glowing? Probably just being a bride-to-be!"

I imagine myself in each of the dresses she has waiting for me and I'm immediately drawn to my wedding dress. "That one."

Malia laughs, "I knew it! Now, how about for your Maid of Honor? I like this one that's a little shorter, but only if it would be knee length. We can get it in any of these colors." She points to the other dresses hanging next to it. I consider Sam and which style would flatter her figure. Malia's right and I choose the one she suggested, I even prefer the traditional white and blue hibiscus print— It's Seals colors!

I take a quick picture of the dresses I have chosen and text them to Sam.

Text from Sam - You're going to be beautiful! I love how you're embracing the Hawaiian theme.

Text from Sam - I never look good in a dress, but that's the best I've seen as far as bridesmaid dresses go.

Text from Sam - What about Rick?

Text to Sam - White suit with a blue sash that matches your dress or white on white print sash that matches mine?

Text from Sam - White on white like you. Blue maybe for best man?

Text to Sam - Maybe aloha shirt for best man that matches your dress.

Text from Sam - I like that, too.

I turn to Malia, "I want these two exactly as they are. Can I try mine on?"

"Of course!" She closes the door behind us, so I can slip into it and it fits like it was made for me. "It's perfect for you. Beautiful bride." I carefully take it back off and hang it up.

"Can I get the Best Man an aloha shirt in the same print as the Maid of Honor dress? How about a sash for Rick that's the same as my dress?" I'm rattling on.

"Yes and yes. Good choices, too. What about shoes?" Malia wants to make sure I'm not forgetting anything.

"I'm thinking of getting a pedicure and going barefoot. Maybe wear an anklet."

"I like it. That fits your style and it's appropriate for a beach wedding. You should get French Manicure and French Pedicure, it'll be perfect!" I love how excited Malia is for me. "I'll keep the dresses, so everything is together and matches. My seamstress friend will make sure everything is perfect, wedding ready."

"What about a dress for Pia?"

"Already handled, just waiting to find out which print to make it in." Malia smiles at me. "No worries for you. This is right for you. He's the one. Be happy and love."

"Thank you, Malia. For everything." We go back to the gift shop to find Malia's sons talking baseball with Rick, and Rick texting. I walk up to him and place my hands on his cheeks pulling his face down for a quick kiss.

Rick smiles at me with a gleam in his eye, "Does that mean you found a wedding dress?"

"It means I love you. But, yes, I found a wedding dress and a dress for Sam and a shirt for Chase and..." I stop and turn to Malia, "What about an aloha shirt in the same material as my dress for Rick instead of a suit and sash?" I gaze up at Rick, "Do you have a preference?"

"I want whatever you want, baby. I don't care as long I get to marry you." Rick kisses my forehead.

Malia sighs, "Where did you come from? You're perfect for her. Why wear a suit if you don't have to? I'll add the shirt to the order, but I need sizes for the men."

I watch Rick texting, "What are you doing? You never text."

"I'm having Cross bring me some Seals caps and photos, for these young men and the Hidden Cafe. He says large and I'm extra large." He truly is perfect.

"Don't leave out their sister." I turn to Malia, "How much money do I owe you for the dresses and everything?"

"Should be under $500, but I'll get you an exact price. She'll have it all in a nice garment bag for you, so you can keep your wedding dress in it afterwards." Malia admires us together, "You two are just too cute with the matching aloha print. You really do have a glow, he must be treating you right."

I thank Malia and buy a few things I need from her shop. Rick reaches to shake her hand, but she pulls him in for a hug and whispers something in his ear that makes him smile into his cheeks.

We get back in the Jeep and Rick focuses on me, "What else do we have to do for our wedding?"

"Get our marriage license in Honolulu, you and Cross need white pants, schedule salon services, finish up travel arrangements for our guests, we need wedding rings... I think that's it."

"I already have your wedding ring. So, you can finish the travel arrangements and schedule the salon for you and Sam tonight?" Rick takes out his phone and sends a text. "Cross will bring his white pants. Honolulu and a mall or something tomorrow, then we can lie on the beach for a few days? What do you think, my queen?"

"I'm behind!" I hear myself get whiney, "You have my ring and I don't have yours."

"Babe, I bought your wedding ring as a set with your engagement ring. I've had it for months." Rick pats me on the leg, "Do you need a vacation day tomorrow?"

I laugh at him because he knows as well as I do, I'm not going to relax until I have everything handled for our wedding. I can't imagine actually taking months to plan a wedding and inviting bunches of people, having a reception and everything. It would be nerve-racking! "Honolulu tomorrow. Stop at the grocery store on the way back to the cottage." He's learned his way around, and we take off for Kamehameha Highway.

CHAPTER ELEVEN

We walk into the grocery store, I pick up a basket and head straight for the refrigerator and freezer along the back wall of the store. Rick takes the basket from me and follows along, ready to carry for me. I pick up a jug of POG from the refrigerator, it's passion fruit, orange, and guava juice and more of a punch really. I walk over to the freezer in search of the local made macadamia nut ice cream. I pick up two pints and go back to the refrigerator case after a can of whipped cream. "Dinner and drinks in tonight, my king?"

"Perfect, my queen."

I pick up another jug of POG, a bottle of vodka, crackers, and cheese. Then I go to the deli counter and get the plate lunch family special with ribs, chicken, rice and macaroni salad. "Do you want anything else?"

"Yes, but it'll wait until we get to the cottage," Rick stares at me like I'm dinner and we head to the check out. I hand my kama'aina card to the checker and she keys in the code for locals. Rick pays before I can get my other card out, "It's date night."

We pull up to the valet and wander down the path to our cottage. I manage to fill the mini-fridge and take a pint of macadamia nut ice cream with me to my laptop. "I'm going for a run while you work. Do you need anything?"

"If you see Alika, send him over. Can I use your credit card for Sam's travel? Also, I'd like to have a small Hawaiian Welcome Basket waiting in our parent's rooms when they check in, okay?"

"Use my credit card for anything you want. Yes, please cover everything for Sam and for your mom. Don't get cheap on them." He opens up the cottage to the gorgeous ocean view and kisses me with his don't-forget-me kiss as he runs out the door.

I check my email and get verification from Alika that the villa has eight separate beds if you include the fold out sofas and he adds a rollaway. Unfortunately, the estimate on the private charter is more than twice the cost of the first class airfare. I adjust the plans I have started for Mr. Seno and email him his itinerary along with my direct phone number. I also order a welcome basket to be delivered to their room on Lanai and send Mr. Seno an additional email with links to the resorts they will be staying at including the spa options, and Lanai Excursions website. I check first class airfare for the team again, trying to find a better option with enough seats left in first class for them all to fly together.

I send Cross a message on social media.

To @RookCross - Can you call me? Now would be great? Please and thank you!

Less than a minute later my phone rings, "Hello?"

"Hey, sweetheart. Do you miss me?" It's Chase.

"Of course I do! Hey, Rick is on a run and I have limited time without him in earshot. The villa has eight separate beds, but only if you count the two fold out sofas and a roll-away bed they can bring in. What do you think about that?"

"Book the rooms instead of the villa." Chase says without hesitation.

"Okay." I'm searching airfare while I'm on the call and get lucky, "For airfare I have found a flight with enough first class seats available, but they're not all next to each other. I'll contact the airline and try to get them to reassign seats. Best I've got unless you want to rent a vacation house away from the resort." I laugh and suddenly wish I hadn't offered a vacation house.

"The resort is where we want to be, please book us that airfare before it's gone. I'll text you my payment info. Hey, are you doing okay?" Chase is always looking out for us.

"I'm better than okay. Slightly stressed trying to get everything done quick for our wedding, so we can still have some vacation days. If I can book my mom on the flight with you, will you make sure she's okay? She doesn't usually travel by herself."

"Happy to be her escort. I'll pretend I'm her date. Just let me know."

"I appreciate you. If I can coordinate Sam arriving at the same time, I may get you all in the same car from the airport to the resort. You'll get an email with itineraries shortly. Thank you for everything!" I'm happy he's so easy.

"See you soon!" and he hangs up.

I purchase the airfare for the guys, book their rooms and call my mom.

"Hello?" my mom answers quickly.

"Hi, mom! I'm booking your travel. Is somebody coming with you?"

"Yes. Umm, the guy I'm dating wants to go with me. He already booked our airfare and a room at the resort. He said he's handling it and taking me on vacation. I'll be there the day before and we're staying for a week. Is that okay?" First time I've ever heard my mom say something to me questioning if it was okay. Weird.

I'm a bit shocked because I wasn't aware she was dating, "You're dating? I mean, I'm glad you're dating. You deserve a vacation. I'll see you when you get here. Do you want me to schedule a car to pick you up at the airport?"

"No, he rented a car. It's all taken care of. You take care of your wedding."

"Thank you. See you soon! Lots to get done!" and I hang up in slight shock.

I check flights for Sam and find one that flies in at almost the same time as the team. I send her the info to make sure the travel dates and times will work for her and she's good with it. I tell her she'll be meeting Chase to get a ride over to the resort and book her a room.

I review my checklist and Alika walks up to the lanai. "How can I help?"

We talk about the salon reservations and I update him on the additional guests, so he's prepared and Rick doesn't find out until they get here. I fill him in on some of the other details and make sure we are all on the same page. Everything is handled except the wedding ring for Rick and our marriage license.

I can finally breathe except I have no idea what kind of ring to get Rick. Should it match my ring? Should it be a more manly material? Should it be simple? My pint of ice cream is already half gone, so I stick it in the freezer and search the internet for men's wedding rings. None of them are right. After scouring webpages and webpages of rings, I find what I want. A polished, man-sized gold band with engraving on the inside. I need his size.

Text to Rick - Babe, can you stop at the jewelry store at the hotel and find out what size ring you wear on your left ring finger? Please. :)

My phone vibrates.

Text from Rick - I'll do it now. Just running up to the hotel.
Text from Rick - 12.5
Text from Rick - Want anything from the hotel?
Text to Rick - Just you... Do you like to make my phone vibrate?
Text from Rick - I'm going to make you vibrate
Text from Rick - On my way

CHAPTER TWELVE

I can't contain my smile.

I put away my laptop and set out dinner on the lanai along with a couple of POG-tinis. It's perfect timing for a lazy sunset dinner. Of course it is, it's date night.

I relax on a lounge chair, absorbing the view of the sunset, the breeze off the ocean, and the crashing waves. I close my eyes and embrace it all around me, the way the wind blows across my body leaves me relaxed. All of my worries have been blown away and the mist from the ocean touches me lightly, refreshing me. I sip my POG-tini and stare at the sky as it begins to change color, no longer the bright sunlit blue it starts to change to a dark orange with lavender clouds outlined by the shining yellow of the sun. The clouds look like zoo animals on parade with heart shaped balloons.

Rick joins me on the lounge chair, freshly showered, wet and shirtless. "Hi, baby." He kisses me with desire, pulls back and gazes into my eyes. I don't know what he's searching for or what he finds there. His expression changes from light and sexy to sincere, and I'm not sure what happened. "I'm worried that I pushed you and I don't want you to do anything you're not ready for."

I stop him, "The only thing that will make me happier than being with you, is being married to you. I'm ready for everything you have to give and I want to give you everything you want. Don't worry about me, I'm in this. I'm in love with you." I smile at him and watch his smile match mine. "Now, let's drink our POG-tinis and enjoy the sunset together. No more stress. No more worries. Just us together."

Rick takes my hand and kisses each of my fingers, he entwines his fingers with mine and holds my hand as we sit together enjoying where we are and each other.

We spend the evening drinking and grazing on dinner. I'm buzzed, maybe I'm drunk. I can't stop laughing. Rick keeps looking at me and shaking his head. "Why do you keep shaking your head?"

"I'm not. You're wasted." He laughs and he's at least buzzed. "I should get you to bed, baby."

"Woo Hoo! Take me, baby!" I yell out as he picks me up and carries me to the bed. I'm glad he picked me up because I'm not sure I could stand.

"Damn, baby! Are you kidding? You want sex?" I feel his hand against my breast and he wants it, too.

"Yes! Get the whipped cream!" I realize I'm being pretty loud and they can probably hear me outside.

"I don't think it's a good idea right now. Bad timing for that, but, my bride-to-be, I will not make you go without when you want it. I always want you." Rick closes up the cottage for the night, bringing in the leftovers and getting things put away.

I strip naked and climb under the blankets, while I wait for him. Within moments he climbs under the blankets with me and runs his hand up and down my body while he kisses me, sucking on my lower lip. I reach for his hard cock and guide him in. He moves slowly, in and out while he continues to kiss me, and I wrap my legs around him tightly, meeting him stroke for stroke. He touches my sensitive nub and instantly I'm lit up like a Christmas tree, crying out his name, "Oh, Rick! I'm yours my king!" He strokes into me harder and this is going to go quick, he's more drunk than he wants to admit. He takes my breasts in his hands and searches my eyes. "You want them, don't you?" He takes one in his mouth and sucks hard, biting at my nipple, while he squeezes the other. He licks and sucks while he continues moving inside me deliberately. Pulling as much of my breast as he can into his mouth while he sucks. It's tugging at my need and I suddenly explode, "Oh fuck! Hard, baby, hard!" He pounds into me making me scream and moves to suck at my other breast without breaking his timing. I arch into him as I scream and he's done with a low guttural groan, pulsating hard inside me.

He keeps stroking into me, "Fuck me, baby. You're perfect. I want more. Fuck, I need more of you." He pulls out and flips me over onto all fours. He smacks my ass causing me to cry out and spreads my knees. He explores my wet sex, sliding a finger in to find I'm still coming. He slams into me hard from behind and grips my hips, pulling me onto his cock, stroking himself with my body.

"You're amazing, my king, harder and bigger than ever before, so fucking huge inside me. I'm yours, my king. Oh fuck. Fuck me, fuck me, fuck me! Oh, Rick! Oh!" I scream out as my orgasm hits like never before and Rick follows in seconds. Collapsing and taking us both down to the bed.

He rolls off of me and pulls me over on top of him. "I love you, my queen," and I don't know which one of us was out first.

CHAPTER THIRTEEN

I wake up with Rick wrapped around me, still sleeping, and a raging headache. I pull the blanket up over my head and go back to sleep.

I smell coffee and wake up again to find water and aspirin waiting for me next to some coffee. I hear the shower turn off and Rick walks in to find me still naked. "Oh, what happened last night? You're all bruised."

I look at myself, hickeys all over my breasts. "You happened. I didn't know you were so much of a breast man."

"I'm a fan, but I don't leave marks." He glares at me with an evil grin.

"Try again." I wait for a better response and wish my head would stop pounding.

"Have I ever left marks? You must have fallen down when you were drunk last night." He's pushing his luck or my buttons, I don't know which.

"If you don't remember last night, maybe you were drunk." I tease him knowing he'll bite.

"You told me I'm fucking huge on the second round without time to reload. No, I'm never forgetting that. Then you talking to me this morning in your sleep. I'm going to be walking around like the king of the world for days." He stares at me, like he wants to show me exactly how fucking huge he is right now.

"Just, no more marks until after we're married. I want no chance of any showing in our wedding pictures. Shit! I forgot about a photographer." I sit up straight and wide awake. "Taking me to the Hidden Cafe this morning? I need Loco Moco with runny eggs to recover."

"Aren't we going to Honolulu today for our license? It's the other direction."

"We can stop for breakfast on the way. This island isn't that big and it has more than one road. We can drive the other direction and then cut across the island. Different scenery." I take the aspirin and a big drink of water. I sit up and stand up slowly to test my hangover and I'll be able to maintain until I get food.

I shower quickly, tie my hair up in a knot, and dress in jean shorts and a tank top with my aloha shirt over it. I want to be county building appropriate since we're going to get our license today. I step into my slippahs, grab my bag and I'm ready to go.

I find Rick outside on the phone with his dad and take the opportunity to check my email and messages. Nothing needs my attention, so I ring Malia about a photographer and a jeweler, because she'll have a friend, she always has a friend. Rick is still on the phone and appears to be having a serious conversation.

I lie down on the bed and call Sam, going over everything with her and helping her pack. I text Cross letting him know my mom is handled and that Sam will be meeting them to ride over to the resort.

I close my eyes and relax while I wait for Rick.

———

RICK CLIMBS in bed next to me and brushes my hair out of my face. "Baby, are you feeling okay? Are you ready to go?"

I look at the clock and I've been asleep for over an hour. My head feels better, I'm hungry and I feel like I could sleep all day. "I'm sleepy, but I'm hungry and ready. Is everything okay?"

Rick kisses me on the cheek, "I'll tell you about it on the way," he gets up and offers me his hand to pull me out of bed.

We take off for the Hidden Cafe and Rick finds it without direction. We split a Loco Moco and Mac Nut Pancakes. I keep getting up for water, probably drank five glasses. Next stop marriage license. We get back on Kamehameha Highway and drive 20 miles or so along the shore with beautiful ocean views, turning off onto the Likelike Highway into Honolulu. I use the GPS on my phone to fulfill my navigator duties and get us to the building where they issue the marriage licenses. We were in and out in less than 30 minutes, marriage license in hand. We get back to the Jeep and I offer up some ideas of places we could go while we're in Honolulu, "Do you want to go to Waikiki or drive up to the Puu Ualakaa State Wayside Park or go to Hanauma Bay or..."

Rick cuts me off, "I think we should just go back to the cottage. I think you need a nap, maybe on the beach in the sun. I will rub you down with suntan lotion and make sure you don't stay in the sun too long, basically be your cabana boy. How does that sound?"

"Only a stupid girl would turn that down," I gaze at him and smile because he's right. "So, did you decide not to tell me about the phone call or is it not important?"

Rick taps his fingers on the steering wheel, "I was talking with my Dad and we all know my mom isn't real happy I'm getting married, but she's been going along with it pretty well. Now, she says she's being left out of everything because she's not involved with the planning and my dad's idea to surprise her with an extended vacation backfired because it was all done before she knew about it."

"Let me guess, it didn't help that I'm the one who planned her vacation?" I try to come up with a way to include her without having to spend too much time with her. I don't want to give myself the chance to make it worse with my DOTM. "What if I call her and ask her to help me with something for the wedding?"

"What are you thinking?" Rick is unsure, but wants to hear it.

"Something that doesn't put her in the middle of everything here, but still needs to be done."

"I'm listening."

"What if we have her handle our wedding announcement? She can contact your hometown newspaper and the San Diego newspaper. She can even put together wedding announcements and send them out to family, friends, whoever makes her happy. She's on the proper side and these are proper things that I would probably forget about."

"I like it. But, you need to call and ask her to do it. Also, you need to let her know that I need to approve whatever she's doing before she does it. This way we can make sure she doesn't tell the world where and when we're getting married. She'll feel like I'm in charge and she'll like that. She's got it in her head I'm being controlled by an older woman. Before you say anything, I've never felt like you're older than me and I've always felt like we're equal. Everyone except my mom knows you're not taking advantage of me, my love."

"And, I'll send her some pictures of us together in case she wants them for the announcement."

Rick tosses me his phone, "Might as well get it over with. She'll answer if it's my number. I'm still her baby." He grins at me with a giggle and I call Mrs. Seno.

"Hi sweetie!" She sounds happy to get a call from her son, but I'm not him.

"Hi, Mrs. Seno. This is Sherry, Rick asked me to call you. Do you have a few minutes? I was hoping you might be able to help me."

"Oh, hi. Do you need money for his wedding ring or something?" I grimace at Rick, it's not going well already.

"No, no, nothing like that. The wedding plans have come together quickly, not requiring too much effort really. But, I thought you might be able to help me with announcements."

"What do you mean?" Mrs. Seno doesn't like me at all and seems to think I'm always trying to do something bad.

"Well, traditionally the newspapers in the hometown and current living locations are notified, so they can print a notice or article about it. I'm guessing they might want to do an article on it, possibly even with pictures because Rick is a professional athlete. Also, since we're getting married on such short notice I thought we should send out wedding announcements to our families and friends, maybe you could find something with a tropical theme, get them printed and sent out for us? We don't even have the addresses for everyone. It would mean so much to me, if you were involved with this. I want you to be part of our wedding and there isn't much to do since we're keeping it small." I added some gush at the end for affect and watched Rick shaking his head as I did it.

"Oh! Well, of course dear! I'd love to help."

"You know Rick is private, so he wants to approve whatever you're giving to the newspaper and the announcements before they're printed." I add like it's an afterthought.

"He's always been that way. I'll put it together and send it to him with the details. Thank you for putting together such a wonderful vacation plan for us, I can't wait to go to Lanai!"

"I was happy to, it's my specialty! If you don't mind, I'm going to take your number and send you some texts with pictures from our trip so far. Would you like to see a picture of my wedding dress and the dress Sam will be wearing?"

"I would love that, dear!"

I text Mrs. Seno the picture of Rick and I at Laie Point, as well as the picture of the dresses and I listen as they pop through on her phone.

"Those dresses are beautiful! Perfect for a beach wedding!" She's quiet for a second, "I haven't seen my baby boy as happy as he is in this picture since he was a child." I can hear her get choked up.

"Mrs. Seno, I promise I'm taking care of your son and I love him. I understand this is hard and I'm sure I'll feel the same when my child is getting married."

"Call me Brenda, dear. Did you just say you're giving me more grandchildren?"

"Well, we hope to give you at least one. Not necessarily right now, but soon."

"You can call me mom if you want or when you are ready. Welcome to the family, Sherry. So happy to have you!"

"Thank you, you don't know how much that means to me. Please keep in touch with me, you have my number. I appreciate everything, Brenda."

"Now, you go take care of my baby and enjoy your vacation," and she hung up.

Rick stares at me with a WTF expression. "It's all handled and I can call her mom now."

"You're amazing. Ten minutes on the phone and she loves you, plus she's handling announcements we probably should be doing." He shakes his head.

"Well, I did tell her we're going to give her a grandchild at some point."

"That would do it and it's the truth." Rick's attitude changes, "Should we stop and get you another test on the way back?"

"Yeah. About that, remember you asked me if I was late?"

"Yes."

"How late would I need to be before you think we should be concerned? I mean, how many days late would I need to be, to be considered late?"

"Sherry." Rick pulls over and parks. "Where are you going with this?"

"I'm just wondering, for my own knowledge. I could be a few days late or even longer from stressing out or something."

"Yea, I'm definitely stopping to get you another test." Rick locks his eyes with mine and holds my face with his hands. "Sherry, my queen, what day are you supposed to start?"

"Three days ago. I think. Based on my pills. The test I did was negative." I wait for Rick to process and respond.

Rick stops and focuses on me. It's obvious he's afraid to say the wrong thing.

"Babe, I don't want to get your hopes up. I don't want to let you down. I know this means something to you. Anything can happen and it could just be me whacked out due to stress or being on vacation or who knows what! I'm fine with it either way. Negative just means we have something we can work on later. Positive is unexpected and will make me happier than I've ever been because I get to give you something you want, something we both want."

Rick with his hands still on my face, leans in and kisses me, pressing his lips to mine and showing me how he feels about it without words. We're on the same page, but positive is better.

Rick pulls back out on the road and pulls into the next drugstore parking lot he sees. He leans over and gives me a quick kiss, "Do you want anything?" I shake my head. "I'll be right back." He goes into the store and comes back out less than ten minutes later with a bag. He climbs into the Jeep and hands me the bag. He pulls out onto the road and drives back to the cottage as I shuffle through the bag: Bottle of water, a couple candy bars, two different multi-pack boxes of pregnancy tests, and a tiny white T-shirt that has outlines of the Hawaiian Islands on it and says "Made in Hawaii". I pull my feet up and curl up in my seat, turning sideways to face Rick and leaning my head against my seat.

I'm woken up by the Jeep stopping and we're at the hotel. Rick walks around to my side and lifts me out of the Jeep, carrying me back to the cottage with my head against his chest.

CHAPTER FOURTEEN

We spend the next few days relaxing at the beach or on our lanai, ordering room service and eating at the hotel property restaurants (except for breakfast at the Hidden Cafe, of course) and being inseparable as we take calls and answer messages from friends and family. The warm sand is relaxing, giving me the feeling of warmth on both sides. Rick rubbing me down with lotion is amazing, his hands are so big and strong, yet a gentle caress across my body. The sun beating down on me, turning my skin a tropical golden brown unlike any tan I ever get at home. The ocean is a clear blue-green and you can see everything in the waves as they build and crash. The silhouettes of fish and sea turtles that look like they're trying to catch the wave like surfers. The surfers are out in full force with the current weather system, pipes are forming large enough to get all the way through and waves are hitting twenty feet in some areas along the North Shore. I'm enjoying the time and the personal time with Rick, the rubbing him down with suntan lotion and days of him not wearing a shirt. His hair is shaggy and he hasn't shaved in a week. I get a message from Sam and realize everybody will be getting here tomorrow. I've lost track of time simply lying on the beach with my man. I check with Malia and she has everything ready, including his ring. I check with Alika and everything is under control. I contact Brenda, she's loving Lanai and thanks me for the welcome basket.

I HAVEN'T STARTED. I'm officially a week late. Rick hasn't said a word. The pregnancy test packages haven't been opened. Rick and I are sharing a lounge chair, he has his arm around my shoulders as we both lie there in the sun with our shades on, "I was thinking that maybe you should do a couple tests, my queen. It's a week, right?"

"Yes, it's a week. I'll do one of each kind first thing in the morning." Not wanting to get up and knowing they're more accurate at first pee.

"How about doing one of each of them for me now? You can do them in the morning, too." I get up and go to the bathroom, peeing on two sticks. I set them both on the counter and read the instructions on the boxes.

I hear Rick outside the bathroom door, "You can come in if you want." The door opens and he peeks in uncomfortably, not sure what to expect.

"What are you doing?" He stares at me and I think it's pretty obvious.

"Reading the boxes to find out how long to wait and what the different results mean."

"A plus sign is pretty obvious."

"Yes, it would be. But, it hasn't been long enough for

the test to process and I need to make sure I give it long enough before I read the result."

"Sherry, what does two lines mean on the left one?"

"Umm, box says that's positive."

"Sherry! Will you look at your tests. My queen... We are pregnant!"

"Don't get excited. I'm only a week late and the tests could be wrong."

Rick runs his hand through his hair in frustration. He takes his phone out, sets it on speaker and calls Sam.

"Hello, baby brother. What's up?" Sam answers casually. "I'm kinda busy trying to get ready to go to Hawaii right now."

"Sam, you're on speaker with me and Sherry. Take your phone off of speaker." I hear her phone click off of speakerphone.

"Something wrong?"

"I don't think so, but Sherry and I have a question." Rick says very matter of factly.

"Shoot." I can hear the "oh crap what now" tone in her voice.

"Can a positive pregnancy test be a false result or only negatives?"

Sam takes a deep breath, "It's rare for a positive to be false. If you have a positive pregnancy test, you should take another one to be sure. Also, consider if you're late and how late. Things can change quickly when you're pregnant and you don't always stay pregnant. So, you probably want to keep it a secret until at least three months. Of course, you're never supposed to keep secrets from me, it's the law."

I take a picture of the tests and text it to Sam. "Do you see the picture I sent you?"

"Yes! I promise I won't say a word. I love you guys! Congrats! See you tomorrow!" and she hangs up.

Rick turns to me, "I love you, Sherry." He places his lips on mine sweetly, tasting me and cherishing me. He's overcome with emotion and it's his turn to have a stray tear fall. "I promise to give you and our baby everything you need." He holds me close and ginger, like he's afraid to hurt me.

"I'm not breakable, Rick. It's weird. We'll figure it all out together. I'm so happy to be pregnant with you and giving you something you've wanted for a long time. I promise to do my best to take care of us and stay pregnant. I love you, my king."

Rick picks me up and carries me back to the lounge chair, where we sit together with his arm around my shoulder. There's so much to think about, but I'm not letting it get to me. It's funny, for the first time in weeks I'm peaceful. I'm not stressing over anything. My world is how it's supposed to be.

CHAPTER FIFTEEN

I wake up the next morning to the sound of the crashing waves. The island smells fresh after a rainstorm hit last night. I'm cozy under the warm blankets with my head nuzzled into Rick's neck. He has the blankets pulled up to our heads, it did get a bit cold last night. Our legs are entangled and he has both of his hands on me as usual, but this morning one of them sits possessively on my belly. I take a deep breath and stretch, rolling over so I can see the ocean. His hand stays with me.

"Good morning, baby. Did you know we're getting married tomorrow?" Happiness bubbling in his voice.

"Yes, and everybody is getting here today."

"Do you know how happy you make me? This morning you were talking in your sleep and said the sweetest, funniest things. I almost want to tell you what you said." He never tells me what I say in my sleep.

"Go for it."

"Maybe part. You don't need to hear the sweet part, I think that's just for me."

"Spill it already." I wait, there's no way he actually tells me anything I said.

"You went on this rant in a sweet voice about how her name can't be Elle because it didn't happen in an elevator. You snowballed off into how it could be a boy and then about what should the name be and should it be Hawaiian or a family name. I can't wait to find out what you say next." Rick laughs and I can't believe he told me, but I can believe I said it. Totally sounds like one of my rambles, though I'm sure it was much longer and I asked tons of questions.

It's early and we won't get much alone time today, probably none until after the wedding. "So, what do you want to do this morning before everybody starts to get here? I need to go visit Malia to pick up dresses and stuff."

Rick kisses the back of my neck, "I have a great idea." His breath hot on my neck and his voice raspy sexy in my ear. He rolls me toward him and kisses my eyelids, then my nose and finally my lips. His tender lips and demanding tongue at odds with each other. He moves his hands to my hips and disappears under the blankets. He moves his hands over my body lovingly, as if he is memorizing it and kisses my inner thigh. He caresses my wet folds and I pull his mouth to mine. His hard cock against my leg, I suck his tongue into my mouth while I stroke him. I rub my sex against him and guide his cock to my entrance. He hesitates as he slides in slowly, he's amazing. His demeanor changes, "I love you, my queen." He takes my mouth with his softly, and moves against me slowly. The slow friction, and his mouth as it moves from my lips, to my neck and my collarbone. This must be what it feels like to be worshiped. "Is this okay?"

"It's wonderful. Don't worry, you aren't going to break

me or hurt me. I get it." Offering him reassurance and he slides in further, moving a slight bit faster. I meet his strokes to bring him in all the way and I'm so full. He's exquisite. I massage his scalp with my fingers, playing with his hair and down his neck to explore the muscles in his shoulders. I wrap my legs around him and draw a low groan as he continues to move slowly. He squeezes my breasts, and kisses them, and it tugs at my sexual need.

"Wow, interesting." He squeezes my breasts again, then nibbles at my nipples. "Huh." Next he goes full on for my breasts, sucking and licking at my hard nipples. I cry out as I explode suddenly. "Fuck me. Oh," followed by a loud growl. Rick keeps moving slowly and wraps his arms around me tight, needing me next to him. Our hearts beating together strong and fast. He moves the hair from the side of my face with his nose, kisses me in front of my ear and whispers, "I don't know how I've gotten this lucky. Thank you, Sherry. I never want to be without you." That's all it took and the tears stream down my face, and I mean I flat out start bawling.

"Sorry." I grimace a smile out.

"Don't be sorry, now I understand why." He turns my face to him with his finger to my chin, "Never doubt my love for you." His eyes shine with sincerity. "Get ready and I'll take you to breakfast. We'll get some snuggle time later tonight." That's not what will happen because the guys from his team will be here and they'll be taking him from me for the night. He deserves it. I get up and pull on my bikini with white shorts over the bottoms and my aloha shirt to put on over my shoulders. Rick starts taking photos of me when I haven't even done anything with my hair yet. I run into the bathroom and brush out my hair, it's comforting down on my shoulders and I opt to leave it down today. I walk back into the room and Rick keeps taking photos of me. He grabs me, pulling me back down into bed and takes pictures of us together wrestling and kissing there.

We go to the Hidden Cafe for breakfast, today we order Beef Stew Omelets and enjoy talking with the waitresses. We stop at the Kahuku Swap Meet on the way back from breakfast and buy a bunch of North Shore T-shirts from the 5 for $20 guy. Rick talks to the carvers while I browse a couple other booths. He buys a tiki that means love and happiness, and looks like it's holding hands. The carver engraves it on the back with the date of our wedding and R+S.

I check flight statuses when we get back to the cottage and everybody is on time, Sam is actually running a few minutes early. I don't know which flight my mom is on. I expect everyone will be here in less than three hours. We take advantage of the end of our quiet time together and relax on our lanai under the tropical sun.

CHAPTER SIXTEEN

That moment when your concierge walks up to your lanai with your parents and finds you sleeping in your bikini with your shirtless husband-to-be, and his arms are around you protectively while you use him as your pillow. Alika knocks on the deck, "Hi!" comes out very loud. Rick and I both glare at him like WTF, dude? "These people were trying to find you. They say you aren't responding to their calls and you didn't answer when I called the cottage. They followed me over. I think you know them?"

Can you see my eyes rolling? Well, Rick did and turned my eyes away from our parents, so hopefully they missed it. Yes, our parents! Alika had a line up following him around the resort that couldn't fit in his golf cart! My mom, her guy, Brenda and Mr. Seno, who I've recently learned is Richard and no, Rick isn't a junior. (There's nothing junior about him!) Can you imagine the eyeful they all got? We've been in Hawaii relaxing for a week and have totally adapted to the lifestyle. I mean, who needs underwear when you can put on your swimsuit? A shirt? Not needed, I have my bikini top on. Even Rick has gotten down to board shorts and an aloha shirt he puts on when necessary, and doesn't usually button it. So, great that they all walked up and saw us lying there with Rick possessively palming my belly. They probably didn't think anything of it or even notice the detail, considering the visual they were getting. I'm not ready for this today and I know we're the ones who invited them here. I'm content to be where I am with my man and don't want to get up. Time to suck it up!

Rick saves me and sits up, pulling me with him. He puts on his huge happy grin, "I'm so happy you all made it. Sorry, about that. Naps on the lanai have become a habit." I reach under the lounge chair for my phone to check the time, and sure enough it's lit up with texts and missed calls.

Text from Mom - We just landed in Honolulu!
Text from Brenda - In our rental car and on our
way to the North Shore! See you soon!
Text from Mom - We just got to the resort.
Text from Mom - Where are you?
Text from Malia - Called and didn't get you. I have
the dresses etc. Are you picking them up today?
Text from Brenda - Checking in at the hotel.
Text from Brenda - What room are you in?
Text from Sam - Hey mama! Landed early and got
lei'd! LOL! Where do I meet Chase for my ride?
Hmm... That sounds dirty. I'd rather ride Kris
Martin.
Text from Chase - Hey! Looking for Sam. Where is
she meeting us?
Text from Chase - Never mind, she found
Kris. smh
Text from Sam - I'm guessing you know about the
team and Rick doesn't? It's a good surprise for
me, too!
Text to Malia - Sorry! Coming to visit and pick up
when Sam gets here. Going to bring the moms with
me. More customers for you. ;) Expecting Sam
soon.
Text to Sam - Sorry, fell asleep. All is well? Where
are you?
Text from Malia - Perfect
Text from Sam - On a road and I can see the beach.
I know, not helpful. Left airport about 20 minutes
ago.
Text to Sam - You should take photos in the car,
maybe a panoramic! LOL!

I stand and hug my mom, Richard and even a willing Brenda. "Thank you so much for joining us in Hawaii. Sam will be here in about 20 minutes. I thought the four of us ladies could drive into Haleiwa, pick up the dresses, do some shopping and maybe stop for shave ice." Rick stands and follows suit, but makes a face at my plan to leave him behind. "Babe, you can't see my dress." Besides, the San Diego Seals are about to take over this resort.

"Sounds lovely, dear." Brenda is the first to speak. My mom nods along.

"Alika, how about you show them around the resort and we'll meet you all in the lobby in about twenty minutes? Give us a chance to change." My eyes willing him, hoping he has an idea to keep them busy for a bit.

"You got it!" He turns and leads them down to the beach, telling them about the resort and leading them back to the hotel.

Rick and I go in to change, but he's ready to dig his heels in, "I should take you ladies into town."

"We'll be fine, babe. This island might as well be home for me, especially the North Shore." Rick gives me a new, concerned expression, "You can't be with me every second."

He kisses me and sighs, "I know, my queen. I should spend some time with my Dad. When is Cross getting here?"

"Cross is sharing a car with Sam, and they'll be here any time." I thumb through the clothes I have available and pull my white shorts back on over my bikini bottoms, then pull on my aloha shirt and leave it unbuttoned. I brush out my hair and tie it up in a knot. Rick pulls one of the cheap Hawaii T-shirts we bought out of the closet and puts it on with his board shorts. A more relaxed look for him. I love the contrast of his tan to the white of the shirt, as well as the way the shirt is at it's limit across his chest and around his thick upper arms.

Rick inspects me, "I'd be happier if you'd put a tank top or something on over your bikini top since I'm not going with you."

I shake my head, unsure what he's worried about. But, I appreciate his desire to protect me and switch the unbuttoned aloha shirt and bikini top for a bra and strapped tank top. "Better, my king?"

"Much. Thank you."

He takes my hand and we walk up to the main hotel, getting to the lobby at the same time as a stretched Hummer limousine pulls up and I'd bet money on who it is. The first person to step out is Sam, grabbing us and giving us a double hug. Next Cross steps out and shakes Rick's hand. "You two needed that much car to bring you over here? A little bit overkill, don't you think?"

Then the windows all roll down and the guys yell out "Surprise! Bachelor Party time tonight!" Rick walks to the Hummer and shakes hands with the guys hanging out the windows, clearly happy to have them here and approving of the gesture. He gazes at me knowingly as the guys unload and get checked in. He takes Sam's things, so she can take off with me and the moms, and checks her in to her room. Sam and Rick are communicating privately by text, I'm guessing he assigned her to be my babysitter.

The ladies and I take off, leaving the men behind and I fill Sam in on the plan. We stop to visit Malia and the moms shop, while Sam and I get the dresses, and everything else that Malia has for me. Rick's wedding ring is perfect. I get cash out to give Malia, to find Rick has added money to my wallet, $5,000 in cash to be exact.

While Sam is trying on her dress, Malia smiles at me, "Show me your hand." I hold out my left hand palm up. "It's a girl."

I stare at Malia in shock. "What are you talking about?"

"You're pregnant. It's a girl because you showed me your hand palm up. Didn't you know?"

"I found out yesterday, but haven't had it confirmed by a doctor or anything yet. Keeping it a secret for now, okay?" I gaze at Malia imploringly. "Rick knows."

"No worries. It's a good thing. She'll be loved."

I stop myself and ask, "How did you know?"

"I see it in your happiness and peaceful demeanor. You have a special shine to you. I thought I saw it before, but today I am sure." Malia hugs me, cupping the back of my head and whispers in my ear, "Everything will be fine. You will have no worries with this little one."

I'm at ease as we walk back to find the moms. Malia's words float through me and I believe every one of them to be true.

The ladies finish shopping and we load the dresses into the Jeep. I take them for Shave Ice and we wander Haleiwa, exploring the galleries and shops, before I drive us all back to the resort. We all get along well and it was an enjoyable trip, which wasn't expected. I never in a million years would've guessed my mom and Brenda would get along.

The moms go to spend time with their men, while Sam hangs out with me. We go to her room, so she can get unpacked and then to the cottage, to find out what's going on and relax for a few minutes.

Text to Rick - Back from Haleiwa. With Sam at the cottage.

Text from Rick - Is everything okay?

Text to Rick - Yes. Errands handled. Everyone got along.

Text to Rick - Having fun with the guys?

Interesting, no response.

Sam starts rattling out of nowhere, "I was thinking, I should stay here with you tonight. You shouldn't spend the night with Rick tonight. He should have to wait until the wedding tomorrow."

Before I can say anything, Rick is there with his hands on me, "No."

"Well okay then, baby brother. Where did you come from?" Sam says with an irritated older sister tone.

"Sherry said you were back and I wanted to see her. You have a spa and salon day with her all day tomorrow. Guys are all at the pool, talking about surfing lessons and how much we're going to drink tonight." I love how he just shows up, we've been together so much on vacation—I missed him.

Sam flips through the resort book, "Dude, you've got it bad. But, I guess that's okay since you're getting married tomorrow and sending me for a spa day. Hey, they have karaoke tonight in the bar."

"Karaoke? We should go while the guys are off doing whatever the guys are going to do!" Excited for something fun to do when I won't have my Rick.

"Better idea, I'll get the guys to go there and we can all hang out. My pregnant bride-to-be isn't going to a bar without me." There's some sibling communication happening that I don't understand and it's fine with me, it all sounds fun. Besides, I'm going to bed early and he'll catch up.

"Fun. I'll tell the moms, so they can join us. Please go play with your boys." I send him back to the pool.

Sam glares at me with wide eyes, "My brother is a handful! Talk about possessive!"

"Protective more than possessive. He wants me safe. I kind of like it." I correct Sam.

Text to moms - We are all going to karaoke tonight at the bar.

"Is there something we're doing here that we can't do at the pool?" Sam is stretching to get a view of the pool from the cottage. I'm guessing she wants to ogle Kris.

"No, let me change to my bikini," we walk over to the pool. I get another disapproving glance from Rick when I walk up to the pool. Apparently, my attire is somehow unacceptable. I guess I could've worn shorts or a cover up to the pool. Instead of worrying about it, I dive into the pool and swim to where Rick is sitting on the edge. Sam does the same thing, but swims up to Kris Martin. I'm beginning to wonder if there's something going on there. Sam and I play in the water, doing handstands and somersaults. Chase jumps in cannonball style to splash us, then has each of us hold one of his feet and takes us for a ride around the pool. This started something, but Rick jumps in the pool and claims me completely, finishing it before all the guys decide they need to outdo each other. The sexy scene Rick causes in the pool with me, my arms and legs wrapped around him, our bodies plastered together, kissing me deeply with his hands in my hair, gets a hooting and hollering reaction from everyone around the pool and some standing on their hotel room balconies.

Sam yells, "Get a room!"

Rick breaks our kiss and laughs happily, "I love you, baby." Then he whispers quietly in my ear, "I'm so happy to be marrying you tomorrow." I shiver, he goes into protection mode. "Going to shower and meet you guys at the bar in a bit." Nobody questions him, as he lifts me out of the pool wrapping his towel around me. He climbs out of the pool and takes my hand, leading me back to the cottage. He immediately turns on the warm shower to get me warmed up and it's just what I need. I get out of the shower, wrap a towel around my hair and put on my robe. I sit down on the couch to relax for a few minutes and watch the waves crash.

CHAPTER SEVENTEEN

"**B**abe," Rick is rubbing my shoulder to wake me up and I'm in bed, "The guys are all at the bar, you've been asleep for almost two hours. Sam is on her way, so you two can get ready together and meet us at the bar." He kisses me sweetly.

I don't remember how I got to the bed.

"Okay," but I don't even open my eyes.

"Sherry, are you okay?" Rick is worried about me.

"I'm fine, we didn't get our long afternoon nap today and I'm on the emotionally drained side." I open my eyes and gaze at him lovingly, his clear blue eyes focused on me. "I hope she has your eyes."

"She?"

"Malia said congrats and she will be loved." I probably sound like a fool. Rick furrows his brow, waiting for more. "As soon as I was alone with her in the back to get the dresses, she looked at me and told me congrats, it's a girl. She just knew. It sounds crazy, but Malia has never steered me wrong before."

"Huh, so you want our daughter to have my blue eyes and she'll have your blonde hair. I'm going to jail for beating off the boys." He laughs as he turns to leave and runs into Sam coming in. "Good timing, sis. See you ladies in a bit. Sam, take care of her, she's tired. Love you, babe!" and he's gone to the bar.

I call across the room to Sam without getting up, "How was Martin?"

"Shut up!" Sam laughs, "Get up, so we can get ready."

"Better idea, get the ice cream from the freezer." Sam nods, then sits Indian style on the bed next to me with two spoons.

"OMG, this is the best ice cream ever!" Her eyes are big and she shovels a spoonful into her mouth. I laugh and try to get bites in between Sam's spoon. "So, are you ready for tomorrow?"

"Yes! Let's get ready, go eat at the bar, do some karaoke and go to bed early. We can go to breakfast in the morning and be back for our 11am spa appointments. I bet all of us who aren't hungover end up at breakfast." I laugh, Rick isn't willingly going to let me go to the Hidden Cafe without him.

"I like it." Sam gets the hanger of clothes she brought with her and starts to change. I drag my butt out of the warm bed and thumb through the few pieces I have in the closet. I slide the tube top sundress on with my lightweight sweater and slippahs. I put on the leaf necklace Rick bought for me and comb through my damp hair. Sam braids a few parts of my hair and puts it up in a chignon, so I don't have to blow dry it. It's loose and fancy. Sam changes into a short denim skirt with buttons up the front, a red tank top with a feminine ruffle collar, and leaves her hair down. We're both ready and find Alika waiting for us with his golf cart as we step out of the cottage. He was obviously sent to get us, didn't even ask where we're going.

Sam and I are the last to arrive at the bar. The parental units are all sitting together and in deep conversation. Rick and the team have spread out around a section of the bar, or I should say, they have taken over. Chase appears to be in charge, somehow leading the group to an organized state of drunkeness while they harass Rick as part of the bachelor party process. Chase meets us at the door, "My lady," and he bows to me as he takes my hand and leads me to Rick. Sam follows right behind me with a full belly laugh going.

I give Chase a hug and whisper in his ear, "I'm going to bed early, so you guys can have guy fun. You're in charge of getting him dressed and to the wedding at least fifteen minutes early. Not hungover, please. Sam and I are going to breakfast in the morning and spending the day at the spa. Got it?"

"Mission accepted." Chase salutes me, so I was probably being the Vacation Commander again. Then he whispers in my ear, "Being a bride agrees with you, you're glowing. Seno got lucky." He chuckles, "Are you sure you don't want to trade up?" Cross keeps it up because it bugs my Rick.

"Cross! Stop hitting on my woman." Rick is standing right there while all this is going on.

"I'm giving him instructions for tomorrow, my king." I kiss Rick solidly on the lips, taking control with my hands and my tongue. Then I turn and walk away with Sam to order food, and check out what the karaoke options are. He's watching me walk away, so I glance back at him quickly and wink like I'm sexy. He admires me full of happiness and we play a game with each other, flirting across the bar.

Sam and I sit next to the moms. We order a rib eye steak burger, garlic parmesan fries and a wedge salad, and share. I read through the list of songs and all I want to sing are love songs. I try to get my head straight, but it kind of makes sense. I have spent pretty much every waking (and sleeping) moment with my Rick for days, I just planned our wedding, and we're getting married tomorrow. I'm female and I picked up my wedding dress this afternoon. Besides, your brain would be sex-fried too, if you'd been spending afternoons napping in the sun with a shirtless hottie and getting sexed multiple times per day! I turn to Sam, "I'm going to need help here. My brain is in wedding mode. You pick for me." I push the list over to her and wait to find out what she chooses. Luckily, Sam asks me if I know songs before she submits them for me to sing. She also set us up to do a duet.

Little do I know, she submits for us to do multiple duets and nobody else is singing. We are first and this is going to be interesting singing "Islands In the Stream" by Kenny Rogers and Dolly Parton with Sam. We're also second to sing, luckily they start playing "Summer Nights" from *Grease*. It's a lot of fun and appears to be annoying the guys in the room.

The young guy on KJ duty calls me out by myself and Sam hunches her shoulders at me, not having anything to do with it. "So, yea, bra, I've been bribed to have Sherry do this next one. So, yea."

I hear the music load up and start to play for "Thinking Out Loud." My emotions hit me and I know singing this song will be the end of the night for me. I'm okay with that. Rick has been enjoying time with the team, but stops what he's doing and focuses all of his attention on me when he hears what song is coming on. My eyes focus on him, "This is the end of the night for me. I love you and can't wait to marry you tomorrow, King Seno." I watch Sam out of the corner of my eye, getting ready to leave with me as I start to sing the song. By the end of the song, Rick is on the stage with me and standing behind me with his arms around me, kissing my cheek and a stray tear is trickling down my face. Everyone claps at the end of the song and it quickly turns to clinking on glasses. Rick turns me to him and kisses me right there on the stage. I'm not talking about a quick peck or even the show from the pool earlier today. No, this is take me in his arms, hold me tight, claim my lips with his and dip me taking me off my feet and leaving me light-headed, an in-case-you-had-any-doubt-in-your-mind-you-belong-to-me-baby kiss. It should probably be given it's own classification, kiss doesn't seem to be enough. I guess I'm Seno'd.

Rick brings me back to my feet and embraces me, "Are you sure you're okay, baby?"

"Yes, I need extra sleep so I can be a beautiful bride for you tomorrow." I smile at him, "Besides, Sam and I are getting up early and going to the Hidden Cafe before our spa day starts. Have fun with the guys." I turn to Sam, "Let's go! I'm going to get you drunk on POG-tinis." She hops up and Alika's replacement is waiting at the bar door for us, it's like having my own personal golf cart driver.

Sam and I sit up, enjoying some girl talk. I ply her with POG-tinis, using up the vodka and we both fall asleep in the bed.

CHAPTER EIGHTEEN

I wake up in the morning with Rick wrapped around me, but today I'm squished between Rick and Sam in the bed. It hits me, it's my wedding day and I want out of bed. I kiss Rick on the nose, "Good morning, baby. I'm getting up and getting out. I love you and I'll meet you at sunset." I nudge at Sam, "Get up, get up, get up!" Until she finally moves, fine, I pushed her. Either way, we were up and getting ready for breakfast and the spa.

Sam enjoys her Hidden Cafe adventure. I order the macadamia nut french toast and make Sam get the beef stew omelet. She thinks I'm crazy, but comes around just like Rick. We talk with the Hidden Cafe ladies and warn them the Seals are in the area, since I suspect they'll be going there for food as soon as they're moving. Rick did have baseball caps and photos brought over for them.

We have some extra time, so I take Sam out to Laie Point. It's the place to be this morning. Peaceful, relaxing, surrounded by the ocean's strength and beauty. Almost meditative for me. It makes me centered. Sam and I take selfies, texting them to everybody and posting them on social media like fools.

Driving up to the valet, the resort van is waiting and baseball players are gathering.

Sam and I go directly to the spa and check in, to find we really do have a full day of spa treatments: manicures, pedicures, body wraps, massages, mud treatments, waxing, full hair treatment and styling, even make-up. Alika has made sure our dresses are here waiting for us and notified the stylist about the flowers that are being delivered. The receptionist directs us to a changing room and gives us assigned lockers to leave our things in. My locker has a really soft robe in it that's embroidered "Bride" and Sam has a robe embroidered "Maid of Honor". We also have boxes and cards left for us from Rick. He bought us white fresh water pearl jewelry sets to wear for the wedding. My card reads:

Sherry,

This is our special day and I want you to know that you're special to me everyday. Married or not, I will love you forever. See you at sunset, my queen.

Love,
Rick

I look up at Sam and she's crying after reading her card, "Is he always like this with you?"

I nod at her and join the tear fest. The poor young girl who's in charge of our spa day today walks in to find us because we're taking too long and has no clue what she's walking in on. The expression on her face says "it's going to be one of those days". Sam and I enjoy the day of pampering, relaxing oceanside between treatments and getting waited on with snacks, drinks, basically whatever we want. I'm sure that was explicit on our spa day reservation, I can see it: Give them everything they want and be at their beck and call.

Everyone is leaving me alone today. Malia checked in with me to let me know everything is as expected and she would be here later. No messages from moms. Only me and Sam, chilling out at the spa. That's not as good as napping on my shirtless man in the sun, but it works. I watch the sun in the sky out over the ocean and the time is getting closer as the sun turns down out of the high position. Alika stops in to check on us and tells me the flowers arrived, everything is as planned. I realize I don't have Rick's ring and message Cross to check on Rick and ask him to bring the ring for me.

Our attendant for the day escorts us to a private dressing room where they have everything hung up for us waiting. Our dresses are not elaborate wedding dresses, they are both pretty and perfect for a beach wedding. Sam's dress is a traditional hibiscus print in blue and white with a halter style top and a slight flounce to the knee length skirt. My wedding dress is white tropical printed flowers on white with a crisscrossing empire waist, a deep V-neck and hits me perfectly at tea-length. It's gathered at the shoulders and is perfectly fitted from the empire waist down. Looking at it on me now, I like it even better with my week worth of Hawaiian tan. I put on the freshwater pearls and they dance across my tanned skin. My French manicure and French pedicure are the perfect match. Only in Hawaii would a set of fresh water pearls come with a necklace, earrings, and anklet. My hair and make-up is already done, I need my flowers added to my hair and my bride's lei.

I watch the location of our vows quickly coming together. Chairs getting set up, Malia helping Pia get ready, Alika directing and supervising, flowers waiting on a table with a guest book, a photographer roaming about taking photos. Then I watch Cross walking towards everything with my Rick.

Rick is breathtaking, a gorgeous man in white linen pants and a white on white aloha shirt that matches the print of my dress. I have wanted him since the day I first saw him on the baseball field. I remember sitting in my seat and cheering for him when he didn't know who I was. I remember being distracted when I was simply within twenty feet of him and watching him do an on field interview. I remember the first touch of his hand and his lips on mine greedily for the first time and unexpected, when I met him at the Locale. I remember waking up the first morning after meeting him and finding him in my bed, wanting me. This man. This perfect man. And today, he's cleaned up, beard trimmed, freshly shaved and still has his grown out Hawaii hair, and a tan to match mine—because today he's marrying me. Our small group of guests start to show up and I watch as Malia greets each one of them individually, placing a lei on each of their shoulders and has Pia start playing as soon as the first guest arrives. The photographer starts by taking a video of Pia.

My quiet moment of observation is disturbed by a knock at the door, Cross walks in, "You're a gorgeous bride," he kisses my cheek carefully to not mess me up. "Here's Rick's ring. Can I do anything else?"

"Thank you. Stand by Rick. This is all because of you, Chase." It's true, Rick never would've met me if Chase hadn't encouraged him and put in a good word for me. Chase heads back to Rick. Sam and I watch, as soon as everyone is seated we make our way out of the spa and across the grass toward Rick.

As we approach my wedding guests, Malia makes eye contact with us and directs Sam to walk in front of me to her and for me to stay behind. The sunset is pink with orange hues, and I hear Pia playing and singing "Thinking Out Loud," it's perfect. I gaze forward as Rick turns and pores over me adoringly. His smile shines from every part of him. He has his green leafed lei on over his white and he's strikingly handsome. Malia stops Sam and places her lei over her head. As Sam walks to the front by Rick, Pia starts playing a ukulele version of the Wedding March and everyone stands as they turn to observe me walk down the aisle. I walk to Malia, "You're beautiful and will have a long, happy life together," she says as she places my lei on my shoulders and makes me wait a moment before completing the short walk to the beginning of the rest of my life.

The twenty-five feet between Rick and I feels like miles, he reaches for my hand as I approach and kisses it sweetly. We exchange leis while our Hawaiian minister defines aloha. Rick gazes into my eyes and nothing has ever been as right as this moment. The minister asks for the rings and performs a Hawaiian Ring Blessing with ocean water in a koa wood bowl and a Ti leaf. I'm missing everything and distracted, simply by the touch of Rick's hands holding mine. Rick turns to me, "Sherry, I knew you were the one for me the first night we met. I could feel it in my heart. I want nothing more than to spend the rest of my life with you. I promise to cherish you, love you, honor you, prove to you everyday that you're special, and fill your life with aloha just like you do for me." He slides the most beautiful wedding band on my ring finger. Gold to match my crown engagement ring, together it's a crown of jewels with channel set diamonds more than halfway around it and a round solitaire in the middle.

It's my turn and I gaze into Rick's eyes and say everything that's filling my heart with love for him, "You make my dreams come true. You've been in my life longer than I've been in yours, and it's beyond all reason. Good or bad, I'll always be with you wherever you are. You're not a baseball player, you're my love and I promise to cherish you, love you, honor you, give you myself whole-heartedly and to keep filling your life with aloha." I hold his ring up, so he can read the engraving on the inside with the date, R+S and the last line of "Thinking Out Loud," singing the line to him as I slide the ring on his finger.

The minister goes through the formalities and we both say, "I do." Rick pulls me to him dramatically, pressing his lips to mine and not in his don't-forget-me kiss way. He's confident, knowing we belong to each other and will always be together.

STAR CROSSED IN THE OUTFIELD
AN ALL ABOUT THE DIAMOND ROMANCE
BOOK 4

Rookie Centerfielder, Chase Cross, flies across the field to make diving catches like a superhero. He's solid muscle, fast, tan, and has the drive to win.

Baseball players suck. I don't know why I'm attracted to them. They're not an option for me.

He doesn't listen. He's a distraction that will hurt me. I'm after my dream, not a man.

Chase the ball. Chase your dream. That's how I made it to the big leagues. Chase the girl had never crossed my mind. Chicks find me.

I'll do anything to be near her.

She's got me Star Crossed in the Outfield.

THE CLOSER

AN ALL ABOUT THE DIAMOND ROMANCE
BOOK 5

You don't choose love, it finds you...

Super D is the closer for the San Diego Seals. He's been my best friend since college, but I haven't seen him in years. My business partner is getting married. She's convinced that D is the one for me. I've been kicked me out of the office until I find out.

Angie is independent. She's never needed a man. Men just get in the way. I've loved Ang since the day we met. No other woman compares. I'll always be there for her. She's not interested in me, or is she?

When love finds you, you don't have a choice.

UP TO BAT

AN ALL ABOUT THE DIAMOND ROMANCE
BOOK 6

She writes sci-fi serials for a living. Her high school sweetheart is her critique partner.

He's the hottest player on the team... gorgeous eyes, perfect lips, built shoulders, and assets filling those baseball pants like no other.

She's been his since the night they met.

He won't give it up.

He's a major league hitter, but with her there's been no attempt at first base. He's still... Up to Bat.

MUFFIN MAN
A STANDALONE NOVELLA

Robbi

"Everybody out!" The manager yells, running through the salon as we all ignore her. She's not the owner. Problem is the owner is out of town and she's in charge. She stops and at the top of her lungs, "Evacuate now! It's going to explode!"

The salon freezes instantly, the calm before the storm. There's a sudden frenzy of women gathering their necessities, and their clients as they run outside hysterically. I casually get up out of the salon chair and walk out with Deanna, my stylist, close behind me, and avoid the trampling stampede of frantic, high-pitched women.

We all gather outside for the details, but the manager is still in there! She comes running out with the massage therapists and their clients wrapped in robes. It triggers me to survey the scene for what stages of beautification we're all in. I mean, we all go to the salon for different things. Personally, it's how I stay blonde and that's not changing any time soon because I can prove blondes have more fun. The stylists are brushing out their hair, fixing their make-up, taking off aprons. I overhear what's happening and empathize for some of the poor women in the middle of getting services, when it hits me—I'm one of them.

The building had started to make a banging noise. The manager, Shawna, had taken it upon herself to find the problem. She was left in charge after all and the ship was not going to sink under her direction. This isn't some basic barbershop, this is Michelle's Salon and Shawna would not be responsible for damage to the custom European style decor Michelle has taken years to refine. It was the water heater. The water heater was making the loud noise, like it had air in the line or was trying to pass bad Chinese food. It was also emitting gas fumes and sparked every time there was a bang. The bangs were getting more frequent.

Which brings us to the bunch of women now standing outside in the shade of the building's front awning. It's almost lunchtime and the parking lot of the strip mall is starting to fill up with patrons to the food establishments, eyes peering at the motley crowd of women in smocks milling around helplessly. Shawna's on the phone with 911 trying to get, yes, you guessed it, the fire department.

911: What's your emergency?
Shawna: There's going to be a fire
911: Is there a fire now?
Shawna: No, not yet.
911: Sorry, we can't help you yet
click

At least, that's how I imagine it from the story Shawna told. There were others calling, it would be fine. Help would show up. Hopefully. Deanna, the only person I will let near my hair, is getting fidgety and twirling her soft brunette curls between her fingers. "I'm sure they'll be here quick. We still have ten minutes before we have to wash the bleach out of your hair. Everything will be fine." For those of you who are not salon savvy, leaving chemicals on your hair too long isn't good. Hair will break off, fall out, burn. I've seen it smoke. All kinds of horrible things, and I take pride in my long platinum blonde hair. So, let me translate what Deanna said: Ten minutes until utter disaster. Others have half a haircut, shampoo or conditioner in their hair, extensions partially tied in. The people who were getting massages are relaxed, even if their clothes are inside the building and they're outside wearing only a robe.

Everyone that could primp, had primped for the firemen to show up. It's a lineup and I can imagine the firemen walking the line, *"I'll take this one, and this one. You don't mind sharing, right?"* The senior firefighter steps up and says, "Sorry, I get first choice. Seniority gets perks. I'll be taking this one from you." Anyway, you get the idea. It's a beauty pageant and then there's me with a plastic bag on my head and a lady with foils sticking up off her head like she could receive radio transmission.

The sound of sirens fill the air as the long red ladder truck pulls into the parking lot, stopping in front of the salon. The important thing here is the possible fire, but I appreciate firemen as much as the next girl, maybe more. Definitely more. I love a hot guy, even on days like today when I only get to drool from a distance because I look like a bag lady compared to the stylists. The first guy is a bit older with short salt and pepper hair. He's fit and fills his navy blue uniform nicely. The second guy is shorter, still at least 5'9" and wearing one of those bulky yellow jackets with reflectors. His face is adorable, but the jacket hides everything else—not a hint of a single ab or muscular arm. The third reminds me of Goldilocks, he's just right. Thick, dirty blonde hair and the mustache to match. His navy blue uniform pants are topped with his station T-shirt which stretches across his chest and shoulders, yet loose where it's tucked into his Dickies. I'm busy imagining the things I could do to him. Naked. With my tongue. Deanna stomps her boots and drags me into the dog groomer next door.

"Firemen? Hot firemen?" I whined questioningly, not wanting to give up my view.

NAOMI SPRINGTHORP

USA Today Bestselling Author Naomi Springthorp is a born and raised Southern California girl who believes that life has a soundtrack and half of each year should be spent cheering for her favorite baseball team. She loves music and spending time with her feline fur babies.

Naomi writes Baseball Romance, Romantic Comedies, Contemporary Romance, and 90s Throwback--all with heat and sometimes a little sweet.

Sign-up for Naomi's newsletter at
www.naomispringthorp.com/sign-up
to get updates on everything she has going on.

Join Naomi's reader group Naomi's Naughties at
Facebook.com/groups/naomisreaders for fun, baseball, and
hotties.

facebook.com/naomithewriter

amazon.com/author/naomispringthorp

instagram.com/naomispringthorp

bookbub.com/authors/naomi-springthorp

goodreads.com/naomithewriter

twitter.com/naomithewriter

pinterest.com/naomispringthorp

snapchat.com/add/naomithewriter

ALSO BY NAOMI SPRINGTHORP

Anthologies & Box Sets

Sacrifice for Love

Storybook Pub

Storybook Pub Christmas Wishes

Storybook Pub 2

Young Crush

Hate to Want You

Tricks, Treats, & Teasers

Caught Under the Mistletoe

Game On

Imperfect Date

Hopelessly Devoted

ACKNOWLEDGMENTS

Thank you to my original support system. Without you, I never would've done any of this.

Brenda, you'll always be the sister I chose.

Irene, I can't imagine anyone else putting up with me. You are more to me than what you think.

Ro, this is still your fault! I had no idea what I was getting into.

Megs, I'm so happy to have you in my circle. I don't know what I'd do without my keeper.

Tonya, my partner in crime. You push me and I thrive on the challenge and your support.

Sara, thank you for keeping me in line and supporting my special brand of crazy.

Naughty Admins, you all rock and support me in different ways. I'm lucky to have you from the beginning.

www.ingramcontent.com/pod-product-compliance
Lightning Source LLC
Chambersburg PA
CBHW032250020726
47495CB00001B/44